TIMEKEEPER

TIMEKEEPER

Praise for *Timekeeper*:

*A Paste Magazine: Best Book 2016

*A Barnes & Noble Teen Blog Best Queer Fantasy 2016

"*Timekeeper* is an extraordinary debut, at once familiar and utterly original. Between its compelling world, its lovely prose, and its wonderful characters, the pages flew by."

—Victoria Schwab, #1 *New York Times* bestselling author

"Alive with myth, mystery, and glorious romance, *Timekeeper* will keep hearts pounding and pages turning til the stunning conclusion. Reader beware—there's magic in these pages."

—Heidi Heilig, author of *The Girl from Everywhere*

"*Timekeeper* is a triumph . . . If you read only one such book . . . let it be this one."

—*Bustle*

"*Timekeeper*'s premise is original and its world unique."

—*EW.com*

"While the world is wildly interesting and fantastic, with broken clock towers that have left towns frozen in time, it's the emotional impact and diverse cast of characters that make this book soar . . . The resulting story is an exciting and inclusive one, drawing in elements of magic, mystical spirits, swoon-filled romance, and just so much more."

—*BookRiot*

"Part mystery and part romance, this fantasy novel delves into what it means to grow up and make important decisions. With an easily relatable main character struggling to fit in, the novel has a realistic and contemplative voice. VERDICT: A must-have richly written fantasy novel that will have readers eagerly anticipating the next volume."

—*School Library Journal*

"Sim creates a cast of complex and diverse characters, as well as a mythology to explain how the clock towers came to exist . . . an enjoyable, well-realized tale."

—*Publishers Weekly*

"Mystery, LGBTQ romance, and supernatural tale of clock spirits and sabotage that explores how far people might go for those they love. Its strongest elements are the time-related mythology and the supernatural gay romance."

—*Booklist*

"This LGBTQ steampunk romance sports a killer premise and admirably thorough worldbuilding, helpfully annotated in the author's afterword. The characters—even the bad guys—are sympathetically drawn and commendably diverse in sexuality and gender."

—*Kirkus Reviews*

"An enjoyable start to a promising new trilogy."

—*BookPage*

TIMEKEEPER

TARA SIM

Sky Pony Press
New York

Visit our website at www.skyponypress.com.
www.tarasim.com

10 9 8 7 6 5 4 3

THE LIBRARY OF CONGRESS HAS CATALOGED THE HARDCOVER EDITION AS FOLLOWS:

Names: Sim, Tara, author.
Title: Timekeeper / Tara Sim.
Description: First edition. | New York : Sky Pony Press, [2016] | Summary: In an alternate 1875 England, seventeen-year-old clock mechanic Danny, aided by the boy he loves, must discover who is sabotaging the towers that control the flow of time and stop him or her before it is too late.
Identifiers: LCCN 2016021334 (print) | LCCN 2016051478 (ebook) | ISBN 9781510706187 (hardcover) | ISBN 9781510706224 (eBook)
Subjects: | CYAC: Time—Fiction. | Clocks and watches—Fiction. | Supernatural—Fiction. | Love—Fiction. | Gays—Fiction. | Great Britain—History—Victoria, 1837-1901—Fiction. | BISAC: JUVENILE FICTION / Fantasy & Magic. | JUVENILE FICTION / Historical / Europe.
Classification: LCC PZ7.1.S547 Tim 2016 (print) | LCC PZ7.1.S547 (ebook) | DDC [Fic]—dc23
LC record available at https://lccn.loc.gov/2016021334

Paperback ISBN: 978-1-5107-2660-4

Jacket design by Sammy Yuen
Jacket photographs Thinkstock

Printed in the United States of America

Interior design by Joshua Barnaby

For those who are still searching,
and for those who are waiting to be found.

Bedford

E

St. Albans

Chel

Hertfod Shire

Enfield

Harrow

Middlesex

London

Tha

Guildford

Shere

Surrey

SOUTH EASTERN
ENGLAND, 1875

Rother

East Su

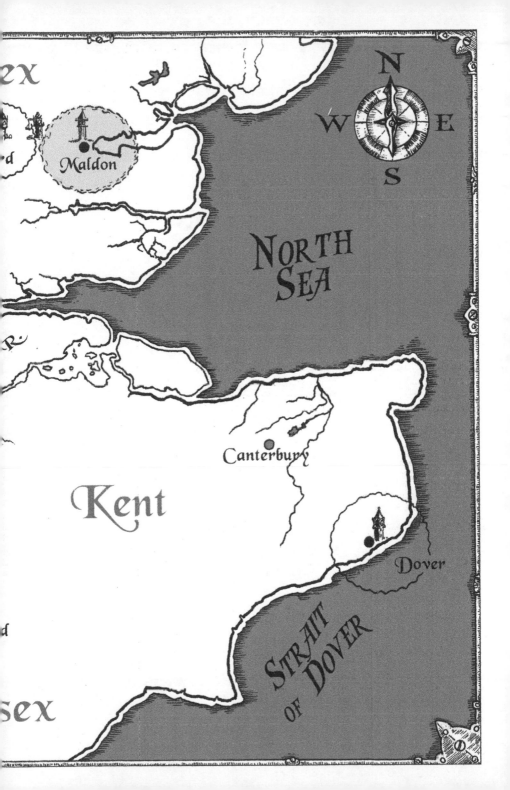

"To see a World in a Grain of Sand,
And Heaven in a Wild Flower,
Hold Infinity in the palm of your hand,
and Eternity in an hour."

— "Auguries of Innocence" by William Blake

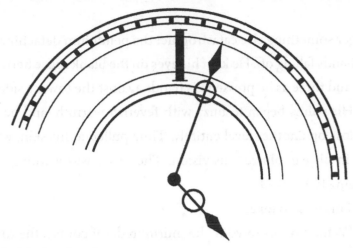

Enfield, England
September, 1875

Two o'clock was missing.

Danny wanted it to be a joke. Hours didn't just disappear. But the clock tower before him and the silver timepiece in his hand read 3:06 in the afternoon, when not fifteen minutes before they had read 1:51.

Because the hour between no longer existed.

A single thought registered, stunned and succinct: *Oh, hell.*

Colton Tower was a pillar of limestone and cast iron with a brick base and pointed spire. The iron gleamed gold in the weak sunshine, illuminating the sentinel-like tower that rose above the shingled roofs of Enfield. It stood apart from the other buildings as if to showcase its power, easily visible at the heart of town. The clock face shone yellow, its numbers and hands black against the opal glass.

Danny approached the tower slowly, as if his presence would

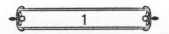

trigger something else catastrophic: the pendulum detaching, or the hands falling off. He kept his eyes on the blank space between one and three as he pressed his hands against the tower's side.

His palms began to buzz with feverish warmth, and he felt the loss on another level entirely. Time pulled at his skin, whistled in his ear, blurred his vision. The tower was warning him, begging to be fixed.

This was no joke.

"Who did this to you?" he murmured. Of course, the tower couldn't answer.

The hum of the crowd grew louder, breaking his concentration. Danny looked over his shoulder. The small homes and shops along the street were empty, their owners huddled near the village green. The townspeople had come not only to stare ineffectively at the clock, but for a glimpse at the young clock mechanic who sensed time in a way they couldn't.

The back of Danny's neck prickled. He looked up again, but saw nothing.

The mayor of Enfield wrung his hands nearby, glancing between Danny and the tower. The thin man cleared his throat with a sound like an engine stalling.

"Can it be fixed?" he asked. The mayor was sweating, but then again, so was Danny.

Danny wrenched his eyes away from the tower and lowered his hands. "Uh, yes," he said, trying not to make it sound like a question. "Yes, it can be fixed."

The set of the mayor's shoulders relaxed, but not by much.

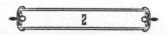

"Then, please, by all means." He gestured to the tower as if Danny had forgotten where it stood.

The mayor was on edge for good reason. Blue uniforms flashed in the corner of Danny's eye as the London authorities combed the town, searching for the missing numeral. They rummaged through houses without a care for the citizens' belongings, if the crashes were anything to go by. Danny watched as a woman in a rose-colored dress was pulled away by a constable. Her son tried to cling to her skirts.

"Where are you taking Mummy?" the boy demanded.

"I'll be back shortly, love," the woman said. She pried his hands off with a smile that barely concealed the worry in her eyes. "They just need to ask Mummy a few questions."

The police would be asking everyone questions. This wasn't a simple matter of a clock falling to bits; otherwise, the numeral would have been found by now. No, this was far more complicated. This was an act of burglary or vandalism.

Stolen. An entire hour taken like it was the last piece of cake on a neglected platter.

The clock ticked on despite the malfunction, but Danny felt the hour's absence as he would a missing finger. Enfield's web of time shivered around him in agitation. That wrongness bore down on his body, his lungs squeezed by the pressure, until it became difficult to draw his next breath.

The threat wasn't as simple as missing an appointment or rushing through afternoon tea. If one hour was subtracted every day, Enfield would slide out of alignment with the rest of the

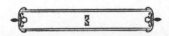

world. There was no telling what would happen to the town then—no telling what would happen to the people who lived here.

Enter Danny, the clock mechanic. The healer of time. Enfield's supposed savior.

Damn.

He snapped his timepiece closed with a loud *click*. This was his first assignment since the accident, and they had given him the most difficult one they had.

I asked for it, he reminded himself. *Now I just have to prove I can do it.*

Turning back to his auto, which sat dusty and exhausted beside the village green, he bit the inside of his cheek. His sweating had progressed from mildly uncomfortable to downright disconcerting. A gust of wind carrying the smell of rain ruffled his dark, unruly hair. Because that was just what he needed: a sheet of rain pelting him while he worked.

He dragged a heavy, rectangular package from the auto's backseat and hoisted it onto his shoulder. The steam auto was a black, five-seater hunk of metal with wheels as wide as sewer manholes. The fabric of the roof was damaged, causing minor flooding when it rained too hard, and the paint was chipped and peeling. Still, he touched the side door for luck. The auto had been his father's, and Danny hoped to feel his presence somehow.

"Do you need assistance?" the mayor called, still wringing his hands. There was something in the man's eyes Danny didn't like,

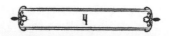

a familiar question: *Why did London send a seventeen-year-old boy instead of a real mechanic?*

Danny tried to smile, but only achieved a grimace. "No thank you, sir. I'm sure the apprentice is waiting for me inside."

He turned to the tower. The closer he drew, the harder the pressure grew in his chest, and he wondered if this was what Atlas would have felt had the world rested on his sternum rather than his shoulder. Opening the tower door, Danny's foot nearly collided with the first step in a long flight of wooden stairs. The rest of the bottom floor was only shadowed corners and cobwebs.

Danny looked up the stairs. The memory of the last clock tower sat heavy on his mind, tightening the cords of his neck. He had ascended those stairs without a care, even swinging his key ring around one finger as he climbed. He grasped at that effortlessness now, desperate to mimic its stride. But it fell away like fog through his fingers.

He had fixed clock towers before, he told himself. He could do it again.

Danny climbed toward the belfry, each creaking step raising small clouds of dust. The tower smelled of moths and age, the scent of a forgotten memory. He counted fifty stairs until he reached the bells. The jack, a mechanical manikin, stood motionless with a hammer poised to strike the bells at the next hour. It had already mistakenly announced the hour of three.

Farther up, Danny reached the churning clockwork, the bronze wheels and gears that turned the hands around the face.

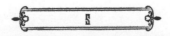

Below his feet swung the pendulum that swayed diligently side to side, beating every two seconds.

As he watched the clockwork turn, the pressure returned and constricted his throat. His breaths came too fast and his vision darkened at the edges. This wasn't just the tower's effect on him. This was—it was panic. He was panicking. *Again.* He couldn't, not now, not when he had so much at stake.

He wanted to run. He wanted to cover his ears and block the echoes of screeching metal, stop breathing in the ghost of smoke that followed him everywhere he went. It was worse inside the towers, this urge to fall to his knees and throw his arms over his head in defense.

One of the reasons he had volunteered for this assignment: to get over this reaction.

The room dipped beneath him as he took a quick step back. He closed his eyes and pushed the panic ruthlessly down, down, down. Tried to convince himself it didn't exist. He was Danny Hart, and he was a clock mechanic.

A clock mechanic who was now afraid of clocks.

It won't be like last time, he thought, touching the scar on his chin. *It can't be.*

His pounding heart was not convinced.

But this wasn't just about him. The tower was hurt in a way he could feel in his bones. A sharp twinge in his side, like a cracked rib. They were both in pain.

Danny hugged the parcel to his body and repeated what the

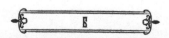

doctors had told him to say over and over again: *I was in an accident. I got out. I'm safe now.*

Whirs and clanks and ticks echoed throughout the tower, a symphony both familiar and new. The sounds vibrated through the wooden floorboards, traveled through the soles of his boots, up his legs, to his heart. Strangely, they calmed him. They loosened his throat and slowed his breaths.

Each tower sounded different to him, like a voice. This one was curious, bright, unassuming. He listened to it speak, gathering his courage until his arms screamed a reminder that the package they held was rather heavy.

Danny climbed higher on unsteady legs and finally reached the clock room. It was cluttered with dusty boxes, better lit than the rest of the tower thanks to the windows cut into the side walls. Out of breath, he put the package down and studied the near side of the clock face. The hands made long shadows through the glass. One rested horizontally, the other diagonal on its journey around the circle.

He wondered who in their right mind would steal an hour from a clock tower. The twinge inside him was a physical warning, like the missing two o'clock demanded an hour of his life in compensation.

As his father used to say: anything was possible.

He looked around again and nearly jumped out of his skin. Someone sat on a box near the clock face. Danny could have sworn no one had been there a minute before.

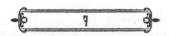

"Oh," he breathed as shock faded to annoyance. "You must be Brandon." The Lead Mechanic had mentioned his new apprentice would be Brandon Summers, a name Danny had never heard before. That was fine with him; his apprentices never lasted very long anyway.

The apprentice turned from his examination of the clock face and examined Danny instead.

Danny tried to mask his surprise. He had expected a fourteen-year-old brat, not someone his own age. Brandon's blond hair made a halo around his face, his skin a soft shade of bronze. Danny wondered if he came from one of the colonies. Australia, maybe. A break in the rain clouds resulted in a brief flare of sunlight that gilded the room around them, giving the apprentice a preternatural glow. The eye Danny could see was light brown, like amber. The other was shut tight.

They stared at each other. Danny wanted to stay annoyed, but couldn't stop his own eyes from traveling over the apprentice's face. The shape of his eyes, the slanted slope from his cheekbone to his jaw. The width of his shoulders and the straight line of his back.

Danny had never seen this apprentice at the office before. Then again, he'd been away for a while.

"Hello," Danny said when the silence stretched on. His nerves hadn't settled, and his face grew hot.

It might have been the way the apprentice looked at him, somber and curious, like Danny had spoken a foreign language.

"Is there something in your eye?" Danny asked.

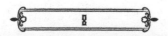

Brandon nodded.

"Must be all the dust."

Brandon remained silent.

Danny tensed, wondering if he was about to contend with yet another apprentice who resented being assigned to a mechanic barely older than himself. Danny couldn't count all the times he'd been tripped, had his tools stolen, or been laughed at behind his back—and all that within months of becoming a full mechanic, the youngest mechanic on record.

But he'd never had an apprentice so utterly silent before. Brandon could have at least mustered up a "Yes, sir." Or better yet, not been here at all.

Danny stripped off his gloves and rubbed sweaty hands against his waistcoat. He couldn't let this silence unnerve him. "My name's Danny. You *are* Brandon, correct?" That should have gotten a response, but the other boy only nodded after a slight hesitation.

"Cat got your tongue?" Danny gestured toward the parcel. "Help me with this. Please."

He knelt before the package to unwrap it, and Brandon came to his side. The apprentice wore tight brown trousers and a baggy white shirt, which he hadn't bothered to tuck in. Danny tried not to look too long at the way the collar of his shirt drooped low enough to reveal the sharp corner of his collarbone. Mechanics and apprentices were required to wear proper trousers, shirts, and waistcoats, along with sturdy boots and gloves. Not . . . this.

Brandon hadn't come prepared. The blatant disregard heated

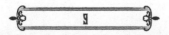

Danny's blood. This assignment was a test, and the new apprentice was going to make him fail.

Just focus on the clock, he thought. *Focus on Enfield.*

They unwrapped the package, which the Lead Mechanic had given Danny that morning. A large black iron Roman numeral II lay within the wrappings.

Shuddering, Danny said, "We'll have to use the scaffolding."

In the clock room, the scaffolding—a wooden slat with metal rails that suspended mechanics in front of clock faces—was stored on a platform above the face, which could be reached by stairs. Danny found even this small height problematic.

He opened a latch above the face and asked Brandon to lower the scaffolding down. Danny looked out and tried not to groan. He could see almost all of Enfield from up here, including the village green near St. Andrew's church. He could also see the dirt road where his skull would crack, should he fall.

"Here's what we'll do," he said, more to himself than to the apprentice. "I'll . . . er . . . you go first, and I'll bring the number down."

The apprentice's fair, nearly nonexistent eyebrows rose, but he did as he was instructed, tying a line to the belt sitting beside the equipment. Danny tugged the rope to make sure it was secure, and without waiting for approval, Brandon climbed out onto the face like he'd been a squirrel in a past life.

"Hey!" Danny called down. Brandon paused, his left eye still shut tight. "Keep both eyes open." The apprentice waved and continued to lower himself until his feet rested on the scaffolding. The cables creaked, but there was no sudden snap or scream.

His own line secure, Danny grabbed the Roman numeral and slung his tool bag over his shoulder. He hesitated long enough to raise sweat on his brow before he followed the apprentice down.

Danny's father used to say the most interesting sights in the world were right before your eyes. That was just his way to keep Danny from looking down, but Danny always did anyway. He snapped his eyes back to the rope and swallowed a small gasp. *You didn't see it. There's nothing to be afraid of. You're not dangling helplessly in the air.*

The boards groaned. He worried the structure might not bear their weight, but by some miracle, the scaffolding held. The wind tugged at their clothing, pressing Brandon's shirt against his slim torso.

"One thing down," Danny said, trying to sound hopeful. "Hold this, will you?" Danny passed him the Roman numeral and laid out his tools. The scaffolding was positioned directly under where two o'clock should have been. He put a hand against the empty patch and flinched as the pull in his belly turned into a hollow, aching emptiness. He closed his eyes to better focus on the image that his normal vision couldn't conjure.

It was as if someone had burned a hole in a woven tapestry. The fibers of time were all attached to one another, the golden threads weaving in and out in the natural flow of time that only the clock tower could produce. It spider-webbed across all of

Enfield like a blanket. But there, in the corner, was a hole. The fibers were broken, and without that connection, time distorted around them.

Memories crept in. Smoke, blood, a gaping void in time.

Danny's eyes shot open and he snatched his hand back. He was breathing fast again, and Brandon eyed him warily.

"H-hand me the micrometer, please," Danny said, but his voice cracked on the last word.

Brandon shuffled on his feet and looked at the tools. At first Danny thought he was dawdling on purpose, but the pained look on the apprentice's face revealed the truth.

"You don't know what a micrometer is," Danny said flatly. The memories, the missing hour, the height, the incompetent apprentice at his side—it all rose like an ocean swell within him, crashing up his throat, and the words poured out before he could stop them. "Great. Bloody brilliant. You don't know a thing about clock repair, do you? You don't dress properly, you don't talk, and now you don't know what a micrometer is. What the hell kind of apprentice are you?"

Brandon lowered his eyes. Danny looked down as well, ashamed of himself as his frustration began to ebb.

While he struggled to word an apology, Brandon knelt beside him. One of his hands hovered over the tools as Danny looked on. The apprentice tentatively grasped the steel caliper used for measurements and held it up, hopeful as a puppy learning its first trick.

The anger that had seized Danny quickly let go. "Yes, that's

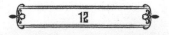

a micrometer," he said, pleasantly surprised. "Well done." The apprentice grinned, and blood rushed to Danny's face.

Danny took the proper measurements and made small marks for the repair, explaining each step. Brandon seemed to have moved on from the outburst, nodding with interest at everything Danny said. Danny had to admit that perhaps his first assessment had been unfair. Here, for once, was an apprentice willing to learn. It eased some of the strain in his limbs.

Tongue poking out between his teeth, Danny focused on the frayed threads attached to the clock tower. He grasped them carefully, using not his hands, but his innate ability as a mechanic to touch time. The fibers were alive and pulsing in his grip, confused and directionless.

This was familiar. This was what he had missed most in the months he'd been away: the thrum of time, the beating of clocks. He used to spend hours in clock rooms before the accident, syncing his heartbeat with that of the clock tower. There was something else, too—a surge of power that felt like sunlight on skin, warming him from the inside out. Time grew stronger all around them, thickening the fibers.

In fact, the power was so strong he faltered. The fibers began slipping away, sensing his uncertainty. Before they fled his grasp, Brandon put his hands on the numeral and something jumped like an auto backfire. Danny jumped with it, eyes wide. Brandon focused only on the numeral, adding his power to Danny's, to the clock's. The fibers rushed back, stronger than ever.

Danny attached the broken ends of the fibers to the numeral

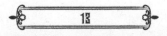

in his hands, allowing the unremarkable slab of metal to join the connective web of time created by the tower. Then he asked Brandon to hold the power-infused numeral up to the clock face. His pale, thin hands looked even paler next to Brandon's bronze skin.

Tools in hand, Danny fastened the numeral to the face. At first nothing happened, and he worried it hadn't worked. Then, gradually, the fibers attached to the numeral filled the hole until it sealed. Time shivered, then relaxed; or maybe that was his own body's reaction.

The tower bells rang in a sudden frenzy, calling out the hour of two before the hands moved to the correct time on their own. Danny tensed, momentarily deafened by the clamor. When his hearing returned, he could make out the crowd cheering in the street below. He breathed a sigh of relief.

"You're all right now," he murmured to the tower, pressing his fingers to its face.

"How long have you been a mechanic?"

Brandon's voice startled Danny, and his fingers skipped against the glass. The apprentice was looking at him the same way he had in the clock room, except now both eyes were open. They were amber in the daylight, bright and curious. His voice was light and smooth, flowing, like the well-oiled whirring of gears.

"And here I thought you were mute." Danny's own voice sounded low and clumsy in his ears. He began to put away his tools. "I was an apprentice at twelve. I'm seventeen now. Became a full mechanic seven months ago."

"Only seven months?"

Danny wasn't surprised by Brandon's disappointment. Most people were convinced that someone so young shouldn't even touch the clock towers, let alone fix them. But that didn't change the rule that one could be a full mechanic by seventeen, if you worked hard enough.

Danny glanced up to find the apprentice's expression hadn't changed. "My father started teaching me when I was six."

The small frown disappeared and Brandon's almost-invisible eyebrows lifted. "He's also a mechanic?"

"Was," Danny corrected, the single word heavy in the air between them. Before Brandon could ask anything more, Danny stood and grabbed the cable attached to the scaffolding. "Let's go up."

They pulled in silence until they reached the wide door above, right as the clouds broke open and spilled their promised rain. Danny almost fell to his knees to kiss the solid wooden floorboards beneath him, still dizzy from the height and the touch of time.

"I need to head back to London before the rain gets worse," he said. "What about you?" There were no other autos parked outside, and the Enfield railroad station had been demolished a few years before.

"I'll be all right."

Danny reached up to fix his hair. His hands were trembling. Brandon noticed and gave him a sympathetic smile.

"I won't tell anyone," he said, putting a secretive finger to his lips.

"Oh. Um . . ." Of course Brandon must have noticed his fear. Danny looked down. "Thank you. Look, I'm sorry for snapping. I didn't mean to. I have a lot depending on this assignment, and I didn't want to ruin it."

"You didn't," Brandon assured him. "I'm sorry for not knowing what a micrometer was."

"You did well with the numeral. Just study a little more, all right?"

He expected the apprentice to leave before him, but as he shrugged on his coat, Brandon hung back and watched the clock face.

"Are you sure you don't need a ride?"

The apprentice smiled and shook his head. Danny hesitated. He wondered if he should offer him a drink as an apology, even if the idea made him shake worse than the thought of jumping back onto the scaffolding. He opened his mouth to ask.

"Goodbye," he mumbled instead. *Coward.*

He headed for the stairs, shoulders hunched.

Brandon stayed in the same spot, staring at the clock face.

When Danny looked over his shoulder, the apprentice was gone.

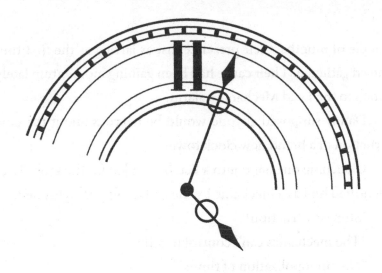

The auto acted up as soon as Danny reached London, the frame jerking until it puttered up to the Mechanics Affairs building across from Parliament Square. It would be a miracle if he reached home before nightfall.

The angry drone of men and women assaulted his ears as soon as he stepped foot outside. They blocked the entrance of the tall stone Affairs building like watchdogs, an odd assortment of middle-class men with canes and working-class boys with threadbare caps, women in taffeta walking dresses and girls with coal smudges on their faces. Whenever someone walked in or out of the building they shouted:

"No support for the unnatural!"

"Take it down!"

"Stop construction now!"

The protesters had become a regular fixture over the last

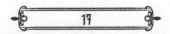

couple of months, their presence just as jarring as the first time they'd gathered. Their cause had been gaining momentum lately, much to the Lead Mechanic's alarm.

Danny supposed anyone would be nervous about the construction of a brand new clock tower.

Clenching one hand into a fist, he headed for the mob. They identified him as a mechanic by the badge clipped to his belt.

"Stop construction!"

"The mechanics can't control us all!"

"No monopolization of time!"

The mob didn't reach out to grab him—didn't touch him at all—but he felt phantom hands at his clothes, his arms, his throat. Their glaring eyes strangled him.

The raised voices cut off when the doors closed behind him. Danny leaned against the nearest column and closed his eyes for a moment, willing his heart to stop beating so fast.

Monopolizing time, he thought with a scoff.

It was true that mechanics kept the specifics of clock towers away from the public, but it was for their own good. They wouldn't understand, not when they didn't have the ability to touch time the way mechanics did. Without the mechanics, the towers wouldn't function. Without the towers, the world wouldn't function.

The very thing they protested was the thing they needed most.

He shook off the thought and walked into the atrium. The wide marble floor shone, reflecting light from the crystal chan-

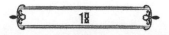

delier above. It hung suspended from a glass dome in the epicenter of the curved roof, which branched out into plaster moldings depicting the four seasons, one in each corner. Danny spotted a couple of mechanics leaning against the railing of the mezzanine above. Their laughter echoed across the atrium.

Danny climbed the long, winding flight of stairs that led to the first-floor offices. He bypassed them as the stairs curved again, away from the atrium, toward the back of the building where the classrooms were. The hallways here were long and wide, painted a shade of citrine the older mechanics insisted was once gold.

He passed murals and framed paintings, classrooms full of chattering apprentices and lecturing professors, before he climbed one more flight of stairs and found himself at the Lead Mechanic's door.

The secretary saw him and waggled her fingers toward the office. "Go on in," she said. "He'll be along shortly."

In the Lead's office, Danny sat tapping his fingers against his knees. He told himself not to be nervous, that he was just submitting the assignment report. They were normally turned in to the secretary, but the Lead had requested this particular report in person.

Danny hoped he had done enough.

The Lead's desk was wide and cluttered. One corner was occupied by a kinetic toy that dangled four metal balls from cords. Danny's chair groaned as he leaned forward and lifted the ball farthest on the right, then let it fall. He watched them bounce back and forth until the door opened behind him.

"Hello, Daniel." The Lead was short but broad, with a dark mustache and a balding head. He looked like the sort of man who would wish you a good morning whether you were an acquaintance or a stranger.

The Lead tossed a pile of papers onto his desk, glanced at the source of the clicking noise, and wrapped his hand around the metal balls to make them stop.

"Was it all that bad?" the Lead asked.

"What do you mean, sir?"

"Your face gives away everything. It always has." The man settled at his desk. Behind him stretched a wide window painted with the colors of approaching dusk. "Tell me what happened."

Danny gave a verbal report as he handed over the written one. It had come out to only one page, hastily scrawled on crumpled parchment he'd found at the bottom of his bag. He hadn't had time to find real paper; he was much too anxious to find out what the Lead had to say.

The Lead skimmed the report with a critical eye, then set it down. "It sounds as if everything went well." Danny wondered if he caught a hint of surprise beneath the words.

"I suppose it did."

"Don't be modest, Daniel. This was a medium-risk assignment, and you pulled it off. That's something to be proud of." He smiled, and Danny started to smile, too. Before, he had never questioned praise. Now, it sat tepid and uncertain at the bottom of his rib cage, afraid to rise too high lest it pop like a bubble under atmospheric pressure.

"I was afraid it would be too much for you," the Lead continued. "This is certainly a successful first step."

The bubble popped and Danny's smile vanished. He resisted the urge to slip down into his seat. *First step.* He'd made so many steps since becoming a mechanic, followed by several large steps back. Now he was lost somewhere in the middle.

Still, he forced himself to reply with a small "Thank you, sir."

The Lead read through the report again. "Was the apprentice agreeable?" It was known throughout the ranks that Danny Hart never got along with his apprentices. Several were on a list of those never to be reassigned to him again due to back talk, piss-poor attitudes, or in one case, body odor.

Danny regretted yelling at Brandon. He hadn't deserved it, not really, even if he was a dalcop who didn't know what a micrometer was.

"No," Danny said. "But too quiet, if you ask me."

The Lead rested his arms on the desk and leaned forward. "You look peaky."

And there it was. He couldn't avoid it. As soon as word had spread that he'd been hospitalized, people had started looking at him differently. Talking to him differently. Quiet, cautious, like he would crumble to dust at the slightest provocation.

"I'm fine, sir," Danny said, "although it wasn't the assignment I expected."

"Don't dip your toe in the water to get used to it, jump in headfirst."

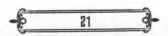

Danny had some things to say about that, but wisely kept them behind sealed lips.

"Now, about the missing numeral," the Lead went on. "I've heard nothing from the investigation crew. Did you happen to see anything suspicious while you were there? Anyone lingering near the tower or avoiding it?"

"I couldn't tell with the crowd. I got a good look at the clock face, but I didn't see any marks or scratches."

The police were still investigating when he'd left, though. They wouldn't stop until a suspect was found.

The Lead chewed his mustache. "The only way the numeral could have detached so cleanly is if a mechanic committed the theft. I suppose the numeral could have dropped from the tower and someone picked it up, but all the same, we should be careful. We don't want clock parts popping up on the black market, if they haven't already." He sighed and drummed his fingers against the desktop. "First Maldon, then your accident, and now this."

A beat of his heart. An intake of breath. Danny scooted forward. "Sir? Has there been any news about Maldon? About the new clock tower?"

The Lead rolled his shoulders back and cleared his throat. "I'm sorry, Daniel, not yet. It's a bit tricky, you know. This is the first tower we've attempted to build in hundreds of years. And what with the protesters, it's making it even harder. You must be patient."

"But what about the mechanics working on the tower? What I mean is . . . Because of what I did today . . ."

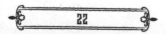

He clasped his hands between his knees as the Lead gave him that familiar look of sympathy.

"I know you want to go, Daniel. It's a big job, and there are several things I need to take into account. You did well in Enfield, and I'm happy to see you haven't lost your spark, but this is something altogether different. We'll see."

He was stalling. The decision should have been simple. What wasn't said was plastered all over the walls: Danny had to overcome his fear before the Lead would let him near such an important assignment.

Based on his behavior today, Danny's hope dwindled even further. He grabbed his bag to leave when the Lead stopped him.

"I just wanted to remind you," he said slowly, each word like a step toward a cliff, "not to give up hope. About Maldon, or your father."

Danny couldn't look him in the eye, so he turned to the door and swallowed. "Yes, sir."

"Daniel?"

He turned back.

"I know you have your heart set on this. Just give it some time. I'm still considering you for the job, don't worry."

"Thank you, sir."

Danny took his time on the stairs and hesitated at the doors. Holding his breath, he rushed outside, but at this late hour the protesters had thinned. Even so, he hurried down the street to where he'd parked his auto.

The rain had stopped long enough for the clouds to part.

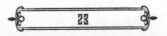

Sunset made the sky blush and set low-hanging clouds on fire. Danny took a moment to breathe in the autumn air and spotted a dirigible airship passing overhead, leaving a contrail of steam in its wake. He watched the ship until it passed above the massive clock tower across the square.

At one end of Parliament stood the tower some called St. Stephen's, others called Big Ben. The feud about the tower's real name was well known, especially among the mechanics who worked there on a regular basis. Ben, of course, was the name of the enormous bell within, but Danny preferred it over the stuffy-sounding *St. Stephen's.*

Much of his training had taken place within that very tower, where the smell of oil and the whir of automation had become as natural as drawing breath. He had once noticed a man standing at the back of the class, taller than the others, with a dark blond beard. The man had caught Danny staring and winked.

While the others debated, fourteen-year-old Danny had quietly stepped aside and asked him which name he preferred. The mechanic had thought about it, listened to the clockwork for a while, and smiled down at him.

"Big Ben. It has more presence."

Seventeen-year-old Danny now slid into the driver's seat, willing the auto to start. It did, although an ominous ribbon of dark smoke coiled through the engine's white steam. He pulled out and drove by the Gothic cathedral of Westminster Abbey, past each scowling gargoyle. A couple of mechanical gargoyles prowled the upper lip of the roof, guardians made of gears and springs rather than stone.

He passed the clock tower to cross Westminster Bridge, congested with autos that released a heavy fog of steam. Whenever he was close enough, he could sense Big Ben's natural energy, the fibers of time ingrained in every living thing around it. It felt bright, powerful. It felt like life. One moment of time could be enjoyed before it drifted into another, and another, until it became the future, present, and finally the past. It was the sole reason London thrived.

If anything irreversible were to happen to the tower—or to any clock tower, for that matter—time in that city and its surroundings would simply stop, its inhabitants trapped until the clock was fixed. It was no wonder the protesters hated them.

Sometimes, Danny hated the clock towers, too.

He drove through Lambeth and reached home just after dark. The street was draped in shadow, relieved only by the soft glow from the row house windows, including his own. That meant his mother was home. She tended to work later hours now, something she would have never done when he was younger. When his father was still around.

The last few meters were the toughest for the auto, but it made it all the way to the curb before sputtering to a halt. Smoke billowed from the bonnet, like ghostly visitors had hitched a ride and this was their stop.

Danny unlocked the front door and threw his things on the

floor. The house stood tall and narrow, with a treacherously steep flight of stairs leading to the bedrooms above. Green wallpaper ran from floor to ceiling, a color long since faded from emerald to celadon. The kitchen on the right was separated from the hall by a push-through door that tended to stick. He had to shoulder his way inside.

His mother sat at the kitchen table reading a newspaper in the dim glow of a lantern. The light caught her mane of curly brown hair, unmanageable even in the best of weather. She held a half-burnt cigarette between two fingers yellowed by years of addiction.

"Hello, darling," she said. "How was it?"

Danny answered with a shrug and walked by a pile of dirty dishes to check the pantry. His mother drew his attention to a sausage roll on the table. He tore into it at once.

"Thought you'd be out later than this," Leila said, resting a pointed chin on one hand as she blew smoke from her slightly puckered mouth. His father had often joked she had sucked too hard on a lemon as a child.

"Thought so too, what with that rubbish auto I've got."

Leila's eyes flashed. They were dark brown and lined with crow's feet. Danny was more an image of his father, from his green eyes to his gangly limbs.

"You best be taking good care of it."

"It's not *me* making it break down, it's the bloody engine." He wanted a new auto, and was secretly saving his money, but his mother refused to be rid of this one. His father had worked hard to afford it, and it was a miracle they had one at all. Families like theirs, in the lowest rung of the middle class ladder, usually couldn't boast such a luxury. "I'll have Cassie take a look tomorrow."

Leila dropped her eyes to the paper spread out before her on the table. He spied a report on recent events in India. Beside that were job adverts.

Nothing about towers.

"Mum," Danny said carefully, "the Lead told me there's no news. About Maldon."

Leila paused, then took another drag from her cigarette. She let it out as a smokey sigh.

Just as easily as Danny could sense the fibers of time, so too could he sense the strain between them. He never understood what his mother needed, especially now, when they were two boats drifting into separate currents. Danny could fix clocks, but he didn't know if he could fix this. Not on his own.

He inhaled as if to speak, but remained silent. Eventually Leila lifted her head.

"I'm off to bed. Douse the light, will you?"

He flattened the rest of the roll between his fingers, leaving imprints in the thick dough. "Mum? Don't work so hard. The job today was worth at least five pounds."

Leila paused again as she stood up, one hand resting on the tabletop as she studied her son across the seemingly immeasurable distance.

"It's all right, Danny," she said. "Don't you worry about me."

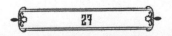

He listened to the clack of her high-heeled boots on the stairs and the muffled closing of her bedroom door. Sighing, he stuffed the last of the thick bread in his mouth and turned to the pile of dirty dishes. His jittery hands scrubbed and soaked until he found some minor relief in the chore, his mind filled only with suds. One less thing for his mother to worry about.

He stared at the empty counter for a few minutes, then doused the lamp.

The clock tower hummed all around him. His hands were on the clockwork, admiring the design of the cogs, the punctuality of it all. Every second tripped onward, one after the other, each tick a breath of air. It filled his lungs, his chest. Seeped through muscle and bone until it fused with the beating core of him.

He was connected to time. It was the greatest feeling in the world.

But something was wrong. A shift in the air, a crook of misfortune's finger. As he reached for the nearest gear, it exploded outward, cutting his hand. He scrambled back, but not before the rest of the clockwork blasted away from the wall—all the metal, the smoke and splinters, rushing at him like a tidal wave.

He was smothered in gray. He choked on blood. Copper filled his mouth, chipped his teeth, gouged his eyes, seared his skin. A gash on his chin seeped crimson onto his white shirt. He couldn't hold it in, couldn't stop it, couldn't reach for time any longer. It

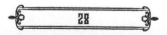

danced out of his grasp, wild, unobtainable. He couldn't breathe. He couldn't. He couldn't. He couldn't—

Danny's scream cut off when he hit the floor. Struggling, he realized he was tangled in the sheets. His bedroom was dark.

As he always did when the nightmare came, he fumbled for his timepiece, the one his father had given him when he became an apprentice. His hands shook so badly that he dropped it twice, but when it opened, he made himself stare at the hands going around the clock face. *Tick. Tock.*

Time hadn't Stopped.

I was in an accident. I got out. I'm safe now.

He touched the scar on his chin, counted the spaces where the stitches had been. There was another scar on his chest, and one on his right thigh, but this one bothered him most. This was his daily reminder, the one the world could see.

It had been three months. Three months since he had been assigned to a small, out-of-the-way clock tower in Shere, a village outside of London. It should have been easy, quick, uncomplicated.

As he worked on the clockwork for a much-needed cleaning, the mechanism had exploded.

For one hair-raising moment, the village had Stopped.

He still didn't know how he'd walked away from that place. The Lead said only Danny's quick work had prevented Shere being Stopped for good. Acting as if someone else controlled him, Danny had reattached the cogs and wound the clock, desperately nudging time to start again.

And it had.

But something else happened that day. The world itself had trembled. An unfamiliar energy had overtaken him, flooding the tower. He couldn't explain it, but he was sure it had played a part in time starting again.

He crawled back into bed and wrapped the blanket around himself. He listened to see if his mother would come, if she'd heard the screaming, but there was no sound on the other side of the wall. Closing his eyes, he clutched the timepiece to his chest, where it ticked above his rapidly beating heart.

The next morning, Danny woke to the shrill ring of the telephone downstairs.

"'Lo?" he croaked into the mouthpiece, rubbing gritty sleep from his eyes while holding the receiver to his ear.

"Daniel? I'm sorry to call so early, but it's important."

The voice belonged to the Lead Mechanic, and he sounded worried. Danny was instantly more awake.

"What is it, sir?"

"Someone's discovered the missing Enfield numeral."

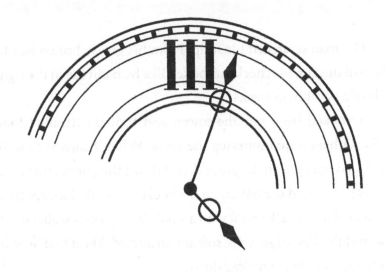

The man from Enfield stood clutching his felt cap in a white-knuckled grip. He fiddled with it as the Lead read the report, turning it over and over in his callused laborer's hands. Danny watched until he was dizzy.

They were in the Lead Mechanic's office, the Lead seated behind his desk and Danny standing to one side. A beam of sunlight struggled to escape the clouds and shine through the window at their backs. It gleamed on the goggles that hung around the man's thick neck.

"Tell us again how you heard about the tower," the Lead said.

The man swallowed, and his Adam's apple bobbed. "I 'eard only that the tower was broke, and that the two was missing. Couldn't tell you how. We all went by to take a peek. I was one of the first, since I wake sooner than most." He hesitated.

"Go on," the Lead said.

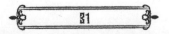

The man scratched his scalp. From his greasy brown hair to the coal dust on his cheek, he looked like he hadn't seen the right side of a bathtub in weeks.

"I walked over, saw the tower, and thought it didn't look right. Others were muttering the same. When I turned to walk back I 'ad me eyes on the ground, and down the street I saw this."

He crammed the felt cap in his pocket and lifted a large rectangular slab of black metal with a small, barely perceivable slit in the middle. The edges were soft and distorted, like it had been in the process of being melted down.

Danny and the Lead inhaled sharply. A tug of something familiar emanated from the metal, like time fibers around the clock towers. The air around Danny shivered and the hairs on his arms stood on end.

"What have you done to it?" he demanded.

"I didn't do nuffink! I'm an ironworker, and I look for pieces like this to use in the workshop. When I walked back to the shop, I saw this on the ground, all mangled up and melted. Couldn't think of what'd done it, and I couldn't know it was from the tower, could I?"

The Lead rubbed his forehead. "Only mechanics would be able to feel the properties of the clock's power in that numeral."

The ironworker's shoulders sagged in relief. "The London peelers were going about asking questions. So when they came to the door, I showed them the block readily enough and they led me 'ere. 'M terribly sorry if it's made a mess."

The Lead glanced at Danny. "The issue's fixed now, at any

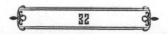

rate. Are you quite sure you found the numeral as you're holding it? You didn't alter it in any way?"

"No time to," the ironworker said. "I'd another project to get on with, and the police showed up in the middle. Probably need to start that over, now."

"I apologize for that, but I'm sure you'll agree your town's well-being is of slightly more importance."

"O-oh, well, yes, of course. 'Course it is, sir."

The Lead sighed. "Very well. Please leave that on my desk and follow your escort out."

Once the ironworker left in the company of the policeman who had been waiting outside, Danny turned to the Lead. "He has to know something."

"He doesn't, Daniel. There was even a witness who saw him find the numeral down the street from the tower. His story seems sound, although I'm sure he must have realized it was a numeral at some point."

"If it can still be called one." Danny picked up the lump of metal, wincing. It felt wrong. Warped. "If it wasn't the iron-worker, then what happened? What could have done *this* to a piece of time?"

The Lead frowned at the ruined numeral, then shook his head. "Perhaps time itself will tell."

"Blazes, what did you do? Feed it gin?"

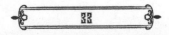

Danny crossed his arms and glared at the auto bonnet, which his friend Cassie had peeled open to reveal the steam engine underneath. The boiler was rusting in places, forming patches of brownish orange like diseased flowers. With months away from work, he didn't have the funds to replace it yet.

"The pressure's off," Cassie muttered to herself as she knelt before the boiler. Her frizzy auburn hair was tied back, and it gleamed in the watery sunshine. "Have you been forcing it to go on low temp?"

"I don't drive it cold," he said. "It's old, that's all. My father bought it years ago. One of the very first models."

Cassie hummed in reply and leaned forward to tamper with something on the side of the boiler, one hand absently twirling a wrench as she worked. He had no idea how she knew all of this. For her, it was like reciting the alphabet. He preferred the familiarity of a clock, the mechanics of which made Cassie cross-eyed.

She turned those blue eyes on him, a smudge of dirt on her freckled nose. "Have you thought about installing a condenser?"

"A what?" He used a sleeve to wipe away the dirt, and she wrinkled her nose at him.

"They've just patented it, and it saves you the trouble of the feedwater. It's a lot more weight for the auto to take on, but it's useful."

"How much does it cost?"

She shrugged. "Twenty quid?"

"Twenty *pounds*? I'll take my chances."

Her face fell a little. "A condenser would be safer. Or even a

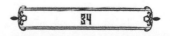

new model. This old thing won't be around much longer." She patted the door as she would a dog.

"Don't talk about it that way."

"What, you're allowed to whinge about it and I'm not?" Her tone had been joking, but seeing his face, Cassie stood and wrapped an arm around his waist. "Calm down, Dan, it's just an auto."

"You know it isn't." He slipped away from her and leaned against the auto door as Cassie leaned on the fence surrounding the Harts' dying front garden. Danny had thought about maintaining the garden during his time off, but one spider bite had driven him away from it forever.

"What's happened, then?" Cassie asked.

The neighbor's tabby slinked around the corner and rubbed itself against Danny's legs. Wanting to avoid Cassie's eyes, he bent down and scratched behind the cat's ears, burying his fingers in its soft fur.

"You and your mum had a row?" Cassie guessed.

"Not quite." Unless you considered three years of resentment a row. Leila had grown distant after what had happened to his father, so wrapped up in her loss that she didn't have the capacity to comfort him in his. Now they could barely last two minutes together.

He had never told Cassie the reason why. It sat like an unmovable stone in the pit of his stomach. If he tried to pull it free, if he even brushed against its sharp edges, he would be cut open and his shame would pour out.

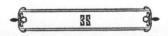

The cat took off in pursuit of a pigeon down the road. Danny stood and decided he couldn't touch that stone. Not yet.

He turned to another problem instead, one Cassie already knew. "Things have just been odd. Ever since I told her . . ."

He trailed off, and Cassie nodded. It still made him uncomfortable to say it out loud, but Cassie, his friend since childhood, never needed words to understand him.

A few months ago—before the disastrous job that had given him his scar and his nightmares—Danny had finally announced what he had known since he was eleven: that he preferred boys over girls. It used to be a capital offense, punishable by hanging or worse, but that law had been abolished in the last decade. While the rural parts of England were still offended by the notion, more civilized areas such as London accepted it with barely a "good heavens."

But much like the protesters condemning the clock towers, that didn't prevent some from thinking it was unnatural.

He supposed he should feel lucky. The ghosts of those before him, the ones who hadn't been so lucky, were a constant weight reminding him he had to make the most of this new freedom.

So he'd told others the truth, his heart knocking against his chest and his breaths like daggers in his lungs each time. The reactions had ranged from wide-eyed "oh"s to sage nods, as if they had known all along. Most people, like Cassie, treated him the same.

His mother hadn't reacted at all. She'd merely sat at the kitchen table and stared at a point over Danny's shoulder, as

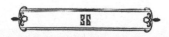

though she couldn't bear to look at him directly. The space between them had grown tight and still. It was the hollow ache of air devoid of words, a breathless subtraction. He'd swallowed that air until pockets of silence sat cancerous in his bones, threatening to expand. To crack.

He knew she kept her distance for another reason. The stone that Danny could not touch. This new information was only another cog in their complicated clockwork.

Cassie gently kicked his boot. "Don't worry, she'll get used to it. She'll have to, or else what'll she say when you bring a handsome young man home?"

"Shove off."

"Not quite what I had in mind." She laughed and noisily kissed his cheek. "Now then, about this boiler. You got two quid on you?" He dug in his pockets for the money. "There's a good lad. Oh, you haven't said if there's been any news."

"News?"

"You know. About the Assignment?"

Danny thought back to the heaviness in the Lead's eyes, the pity he was tired of seeing. His stomach dropped. He wanted the Assignment so badly it hurt.

"The Lead says there's been no progress. He won't make a decision yet."

"I'm sorry, Dan. I know how much it means to you. It'll probably take time, though, won't it? Building a brand-new clock tower?"

Not just that: the first clock tower to be built in hundreds of

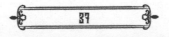

years. The time zones of every city were firmly locked in place by the towers, which had been built to regulate time more efficiently. But the builders had destroyed all knowledge of how to create them. The idea of a new tower had first been met with scorn, but the Lead was determined to see it through.

"No one knows how to build them anymore," Danny said. "Just how to repair them." He dropped his voice to a bitter murmur. "Fat lot of good that does us now. If we don't get this tower to work . . ."

I'll never see Dad again.

Cassie watched him somberly. The stone inside him ached, begging to be pried free.

Cassie knew what it was like to live with guilt. Danny saw it in the way she kept glancing at the auto beside them, her fingers twitching to double-check the engine.

But he remained silent, and Cassie wrapped a hand around his arm. "It'll all work out. At least you did good with the Enfield job, yeah?" He nodded. "Then that's something. They'll see you're back in the game. Do you think you'll have to go there again? To Enfield?"

He remembered the fear that had choked him, the sense of dread he felt just from looking at the clockwork. Maybe the Lead was right to keep him away from the new Maldon tower.

"Not if I can help it," he said.

Fate must have taken a dislike to Danny, because he was called into the Lead's office a couple of days later.

"Colton Tower?" Danny said. "But I was just there."

The Lead raised his hands, just as confused. The little amount of hair he still possessed stuck out awkwardly, as if he'd run his hands through it several times.

"The maintenance crew's phoned in with another problem."

Danny's heart gave an extra-hard thump. "Which is?"

"The minute hand's gone missing."

Fate didn't dislike Danny. Fate despised him. He took a moment to rub a hand over his face, hoping that when he was done, the world would be a little less upsetting.

"Well, the minute hand's not exactly missing," the Lead continued. "They found it at the bottom of the tower, bent at a right angle."

Danny choked on his own saliva. *Bent?*

"But what's happened to the town?" he asked, not bothering to conceal the worry in his voice.

"They're fine, so far as we know, but it's interfering with daily life. Time is moving in quick bursts once an hour. Mayor Aldridge said it's like tripping. In any case, we've commissioned a new hand to be made. As soon as it's installed, it'll fuse with the power of the clock tower and time should go back to normal. The hand will be ready for pickup soon. Do you think you can handle this, Daniel?"

Despite his instinct to say no, Danny told the Lead that he was more than willing. It wasn't entirely a lie. He wanted to make sure the tower was all right. Maybe he could learn something more about the vandalism. Maybe, if he figured out what was going on, he could finally convince the Lead to put him on the Assignment.

As he was leaving, he hesitated on the second floor and turned away from the stairs, toward Matthias's classroom.

Matthias was an old friend of his father's. He and Christopher Hart had started off as apprentice mechanics together, and it hadn't taken much time for them to grow inseparable. From shared assignments to orchestrating pranks on the other apprentices, they had done everything together. As a result, Matthias had been a big part of Danny's life as well, a regular figure at Sunday dinners and birthday parties.

What Danny remembered most was Matthias looking after him when his parents went out. The man would feed him stories as the night grew long, stories of his travels—some true, some nothing more than fancy. ("Did I tell you about the time I met a witch in the Białowieża Forest? She said she would put a curse on me if I hurt any of her bison.") And when Danny was lonely or scared, Matthias would drape a strong arm over his shoulders, keeping him safe and close. Danny needed to feel a measure of that safety right now.

Matthias was teaching a room of apprentices when Danny found him. Matthias was a tall man with a wide chest and a strong jaw, and he normally braided his brown hair, which would have been a source of humor for the younger mechanics if it weren't for his reputation for winning pub brawls.

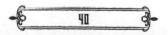

But though Matthias could be strong and bold, what Danny liked most about him was his calm, easy manner, so at odds with his own. Even now Danny saw the room of teenagers barely younger than himself and hung back.

"When the pieces of the clockwork are removed, you *must* be careful to wrap them up and store them, or else they might go missing." Matthias stood before a sketch of clockwork drawn across the chalkboard, pointing sternly to a cog drawn to one side. A metallic whirring box on the teacher's desk recorded every word of the lecture, inscribing them with a tin wheel. "The bits of clockwork are still powerful, even when they've been removed from the main frame, so these need to be taken back to the office. Never toss pieces away. You get that, you lot?"

He was chorused with yesses and nods. Danny smiled. He had never been in Matthias's classes as an apprentice, but wished he had been.

"Now then, one last thing before I let you loose. We have a special visitor today who's going to tell you a little more about how assignments work."

Matthias nodded to a corner Danny couldn't see. A tall, blonde girl walked up to the front of the classroom, her broad shoulders held straight and her gait steadfast. When he recognized her, Danny held back a curse.

Daphne Richards. A full mechanic only a year older than himself. She and that snob Lucas Wakefield had been the youngest mechanics on record at eighteen before Danny had snatched the title away, painting a target on his back at the same time.

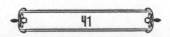

Since then, the three had used their strengths to demand the most challenging assignments in an effort to outdo one another: Daphne with her intellect, Lucas with his looks and his money, and Danny with his sheer, if sometimes aggressive, determination. It had driven the Lead mad.

Then Danny's accident had happened.

A twinge of jealousy ran through him. Why hadn't Matthias asked him to speak to his class? Then again, Matthias had been Daphne's mentor. Just as Danny's father had taken it upon himself to teach Danny all he knew, Matthias had chosen Daphne as his junior apprentice. That sort of bond was hard to sever.

Daphne gave Matthias a small smile and turned to the class. Like some of the younger women in London, she chose to wear trousers and a blouse. Her dark jacket helped conceal her curves, but it couldn't hide the purple diamond-shaped tattoo beside her right eye. He'd once heard an older mechanic call her a walking scandal.

"As many of you know," she began, "London is the central headquarters for clock mechanic affairs in England. When you've passed your assessments to become full mechanics, you'll have the option of staying here and receiving assignments for towns in and around Greater London, including Essex and Kent. Or, if you prefer, you may relocate to another of the branches, such as in Manchester.

"We're also developing a new foreign exchange program with clock mechanic unions in China and America. The latter, for example, would allow certain apprentices to visit one of the American union hubs, such as the one in New York."

As she discussed the exchange program, Danny scanned the room. The boys weren't paying attention to her; they were either scribbling in their books or staring out the window. The girls, however, were enraptured. One girl was furiously writing down everything Daphne said, getting ink splotches all over her hands.

"We're also in the process of beginning an exchange program with India," Daphne went on, and Danny's attention snapped back to her. "Indian apprentices can come to London to learn, and London apprentices can go to Delhi, or one of the other large cities, to study Indian tower design."

Danny watched her face as she continued to discuss plans for the new program. He knew—was one of the few mechanics who knew—that her father had been half Indian. No one would guess it, looking at her skin and her hair and her eyes. Danny certainly wouldn't have known if Matthias hadn't accidentally let it slip years ago.

There were many who opposed the idea of a female clock mechanic at all, let alone one with foreign blood. Despite their history, Danny couldn't help but feel an unspoken understanding. There were some things you were better off keeping to yourself, if you could.

Daphne finished her speech just as a steam whistle blew, signaling the end of class. The apprentices rose with a rustle of papers and the scraping of chair legs while Matthias thanked

Daphne for her time. As she headed out the door, her pale blue eyes locked onto Danny's.

"Mr. Hart," she said coolly.

"Miss Richards."

When she and the students had all gone, Danny slipped inside the classroom. Matthias flipped a switch on the recording mechanism to power it down.

"Danny Boy." Matthias grinned. "How was your assignment? We heard about the missing numeral."

Danny rubbed the back of his neck. "Could've been worse. How are you, Matthias?"

"Could be worse," he echoed. "What happened?" Danny told him about the melted numeral and how it had been found.

Matthias whistled. "And it just happened to be found by a man who melts iron for a living?"

"It's fishy, isn't it?" Danny sat on top of a wooden desk in the front row. "Now there's a report that the minute hand's been bent. I still think it's the ironworker, but the Lead doesn't suspect him."

Matthias started erasing the clockwork sketch. "You've been reading too many detective books."

"Says the man who got me to read them in the first place."

Matthias shrugged in mock guilt.

"Do you think I should do something? About the ironworker."

"If the Lead doesn't suspect him, I doubt there's anything you can do. Just complete the assignment as best you can."

Not quite the answer Danny wanted. If it hadn't been the ironworker, then who could have stolen the numeral? He thought

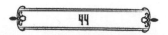

about the protesters outside and his shoulders tightened. He thought also about the mechanics who had been at the Shere tower before him, who would have had plenty of time to hide a bomb within the clockwork.

Someone had carved the initials *E.B.* into the desk on which he sat. He traced the letters with his fingertip, trying not to think about his scar, where the clock had carved its own initials into his skin.

Matthias noticed the shift in Danny's mood. "Was the assignment hard for you, after what happened?"

"It wasn't hard at all," he lied. "It's my job."

"Danny."

He sighed. "Yes, it was hard. Would you be surprised if it wasn't?"

"I don't blame you for being scared." Matthias sat on the professor's desk, facing him. "It's only been a few months since the accident. Your mother says you're still having nightmares."

Of course his mother heard him screaming at night. Not like she would bother asking him about it in the morning.

Matthias frowned. "We're worried, Danny."

"Look at me. I'm fine."

Matthias studied him a moment, then stood and walked up to Danny with his little finger extended. "You'll swear on it?"

It was a custom Matthias had learned in China when he'd visited as a much younger man. He had taught it to Danny a long time ago.

"Matthias," he groaned. "I'm too old for that sort of thing."

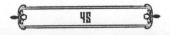

"You're never too old to tell the truth."

Danny rolled his eyes and held up his own little finger to entwine it with the man's thicker one. They shook.

Matthias lightly cuffed his head. "You should be off. You have menacing ironworkers to question and clocks to save."

Danny noted the rings of exhaustion under Matthias's eyes. The man had had a scare when he heard of Danny's accident. Matthias didn't have many people in his life to fuss over, which meant Danny got the brunt of his protectiveness.

But maybe he looked tired for another reason. Danny wondered if the apprentices had been talking about Matthias behind his back again.

"Go on," Matthias urged with a shooing motion. Danny slipped off the desk and wondered if there would ever come a time when adults stopped treating him like a fragile object.

He needed to go downstairs and wait for the new minute hand. Trying to distract himself from wondering what the protesters would do if they saw the part in his arms, Danny walked down the hall and glanced at the paintings as he went. He slowed to a stop when he came to the one he knew best. His father's favorite.

It depicted a storm-tossed sea in grays and blues and greens, the water parted to reveal a dark ocean floor. In that waterless cavity stood two large figures, one red and one gold. They faced each other, prepared for a difficult fight. Lightning forked above their heads.

Danny touched his fingers to the golden figure and thought

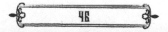

of the golden tower in Enfield. The more he focused on it, the heavier his body grew. What if these incidents meant more? What if they were a prelude to something else?

Away from Matthias's calming presence, Danny's stomach twisted into knots again. Sometimes clocks fell apart with age. It was to be expected when the towers had been maintaining time for hundreds of years.

But this was not the same thing. A numeral had been melted. A hand had been bent.

What was strong enough to tamper with time?

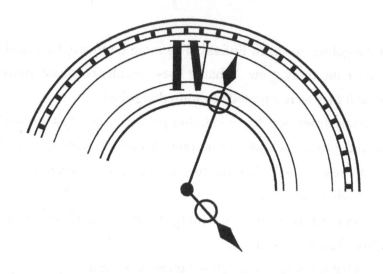

Danny's mother and Matthias had told him stories when he was younger, but his father had kept a few up his sleeve as well. The first time Danny remembered seeing Big Ben, really seeing it and feeling it for what it was, he'd asked his father how the clocks ran in the first place.

"Don't you know?" Christopher had asked, feigning shock. "How on earth will you be a clock mechanic if you don't know your origins, Ticker?"

Every story originated from myth. Different cultures had their own gods. Their world had both.

Chronos was the father of time. After the world was shaped, he awoke within the cosmos, wrapped within galaxies and energy. He saw the earth and how wild and untamed it had become. How it needed to be maintained. So he created time out of the restless power within him, a tiny stream that became a raging flood as

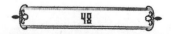

it spun the earth on its axis. Men and women aged, trees grew, plants withered. Time moved all things. Killed all things.

But Chronos couldn't keep an eye on everything, so he cut four fingers from his hand. From his fingers grew the Gaian gods, each one chosen to oversee an element. Terra, earth. Caelum, sky. Oceana, sea.

Aetas, time.

"Aetas was called the Timekeeper," his father had said, one hand resting on Danny's shoulder. He remembered the familiar weight of it, the strength of those fingers gently squeezing his shoulder, the calluses on his father's palm. "He made sure the pattern of time never became unbalanced, never got too tangled. He made sure our pasts, presents, and futures never collided."

While the Gaian gods maintained the earth's elements and humanity advanced, Chronos grew hateful. He saw lives of greed, lives of gluttony, lives of pride and blood and sin. Weary of this corrupt world, he retreated into slumber.

Aetas also grew weary, and mad with the power of time, which was too enormous for him to bear alone. His sister, Oceana, begged him to return his domain to Chronos. When he tried, Chronos turned him away and told him to forget the burden. The world could burn. He no longer cared.

But Aetas cared.

Desperate, he gifted some of his power to humans so that they might help him control the wild beast that was time.

"Chronos found out, and *oof*, was he mad." Christopher smacked the side of his leg for emphasis. "He woke and confronted Aetas. Said that humans should never have been given such power."

Chronos descended to where Aetas lived within the ocean. The water parted for their battle, roiling walls of gray and blue, the crash of lightning and waves above. They fought among dry coral reefs and seashells that broke beneath their feet, the sea a raging storm for three days and three nights, until Aetas grew weak enough for Chronos to land the final blow.

Danny had looked up, his eyes wide. "Chronos killed Aetas?"

"Yes. And when he did, time shattered. No one could control it. And so we built the towers." Christopher had gestured to Big Ben. "The towers are conductors of Aetas's leftover power. Through them, we can control time—or give ourselves the illusion we can. The burden is ours now. We are the Timekeepers."

There were no Gaian gods to help anymore. The other three had receded, choosing to fade to little more than myth. The demand for technology grew in their absence, a demand for humans to control what was once out of their grasp. People held fast to their Bibles and their churches, to the belief that perhaps a benevolent creator looked on, and did nothing.

Everyone leaves, in the end.

It took an hour to reach Enfield. As he got closer, Danny nearly hit a bump in the road and swerved to avoid it. He cursed as his heart jumped into his throat. This bloody town would kill him.

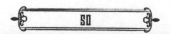

The town was holding its weekly market, and people were clogging the path. He parked on the outskirts and lifted the thin, long parcel containing the new minute hand from the back of the auto.

Immediately he sensed the cracks in time, the empty pockets of missing seconds and moments. It made the air heavy and the sky appear frozen, as if the town were being forced to slow down until the next hour. Time wanted to move in leaps, just as the Lead had said.

Why on earth were they holding the market *now*? He peered at their faces and noticed tight mouths, narrowed eyes. They were putting up a brave front.

Danny walked across the village green and caught glimpses of wares for sale: timepieces, crockery, flower-pulp paper—even a large, clunky photograph-taker. The black camera box sat on its three-legged stand like a raven perched on a fence. Danny longed to have one of his own to play with. The lightness of his pockets kept him away.

He examined the timepieces for sale. They hadn't stopped, exactly, but the minute hands were stuck at eleven, the time when the minute hand had been detached from the tower. At least the hour hands were all correct.

"How do you know what time it is?" he asked a woman passing by.

"We guess," was her terse answer.

Fair enough.

Someone touched Danny's shoulder and he turned, com-

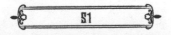

ing face-to-face with Mayor Aldridge. The mayor's mouth was creased from a lifetime of frowning.

"Mr. Hart, thank you for coming back so soon. I'm sorry for the trouble."

"That's all right. I've brought a new minute hand."

"Brilliant," Aldridge said distantly, glancing at the parcel under his arm. "The sooner we return to normal, the better. We've tried to keep things as routine as possible, setting up the market and all. Don't want them to think too much about becoming another Maldon." The mayor mustered up a nervous laugh, and Danny's cheek twitched. "The, ah . . . police will be here again, won't they?"

The Lead had mentioned there would be an investigation, and Danny said as much to the mayor. Aldridge sighed. "Nothing for it, then. Such a disturbance . . ."

Danny nodded in a vaguely sympathetic way and excused himself. He walked past the church to the tower beyond the green, eyes on the missing pivotal line of the minute hand. Walking through the town was like walking through a bog. Time dragged him down, willing him to stop where he stood until the next hour rang. He gritted his teeth and pressed on.

The tower sent a hollow ache through his chest when he crossed the threshold. Danny grunted and braced himself against the wall, wondering if this was how it felt to lose a limb. He climbed the stairs, taking a break in the belfry to wipe his forehead and examine the four bells more closely. None of them were named. That ceremony was reserved for the largest of the towers, like Big Ben.

On the next level, Danny leaned the package against the stair railing and watched the hypnotizing effect of the clockwork's movement. It had been a while since the gears were cleaned; someone would have to come back and do that. The maintenance crew in Enfield was not allowed to touch the clock pieces, only clean and take care of the tower on a basic level, and report anything unusual to the headquarters in London. Like missing numerals and hands.

Fear beat against Danny's rib cage. Sweat dampened his collar.

Don't panic, he told himself. *Don't panic. Don't panic.*

But he couldn't stop thinking about something happening to this tower. The incident at Shere had been investigated, and Danny had been questioned. Though the authorities had found evidence of a bomb, no one could determine the reason behind the attack. Some thought it was terrorism. Some thought it was a misguided prank.

An exploding mechanism was one of the rarer dangers mechanics faced. Still, that moment hovered over him, in his sleep and in the back of his mind. A ghost of terror.

Now clock parts were disappearing from this tower.

You don't even know if it's connected, he reminded himself.

A cog the size of a dinner plate circled in the middle of the clockwork. The central cog was the most important component of the whole tower. Without it, the rest of the clock would refuse to run, and time would Stop until the cog was replaced.

The central cog of the Shere tower had sliced Danny's chin open, turning his white shirt crimson. He could still feel the burn of it, the violent kiss of hot powder against his skin. The jarring skips of time like an arrhythmic heartbeat. Cuts along his body had seeped blood onto the gouged floor created by the skidding of smoking gears, and all the banging, screeching, screaming—

"Stop it," he whispered, closing his eyes tight.

He held himself in busy silence, a stillness that wasn't still, as there was movement in the tower all around him. Danny opened his eyes and gazed balefully at the central cog. He laid his fingers on the gear and left trails in the dust as it turned, like ripples in a pond.

"What are you doing?"

Danny jerked back and nearly tripped over the package. The blond apprentice stood on the staircase, frowning down at him.

"I . . ." How many times had a mentor told him not to touch the central cog, or that his fingers would be crushed if he played with the gears?

"I was just checking it," Danny said. "To make sure it's . . . there."

You're such an idiot.

Brandon's amber eyes flashed, not even glancing at the cog. "It's there."

"Ah, you're right. It is. Good." Danny lifted the package to his

shoulder, attempting to hide his burning face. "You like to arrive early, don't you?" He received no answer. "Let's get started."

When they reached the clock room, Brandon's frown dissolved into his earlier expression of curiosity. Danny noticed that the apprentice wore the same outfit as last time: tight trousers and a baggy shirt. His clavicle peeked out from underneath his collar. Danny swallowed.

"You know," he started, then lost his nerve, unbuttoning his coat instead. When he looked back up, the apprentice was staring at him. "You need to wear different clothes for this sort of work."

Brandon tilted his head to one side, then looked Danny up and down with a small smile. It was such a thorough assessment that Danny felt his earlier blush return like a wave of heat.

"Should I dress like you?"

"Yes, I suppose." Danny typically wore a brown or black work vest, the silver chain of his timepiece hanging from a small pocket. His tall boots were worn, but most of the decorative copper gearwork near the heels remained intact.

The apprentice continued to smile. Danny had no clue what was so funny but wanted to change the subject as soon as possible.

He shifted on his feet and outlined the plan to install the minute hand. Brandon wouldn't have much to do beyond serving as an extra pair of hands, and to observe. Brandon's light eyes flitted around Danny's face as he talked, sometimes glancing down at the chain of his timepiece or the still-wrapped minute hand.

Danny noticed the apprentice was as tall as he was, his waist

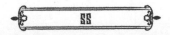

slim under the large shirt, his body made of wiry sinew like a wound mainspring. Brandon had a nice face. Almost too nice. It was lean and smooth, and Danny wondered if he ever had to shave. He suddenly had the absurd urge to touch the boy's jaw. Would that be strange?

His eyes trailed lower, and he barely stopped himself from gasping.

The apprentice's left hand was deformed. It curled in on itself, shrunken within its baggy sleeve.

How did I not see that before? Danny thought, furiously trying to recall their first meeting. Perhaps he had been too preoccupied, but to not even notice . . .

Danny's ears burned with silence, and he realized he had stopped talking. The apprentice watched him warily.

Danny cleared his throat. "Right. Let's begin." He wouldn't—couldn't—mention it now.

They again lowered the scaffolding down the clock face, into the bitter cold. Without his coat, Danny was shivering in no time. Brandon didn't seem affected.

But it wasn't just the cold that made Danny shiver. The height blurred his vision, and he triple-checked that the cables were secure. He remembered the easy way Brandon had scaled the clock face compared to the difficulty he'd had locating the right tools.

"How many jobs have you been on?" Danny asked as they ran the cables down.

The apprentice looked up, as if the sky held the answer. "Just one."

His hand slipped on the rope. "You mean *that* was your first job?" Brandon nodded. Danny cursed himself, wishing he'd handled the situation better, but it was much too late now.

"Hold on," Danny said, "apprentices usually start at twelve or thirteen. Aren't you a bit old to be starting on assignments?"

Brandon looked Danny up and down again. "Aren't you a bit young to be a mechanic?"

Danny tried not to clench his jaw. Maybe this boy wasn't so different from the others after all. "Is that what you think?"

"No. I've only ever seen older mechanics."

"Apprentices can become mechanics by seventeen, if they know what they're doing."

"Well," Brandon said, "you certainly know what you're doing."

Danny waited for the sarcasm to register, but it never did. He felt a curious lightness, momentarily driving away the pang of the damaged tower. Danny ducked his head and muttered a sheepish thanks.

He watched Brandon as they worked. He wasn't using his left hand much. How had he held up the Roman numeral the last time? Danny tried to remember and found that he couldn't.

"Are you ready?" Brandon asked, putting on his abseiling belt.

"Er, sure." Danny couldn't have sounded less certain if he'd

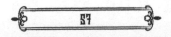

tried. Biting his lip, he peered down at the scaffolding. Brandon glanced at him out of the corner of his eye.

"You look like you know interesting stories," Brandon said suddenly. "Do you?"

"Do I ... know stories? Make-believe ones, you mean? I think everyone knows at least one story."

Brandon gave him a sly smile. "Tell me your one story, then."

It was a strange request, but Danny racked his brain anyway, tiptoeing away from the cruder stories that Cassie knew by heart. Riffling through his childhood memories, he recalled the fairy tales his mother would read him from a green leather-bound book they still kept somewhere in the house. He snatched the first one that came to mind.

"Have you heard the story of Rapunzel?" Brandon shook his head. "I won't tell it very well, just to warn you." He cleared his throat. "There was once a witch who lived in a tower ..."

As they scaled down the clock face, Danny told the story of Dame Gothel, who kept the girl Rapunzel in a tower until her hair had grown amazingly long. Then a prince heard her singing, and saw the way Rapunzel pulled the witch up with her hair. Thinking to try the same, he called for Rapunzel to lower her hair.

"And when she pulled him up and they met, they fell in love, and he came again and again to see her. He asked her to marry him, and they escaped the tower and were married in his kingdom."

Brandon listened quietly the whole time. Danny realized

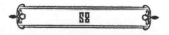

they were already on the scaffolding, the minute hand resting heavily at their feet.

"What about the witch?" Brandon asked.

Danny had asked the same question when he was young, as his mother closed the book. She had paused to think for a moment.

"The witch never bothered them again," she'd said, brushing back his hair to kiss his forehead. "Rapunzel and the prince were careful. And they were together. From there on out, the world was theirs."

But Danny had gone back to read the ending for himself. Remembering it now, he took a deep breath.

"Rapunzel accidentally mentioned the prince, and the witch was furious, so she cut off all of Rapunzel's hair and cast her away. When the prince came, the witch used Rapunzel's hair to hoist him up. Then she dropped him onto a bed of thorns, blinding him."

The apprentice barely blinked, so Danny continued. "The prince wandered for days until he heard Rapunzel singing. He followed the sound, and when they were reunited she was so happy that she wept, and her tears healed his blindness. How that happened, I couldn't tell you. It's a fairy tale. All sorts of strange things happen in fairy tales."

"I see." Brandon gazed solemnly at the clock face where the new Roman numeral II had been installed. "I'm glad they were together, at least. Although I feel bad for the witch."

"What? Why?"

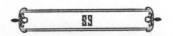

"She must have acted that way for a reason. She didn't hate Rapunzel, or else she would have done something worse to her. Maybe she loved her. Maybe she felt betrayed. Rapunzel and the prince had a happy ending, but she didn't."

"She's the villain. She's not supposed to have a happy ending."

"I know." Brandon's eyes were unfocused. "It just makes me wonder. If she'd done something different, she could have had a happy ending, too."

Danny stared at him until a blast of wind slapped him back into the present. Shivering, he reached for the minute hand. "Can you hold onto this end, here?"

Together they aligned the end of the hand to the cannon pinion, Danny being careful to take most of the weight. He screwed in the industrial bolts, checking the ease of movement. All the while he explained what he was doing and why. Brandon listened as raptly as he had listened to the story.

When Danny fastened the hand, he closed his eyes and tried to grasp the time fibers that flowed around the clock. They weren't frayed as they had been when the numeral was missing, but they were scattered. He gathered as many as he could, pulling them in tight. His fingers twitched as if he were knitting.

Finally, with the twelve main fibers drawn together, Danny screwed in the last bolt. Stepping back, they watched as the longer minute hand slowly traveled around the clock's face until it stopped close to the six position. Just about 12:30. The pain in Danny's chest vanished.

People from the market had come over to watch, and just as

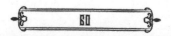

they had the last time, they cheered. The corners of Danny's lips turned up.

There was still the matter of the old minute hand, which had been taken back to the office for analysis. He had half a mind to snoop around the town some more, perhaps take a look at the ironworker's forge.

Maybe he really did read too many detective novels.

But he couldn't deny that the incident was suspicious. And after what had happened in Shere, he felt justified in his caution.

"Do you have a theory?" he asked Brandon. "About the missing tower parts."

The apprentice hesitated. Danny took his silence as a no.

"This isn't normal. There has to be *some* reason why it's happening." At least now, with a second assignment under his belt, he would hopefully be closer to getting the Assignment.

As Danny gathered his tools, Brandon studied the clock face, an unreadable expression on his own. "You mentioned your father last time," Brandon said. "What happened to him?"

Danny couldn't tell what to be more surprised by: that the apprentice didn't already know, or that he'd asked. Everyone knew what had happened to Christopher Hart. But there was something annoyingly sincere about Brandon's gaze as he took in Danny's reaction.

"That's not the sort of story you want to hear," he said. "It's a sad one."

"I like sad stories, too."

Danny's anger flared like wind through a flame, but he

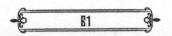

quashed it and gestured to the cables on either side of the scaffolding.

"Let's get inside."

After they dragged the scaffolding back into the tower, Danny smoothed down his runaway hair. He glanced several times at his apprentice, who was taking in the view of the still-bustling marketplace.

"He disappeared three years ago."

Brandon turned, surprised. He lifted a hand, like he would touch Danny's arm in sympathy. Danny turned away before he could. He wasn't sure what would happen if Brandon touched him now.

"How?"

Danny brushed the dust from his trousers. "Not disappeared, exactly. He was a mechanic, like me. One of the best. Worked on Big Ben all the time." Some of his favorite childhood memories were when his father and Matthias told him about the massive clockwork inside Big Ben and the four gleaming faces at the very top, staring out at all of London.

"He started training me when I was young. We took apart clocks and timepieces, and read books about clock towers around the world. Mum had hopes of sending me to Cambridge or Oxford, but I refused. I wanted to be like Dad. I wanted to be a clock mechanic." He smiled as a memory unfurled within him, a memory of his father and him laughing when a spring had become lost within his mother's curly hair. But as he continued, the smile died.

"We saved up to go on holiday to France, since Mum's always wanted to go, but something happened to Evaline Tower in Maldon. They needed someone to look into it."

Danny swallowed. His throat felt tight, like the hand of the past gently squeezed it. "My father volunteered. Mum wouldn't leave for our holiday without him, so we were stuck at home. He went to Maldon and didn't send any word back to us.

"The next day we heard the town was Stopped."

Brandon cocked his head to one side. "Stopped?"

"Lord, don't you know anything? It's when the clock stops working altogether. Until it's fixed, the town Stops, and the people inside are trapped. Time can't move forward. No seasons pass, days don't transition to night, people don't age. And no one can speak to the ones trapped inside, not even through a telephone. They're all just . . . stuck there, caught in an endless loop."

Danny again recalled the horrifying moment in Shere when the clockwork exploded. If he hadn't fixed the clock in time, he would have suffered the same fate as his father.

A voice in his mind whispered that maybe he should have.

"We don't know why the town Stopped, or how the clock can be fixed. We don't know anything. All we can do is wait and see if there's any change."

Danny sat on the staircase leading to the platform and rested his arms on his knees. "Mum keeps waiting for him to walk through the door, but I know he won't. Once a town is Stopped, it's Stopped until the clock is fixed."

Everyone leaves, in the end.

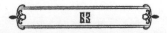

The apprentice settled next to Danny, his eyebrows furrowed. "I'm sorry. You're right, that is a sad story."

"You asked to hear it," Danny reminded him, cross. He wasn't even sure why he had bothered to tell him. But if Brandon didn't hear it from him, some other mechanic or apprentice would have been all too pleased to trade gossip.

There was also something about the apprentice that made Danny feel his words would not be judged. That it was safe to tell his story here.

"Are you sure nothing can be done?" Brandon asked.

"Well. There is one thing. They're building a new clock tower just outside of Maldon. It's almost complete, but the clockwork needs to be forged and installed. The Lead thinks that if this tower creates a new area of time, it'll cross into Maldon's time zone and free the town. Some of the mechanics say it won't work. Others don't want the tower built at all." He rubbed his eyes. "But it has to work. It *has* to. If they can't find a way, I will. I have to see Dad again."

I have to tell him I'm sorry.

Brandon mulled over the story. "I think you'll see your father again."

Others would speak such platitudes with caution, knowing in the back of their minds that it was possible Danny would never be reunited with his father. The words were cardboard condolences, spoken over and over in a bland, frustrating mantra: "Keep faith. It'll be all right. Be strong, Danny."

He looked at the apprentice and saw no pity in his eyes. Just

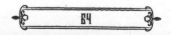

concern. "We'll see," he said, standing. He stretched his arms above his head and heard his shoulder pop. "What do you think, drinks to celebrate the repair?"

Brandon's head shot up. "Drinks?"

Danny glanced outside. "I guess it's a little early. Still, why not?"

The apprentice hesitated, then shook his head, his eyes averted. "No, thank you."

Danny lingered, hoping Brandon would change his mind. When it became clear he was on his own, he reached for his coat.

He heard his name and turned around. Brandon still sat there, hands on his knees. Danny had to look twice; his left hand was now identical to the right. Unmarred. Whole.

Then what the hell had he seen? A trick of the light?

"What is it?" Danny asked when Brandon remained silent, heart beating a little faster. He willed him to change his mind. To jump up and say that drinks were a good idea after all. To explain his damned hand.

The apprentice chewed his lips and shook his head again. Disappointed, Danny slung his bag over his shoulder.

"'Bye, then." He started down the stairs feeling Brandon's eyes on his back. It wasn't until he reached the bottom that he realized something.

He had been too busy reciting the story of Rapunzel to focus on his fear of the scaffolding—or his fear of the clock.

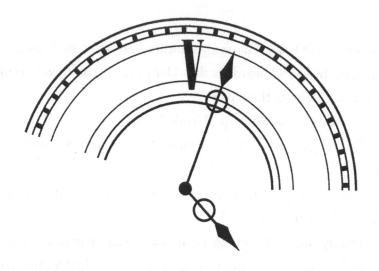

Danny gripped the steering wheel so tightly his hands looked bloodless. Every exhalation rattled from his chest.

"Calm down," he whispered. "It won't happen again."

He was parked outside of Shere. He'd suffered nightmare after nightmare about this place. Now that he was back, the first time since the incident, he realized what a horrible, stupid, idiotic idea this was.

No one had given him an assignment. No one had forced him to come. He was here on his own, because he had questions.

Swallowing painfully, Danny untangled himself from the steering wheel and walked into the village, the roads too narrow for his auto. The buildings were old, but in a way his mother would call "charming." Ivy grew up the sides of houses, and the steeple of the church roof was wet after the recent rainfall. Children laughed nearby, playing a game with hoops.

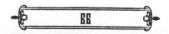

He wanted to run.

He stopped in front of a statue and leaned against it. The stone was cold and made him shiver, but its solidness was reassuring. He focused on breathing as he stared first at the ground, then at the statue. After a moment he realized it was a shrine.

It was common to see relics of the Gaian gods following in small towns and villages. Some probably still held fast to the old religion, but Danny had yet to meet anyone who actively prayed to the lost gods. Even some of the clock mechanics rolled their eyes at the mention of Aetas.

Danny himself wasn't sure if they had ever existed, despite his father's stories. Sometimes a story was simply a way to put the extraordinary into perspective. To embellish a truth so much that it became nothing but fabrication.

The goddess he was using as a prop was Terra, of the earth. Of course—Shere was surrounded by farmland. Farmers would sacrifice livestock as offerings to Terra in ancient times. Danny certainly hoped that practice had died out.

Terra sat cross-legged, her weatherworn hands pressed to the ground. Her face had long since eroded, but it was tilted up as if receiving strength from the sun. Her long hair fanned over her shoulders, stone strands chipped and pockmarked. Ivy snaked around one of Terra's arms.

Danny patted her shoulder in awkward apology and stepped away from the shrine. He turned toward the village square where the clock tower stood in the center, gray stone stretching up to a white face. The ivy had even found its way here, the whole village choked with it, creeping up the tower walls. It looked more like a grave marker than a clock.

The bomb had done the most damage inside, blasting apart the clockwork and breaking wooden beams. Nothing permanent; nothing that a few replacement parts and some carpentry couldn't fix. The central cog—the most important part of all—had remained intact.

If it hadn't, he would have never made it out.

Danny didn't trust himself to draw any nearer, as if getting too close would make the clockwork explode all over again. Instead, he forced himself to approach the people around the square. Luckily, no one recognized him.

A woman bounced a baby on her hip as Danny asked about the tower. "Missing parts?" she said. "No, I don't think so."

"You didn't see anything strange beforehand? A lost numeral, perhaps? Or something wrong with the hands?"

"Not that I recall."

He asked a few others, but they all said the same: everything had been running smoothly until the bomb went off. No one could remember seeing a suspicious person, not even when Danny described the Enfield ironworker.

"There was a mechanic who came before the bombing," a man with long sideburns said. "A big man with a strange walk."

Danny recognized the description of Tom Hawthorne, one of the older mechanics. He had worked on the Shere tower a week before Danny, and had been the first suspect. After an inquiry, the authorities had declared him innocent.

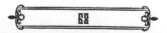

The clock struck three. The pealing of the bells shook Danny's heart.

He hurried back to his auto, breaths fast and shallow. Sitting in the driver's seat, he closed his eyes as sweat rolled down his temples. He swore he heard the clock ticking even from here.

I was in an accident. I got out. I'm safe now.

Twenty minutes passed before he could drive home.

Danny set his mug down with a loud sigh.

"That good, is it?" Matthias asked, smiling.

Danny sloshed the golden liquid, careful not to spill any. The color inanely reminded him of Brandon's eyes. "You taught me how to drink, remember?"

"I did, didn't I?" Matthias laughed. "Shame on me, then. What'll I say to your poor mother?"

"That her son is now a drunkard." Danny drained his mug and banged it on the table. The unimpressed barmaid snatched it up. The only thing preventing Danny from being thrown out was that he was sitting with Matthias, arguably the pub's most frequent patron.

Matthias set down his own mug, his first of the night and barely half-drunk. "Danny, I know something's the matter."

"The truth, then?" Matthias nodded, so Danny leaned forward in a conspiratorial manner. "I'm actually Queen Victoria. Fooled you, didn't I?"

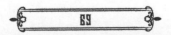

He snickered, but when a muscle in Matthias's jaw feathered, Danny silenced himself.

"S'nothing much," he mumbled to his hands, which were curled on the sticky tabletop. "Just thinking about Dad."

The barmaid came and left. The newly filled mug of beer sat within easy reach, but Danny didn't touch it.

"Been three years," Matthias said, taking a sip of his own pint. "I can hardly believe it." He shook his head slowly, blue eyes darkening.

"I suppose you haven't heard anything more about the new tower?" Danny asked.

"It isn't coming along the way the mechanics want it to. They say there's something off about it. Doesn't help that the protesters are being tetchy, demonstrating all around the construction site."

Danny frowned. "I want to help, but the Lead won't let me. He doesn't believe I'm . . . recovered." When Danny had approached him after installing the minute hand, he'd been rewarded with the same string of words: *patient, wait, sorry.*

Matthias kept his hands clutched around his mug, gaze fixed on the murky drink. He took a breath as if to speak, then let it out again.

"I know," Danny said, finally collecting his mug. "'Don't despair.' 'It'll come to rights, Danny.' 'You're being too pessimistic, Danny.' Well, Danny knows the truth, and he's not an idiot."

Matthias put a strong hand on his arm. "It's good to be realistic. No false expectations. But don't give up hope."

Danny nodded and the hand slipped away. He took a sip, but found he had no desire for the drink anymore.

Matthias knew all about grief. Danny remembered when his father had sat him down and explained that he should never ask Matthias about his late wife, Alice. She had died young, just four years after their wedding, leaving Matthias to grieve for twenty more. Christopher had told his friend to take a new bride, but Matthias had stubbornly refused.

Then Matthias had been assigned to Maldon's clock tower just over three years ago. People believed that while he was there, Matthias had fallen for a woman and lost focus of the job he was sent there to do. While distracted, he had done something irreparable to the clock—something grave enough to be fired as a mechanic and exiled from Maldon, although nobody could say what that was. A private meeting had occurred between Matthias and the Lead, where Matthias had entered the office as a mechanic and left only as a teacher.

That was the story everyone knew. The one Matthias told went a little differently.

In his version, Matthias claimed to have met the tower's clock spirit.

He told the story the same way he told all his stories, in that slightly lilting voice, his eyes dark and turned to something distant. Danny might as well have been a child again, sitting at his side with the man's arm across his shoulders.

"She was lovely," Matthias would say. "And she could feel time in a way no one else could, not even me. She *was* time."

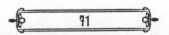

Danny had grown up with the myth of clock spirits. Some claimed that each clock's power over time manifested itself into a spirit that guarded the tower and the delicate clockwork within. Others said it was leftover power from Aetas that clung to the towers when the god died. That's what his father believed.

Danny wanted to believe it, too, but never could. As much as he devoured stories, he always held a kernel of doubt in his pocket.

Still, superstitions were hard to snuff out. No one liked to be reminded of the mechanic in Glasgow who had fallen so in love with his tower that time reversed every time the sun set, making the day start over and over again in an endless loop. Or the mechanic in Paris who had caused a citywide disaster when time crawled almost to a stop within a one-mile radius from the tower where she had been secretly living.

It wasn't an official rule in any handbook, but it didn't need to be. Everyone knew forming an emotional attachment to a clock was forbidden.

Matthias had fallen in love, he said. The weak muscle of his heart had grown strong again. But as he tried to keep this supposed clock spirit affair a secret, something within the tower had broken. He had been unable to repair it, and time skittered wildly.

Danny's father had been sent to Maldon to fix things. Days later, the town Stopped.

It was just another of Matthias's stories, a fabrication built layer upon layer until the truth was so buried that Danny couldn't see it. There was no witch in the Białowieża Forest. There were no man-eating dragons in China.

There were no clock spirits.

Danny understood that Matthias wanted to protect himself from his mistake, that his shame could momentarily be disguised with wonder. So Danny let him tell his stories. He pretended to believe.

But he knew better. It didn't matter how many stories you told if you were still at fault in the end.

"Here," Danny said, pushing the mug toward Matthias. "I think I'm finished."

Disappointment creased Matthias's eyes, or perhaps it was guilt. He often looked that way, even though Danny had forgiven him a long time ago.

"Heading home? Give your mother a kiss for me."

Danny knew she wouldn't accept a kiss from her own son, let alone him. He was about to pay when Matthias waved his hand away.

"Go on, get some rest. I'll take care of it. And Danny? The next time you have these thoughts, don't hesitate to ring me. I'll always be on the other end of the line."

Danny managed a small smile. "I know."

The pub was not far from home. Kennington was loud with the sounds of autos, carriages, horses, and the cries of coster-mongers selling matches and rat poison. He kicked an empty tin toward the street. It would be picked up in the morning by the cleaning crew, a new development since the sanitation reform had kicked in. A young crossing sweeper with a broom in his hand shot Danny a nasty glance.

Some thought the city was chaotic, yet Danny loved it. The cobbled roads, the tall buildings, the history, the technology. London was the thriving pulse of the civilized world. He weaved through ladies with spotless white gloves and grimy chimney sweeps dropping soot wherever they went. Steam and smoke rose from chimneys and engines, forming a gray cloud that loomed over them all.

As he walked through the front door, Danny saw his mother on the telephone. She stood hunched over the holder, the chartreuse-colored receiver clutched in one hand.

Danny's heart stuttered. His mother had been in this exact position when they'd received the call about his father. This was the position of the world ending.

But then he realized she was simply writing something on the pad beside the telephone.

"Yes. Of course. All right. Thank you very much."

She hung the receiver back on its holder and ripped the paper from the pad. Leila turned and jumped at the sight of him.

"Danny! When on earth did you get here?"

"Just now. Who were you speaking to?"

"Who . . . ?" She pointed uselessly at the telephone. "Oh, that was nothing. Nora called to tell me about a new boutique on Piccadilly I might like." Leila peered up at her son, the paper clutched in her small hands, as if waiting to be dismissed or told that her lie was good enough. Danny was too tired and too tipsy to argue. He shrugged and shucked off his coat. She disappeared into the kitchen and he followed slowly behind.

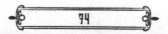

A container of milk had been forgotten on the table. "Mum, put this in the cold box, for Christ's sake."

"Don't use that language," she snapped, distracted as she cut up carrots at the counter. She had thrown on a stained apron and her eyebrows were knotted in concentration, as if she were performing surgery, not crookedly mincing root vegetables. Something had filled her with an almost manic energy. "Which reminds me—you should come to church this Sunday. An out-of-town bishop's coming to give a lecture."

She hardly ever spoke this much to him. She was definitely in a good mood. Danny hid his face as he returned the milk to the cold box. "I'll see if I'm free."

"You smell like the pub," she murmured. "I think church'll do you some good, Danny."

"Church won't earn us money." *Or get Dad back.*

His mother sighed, but when she said nothing further, he escaped upstairs to his room.

As it so happened, he was busy on Sunday after all. During a breakfast of crumbs he'd found at the bottom of the bread box—his mother hadn't bought a new loaf—the telephone in the hall rang.

"Hullo?"

"Ah, Daniel?" The Lead Mechanic's voice came through tinny and crackled. Danny automatically stood straighter, although the man couldn't see him.

"Yes, sir."

"Good, I've caught you in time. There seems to be another issue with the tower you've been fixing this week, the one in Enfield."

"Again?"

His mother, coming down the stairs dressed for church, threw him a startled look.

Danny cleared his throat. "Haven't they caught the person doing this?"

"We're not sure if it's a vandal or if the clock's simply falling apart. The Enfield maintenance crew hasn't reported anyone suspicious."

Danny imagined the ironworker in the dead of night, tiptoeing away from the tower with a sinister chuckle. "What's wrong with it this time?"

"There appears to be a crack in the face. We think it was caused by the minute hand's removal. Nothing substantial, the time's not skewed much; it's just a nuisance. Don't want it disturbing the structure, you understand."

Danny gazed heavenward, wondering if he should go to church after all. "I'll drive out as soon as I can."

"Good show. I'll ring up the apprentice."

Danny hung up the receiver and stared at the telephone, the bottom of his stomach feeling strange as he thought about the blond boy. Or maybe that was hunger.

Danny enjoyed his work, or at least he used to; most mechanics were passionate about their field of expertise. But he had never heard of a clock having this many problems in such a short amount of time. Usually his jobs were spaced out to once a week, perhaps once a month in lean times. Thrice in one week was virtually unheard of.

Especially three times for one small clock tower.

Something was off. Sabotage? A bad attempt at a practical joke? Whatever the reason behind these incidents, Danny was getting more and more frustrated. And scared.

The auto sputtered and rumbled as he drove into Enfield. Some people waved while others called hellos. Danny was so used to the anonymity of London that it hadn't crossed his mind that the townspeople would know him by sight now. He waved back, perturbed, but didn't stop to chat. An attractive young man smiled at him and Danny slowed for a moment, then forced himself onward with a scolding shake of his head.

A crack marred the clock face between the numbers three and four. Danny parked the auto across the street and eyed the damage for a moment. It would take some time to fix a crack that big.

The back of his skull pulsed with sudden pain and he rested his forehead on the steering wheel.

He had to prove himself. No more panicking.

Curiously, there was another auto parked near his own. Danny gave it a confused glance before heading inside the tower. He reached the familiar clock room and set his bag down with a sigh.

"Here we are again." He turned and unbuttoned his coat. "There's something seriously wrong with this ruddy old—Who the hell are you?"

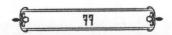

The boy standing in the clock room blinked at him. "I'm the apprentice. Brandon Summers."

Danny stared at him, unaware his jaw had dropped until he closed it with a click of his teeth. The boy was decidedly *not* the apprentice he had worked with before. This one had dark skin, with a snub nose and hooded brown eyes, his black hair clipped short. He wore a white cravat with his gray vest and trousers.

"You're not the . . . I've never seen you before."

"Can't figure you would have," the boy, also Brandon, said with a hint of impatience. New Brandon was younger, though a couple inches taller than Danny and broader in the shoulder. "I was sick. Didn't you get my note? Would've called, but our telephone is faulty."

"But the office . . ."

"Was I supposed to tell the office, too?"

Danny stood marinating in his own disbelief. Something caught his eye and he looked over the apprentice's shoulder.

Standing just behind New Brandon was the blond apprentice. He grinned when Danny spotted him.

He had a scar on his left cheek.

Just like the crack on the clock face.

"Something the matter?" New Brandon asked.

Danny shook himself and looked again, but the boy had disappeared.

"It can't be," he whispered. His veins throbbed with the force of his heartbeat.

"*What* are you going on about?"

Danny struggled to remember how words worked. He kept

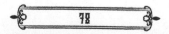

staring over New Brandon's shoulder, but when the apprentice turned around, there was nothing to see.

"Uh, sorry," Danny croaked. "I, er . . ."

Not good. He probably looked like a lunatic.

Danny forced a laugh. "Sorry, I just had a thought, but it's gone now. What'd you say your name was? Brandon . . . ?"

"Summers," the boy finished, the name clipped around his frown. "They should've told you."

"I see." *Brandon Summers.* The blond boy had said his name was Brandon Summers. Danny couldn't recall half the names of his past apprentices, but he had remembered that one.

Danny felt as if eyes were on him, and the space between his shoulder blades tightened. He heard a faint echo of laughter in the whirring of the clock's gears.

"You all right?" New Brandon asked. "You want a lie-down, or—?"

"No, no, I'm fine. Let's . . . let's get to work."

They settled in to discuss the plan of action. Danny could barely concentrate, and his explanation was filled with pauses. He turned to his tools and quickly looked around.

There he was: standing so that New Brandon couldn't see him, wearing his white billowy shirt and tight trousers. The boy met Danny's eyes and smiled, his mouth a mischievous curl. In a blink he was gone again.

"Losing my mind," Danny muttered. "Losing my damn mind."

Thankfully, the repair could be done without having to use the scaffolding. The clock room allowed them access to the clock face, gleaming yellow and white as the sun slanted through. The floorboards had been stripped of color after decades of sun exposure, but the light turned the dust motes floating through the air into specks of gold.

Danny and New Brandon—Real Brandon?—each donned goggles before preparing the sharp-smelling cleaning solution. They wiped the length of the fissure with it, making sure there were no small pieces of glass residue, and waited for the surface to dry. Then Danny sealed the crack with strong resin, which was specially formulated to mimic the glass.

He felt the strange boy's gaze the entire time, resting like a hand upon his back.

Once they'd sanded the resin and chipped the extra away, Danny told the apprentice to watch as he set his hands upon the crack. He closed his eyes and felt the fibers there, intact, but with a line through them that threatened their delicate system. Danny erased it until there was only the thinnest hairbreadth remaining. He sealed the rest of the gap by taking tiny amounts of each thread and pinching them together until time rolled like an air current through the fibers.

He opened his eyes and saw the crack was healed. The apprentice whistled appreciatively as Danny stepped back.

"Nice work, mechanic."

"Uh, thank you. If you would help me clean up?"

With nothing left for him to do, Real Brandon prepared to leave. He hesitated by the stairs.

"You won't tell the office about the mix-up, will you? About

them sending payment for the other jobs?" At Danny's silence, Brandon turned fully toward him. "I normally wouldn't ask. But my family—"

"I won't say anything."

"It's just that I've five siblings," Real Brandon said in a rush. "They need new clothes, and—"

"Don't worry, I won't mention it."

The apprentice had taken something out of his pocket: a tiger's eye marble, a sphere of dark amber with a black slit running down the middle. He fiddled with it, but not nervously, as Danny tended to fiddle with his timepiece. Rather, he rolled the marble around in his fingers as though he was in the practice of doing it often.

"You sure, mate?"

"Yes, I'm sure. You're free to go." He watched as the apprentice galloped down the stairs, eager to be away before Danny changed his mind.

Danny sat on a box near the clock face and listened to the ticking at his back. He took out his timepiece and checked the time, pocketed it, forgot the time, and checked again.

When he looked up, the blond boy was standing before him.

Danny swallowed. He looked like an average boy Danny's age. But there was something about him—something that had been there from the start—that was more than average, like the evasive unknown between the time fibers Danny reached for in the darkness.

It couldn't be true. He didn't want it to be true. But the threads

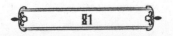

of the story kept unraveling, wanting him to find the truth hidden inside. The question emerged before he could stop himself.

"You're the clock spirit, aren't you?"

The boy didn't respond, but smiled with a glimmer in his amber eyes.

"No. No, that can't right. That's not . . ." Danny stared at him, at a loss. The boy stared back. "Possible."

Anything is possible, his father had said.

"God," Danny breathed. "I didn't think—I mean, when you've never seen one before—Do you really live here? You're actually the . . . ?"

The spirit cocked his head to one side. The scar on his cheek had gone, sealed like the crack on the clock face.

"Silly question, of course you are." Danny was trying to remain calm, but every second only heightened his amazement. "Why didn't you tell me?"

"You thought I was your apprentice. I wanted to help."

"Yes, but, you weren't. And I looked like an idiot." Danny groaned and rested his forehead on his palms.

The spirit sat on the box beside him. "I should have told you earlier. I'm sorry."

Danny dropped his hands and looked up. This close, the spirit's eyes were mesmerizing, almost as striking at the glint of the opal glass behind them.

"What's your real name?" Danny whispered.

"Colton."

Of course. The name of the tower.

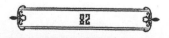

"Another silly question. God, I'm thick." He rubbed his eyes. "Why didn't you show yourself to Brandon? The real Brandon?"

Colton linked his hands together between his knees. "I've never revealed myself to anyone."

"And yet here you are. With me. Why?"

The spirit tipped his head so that some of his bright hair fell forward. "I don't know."

"You don't know?" When the spirit only shrugged, Danny rose and began to pace around the room. "You show yourself to me, help me repair you, but you don't show yourself to anyone else. You speak to me, and yet you . . . Hang on." Danny stopped, his excitement tripled. "Why do you keep falling apart? Who's doing this to you? If anyone knows, it's you!"

Colton looked away. Danny knelt before him, but the spirit wouldn't meet his eyes.

"It's all right, you can tell me. I'm a mechanic, it's my job to know if someone's tampering with your tower. I mean, it's not as if *you're* the one doing it."

No response.

Danny stared at him, heartbeat quickening. "Did you do this to yourself?" When Colton still didn't answer, Danny's frustration boiled into anger. "What's the matter with you? Why would you do that?"

The spirit disappeared. Just *vanished*. Danny gasped and fell on his backside.

Colton winked back into existence a few feet away. "No one comes here," he said, eyes blazing. "No one cares about this place.

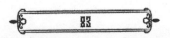

The cleaners come and faff about, and leave me dirtier than before. I haven't had a real mechanic set foot here in a year."

Danny ran a hand over the front of his waistcoat, speechless. Eventually he murmured, "You shouldn't do that to yourself. It harms you, and the town."

Colton lowered his gaze. "The numeral was rusting, and the minute hand was slowing. I had to do something."

They stayed like that, motionless, for a full minute. Then Danny stood up carefully, worried that the spirit would disappear again at any moment. Something had changed between them, and it made his frantic mind slow down. He should have been angry; he should have told Colton what a mess he'd made.

But he couldn't. Because he understood.

Coming nearer, Danny raised his hand.

"Can I . . . Would it be all right to touch you?"

Colton didn't move at first. Then he took a step forward and held out a thin, bronze-colored hand. Danny cupped it with his bigger, paler hand, his fingers first skimming the inside of Colton's palm before their hands clasped.

Danny held back another gasp. A peculiar ripple traveled up his spine, and the hairs on his body stood on end. It was much like touching the time fibers, brushing a finger across them to feel the yawning of time open and swallow him whole. He was scattered across the cosmos and deep within the earth, within himself and outside of himself. A miniscule star in the infinite sky. A tiny speck of life in the flow of time.

He came back to himself a few seconds—hours?—later,

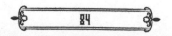

breathless. Their hands were still clasped, a seam of gold and silver. How could something with such a gentle touch melt an iron numeral or bend a minute hand? The spirit was much stronger than he appeared. A dangerous thrill shot through Danny's body.

He tried to imagine being stuck in this tower for years without end. To have no other option than to pretend he was falling apart to get attention.

Danny tugged the spirit forward. "Come with me."

They walked down a level to the clockwork. Danny heard the swinging of the pendulum below, the heavy weight like a beating heart under their feet. Danny tried to feel for Colton's pulse, but the hand within his own was still.

The pendulum was not the heart of the clock. The lungs, perhaps, every swing a breath propelling life forward. But the heart was something else.

The lines made by his fingers were still on the central cog, creating channels in the dust. Danny touched it.

"These gears need cleaning. You can't trust a maintenance crew to do that. Why don't I come back and do it myself?"

Colton narrowed his eyes. "You would do that?"

"I won't be paid for it, but I'd like to. I can tell it's been a while, and if the dust keeps gathering, it'll muck everything up."

"Won't you get in trouble?"

A mechanic was never supposed to accept a job if it didn't come from the Lead himself. But in this instance, what could

Danny say? He couldn't tell the Lead the real reason why the clock was falling to pieces. He'd look mad.

"No, I won't get in trouble."

Colton's face brightened, shining like the clock face above them. He followed the trail Danny's eyes had made across the clockwork a moment earlier. "Can I tell you a secret?"

"What's that?"

"I'm off by about four minutes."

Danny blinked, then smiled. Colton sounded like a boy who had just admitted to trampling his mother's prized flowers.

"Don't worry, I'll fix that, too."

He knelt in front of the clockwork, eyeing it with appreciation, the complex structure forged from cleverness and creativity. And necessity. His tools were laid out beside him, from the soft-bristled brush to the screwdriver he'd need for cleaning and disassembly. Although Danny couldn't stop the flutter of anxiety from being so close to the mechanism, he had to admire it for what it was.

After the incident with his father, Danny had retreated from society. He didn't want to mince words and force smiles while the stone that sat within him wedged itself deeper, cutting and bleeding him dry. Because of his distance, he had developed a reputation for being *odd*. People gave him sidelong looks and whispered as soon as they thought he was out of earshot.

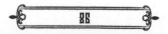

Out in the world, Danny didn't feel himself. There was nothing for him there.

Here, he felt needed. Valued. The tower was a sanctuary, all gold lines and hard curves, glint and glass, standing old and steady under the thrum of time.

Colton stood at his shoulder. As he looked on, Danny found the small components of the clockwork, the cogs that could be removed without interfering too much with the clock's running. Even if time paused, the townspeople probably wouldn't notice if Danny replaced the parts quickly enough.

When he'd driven into Enfield that morning, he'd worried what the townspeople might say, since there was no noticeable problem with the tower. But there was a wedding taking place at St. Andrew's church today, distracting many of them. He wondered what would happen if time warped over the assembly, giving a new meaning to the term "forever hold your peace."

It was something he wanted to avoid. All apprentices were trained to recognize the signs of Stopping: being enclosed by a solid gray barrier, or time skipping repeatedly. One had to move fast to reverse the effects. A retired mechanic who'd once been trapped in a Stopped town had explained to Danny's class that people could still move and speak to one another, but were unable to do much else. Items that were picked up returned to their original positions. A woman had run out her door thirteen times in a row, caught in a loop.

All that training had gone out the window for Danny when the Shere clock blew up. Adrenaline, and what Matthias called his intuition, had prevented disaster then. That, and the strange other power he'd felt so briefly.

"Look at all this dust," Danny muttered, giving the gears a preliminary wipe with a cloth. "How do they expect you to keep running under these conditions?"

"I think they forget," Colton said, leaning down to inspect what Danny was doing.

"Forget! How could they?"

Colton shrugged.

"More like take you for granted. Don't worry, you're in good hands now."

The spirit smiled. It was slow and full. "I don't doubt it, Danny."

The sound of his name set his heart off like a firework. He turned his head and realized how close their faces were. Trying not to blush, Danny quickly turned back to the clockwork.

A clock spirit. A *clock* spirit. He had tried to get his head around the fact, but spent the night tossing and turning—not out of fear, but fascination. They really did exist. They weren't just a myth.

Which meant that Matthias's story might be true. He had always humored Matthias, pretending to believe him, but now Danny couldn't help but look at him differently. Understand him differently.

He could imagine the scene now, in a way he couldn't before. Matthias standing before the Lead. Being told that his relationship with the Maldon clock was forbidden, disastrous, unacceptable. Stripped of his title and his pride.

Knowing no one else would believe him.

Danny removed the first small cog and used the brush to carefully clean its spokes. The weight of the spirit's eyes was still on him; he was certain Colton was just as fascinated with him as he was with Colton. Danny looked over his shoulder.

"You don't have to wait around on my account. Look in that bag, there." Colton crouched and lifted the flap of the satchel with a thin finger. He dragged out a large book with a green cover. "Fairy tales. Figured you might like to read them while I do this."

Colton smiled wider and sat on the floor, the book opened to a random page on his lap. Danny returned to the clockwork.

The pages turned at a quicker rate than he expected, so he glanced over to find the spirit examining the illustrations.

"The pictures are nice, but the stories are good, too."

"I can't read."

"You can't—? Well, of course you can't, you're a bloody clock. Here." He leaned over and flipped to the story of Rapunzel. "Look at those pictures. They're from the story I told you."

Colton did as he was told. Since he seemed to be enjoying himself, Danny resumed his work.

It proved to be a long, labor-intensive process, and he was sweating by the time he cleaned the larger cogs. Time would occasionally slow around them, and he felt as if he dragged his limbs through air turned to jam, but when he replaced the parts he cleaned, it returned to normal.

He stopped to eat lunch and told Colton more stories. He read about Cinderella—the spirit enjoyed the part about the clock striking midnight—and Sleeping Beauty. During the latter, Colton kept asking about the time dimensions used to make everyone in the kingdom sleep for a hundred years.

As Danny finished the last bit of his sandwich, he looked up and started. A brown mouse was perched on Colton's shoulder.

"Uh..."

Colton looked at where Danny was staring. "Hallo. You're probably hungry." The mouse's ears trembled.

"Is this normal?" Danny asked, watching the mouse. Its whiskers twitched, nose sniffing the air. "You being friends with the tower mice?"

"No one else to talk to."

Danny winced. Keeping his eyes on the mouse, he broke off a piece of bread and leaned forward. The mouse grabbed it with tiny paws and began nibbling at once, spilling crumbs down Colton's shirt.

Danny laughed. "I feel like I'm in my own fairy tale."

Colton smiled.

The larger gears couldn't be handled without assistance from at least two other people, so Danny reluctantly used the ladder to reach the higher ones and wiped them off as they moved. He attacked between the spokes with his brush and dust and grit flew off, making him sneeze.

Finally, Danny turned to the main structure of the clockwork. He watched the central cog turn for some time until he knelt to wipe it with an alcohol-soaked cloth. Streaks of grime peeled away, revealing a bright copper surface underneath.

As he dusted off the spokes, he sensed Colton standing at his back. He was silent, but Danny felt his tension like a pulled bowstring. He would be rather nervous himself if someone were laying their hands upon his heart.

"No one's treated me this gently in a long time," the spirit said.

Danny looked up at him. Colton's face was grave, the fairy tales now reduced to nothing but a childish distraction.

"My father taught me to do it this way. The other mechanics haven't been gentle?" Colton shook his head. "I'm sorry. Not all mechanics are careful, I'm afraid. A few aren't even all that good. Just because someone's born to sense time doesn't mean they have any skill with it."

"You're a good mechanic," Colton said. Their eyes met, and Danny fought to swallow. "I want you to be my mechanic."

"Well, that's not really my choice to . . ."

His voice died away as the spirit leaned down and kissed him.

Danny's eyes widened. His chest rioted. Blond hair tickled his forehead, and he could see the curve of Colton's closed eyelids, so close to his own. The spirit's lips were surprisingly soft. It was difficult to remind himself that Colton wasn't really made of flesh, that he was only a manifestation. He felt real enough.

The entire universe was flooding into his chest. Time hugged him, held him, warned him of its strength beyond the gentle touch of mouths.

Colton leaned back and their lips separated with a small noise.

Danny stared at him, out of breath, feverish. He was unsure what to say now. "Thank you" didn't seem like the proper response.

Colton's eyes gleamed like sunshine on metal. "Will you come back?"

Danny remained kneeling by the clock's turning heart, his own beating so hard that he would be shocked if Colton couldn't hear it. The cogs seemed to listen and wait for his response.

But Matthias's pained face flashed across his mind. He knew what happened to mechanics who got too close to the spirits.

Danny refused to turn Enfield into another Maldon.

"Yes," he lied, giving a little nod to convince him. "Yes, I will."

AETAS AND THE EARTH GODDESS

When the earth was quiet and the air was still, Aetas emerged from the ocean to discover land. He walked across red dust and desert weeds, craggy mountainsides and grass so soft he wondered if they rivaled his brother Caelum's clouds in the sky. Time rolled over him, a second and a year, so that he traveled endlessly and within the blink of an eye.

The ocean beckoned to him. His sister, Oceana, was impatient for his return, so Aetas knelt in streams and cupped his hands in rivers to whisper of his adventures to the water. It trickled from his fingers and traveled back to Oceana, and she listened to the vesper of his stories, the breath of him under the calm, deep waters.

Aetas was wandering across a great plain of larkspur and blackthorn when he saw a young woman dancing. She twirled and turned into a shower of violets that dizzied on the breeze, then coalesced and returned back to a maiden's form. Her hair was the color of laurel, her skin the shade of an old mahogany tree.

When Aetas approached, she stood still and let the wind play with the stalks of her hair. Aetas greeted his sister, Terra, she of the earth and living things. She asked after the ocean, and he asked after the sky.

"I'm glad you are here, Brother," she said with the voice of the wind through bamboo reeds. "I'm in need of your assistance."

She led him to a small settlement where humans toiled to build and plant and irrigate. A line of saplings stood as a border between the settlement and the wild hills to the east.

"These trees need to be big and strong," said Terra, "for these humans to benefit from their fruit and their protection."

"They will need time to grow," Aetas replied.

"And that is what I am asking for, Brother. Time."

He understood. Aetas spread his hands and felt the stir of time across his body, wisps and coils of golden light. They snaked around the saplings, twining through their thin branches, hugging their lean trunks. As they watched, the saplings grew and spread.

Time tugged him forward, and Aetas frowned. For even as the trees became large and strong and green, the settlement grew and grew and grew. People aged. Tombstones speckled the landscape beyond.

Aetas carefully pulled back until time reversed. The trees shrank and groveled toward the earth. The settlement contracted. The tombs gave up their dead.

"I cannot do what you ask, Sister," Aetas said. "These trees need to grow on their own. Think of the repercussions that ripple of time will have on other living beings. The humans will all be dead before they can reap the benefits of the fully grown trees. It will cheat the trees out of many years of their long lives. Let them come into their own."

Terra's eyes were the grayish-green of uncut emeralds, shining as Aetas's words opened a well of sadness within her.

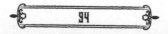

He took her dark hand in his golden one. "Do not fret, Sister. The humans will grow up wise and strong like these trees. They will care for them. And when enough time passes, both will be better for it."

For Aetas should have known that to play with time was to go against the wishes of Chronos, his creator, the originator of the power that flowed through Aetas's body like veins of golden thread. He did not want the wrath of Chronos upon himself or upon his sister. He did not want to do something he would later come to regret.

Aetas said goodbye to Terra and resumed his travels until, weary, he walked back into the ocean to rejoin Oceana, where time was his to keep. Where each thread from his body could push in and out with the tide, touching every shore, running the world.

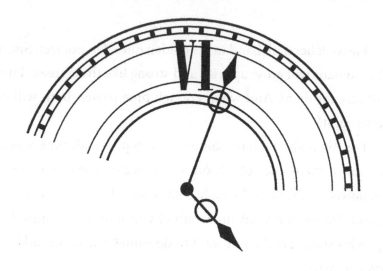

There were several things Danny had never expected to happen to him in the course of his life. Become the King of England, for instance, or have his name written in a history book. The list ranged from the implausible to the idiotic: become a baker, fight in a war, swim in the Thames.

In that entire list, he had never expected to include *be kissed by a clock spirit.*

Danny bit the inside of his cheek as Cassie disappeared under his auto. It was currently propped on a metal bed, its parts exposed like intestines. It had finally broken down on him, and he'd needed it towed to the warehouse where Cassie worked. He didn't trust anyone else to take a look.

He ran a finger over his lips again, as if amazed to find them on his face. He recalled the moment perfectly, even the eyelashes on Colton's face, a dusky blond at the tips that darkened to black at their roots.

It was a thing so strange, so bizarre, so exceptional, that Danny felt he ought to tell someone. But he knew all too well why he couldn't. There would be an investigation, they would find out about Colton, and the *kiss*, and oh God—he would be exiled from Enfield quicker than a door could be slammed in a salesman's face.

"Oh, s'not good at all," Cassie said from under the car, her voice muffled. All Danny could see of her were dark coveralls, which were baggy on her sturdy body.

"Should I hand over my entire life savings, then?"

"Don't be dramatic, Dan."

He kicked the sole of her boot. "Then don't say dramatic things. Tell me what needs fixing."

"Everything."

Danny pinched the bridge of his nose and counted to five. When he looked up, Cassie was sitting with her back against the auto, her auburn hair streaked with oil.

"I just need it to run for jobs," he said.

"Then you may need a new boiler. Dan, I'm telling you, they're making newer models that run like a song. Why don't you try one of those out when you've the money? Loads easier than these clunky things."

"How much for the new boiler?"

"Twenty quid."

He groaned. Due to his leave of absence, his pockets were not exactly bursting with riches.

"Either that or pay for another tow," Cassie said bluntly.

Danny sighed and pulled out his wallet, hoping he had enough. Cassie examined the auto behind her. Danny knew that look. As he expected, she began to disappear back under the framework.

"I think I forgot to check—"

Danny grabbed her ankles and pulled her back out. She glared at him from the floor.

"You've done all you can for now," he said. "Leave it alone."

She huffed a breath that stirred the loose hairs on her forehead, but her expression was strained.

Danny remembered her face on the day her older brother's auto flipped and crashed, killing him instantly. Her skin had been bone white, her eyes hollow and dark like a flame blown out from a lantern. He'd felt the tremor between her body and his as he held her, as she wept and said that it was her fault. That William was dead because of her.

Of course that wasn't true. She couldn't have known it would happen, hadn't thought to check her brother's auto that day. It had been having problems, she said. She should have done more. Her sisters and remaining brother would blame her.

It had been ten months, and Danny still saw remnants of Cassie's terror each time he took off in his auto. He wanted to tell her he knew the taste of guilt, but the bitter burn on his tongue prevented him from saying anything. He knew it wouldn't give her any comfort. Her loss was finite, irreversible. His loss was caught in suspension.

"It'll be all right, Cass," he said gently. "I know you'll do a good job."

Her mouth quivered before she pressed it into a firm line. Nodding, Cassie stood and redid her braid, resettling her mood just as she resettled the strands of hair.

"There's something else, isn't there?" she asked. "You've that look."

"It's nothing." But he considered it again, the thought standing with its toes curled over the very forefront of his mind, waiting to swan dive into the open.

The color of amber. The sweet smell of mechanical oil. Colton's lips.

"Danny Hart, your face is red!" She tried to pinch his cheeks, but shrieked when Danny picked her up.

"I'll find the nearest body of water and toss you in it," he warned her.

"All right, all right!" He put her down. "You're a touchy bloke, you know that?"

Would it really be so bad if Cassie knew? He could still see a fragment of fear caught in her eyes. He could provide her with a distraction at the least.

Ducking his head, Danny mumbled, "A boy kissed me."

Cassie drew in a breath to shout her glee, but Danny slapped a hand over her mouth just in time. She swatted him away to reveal a Cheshire Cat grin.

"Who was it? Where? Do I know him? How old is he? Is he good-looking?"

Danny wished he had a shield against the onslaught of questions. He picked one at random. "It was in Enfield, on assignment."

"Did it *just* happen?"

He nodded.

"Oh, that's marvelous! Who was it?"

He shrugged and looked at his feet. "Just some bloke."

Danny had been kissed before, but only twice. Once by Cassie when they were twelve, to see what being kissed by a girl was like. She'd been offended that he hadn't liked it very much. The second time had been by Barnaby Slacks, a fellow apprentice, a few years later. Danny had liked that much better. But Barnaby had been relocated to Leicester after causing some trouble on his assignments, along with any chance of them growing closer. Since then, Danny had been too shy and too busy, and no one had been willing. Until now.

A clock spirit, of all things.

Cassie's face fell. "You don't even know his name?"

"No. Didn't ask."

"Well, did you like it, then? Did he kiss the way you like?" She dropped her voice to a whisper. "Did he use his tongue?"

"*Cass!*"

"C'mon, I want to know! If you can tell anyone, it's me."

He crossed his arms. He had no idea how to answer, because

he honestly didn't know. Liked it? Yes, of course. Impossible not to. But caution was slowly taking over that curious, shameful feeling initially mistaken for excitement.

He knew what happened to those who became too involved with their projects. Compulsive cleaning, installing unnecessary parts, and excessive tinkering had all landed mechanics in trouble. An entire town had been Stopped because of this sort of misguided enthusiasm.

Now that Danny knew the truth, he had a rather good idea of what happened three years before. The clock spirit of Maldon must have reacted when Matthias left, much in the same way Colton had harmed himself to get attention. Only the Maldon spirit hadn't just harmed herself; she'd destroyed herself, perhaps as punishment, or out of grief, or rebellion.

This would cause nothing but trouble.

"Danny? You all right?"

"Yes, I'm fine."

Cassie's blaze of excitement died down to only the embers of interest. She gripped his arm. "Don't worry, no one's bothered by it. Your mother isn't, despite whatever she says about grandchildren and all that nonsense."

Danny was confused until he realized that she wasn't talking about clock spirits. "That's not—" He rubbed a hand against his face with a sigh. "Never mind."

"Now who's being dramatic? Really, Dan, you've nothing to worry about."

Though he doubted that, he made himself smile for her. He reached into the wallet, but found a humiliating truth awaiting him.

"Cass," he murmured, "I don't have enough."

Her eyes winced in sympathy. "That's all right. We'll do it in installments, yeah?"

Which meant he'd have to dip into his new auto savings. Danny handed her a pound to start with. "Fix it up, all right?"

"You know I will, don't offend me so. You go on home and rest. And Dan?" He turned to find her glowering. "Next time, you better be decent and find out the bloke's name."

He didn't want to tell her there wouldn't be a next time.

Home was not his first stop, despite Cassie's command to rest. That's all everyone ever wanted him to do now. As if he could sleep his life away until he woke one morning to find all his problems solved.

He went to the Mechanics Affairs building to ask if there was any news about the Maldon tower. The protesters were there again, a mix of people complaining about things they couldn't control. One woman held up a sign that read THE GOD OF TIME WILL BE REVIVED! A man with a thick mustache was shouting at her about paganism and how there was only one true God.

Danny ran through the masses and into the building. The atrium was congested with busy mechanics and apprentices. He took to the stairs, first checking to see if he had any new assignments, but he found nothing in his folder. Vexed, he made his way to the Lead's office.

Two older mechanics walked down the hall toward him. Danny's breath caught when he saw who they were. Tom and George were both well-respected, having been mechanics for over thirty years. Tom was tall and broad, while George was short and stocky, but both wore the same look of importance that was not quite arrogance.

Both were on the Maldon assignment.

The bigger one, Tom, walked with a heavy limp. He had lost his right leg to an infected bullet wound in the Crimean War twenty years before. Since then, he'd worn a mechanical prosthetic.

Someone in Shere had recalled Tom's limp, identifying him as the mechanic who had worked on the tower before Danny arrived. Seeing him now, Danny couldn't stop the shiver that rolled down his spine. He'd never liked Tom. Perhaps it was because his father and Matthias had never got on with him. Maybe because Tom had been Lucas Wakefield's mentor, and had always turned a blind eye whenever Lucas decided to poke and prod at Danny. There was something about the man that bothered him, some gruff distance.

The two older men were in deep in conversation, but stopped as soon as they saw Danny. George sighed.

"Hello, Danny," Tom said warily.

This wasn't their first meeting since the accident. They had endured Danny's glares and suspicion. But since they'd been put in charge of the new Maldon tower, Danny had to change his approach.

"Hello," Danny mumbled. "I was wondering—I mean, how are you?"

"Get to the point, boy."

Danny swallowed. He noticed that Tom was holding a long roll of paper in his hand. His heart leapt. "Are those the blueprints for the new Maldon tower?"

The mechanics exchanged a look. George tilted his head slightly, an inquiry, but Tom replied with a slight but clear shake of his own. "Danny—"

"I'd like to know how it's coming along. I'm sure you've been there recently."

"If the Lead hasn't said anything, we can't discuss it with you," Tom said. "Be patient."

Danny, already tipping into frustration, allowed this to be the push he needed. "No. I'm tired of being patient. I have a right to know what's going on."

"Move, boy," Tom grunted, but Danny stood his ground and curled his hands into fists.

"I want to see those blueprints!"

Tom grabbed him by the vest and pushed him against the wall. Danny tried to pry the man's hand away, but it was thick and strong, like Matthias's. He wished his old friend were here to punch Tom in the jaw for him.

"Listen, you annoying bleeder, I don't care if you think you've *got a right to know*. Hundreds of people with family stuck

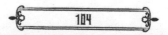

in Maldon deserve to know, but you don't see us lining them up for a rally. Don't think you can try to bully us just because you're the Lead's favorite. I don't *care* if you're a broken little boy who needs to be treated special. That act's not working on me."

"C'mon, Tom," George murmured. "Leave the lad alone."

Tom frowned before releasing Danny's vest.

Danny leaned against the wall, fighting for breath as the two mechanics walked away without another word.

A broken little boy. An act. The Lead's favorite. None of it was true. But standing there, his chest throbbing with anger and disappointment, Danny wanted to believe at least one of them.

He took a steam-run omnibus home, leaving him with only a sixpence in his pocket. The house was empty. His mother was working late again.

Danny stared into the pantry and rubbed a finger over his lips. If only life could be like the fairy tales: a short obstacle to overcome and a reunion at the end of it, with a small chance of blindness or a dragon thrown in to make things interesting.

He jerked when the telephone rang. Thinking it might be Cassie or the Lead, he banged a shoulder against the kitchen door to hurry into the hall.

When he answered, an unfamiliar woman's voice floated from the receiver into his disappointed ear.

"Is this the Hart residence?"

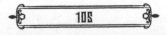

"Yes, who's calling?"

"Elizabeth Collins, over at the McClure and Gambol Firm. I spoke to a Mrs. Hart the other day."

Danny gripped the mouthpiece harder. "This is her son. She's not in. May I take a message?"

"I'm returning her call about the bookkeeping position here in Chelmsford. Will you let her know she's been selected for an interview in two weeks' time? Thursday, at ten o'clock."

Chelmsford?

His throat was too tight to swallow, but he let out a strangled, "Yes."

"Thank you, dear. Have a nice day."

He stared at the telephone until a loud and unpleasant blaring exploded from the receiver, then slammed it down and went upstairs. He couldn't remember how to put away his socks. The rubbish bin stayed overturned where he'd kicked it. Unable to stand the questions that stabbed the backs of his eyes, he retreated to bed.

The front door opened and closed around ten. Danny had dozed off, and his stomach was hollow and vengeful. He went downstairs as if marching to the gallows.

His mother was puffing on a cigarette in the kitchen, flitting about like a worker bee. Smoke streaked the air in gray clouds. Danny waved them away.

"Mum?"

"Still up, are you? How's the auto?"

"Cass has it in the shop. It needs a new boiler."

Leila clucked her tongue. "Can't be helped, the poor thing is getting on in years." She dragged a pot onto the stove. "Had a chat with Cassie's mum. She told me Cassie's going to a social dance. You'll be going, I hope? There's a nice suit in your closet you never wear. I'll straighten it up and make sure it still fits."

"Mum?" He waited until she turned around. Leila's face had become lined around her mouth, her lips pursed as if she always thought she were smoking. Runaway curls had sprung free from her coiffure, giving her a particularly mad look. Her shoulders sagged with exhaustion.

"What is it, Danny?"

He took a deep breath. "Why have you applied to a job in Chelmsford?"

She stood stock-still, her dark eyes like a frightened deer's when the hunter's caught a glimpse of it. She turned and rearranged the pot, then grabbed a few potatoes on the counter.

"*Mum.*"

"It'll pay more than my current job," she said, studying the potato in her hand. "Much more."

"Chelmsford is at least two hours away. How d'you expect to get there every day?" When she remained quiet, he finally understood. "You want us to move?"

"Chelmsford's a nice place, and—"

"My life's in *London,*" he said. "My friends, my job, my—everything's here, Mum! Everything is in London."

"Then you can stay here," she said, "and I'll move to Chelmsford."

Life tilted a bit, and he looked at it from this new angle. Living in London without his mother? Was such a thing possible, or was it on the list of things he thought would never happen?

He knew he could have a place of his own, some grimy flat above a barber's shop—that's where people his age went to live, wasn't it?—but then he would be truly alone. The gaping threat of the future chilled him.

Perhaps his mother simply didn't want to be near him anymore. Perhaps, finally, she had stopped caring.

"You have a job, you have connections," Leila said. "You'll be fine here on your own."

Danny detected something stiff about her, something in the way her eyes moved to the pot to avoid his gaze. He thought of Chelmsford and the towns around it. What the mechanics were trying to build on the very edge of its time zone, right where it met Maldon's.

"You want to go because of Dad." He said the words slowly, his voice hard with accusation. "You want to be closer to Maldon." Danny flinched when she shoved the pot away with a scraping clatter.

"Of course I want to be closer to him! Why do you make it out like that's a bad thing? I *miss* him, Danny. We both do."

Danny was alarmed, and ashamed, to see that her cheeks were wet. She turned and wiped her face around a sniff like paper tearing.

"It won't bring him back," he said quietly. They had lived that first year in anticipation, thinking Christopher would come through the door at any moment. But just because his father now lived where time stood still didn't mean their lives could stand still also.

"I know that," his mother said. "I only want to be closer to him, to see if I can f-feel him, somehow." Her shoulders shook. "If it were you, if it had h-happened to someone you . . . Wouldn't you do the same? Wouldn't you do anything for the one you love?"

Danny felt the wound again, the sharp slide of stone. He clutched his stomach and closed his eyes. He deserved this. He deserved her leaving him.

Nothing would get through to her now.

"A woman named Collins called," he said. "You have an interview in two weeks. Thursday, ten o'clock."

Leila turned her head, her eyelashes formed into wet spikes. "Thank you, Danny."

He went to bed hungry.

The news made the front page of next day's paper:

Rotherfield Clock Tower Bombed—Citizens Alarmed

Danny dropped the paper like it had caught fire. Bile burned the back of his throat.

"Don't leave it on the floor," his mother scolded. She bent to pick it up, but stopped when she read the headline. She turned to Danny, horrified.

He ran to the toilet just in time to empty his stomach.

The Lead didn't waste time calling an assembly of clock mechanics. The small crowd of protesters was more riled up than ever, and police had to patrol the outside of the Affairs building as mechanics filed inside. Danny ducked his head and pretended not to hear the shouts and calls, the yelled questions he couldn't answer.

He bumped into the mechanic in front of him in his hurry. She half turned with a frown, crinkling the diamond-shaped tattoo by her eye. Daphne Richards.

"Sorry," he mumbled.

"Maybe you should keep your eyes off the floor, Mr. Hart," she replied. She slipped away before he could respond.

Solemn murmurs filled the assembly hall, speculating about the recent attack. Tom and George spoke with heads bent close together. Danny often felt eyes on him, on his scar. No one said a word to him.

The Lead announced that there would be further investigations, and that any suspicious behavior was to be reported immediately. Danny thought about Colton's tower. Would the police come back? Would they find out that he'd been there on his own?

He hadn't eaten anything since yesterday, but he felt ready to throw up again.

As the mechanics filed out after the assembly, Danny spotted Matthias in the far back. The man seemed to be looking for him, so Danny hid behind a group of apprentices. He wasn't in the mood to be fussed over right now. He had already endured his mother's particular brand of worry.

That morning, she had knocked repeatedly on the washroom door and asked if he was all right. The first wave of panic had been the worst, seizing his limbs and smothering his lungs. Danny hadn't been able to move for some time, slumped against the tub and staring blankly at the wall.

Again. It's happened again. In his mind, the clockwork gears blasted apart repeatedly, blossoming out like a sharp, deadly flower before retracting to its framework and exploding all over again.

By the time he'd found his way to his room, his mother was sitting on his bed. She'd been pale and frantic, twisting her thin hands together, dried tears on her face.

"Danny, do you need anything?"

He had shaken his head. Better to pretend he was fine; he didn't want to go back to the hospital. He'd been forced to stay there after the incident in Shere, and it had made him feel lesser. Weaker. Alone.

His mother had cried then, too. He didn't want to see her cry anymore.

In the atrium someone tapped his shoulder, returning him to the present. The Lead.

"Daniel, a word?"

He knows about Colton. He knows I went back to Shere.

Danny followed him, hands clenched at his sides. When they got to the Lead's office, they didn't bother to sit.

"Do you know anything about this attack?" the Lead asked.

Danny was thrown off balance, and it took him a moment to answer. "No, sir."

The Lead sighed. "The tower isn't too damaged, thankfully. But we can't let our guard down again."

By some miracle, Rotherfield hadn't been Stopped. The bomb had been misplaced or defective; the clockwork itself was fine. However, a clock face had been shattered and some of the paneling would need to be rebuilt. Time was jumping around the town, and officials wondered whether or not to evacuate residents.

It had been a close call.

"I'm starting to wonder if this is what happened to Maldon," the Lead said. "What do you think, Daniel?"

"Maybe, sir."

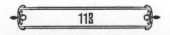

But for once, it wasn't his father he was thinking of. It was Colton.

Did he worry about Colton's tower? Of course. Did he want to go there? Yes. Did he still think about that kiss? Definitely.

Would he go to Enfield?

He shouldn't. He knew now that a clock spirit or a bomb could wreck the tower. Danny could at least prevent one of those.

Instead of going to Enfield, he did something even more absurd. He waited a couple of days until the normal flow of time had been restored in Rotherfield, then drove two hours to the town. When he arrived, he almost turned around and drove straight back to London.

"Don't be a coward," he muttered to himself.

A mechanic was already here. A well-to-do mechanic, by the looks of the auto parked outside the town square. The auto must have come from London; it was much too nice for the country roads around Rotherfield. The black paint was shining and spotless, the wheels perfectly inflated. It looked as though the vehicle had been bought yesterday.

Wary, Danny walked down the narrow street. The smallness of the place unnerved him. He was so used to the sprawling metropolis of London that these tiny towns felt too close for comfort.

Danny passed an alcove carved into the side of a stone build-

ing. Inside stood an old shrine much like the one he'd seen in Shere. This one had been partially destroyed, but whether by the elements or by man or both, it was hard to say. The base of the statue was still visible, as was the scalloped pattern of what looked to be a wing. Caelum, then. The Gaian god of the sky.

Danny reached the square and looked up at the tower. It stood about the same height as Colton's, but had four faces instead of one. The western face had been blown out by the bomb, leaving behind jagged bits of glass like yellow fangs in a gaping mouth.

According to the report, mechanics had stabilized time using the power of the other three clock faces. If this had happened to Colton's tower, with its sole face, the town wouldn't be so lucky.

Police surrounded the tower. Citizens stood a short distance away, muttering among themselves. Danny watched them for signs of protest, but his eyes kept returning to the empty, faceless circle.

"What are *you* doing here?"

Danny jumped. A familiar mechanic stood across the street, glaring in his direction.

"Lucas," Danny said stiffly.

Now the other auto made sense.

"I asked what you're doing here," Lucas demanded, eyes narrowing slightly. Danny had always thought his eyelashes were absurdly long for a bloke.

"I . . ." Danny couldn't say he was on assignment, not with

Lucas here already. "I have a friend here. I was checking up on him."

Lucas smiled. It was the type of smile that didn't mean nice things.

"You have a *friend*?"

"Har, you're so clever. I also wanted to get a look at the tower."

The smile shifted into a frown. "There's no need. I've already had a look, and so have two others." Lucas's gaze dropped down to Danny's chin. "Unless you think you're the expert."

Danny's neck grew hot. "I'm curious," he said, heading for the tower. Lucas blocked his path.

"It's closed off. No one's allowed inside."

"Except for mechanics, right?"

Lucas grabbed his arm when Danny made to step around him. "You're not a mechanic. You're an apprentice disguised as a mechanic."

Danny yanked his arm away. "Shove off."

"What's going on here?" A constable had come to see what the commotion was about. Lucas put on an innocent show.

"No trouble at all, Constable," he said, flashing his teeth in a grin. Unlike Danny, Lucas kept his brown hair neatly trimmed, just bordering on austere. Lucas's clothes were fresh and new, all crisp lines and gleaming buttons. Danny resisted the urge to run his fingers over the threadbare collar of his own shirt.

The officer grunted and moved away, already bored. If Danny had attempted that, he would've been hauled off.

There was something to say for looking like you had money.

"You're not going to figure out anything we don't already know," Lucas muttered. "You think you can take some notes, report back to the Lead, and be showered with praise as usual? It's not that simple. Why are you toadying up to him, anyway? You miss your dear old dad so much you need a replacement?"

Danny's hands curled into fists, but he couldn't do anything in full view of the constables. Instead, he imagined someone pummeling Lucas's face until his teeth looked like the shards of glass above.

He was right, though. There was nothing to be done here that the others weren't already doing.

Fuming, Danny turned to where his auto was parked. Lucas laughed at his back.

He bumped into someone on the street and mumbled an apology. Danny hesitated, then decided he might as well make one last effort. "Do you know anything about the tower?" The man shook his head. "You didn't see anything unusual before it happened, or after?"

The man pushed his glasses up his nose. "Not that I recall."

Danny made to turn away, but the man cleared his throat. "Wait, there was one thing. The night before, I was walking through the square on my way home. When I passed the tower, I thought I heard . . ."

"What?" Danny pressed.

"Well, it sounds silly, but I thought I heard someone crying."

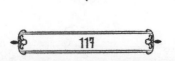

Danny's head was spinning with too many thoughts, and suddenly the house around him felt too small. Grabbing his coat, he decided what he needed was a walk to stretch his legs and some conversation to stretch his mind.

Danny walked through Hyde Park and enjoyed the bracing autumn air. He watched ladies taking a morning stroll with their servants, gentlemen on horses, young girls acting as caretakers for rich children. But he mostly watched the lower-class mothers and fathers chasing after their own children, laughing and making memories. Danny had his own cache of such memories: his father lifting him up on his shoulders to see Punch and Judy shows, giving him crackers to feed the ducks, buying him sweets. Christopher never had much time to spare, focused on work as he was, but he'd still taken Danny out as often as possible.

He remembered trying to fly a kite, throwing it up as an offering to the wind, only to have it sadly plummet to the ground. Christopher had laughed and said the wind currents were probably better at the top of Big Ben.

"Can we fly a kite on top of the tower?" Danny had asked, excited by the notion. "Is that even possible?"

His father had grinned. "Anything is possible."

They'd never had the chance to try.

Danny felt the pull of Big Ben even from here. If he focused hard enough, he could sense the fibers running through the city, enabling it to thrive. They were golden arteries attached to the heart of London, the clock that made sure the leaves fell and the snow would come.

Danny left the park and walked down a couple streets, toward a row house painted a shabby white trimmed in chipping blue. Like Christopher Hart, Matthias was addicted to his work, and could not be bothered with menial household chores like repainting. Matthias lived on the outskirts of Kensington, an admittedly wealthy district, but he had inherited the house from a rich aunt. His neighbors often expressed offense that he didn't take better care of the place.

Danny walked through the creaking iron gate and knocked on the blue door. He heard a distant "Coming!" on the other side and waited with hands in his pockets. The heavy yellow drapes in the window swayed. Matthias sometimes complained about a draft in the old house.

The door was unbolted and Matthias stood in the doorframe, running a hand through his long brown hair.

"Danny Boy! What's the matter?"

"I didn't know if you were busy," Danny said, half turning. "I can go if you are."

"Nonsense. Wait right there."

The door closed and he heard heavy footsteps. Danny burrowed his nose and mouth deeper into his scarf. Matthias never let him inside his house. When Danny had once asked why, he said he was embarrassed by the state of disrepair. Danny tried not to take it personally. Others would just as likely be turned away, if there was anyone besides him who even visited Matthias.

The man emerged a minute later, dressed for walking, his hair tied back. "Where to?"

"The park's fine."

They set off in comfortable silence. Matthias glanced over a few times, but Danny's eyes stayed fixed on the ground.

They followed the stone path through a corridor of trees and sat on an empty bench across from a mother and her young daughter, who were eating a midday snack. The girl crumbled the bread of her sandwich for the hungry pigeons below.

"How's that housemate of yours?" Danny asked. Matthias let a room for extra income.

"Why do you bring him up?"

"Thought I saw him at the window."

"No, it's that bloody draft again. I'll get to fixing it soon." He tapped his fingers on his thigh, then sighed. "You've been thinking about Rotherfield."

"Who isn't thinking about Rotherfield?"

"I reckon it must be difficult, what with Shere and all." Matthias glanced at Danny's scar. "The Lead will find out who's behind the attack."

"But what if he doesn't?" Danny's voice shook slightly, despite his best efforts to keep it even. "What if this just keeps happening until—"

Until another town becomes the next Maldon.

Matthias shifted to face him. "You mustn't think like that. They'll find a way to stop this."

Danny watched the little girl feed the birds, throwing down crumbs like confetti. A boy on a chrome bicycle zoomed by, scaring the pigeons, and the girl shrieked as they all took off in a chaotic flutter of wings. Danny knew how that felt: to be content one moment and terrified the next. For something normal to erupt and leave you senseless.

Danny stuck out his long legs. If only Matthias knew the entire problem. Thoughts and fears frothed under the surface, ready to spill over at a word.

Matthias's story about the clock spirit was true. Whenever Maldon's name came up, the man's eyes dimmed, his face like a closed door to the past.

Matthias losing the two loves of his life was enough reason for Danny to stay quiet. More than that, Danny didn't want to become like him, exiled from Enfield and shunned by his colleagues. To be a lonely man in an empty house, trailed by the ghosts of his mistakes.

As if Matthias had peeked into his thoughts, he asked suddenly, "How have those assignments been?"

"Terrible." Danny ignored the familiar pinch of guilt when he thought of Enfield. "The clock tower keeps breaking."

"Still?"

"It's just one thing after another. The numeral, the hand, the crack in the face . . ." Danny would have asked, "What next?" but was irrationally afraid Colton might hear and decide to do away with his pendulum just to vex him. Danny groaned and rubbed his hands over his face.

"The tower sounds defective," Matthias said, eyebrows furrowed. "I hear the one in Dover's been having problems as well. Has anyone else looked into it?"

Danny shook his head. "The Lead's doing his part, but I'm sure he's got enough to handle without breaking his back over this, too."

"Aren't you worried something might happen to the Enfield tower? You can't afford another accident. I'm worried about you, Danny Boy. You look tired."

Danny swallowed. "I probably won't go back there anyway."

Again he felt the burning desire to tell someone—anyone—about his encounter with Colton, but the words stuck in his throat. *No one can know*, he reminded himself firmly.

But Matthias might understand.

"Matthias," Danny started, "I was wondering if you could tell me what you know about clock spirits."

The man looked at him sharply. "Why?"

"I just . . . I was curious." He lowered his voice. "About . . . you know. What happened to you."

Matthias's tension eased. He looked older than Danny had ever seen him. Danny watched as Matthias closed his eyes and took a deep breath, pulling back the ghosts. "I'm sorry, Danny. I appreciate the thought, but I'm not in the mood."

"But—"

"I don't want to talk about it. Please."

Danny nodded. He should have guessed that would be Matthias's reaction. It only reaffirmed that Colton was a secret he had to keep to himself, whether he liked it or not. He would have to weave his own lies over the truth until it became unrecognizable. Until it became just another story.

A torturous week passed. Each day felt years long. Danny prowled the house like an anxious tiger in a cage, looking for distraction.

He normally busied himself with reading when he wasn't working, but every book he picked up he immediately put down again. He found the collection of fairy tales in his bag, stared at it, and stuffed it back in with muttered curses.

He ended up visiting Cassie at the garage. After he paid her the next installment for the boiler, they sat together for a cup of tea. A steam train roared down the nearby tracks, shaking the garage so that the chipped teacups rattled on their saucers.

"Noisy things, aren't they?" She took a bracing sip. "Auto should be ready by tomorrow."

"You're a godsend, Cass."

She winked. "Don't tell me what I already know." Her smile dimmed, and she began fidgeting in her chair. "Danny? There's a function my mum's making me go to."

"Oh?"

"Some ridiculous dance. It's supposed to be for people our age to, you know, mingle and all that. I don't want to go, but she's forcing me."

If Cassie's mother made her go, Danny knew his mother would urge him again. Their mothers were good friends, and always hoping their children would marry off. Danny's recent announcement about his preferences had barely slowed them down.

"You want me to go with you."

"I'm already planning a way to sneak off," she said. "I know where it'll be, and there's an easy way to slip out if no one's watching."

Danny couldn't help but laugh. "When is it?"

"In a few weeks. Promise you won't leave poor, defenseless me all alone there."

He snorted. Cassie, with a wrench in her hand, was anything but defenseless. "Fine, I'll go with you. But only if you're sure the escape plan is foolproof."

"Foolproof," she agreed. "Thank you, my chuckaboo."

"Don't call me that."

Danny ran a finger around the rim of his cup. He wondered if she would live with him if his mother moved out. But then people would talk, and he would have to convince them that there really were no plans of marriage between them. That might produce an even bigger scandal.

In the end, he couldn't bring it up. Instead he asked, "How do you think I could get a person to not like me?"

She choked on her tea. "Wassat?"

"If someone fancies you, how do you suppose you could get them to *not* fancy you?"

"Who's this, then? The blond boy? You don't like him?"

Danny shifted in his chair. "It's not that, exactly. It's hard to explain."

"But you're sure he likes you?" Danny hesitated, then nodded. "And you like him?" Another hesitation, and a less certain nod. "So what's the problem? Your mum hasn't been on you about it, has she?"

"No." He tugged on his shirt cuff, frowning. "I don't know. It's odd."

"Why? Is he into the weird stuff?"

"Cass," he groaned. She was a bricky girl, he'd give her that.

"What *is* the weird stuff for blokes, anyway?"

"How should I know? I've never . . ." He sank so low in his seat that his eyes became level with the table.

"Get back up here, Dan. I'm only teasing." But he stayed put. "Are you sure you fancy him? Sounds to me like you're confused."

"You don't know the half of it."

Cassie drummed her fingernails on the table. "I know— bring him to the social. That way, I get to meet him and tell you if he seems all right."

"That's not possible."

"Why not?"

He can't leave his town, that's why not. "He's in Enfield, for one thing. For another, I barely know him. Forget I said anything. I might not even see him again."

Despite Cassie's pleading, Danny couldn't explain further, so he left the garage to wander the dismal day alone. Besides, seeing his father's auto strung up for repair depressed him.

He bought bread and milk. The shop blended into meaningless colors, and he hardly paid attention to his transaction with the automaton behind the counter. The figure was man-shaped and made of bronze, although it had no face. Someone, no doubt one of the other shop clerks, had put glasses and a hat on it. The automaton jerkily lifted its hat to Danny when he paid.

The city hummed with energy and insistence—*go here, do this, look at that, step aside*—a pushing, cycling swell of activity. Not like Enfield. Quiet Enfield, where the only push was the wind sweeping across the grass of the village green like an ocean wave. Where people's eyes met and their lips turned up in true smiles. No averted gazes, no hard mouths. *How are you* and *good day* instead of spits and curses. A place to draw a deep breath. A place his lungs ached for.

Back at home, Danny drew a bath. He quickly submerged his body to hide it from the scrutinizing reflection in the mirror on the wall. He curled up in the water and inhaled the steam, slumping against the side of the tub.

His reflection refused to stay hidden. When he turned his head, his own face stared back: thin, sharp, young. Green eyes, dramatic eyebrows. A taunting echo of his father. A ghost that haunted his mother. What he would give for the automaton's harmless blank mask.

The telephone rang around noon, and he rushed to answer it. He craved anything that might break the brooding silence.

"Daniel, thank God I caught you at home," the Lead Mechanic said in a rush. "It's that damn Enfield clock again. Something's happened."

Danny's heart ricocheted off his clavicle. He'd wished for anything to break the silence—anything but this. "S-something's happened, sir?"

"The escapement's gone off, and time is completely warped. It runs slow, then fast. The people can't catch up. And the face has been scratched again."

Danny's fear turned to fury, sharp and hot in his throat. He wasn't going to let this sway him into going. He'd made up his mind to stay away. "Sir, I wish I could go, but my auto's in the shop."

The Lead sighed. Danny could almost see him nodding. "It can't be helped, then. We'll send a driver for you."

"But, sir, another mechanic could—"

"No, no. You're already familiar with the tower, and I trust you. Just try to get there as soon as possible. I'll send Summers as well."

"I . . ." No matter what he said, the Lead wouldn't take no for an answer. Danny exhaled through his teeth. "All right. But let me call the shop for my auto, sir. My friend works there."

"Very good."

Danny slammed the receiver back onto its hook. Clenching his jaw, he thought about the smile he had last seen on Colton's face, full and bright. Then he thought about the ruined clock face in Rotherfield.

He wasn't going to let Colton get away with this.

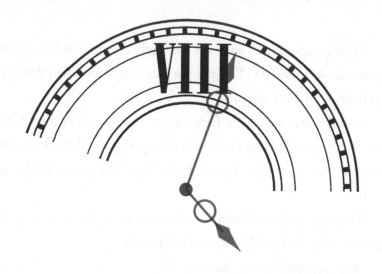

VIII

He felt the wrongness even before he reached the town's perimeter. A violent shudder crawled over his skin, followed by a flash of cold and a flash of heat. Danny fumbled with his timepiece. The hands were zooming around its face. As he watched, they slowed to their normal movement, then sped up again. Danny looked up and saw that, though it was early afternoon, the sky was steadily progressing toward sunset.

Townspeople were muttering and groaning, watching the same spectacle from the green. Someone saw Danny and clapped him on the back.

"Here's our man! Fix it up right, won't you?"

"Yes, I'll just—if I could get through?"

"Clear the way," the mayor said loudly, sweeping his arm to make room for Danny to pass. Still, a few people trailed behind, accompanying him to the base of the tower like some bizarre entourage. How was he supposed to work with these anxious people watching? Danny wanted to scare them off, wondering if they would scatter like the pigeons in the park.

"It's going to take a while," he told them. "You should wait at home." He met eyes with Aldridge, and the mayor nodded before he echoed Danny's words as an order. Some people muttered and walked off, but a few rebelliously stayed across the street, staring up at the scratched clock face.

"This won't be another Rotherfield, will it?" the mayor whispered to Danny.

"No, sir. I should hope not."

Not if he had anything to say about it.

Brandon stood outside the tower door. They nodded in greeting and took to the stairs.

"The escapement's out of order," Brandon reported. "Had a peek while I was waiting for you."

Danny had only visited the pendulum room briefly, but now it was his destination. They walked through the door leading to a wooden platform that hugged the sides of the tower, forming a square around the enclosed, windproof space where the pendulum hung. The pendulum was about three meters long, a dark bronze color, swinging side to side. But the swinging had become erratic. Something in the mechanism above was catching.

The clock tower, like Big Ben, contained a double three-legged gravity escapement that separated the pendulum from the clockwork. It looked skeletal and sinister, the gears making up the body where the pendulum clung. Danny examined it, running his eyes over the gear train. The escapement adjusted the weight attached to the pendulum, and therefore managed the pendulum's speed, preventing the clock from running too fast or too slow.

But with every swing, the gears and escapement caught and the weight dropped. As he watched, the slow *tick tocks* that filled the air increased with sudden and alarming speed. *Ticktockticktockticktock.*

"Why's it doing that?" Brandon demanded.

Danny knew why. "Let's get the mechanism properly wound. We might have to take the gears off and reinstall them."

A platform had been built above the clockwork to allow mechanics easy access, so he and Brandon climbed up and laid out their tools. Danny reminded him how to handle the gears. Another apprentice would have rolled his eyes, but Brandon just nodded.

They worked in silence unless Brandon had a question. Danny removed the smallest gear from the train and rewound the clock, one of the only technical duties the town's mainte-nance crew had; it was too much of a bother to call a mechanic every time a clock needed winding. Danny used a wrench and pulled until the weight was where he wanted it to sit.

His forehead was soon dotted with sweat. He removed each gear, checked it was sound, cleaned it to make sure, and rein-stalled it. Brandon took apart the escapement and did the same. As they worked, Danny sensed time shift and grow tense around them. The *tick tocks* ceased. Even the timepiece in his pocket stilled.

For a moment, he couldn't breathe. He thought of the mechanic who told his class about the jerky movement of time, the gray barrier of a town Stopped.

But once everything had been replaced, the pendulum swung freely again, and the ticking resumed. Danny let out a long breath, but couldn't get his hands to stop shaking.

Just to be certain, Danny checked the very top of the pendulum. A few pennies had been put there to adjust the time. Adding a penny would lift the pendulum's center of mass, increasing the speed with which it swung, just as removing a penny would decrease the speed. Danny was not surprised to see several coins there now. He removed the unnecessary ones until it felt just right.

They climbed the stairs to the clock room to repair the scratches on the face. As Danny approached the scaffolding, he caught a glimpse of white.

Colton stood across the room, a glower on his clawed face. Danny's heart tripped at the sight of him, whether from anger or excitement, he couldn't tell. Colton shone like a lighthouse, his beacon both a welcome and a warning, drawing Danny to his shores even though he knew he would be dashed upon the rocks.

Danny turned away, but he felt the spirit's eyes follow him.

Outside, the sun had returned to its correct position in the early afternoon sky. Time was still a little off, but the fibers would take or add time as they saw fit until the tower stabilized itself. Danny and Brandon used resin and cleaning rags to buff the scratches from the face, Brandon wondering aloud if there was any clock in all of England in such miserable disrepair as this one.

By the time they were finished, the sun was well and truly setting. Danny made sure they checked the clockwork again, just to be sure, but everything seemed to be running smoothly. Both mechanic and apprentice were exhausted, so Danny told Brandon to get a pint. The thought of driving home now seemed agonizing.

With Brandon gone, Danny's face hardened into a determined mask and he took the stairs to the clock room. There was still one thing left to do.

As he expected, Colton stood there waiting for him, his skin now unmarked. His amber eyes gleamed in a silent challenge, a fringe of blond hair falling carelessly over his forehead. He was brilliant in his fury, golden and untouchable.

Danny glared at him a moment, too furious to speak. He dropped his bag and coat on the floor.

"Are you a spirit or a child?" he demanded at last. "I asked you not to do this anymore, and then you turn around and make the town suffer because you don't get to have your way."

Colton looked away, but not from guilt. Instead, he looked self-justified. "You don't know what it's like here."

"What, to be alone and have no one give a damn?"

Colton closed his eyes.

"I understand, Colton. I don't think you realize how much I understand." Danny ran trembling hands through his hair. "But that's not the point. Do you realize what happens to the town if you're not working? If the town Stops, then it's all over. Everyone will be trapped here, cut off forever, and it'll be your fault!"

Your fault.

"I don't want the town to be cut off forever," Colton said.

"Then why did you do this?"

The silence lasted so long Danny almost thought the spirit wouldn't answer. "You didn't come," Colton said at last, his voice almost too low to hear, like the scraping of old gears. "Why? You said you would."

Danny leaned back on his heels. When he didn't say anything, Colton went on.

"I waited. You said you'd come back, but you never did. This was the only way to bring you back."

Your fault.

"My auto broke down," Danny said, his voice hoarse. Although it was the truth, it still felt like a lie. "I couldn't come with a broken auto. And I couldn't very well send a note. 'Yes, please deliver this to Colton Tower in Enfield, attention: clock spirit.'" Danny paced around the room, kicking over a dusty box. He sneezed and tried to sniff indignantly.

Colton stared at the floor. He was finally beginning to look guilty. "You couldn't come?"

"No. My auto was in shop until this morning, but then I got the call that you'd gone and done *this*. Bloody ungrateful fool, that's what you are. Why are you here, exactly? What's your purpose?" Colton looked up, confused. "To keep time running! You're Enfield's guardian. You're supposed to take care of yourself, not—not destroy yourself like some selfish—Goddamned—"

The dust was making his eyes water. He turned away and rubbed at them, but the water escaped past his eyelids and he scrubbed his face to get rid of it.

Your fault.

He wrapped his arms around his stomach. The air was too thin, his shoulders shaking with the need to breathe, to run, to curl up and pretend that none of this was real.

"I'm sorry." Danny felt a hesitant touch on his back. "I'm so sorry. I—I don't want to do that to the town. That wasn't what I was trying to do. Danny?"

He had to answer. To say everything was all right now, that it wouldn't happen again. But the stone that sat inside him grew sharper, heavier, cutting his throat as it pushed itself out as words.

"It was me," he whispered to the floorboards.

Colton stepped around him and touched his elbow. "What?"

Danny closed his eyes. "I'm the reason my father left."

The stone was dislodged, but not completely gone. Colton's fingers on his elbow anchored him to the floor, his eager silence waiting for him to explain.

He still heard the echo of the door slamming in the corners of quiet moments, a faint reminder of what he had done. Still saw his father's green eyes as Danny yelled in the dim hallway.

"You don't care about this trip, do you?" Danny had shouted. "You want any excuse to leave!"

"That's not true," Christopher said. "I just have to check something, and then I'll be back. We'll be on our way to France in the morning, like I promised."

"I don't want you to come with us."

"Danny—"

"No. Go to Maldon, all right? Just *go*. Fix whatever mess Matthias made. Mum and I will go without you."

Then the slam of the door, the tightness of his mother's admonishing eyes, the message that Christopher had decided to go to Maldon after all.

The shrill ring of the telephone the next day.

"I told him to go to Maldon," Danny said. "I was so angry. I don't even know why, now. I can't summon the rage I felt then. But because of me, he left. He went to that tower, and . . . he was . . ."

"Danny." Colton's hands framed his face. "Danny, that wasn't your fault."

Your fault.

His mother's words, pushed over her broken sobs, when she heard the news. The words that were now their foundation. He was the architect of their suffering.

"It *is* my fault," he said. "I pushed him to go."

But Colton was shaking his head. "It sounds like he would have gone anyway."

Danny had entertained the same thought. Anything to

absolve himself. But those reassurances were little more than lies. No matter how logical, his truth was sharp and cruel, edged in blame.

He had never told anyone before. Not even Cassie. Now the stone began to dissolve, its burden no longer only his.

Danny looked up, meeting Colton's steady gaze. "I have to get him out of there," he said softly. "I have to find a way to make it right."

"You will." Colton's fingertips traced the line of his cheekbone. Danny had never given much thought to that small area, but suddenly it became the most pivotal part of him. "I know you will."

"If the clock can even be fixed."

Something in Colton withered then, and he withdrew his touch. He crossed his arms and gave a nearby box a gentle kick. "You're right. I really am a fool."

Danny's shoulders slumped. "You're not."

"I am. I shouldn't have done it." The spirit looked up from under his eyelashes. "I'd thought, because I . . ." Colton touched his lips. "That maybe you didn't want to."

Danny flushed. He was getting very tired of that reaction. "No, no. It's not . . ." He sighed. "There's a part of the story I haven't told you."

They sat on boxes as Danny told Colton about Matthias. About how the clock spirit had destroyed herself.

Colton almost seemed to grow paler as he listened. "I didn't know," he said. "Honestly, I didn't know. Did I do a bad thing? I thought, because the fairy tales said it was nice, that kissing you would be nice, too."

Danny's chest tightened. The spirit could have been old enough to be his great-grandfather ten times down, but Colton's ignorance reminded him how little he knew of the outside world. His realm was Enfield. He could never leave, never experience the things that people were free to have—were lucky to have. A prisoner locked inside a tower.

"What you did wasn't bad," Danny said. "It's just not normal between a spirit and a person. I was surprised. I don't want Enfield to become another Maldon."

Colton lowered his eyes. "I won't harm myself again. I just wanted to thank you because you've been so kind. I'm sorry."

Again came the flood of guilt, strong and painful, crashing down Danny's walls. What could he do? What would anyone else do?

He stood and held out his hand, which Colton took without hesitation. Again he felt time bend around them, stretching the moment into eternity. Colton's eyelashes were long, his lips pink. He looked so human that for one moment, Danny could pretend to forget what he truly was.

He brushed his fingers against Colton's collarbone, and the spirit closed his eyes. Danny wondered how much Colton could feel. How much he understood. If the answers were hidden behind some unmarked door.

Danny decided to open that door. He leaned forward and kissed him.

The clock chimed five. It sounded almost celebratory as they stood there, hands clasped between them like the meeting of continents. Colton's mouth was soft and warm, sunlight on silk. Danny was swallowing light. It dived down inside of him until he imagined it bursting out of every pore.

When he pulled back, he was light-headed and breathless. "You know, before I met you, I'd never kissed a clock spirit."

Colton smiled. "First time for everything."

Worried that Colton would somehow forget his promise, Danny made sure to return to Enfield two days later. The tower was still standing and the clock running smoothly, much to his relief. Inside, Colton was waiting.

"What does a clock do to pass the time?" Danny asked.

"Time usually goes very quickly for me. I know it's been two days since you were last here, but to me, it feels like a few hours."

"A few *hours*?" Danny shook his head. It was odd to be here and not have something to do, but he'd brought his tools anyway. He set them down. "Sometimes I wish time passed that way for me."

"You don't want that," Colton said, suddenly grave. "You're a human. Life goes by too quickly for you. If time went fast, you'd be gone sooner."

Danny cleared his throat. He suspected Colton had no idea

about what humans actually felt about death. "I guess you have a point. How old are you, anyway?"

Colton tilted his head to one side, amber eyes distant. "I don't remember. I feel as if I've always been here." An auto rumbled down the street, and Colton pointed at it through the window. "I remember not knowing what those were."

Suddenly Danny's seventeen worldly years seemed of little importance, long as they had been for him.

They stood for a while regarding each other, uncertain what to do next. Danny had always come to Enfield with a purpose, but now that he'd come merely to see Colton, things were rapidly turning awkward. What did one talk about with a clock? None of his classes had ever covered that particular topic.

You shouldn't even be here, he thought with a rush of nervous energy. *Someone's going to start wondering why you come so often. The Lead's going to find out. It'll be Maldon all over again, it'll be—*

He started when Colton touched his chin.

"There's a scratch here," Colton said.

"A—? Oh, no, that's a scar." He rubbed a finger over the raised line in his skin. "People get scars when things hurt them."

Alarm flickered in Colton's eyes. "You were hurt? How?"

"Something cut me open."

Colton frowned at it distastefully, like it was Danny's chin's fault for the blemish. "When will it go away?"

"I couldn't tell you. Some scars never fade."

Colton glanced at the clock face, and Danny read his thoughts. His scratches had been healed with resin and buffing.

It didn't make sense to Colton why Danny's skin would be any different from his own.

The spirit stared at Danny's chin again. Colton touched his thumb to the scar, following the slant of it.

"I wish I could heal it for you."

"You are." At Colton's confused look, he explained, "Time heals scars."

Colton grinned. The smile washed over Danny's worry, making him forget what he'd been anxious about in the first place.

They ended up standing by one of the small windows, which provided a view of Enfield to the east. There wasn't much to look at, but Colton stared for a long while in silence. His eyes were fixed on a point Danny couldn't see, drawn to something intangible. Going somewhere Danny couldn't follow.

"Are you allowed to leave the clock tower?" Danny asked.

"I can't go very far."

"That's a shame. There are so many interesting sights out there. You should see London, it's brilliant." He caught the look on the spirit's face and could have hanged himself. "I'm sorry. I wasn't thinking. Here I am, making it all worse."

"It's all right. I know I can't leave, and I can't see anything beyond Enfield, but I enjoy it here. It's quiet, and it's peaceful. I see the people come and go, and learn about their lives, and listen in on their problems. Sometimes, I wish they knew I was here. Do you remember the wedding not too long ago?" Danny nodded. "I've wanted those two to end up together since they were children. It makes me happy, seeing these people live their lives. I like to think I'm living it with them."

It did seem a nice way to pass time, to watch people and become invested in their lives from a distance, like God parting the clouds to observe his worker ants below.

"I want . . ." Colton paused, then shook his head. "Well, it doesn't matter what I want. Still," he said, his voice distant as he turned back to the window, "it would be something, being in another place."

A spark of an idea caught tinder. "Where would you most like to go?"

"I don't know. I only know the names of what's around Enfield—London, the towns. I know nothing about the world. Enfield is my world."

It was the saddest thing Danny had ever heard. "How about this: when I come next time, I'll bring the world to you."

Though he didn't understand, Colton looked interested. "Is that possible?"

"Anything is possible."

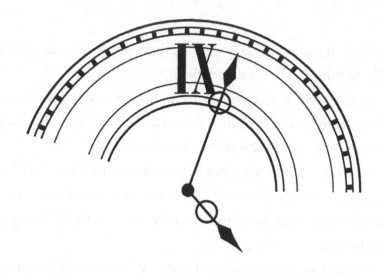

There were no leads about Rotherfield over the next few days. It was like Shere all over again—the endless questions, the uncertainty, then, gradually, the giving up. No one could trace the bomb back to any person or organization.

Danny skulked around the offices waiting for the Lead. He wanted to ask about Maldon and how the clock tower was coming along. As he waited, Tom and George came out of an office down the hall.

Something wasn't right. Tom's face was mottled, his eyes red. Had he been crying?

It sounds silly, but I thought I heard someone crying. That's what the man in Rotherfield had said. Danny edged in closer to hear them.

"—difficult, but you know it needs to be done," George was saying.

"I know." Tom stared at the wall, his eyes hard. "Lord help me, I know."

George gripped the taller man's arm in sympathy. They turned and walked down the hall. Danny was about to follow when he heard a snort behind him.

"Eavesdropping, Danny?"

Lucas held a report in one hand, his face marred by a smirk.

"I don't know what you're talking about," Danny replied.

"Cut the act. Tell me why you were at Rotherfield."

"I told you, I was visiting a friend."

"Everyone knows you don't have friends."

Before he could think of a response, the Lead's door opened. He saw Danny and sighed. "Daniel, I don't have anything for you. I'm sorry."

Danny pushed himself away from the wall and headed for the stairs. He heard the Lead ask Lucas to step into his office and paused, wondering what they could have to discuss. A telling off, he hoped.

He couldn't get Tom's face out of his mind. As he slowly made his way down the stairs, a young apprentice flying past him and trailing papers in his hurry, Danny wondered what Tom and George could have been discussing.

On the second floor, Danny turned down the hall. He needed to find out.

Tom's office was next to George's, right at the end of the corridor. Danny kept turning his head to see if anyone was around, but he only heard voices echoing from the classrooms farther

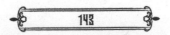

down. He knocked softly, and when he received no answer, he tested the handle. It was open.

Danny stepped inside and soundlessly closed the door behind him. Tom's office was neat, unlike Matthias's with its precarious towers of paperwork and unorganized files. But there was no personality in this small space, no portraits or trinkets or even a kinetic toy like the Lead had.

Danny didn't know if Tom was gone for the day or if he'd be back any moment, so he quickly began opening drawers and riffling through their contents. It was the usual sort of nonsense: pens, clips, reams of paper, loose screws and springs. Danny looked under the desk and pulled a few books from the shelves. Nothing. Not even a sign of the Maldon tower blueprints.

Then something caught his eye beside the bookshelf. He knelt and found a canvas bag that clanked when he touched it. Frowning, Danny opened the top and found pieces of metal inside. He took one out.

"A pipe?" He examined it from every angle, even looking at the desk through the hole as if it were a spyglass. It told him absolutely nothing.

Frustrated, Danny kicked the bag back into place and slipped out the door. He was listening for the click of the latch when a familiar voice asked, "What are you doing?"

Danny whirled around. Daphne stood with one hand on her hip, looking down her nose at him. She held a file in the crook of her arm.

"I . . . that's . . . a good question." Danny resisted the

urge to wipe his damp palms on his trousers. "What are *you* doing?"

She raised an eyebrow. "I'm on the foreign exchange committee for the new India program," she replied easily. "I'm turning in some research. But what I'm most curious about is why you're not answering my question."

"Tom was—that is, he—wanted me to drop off something. So I've dropped it off." He inclined his head. "Good day."

Danny edged past her and headed for the stairs, but she followed.

"What were you dropping off?"

"I don't see how that's any of your business."

"Was it for an assignment?"

"That's not—"

"Or were you hoping for a glimpse of those blueprints?"

Flushing, Danny grabbed the top of the banister and spun around, coming within inches of Daphne's self-assured face.

"It's none of your business, Miss Richards," he ground out. "We're both too busy for this stupid game. Good day."

He hurried down the stairs and felt her eyes on him the entire way down.

Danny and his mother hardly used the sitting room anymore, the banged-up couch and armchair sagging with dust and neglect. Danny was currently raiding it.

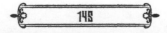

He grabbed trinkets off the mantle, gifted to them by friends and family: a jeweled elephant sent over from a cousin who had gone to India, a miniature flag of Australia, and a ceramic figurine of a dancing German, complete with lederhosen and a mug of beer in one pink hand.

He stuffed whatever he could into his bag, careful not to break anything. He ran his eyes over the bookshelves and grabbed a couple of titles he thought would be interesting. Then he ran out of the house, right past his mother, who asked him how her interview dress looked.

"Good, fine, very professional," he called over his shoulder.

"Where are you going with all you've nicked?" she demanded before the door closed behind him.

In Colton's tower, they sat cross-legged in the clock room as Danny removed everything from the bag, including a book of Greek mythology that still had a layer of dust on its cover. He blew the dust off and handed it to Colton, who held the book as if he'd been given the most valuable artifact in human history.

"It's all right, have a look."

Colton examined the cover, which featured a drawing of Pegasus flying toward Mount Olympus. Danny watched as Colton ran his long, nimble fingers over the golden lettering before he opened the cover and began flipping through the pictures. Danny explained the stories when he could remember them.

"The Greeks loved the idea of fate. In a completely morbid way, of course. Most of the stories are about people trying to change or avoid their fate, but everything they do just brings them that much closer to it." Danny tapped a picture of three women holding a long thread between them. "The Fates spin out the thread of your destiny, whatever it is—killed by stampeding rhinoceroses, let's say—and you think, right, well, I'm never going near a rhinoceros ever again.

"But it's not really your choice anymore. The Fates assign your destiny, and even though you have no desire to see a rhinoceros, all of a sudden you're whisked away to Africa because you're now governor of a colony. And when you're there, you will most certainly be trampled by rhinoceroses. The thread is cut." He imitated the motion of scissors with his first two fingers. "And that's that."

"Is that what you believe?"

"Me? Not at all. I can change my fate whenever I want. Or maybe that's what the Fates want me to think."

Colton laughed, and it lit up the room. Sitting so close to him, feeling this tenuous thing between them, Danny realized now that something had been stripped away from him in the last three years. He'd been eroding. Losing the things close to him. Sanded down to a pale, exposed nerve.

And here . . .

Well, he was *more*. It was the only way to describe it. It wasn't shedding weight, but rather putting it back on, padding himself against the elements and the world. He wasn't the ghost of a boy who once was happy. He *was* happy.

Happy.

It was an odd concept.

But Colton's smile seemed to creep across his own mouth, pushing up the corners of his lips. Here, he was the opposite of eroding.

He was living.

Colton turned a few pages. "What's *that*?"

Danny roused himself from his thoughts and focused on the book. Colton was pointing to a picture of a woman's hideous face, her hair a riot of crawling snakes.

"That lovely lady is a Gorgon. Her name's Medusa. With one look, she could turn you to stone." He turned the page to show him a picture of a dark-haired, handsome young man holding a sword and shield. "This is Perseus, the only one who could kill Medusa. He couldn't do it on his own, of course. He had help from the Greek gods, like Hermes." Danny flipped to the back of the book, where the gods were depicted, and pointed at a curly-haired youth with wings on his sandals. "With their help, Perseus was able to chop off Medusa's head."

Colton lifted his thin eyebrows. "That's rather violent."

"A lot of Greek stories are violent. Best not tell you about Troy, then."

"No, no—tell me."

So they spent the afternoon talking about the fall of Troy and Achilles's wrath, of Theseus's heroism in the Labyrinth, and how Cupid and Psyche had fallen in love. Colton would have demanded more, but Danny wanted to show him the other things he had brought.

As he handed Colton the figurines, their fingers occasionally brushed. Each time a flash of heat started at Danny's fingertips and traveled all the way to his stomach, where it sat like a hot coal.

Colton laughed over the drunken German, although Danny told him that not all Germans looked like that; they actually had a very nice German family on their street who did not wear lederhosen. He talked about the colonies in Australia, the American Revolution, and the Irish Question. Scotland was a land of kilts and bagpipes, and Italy of wine and art.

Danny took out the second book he had brought with him. An atlas.

"This shows you the world," he said, opening it to reveal the maps within. He pointed at Greece. "That's where all those storics come from. Here's where Troy would have been, near Turkey." He turned the page. "That's Egypt, in Africa. Long ago, they built pyramids to appease their Pharaoh." Danny drew a pyramid in the dust.

"They have their own gods, too, but not like the Greeks. Some Egyptian gods have animal heads." He attempted to draw jackal-headed Anubis, but failed utterly. "There are different gods for each religion, for the most part. And then there are the Gaian gods."

"What are those?"

Danny fiddled with the chain of his timepiece, thinking back to when his father had first told him the story of Aetas's demise. "The Gaian gods once protected the earth. They were cast-offs

from Chronos, the creator of time. One of them, Aetas, inherited the running of time from Chronos.

"But it went wrong. He gave the power to humans, and Chronos wasn't pleased with that, so he confronted Aetas on earth. They fought in the sea, a storm raging all around them . . ."

Colton was staring at him so intently that Danny trailed off, mesmerized by the gleam of his amber eyes.

"And?" Colton prompted.

"And . . ." Danny shook his head. "Aetas lost. Some say that Chronos chopped off his head and fed it to a kraken. Other stories say that Chronos took away Aetas's powers, turned him mortal, and then burned him alive."

"But the version I like best," Christopher would say as Danny sat on his lap, listening raptly, "is the one where Chronos tried to reattach Aetas as a finger on his hand. Aetas resisted. He took out his own beating heart and crushed it into dust, scattering time around the world. That's why some parts of the world run on different times. Aetas's blood pooled into the sea—"

"And that's why it's so salty!" a younger Danny would finish.

Danny took a deep breath, returning to the present. "So that was the end of the Timekeeper. We're the Timekeepers, now."

Danny felt a touch at his jaw and raised his head. Colton, golden and solemn, regarded him as though he was trying to read Danny's story. As if everything was printed on his skin, his face a picture in substitute of words.

Danny ducked his head and pulled the atlas closer, turning the pages quickly. He stopped at random and pointed.

"This is India."

Colton watched him a second longer, then leaned closer to take in the map. "It's big."

Danny picked up the elephant and handed it to Colton. The spirit tilted it this way and that, making the sunlight spark off the tiny jewels.

"Those beasts are huge up close. People ride them. From what I've heard, India is so different from England that it's like stepping into another world entirely." Danny turned back to the atlas. "Britain's taken the place over, though."

Danny's schoolbooks had always painted India as a savage place, one in dire need of help, as the people barely knew how to run themselves. He doubted that was true. He wondered, not for the first time, what it was like to suddenly have your entire country snatched away from you, to have foreigners pressing their ideals on you in the hope you could change to be something you weren't.

His thoughts briefly flitted to Daphne and her exchange program. He wondered what Daphne thought of those schoolbooks, or if her father had drawn distrustful looks. If she thought her pale skin was a blessing or a curse.

"And there are clocks there, too?" Colton asked, setting the jeweled elephant down.

"Of course. I'm sure there must be hundreds of towers controlling Indian time. I've always wanted . . ." It sounded stupid, even in his own head, but Colton's look urged him on. "I've always wanted to travel abroad. To see clock towers elsewhere. I'm fond of London, but I'd like to see other things."

Danny turned back a few pages and tapped his finger on France. "My family was supposed to go here on holiday. Mum was so excited. She even tried to teach me French, but I'm no good with languages. We would practice with a man she knows from work. Once I tried to say 'the green chair,' but it sounded exactly like the word for *worm*, so I ended up saying 'the chair worm.'" Colton laughed softly, the sound like chiming glass.

"But then my father left." Danny's finger slipped off the page. "And that was that."

France and Spain blended into one country as Danny's vision blurred. He huffed at himself and closed the atlas.

"Never mind, that's depressing stuff. You don't want to hear about that." He grabbed the book of mythology again. "Have you heard of the Labors of Heracles?"

Colton touched the back of Danny's wrist.

"If it hurts," the spirit said, "then why not talk about it?"

Danny shrugged. "It hurts more, talking about it."

"Are you sure?"

Danny thought of his mother sitting by the window when she thought she was alone, her eyes faded, her face aging. The pity from his superiors and his peers alike, the way they tiptoed around him. The Lead telling him that there was still no way to fix Maldon.

"Sometimes, I . . . I don't know if I can save him." He opened the book to the picture of Perseus about to slay the Gorgon. "At this point it might take the gods themselves."

The touch on the back of his wrist traveled down until Colton pulled Danny's hands away from the book. Colton stared at Danny's palms, rough and dry. His fingers skimmed the life and heart lines, the map of pale blue veins on Danny's wrist. Like he wanted to put away every detail, the same way Danny took inventory of his clockwork, the pieces and gears that held him together.

Danny had never been so aware of anyone else in his life. Everything shrank from a universe to a pinpoint, every turn of the earth dependent on his next breath, each touch lingering until those eyes found his.

Colton pressed a hand to Danny's chest and laid his mouth gently against his. Danny wasn't prepared for it—the reminder that Colton was not like him, that his palms were smooth and free of flaws, that his wrist showed no veins, that his mouth tasted of copper and of sweet clean air.

He was a boy of air and dust and sunlight. Everything that had gone into the making of the world.

Danny sat at his desk, scribbling on a piece of parchment paper that had once been a grocery list. He propped his head on one hand and stared at the lines without seeing them, occasionally stopping to gaze out the window at the bland view of the next house over. The soft patter of the rain was soothing, and he left his window slightly ajar for fresh air to come through.

The breeze blew up a corner of the paper and he smoothed it down again. The paper was riddled with drawings, the mechanism sketches he'd learned to do as an apprentice, and the full-face clock sketches he did on his own. At the top of one of these he had drawn a small figure reclining on the minute hand, gazing down at another figure at the foot of the tower. He started to add Rapunzel-like hair to the figure at the top, then snorted and crossed it out with a few swipes of his pencil.

He had gone to Enfield again, this time bringing a storybook in the hopes of teaching Colton how to read. He'd caught on quickly, sounding out words until he had them memorized and could recognize them throughout the book. Danny was pondering which book to bring next when the telephone rang.

He leapt down the stairs, hoping it was Cassie, even though she'd pestered him the other day about his secret love affair in Enfield. She begged for the boy's name, but he refused to tell her, so they continued to call him "the blond bloke."

"Hullo," he sang into the receiver.

"Daniel?"

The Lead. Danny swallowed his usual crude greeting to Cassie—*What's up yer bum?*—and endeavored to find a professional tone. "Oh, sir. Good morning."

"I'll need you to come into the office today. Is that all right?"

His chest fluttered. "Perfectly all right, sir. Is it another Enfield assignment?"

He had said it lightheartedly, almost jokingly, but the Lead's unnerving silence wiped the smile from his face.

"Something of the sort. Come down when you can."

Danny began to sweat on his way to Parliament Square. Had the officials heard about his extra trips to Enfield? Had someone seen him talking to Colton? Was there news about Rotherfield or Shere? The wind bit and rain splattered his goggles, but Danny barely noticed. He nearly caused two major collisions before the auto came sputtering to a stop in front of the large gray stone building.

There were only a couple of protesters out today, soaked and discontent. Danny hurried past them into the atrium, where he slipped a little on the marble on his way to the stairs.

The secretary was out, so he knocked on the Lead's door and waited for permission to enter. When he did, he found the man seated behind his desk. The kinetic toy in the corner was pattering away, the metal balls jumping back and forth. Danny took that as a bad sign; the Lead only did that when he was stuck on a problem.

The Lead stopped the toy and regarded Danny, his look more kind than stern. "Sit down, Daniel." He did. The Lead stroked his mustache, though Danny wished he wouldn't. It only made the situation seem more sinister.

"Daniel, how have you felt about your assignments in Enfield?"

Danny sat back and tried not to stammer into apologies. "They've been fine, sir. A bit labor-intensive, but that's to be expected."

"Yes, that's what I was afraid of. I thought the best way for you to return to work was with a difficult assignment. And it seemed to do the trick, but then more followed. I can only imagine how tiring it must be for you."

Danny's hands curled into fists on his knees. He imagined trapping the pity against his palms, crushing it like Aetas had crushed his own beating heart.

"No, sir, it's nothing like that. I've actually enjoyed my time there. The people know me now, and the town is—"

"You don't have to pretend. I know it's been a strain on you."

"But it hasn't. I've—"

"I don't want to exhaust you so soon after your return to work. I've heard that this town is not the best fit for you."

Danny's stomach hardened into a cold, heavy ball. He licked dry lips and tried again. "Who's been saying that?" He thought about Brandon and how he'd looked at Danny like he had come to England directly from the planet Neptune. He thought about Daphne's look of suspicion as he'd slipped out of Tom's office.

"I would rather not reveal identities, but it's an opinion I trust, and I want to make sure you're well. Enfield is too difficult for you. I'm reassigning it to someone else."

"Someone else?" The room grew hot and close. Danny smelled smoke. It burned his eyes and wove into the fibers of his shirt, a smell he couldn't get rid of no matter how many times he washed it. He tasted copper on his tongue, rich and thick, cloying like blood.

He imagined the destruction that Colton Tower would face if he didn't return, his threat of finding another mechanic turning the spirit toward grief, just like Maldon.

Colton, pulling apart his clockwork.

Enfield, Stopped.

"Daniel? Daniel!"

He must have fainted, because he awoke on the floor a moment later. His cheek was pressed to the maroon carpet that smelled of musk and canvas. His heart pounded, and he pushed a hand against his chest as if to prevent it from bursting out of his body.

"Sir, you can't do that," he croaked. "He'll be upset."

The Lead knelt beside him. "You're not talking sense. Come on, up you get."

Danny raised himself up and rubbed a hand over his numb face. "Please, listen to me. I . . . I like Enfield. I really do. I didn't think I would, but—"

The Lead shook his head. "No, I see now that this was not the right assignment for you. I'll find someone else to go up next time. You rest at home for a bit, take your mind off things. Take a holiday."

"Sir, please—"

"I've had my say, Daniel. Your father would have wanted the same."

You don't know what my father would have wanted.

Danny was ushered to an empty sitting room and ordered to lie down on the couch. Tea and biscuits were brought in, but he didn't touch the tray. At least, not at first; he couldn't avoid the tea for long, and drinking it helped steady his shaken nerves.

Standing at the window, he looked at Big Ben through the rain. He couldn't let this happen, even if the Fates themselves had woven this turn of events. No matter where his thread ended up, he would spin it in his favor.

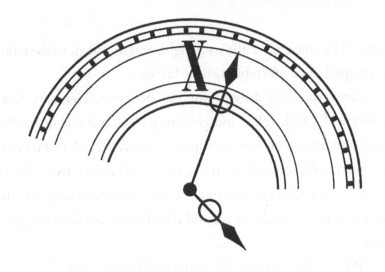

"Y ou don't look happy at all," Cassie complained, fiddling with the buttons of her dress. "I don't want to be seen with a dismal Jimmy. At least try to smile, Dan."

"Hark who's talking," he mumbled. "You look ready for your own execution."

They stood beside his auto, which was parked on the street alongside a dozen others. The moonlight shone against the auto's black paint—paint that was scraped and chipped, with a large scuff on the passenger-side door. A lantern over their heads flickered, its indecisive light showering them with flashes of sodium yellow glare.

Although Danny had no desire to attend a social, Cassie had reminded him numerous times of the promise he had made her. His mother had even taken the mothballs from his suit and smartened it up. It still smelled like dust and the sour odor of old things. The collar and cuffs were tight, and the fabric of the trousers rasped uncomfortably against his legs.

Cassie was also dressed for the occasion. Her dark blue bodice had a high collar and gleaming black buttons down the front, and flared out over her hips above a ruffled skirt. Her hair had been coiled behind her head, her rough brown work gloves replaced with dainty white ones. It was so strange to see her without her usual coveralls or a braid that Danny couldn't help but stare.

"What?" she snapped. She unpinned her grandmother's rose brooch and fumbled to re-adjust it. "Do I look silly?"

"No," he said honestly, reaching out to help her. "You look nice." He glanced at the back of her skirt, where he knew she wore a bustle to make her dress flare out. "Your bum looks big, though."

Though he was teasing, she smacked him hard on the arm anyway, as if she'd been waiting for an excuse. A pair of girls walked past and hid their giggles behind white fans. Cassie's face turned pink.

"I don't want to be here long," Danny said. "You have your escape plan ready?"

Cassie shifted on her feet. "Yes."

"Then let's get this over with." He held out his arm, and she took it.

It wasn't just the social. Danny didn't even want to be in London. He wished he were on his way to Enfield to see Colton. But now a visit there would be suspicious, and he needed to toe the mark until he was deemed fit for the Maldon assignment.

You haven't even been thinking about the Assignment, he scolded himself, guilt flaring uncomfortably in his chest. *Get your act together, Danny.*

The old stone building where the social was being hosted was tall and wide with Gothic windows, and the open doors spilled light onto the street. Boys and girls chatted and laughed and flirted inside. Danny grimaced and Cassie pinched his arm.

The chaperones at the door asked for their passes. "Daniel Hart and Cassandra Lovett?" They both nodded. "In you get."

They shuffled across the threshold. Inside, a wide ballroom had been adorned with green and blue streamers, tables of finger food, and crystal bowls of punch. A piano, violin, and cello warbled out songs in the corner. A set of double doors stood open to their right, allowing them a view of the card room where games like whist and speculation were being played amid bursts of laughter. A massive chandelier hung over the marbled floor, casting light onto the partygoers. Candle wax dripped onto the beeswax-polished floor below.

"Coo. Bit butter upon bacon, isn't it?" Cassie said under the noise. "What should we do?"

Danny watched as a well-dressed group took to the dance floor, their loud chatter like the squawking of seagulls. "Use your escape plan, of course." Her sheepish frown confirmed his suspicions. "Let me guess: you don't actually have an escape plan."

"You know they'll have chaperones guarding the place.

Otherwise all the couples will be off to find themselves a private moment."

Frustration welled up inside him. He hated that Cassie had dragged him here, forcing him to mingle with people he didn't like. People who would turn their noses up at his old suit and laugh behind their fans at his clumsy dancing.

He looked at Cassie and found her to be equally miserable, and that made him feel better, in the worst way possible.

"I'm sorry, Cass. I don't feel well."

"Will you tell me what's the matter?" Someone bumped into them from behind. Realizing they were crowding the entrance, they moved toward the tables laden with food.

Danny took a deep breath. "It's about my job."

Her fingers tightened on his arm. "You weren't sacked, were you?"

"No, not that. But Enfield's been assigned to someone else. The Lead doesn't think I can handle it anymore."

"That's not so bad, is it? You said yourself Enfield was small and—" Her eyes widened. "Oh. Your blond fellow."

Danny nodded.

"Can't you still visit him? Or could he come to London?"

"It's more complicated than that."

An automaton stood behind the table, its blank face decorated with a ridiculous black mustache. As they approached, the automaton lifted its head. "*Refreshments?*" it asked in monotone.

"Oh, ah, sure," Cassie said. She checked her hair as the automaton made up a plate, its arms whirring with movement. When

Cassie was certain no lock was out of place, she gave Danny another frown. "You're being this way on purpose, aren't you?"

"You caught me. Miserable, brooding Danny, available for one night only! Come on, Cass."

"Why don't you just tell me what's got you so bothered?"

The automaton handed her a small plate loaded with sugared fruit and a colorful assortment of canapés. "*Drink?*" it asked.

"No, that's quite all right. Listen, Dan—"

But she was interrupted yet again, this time by a young man with a green silk ascot at his throat. He sent a cool glance in Danny's direction before bowing to Cassie. "May I have this dance?"

Cassie looked as though she'd been told she would be the next Queen of England. Her eyes met Danny's, but he just shrugged.

"All right," she agreed faintly. Danny wondered if she had ever danced with a boy other than himself. He suddenly recalled clearing away the furniture in the sitting room when they were younger, Cassie directing him through the steps she'd seen her parents dance at a party.

"Here," she hissed, shoving the plate of food at him. "Don't you dare laugh at me!"

She took the young man's arm and they walked off, Cassie a little unsteady beside the confident gait of her partner.

Cassie proved to be somewhat graceful, and she even let the boy lead. Danny picked at her food as he watched, and his bad mood nearly snuck away from him. But then he wondered what it would be like to be here with Colton. If he weren't a clock spirit, but a human boy, living and breathing and able to eat delicious, if impractical, finger foods.

He imagined leading Colton across the floor, stepping and swirling in time to each sprawling note, the bend of a smiling mouth, the glimmer of golden eyes. His hand on Colton's waist to draw him close. The glow of the chandelier catching their edges and setting them alight.

Danny set the plate down, no longer hungry.

The song ended and Cassie curtsied awkwardly to her partner. They exchanged a few words before Cassie made her way back to Danny, flushed and out of breath.

"*That* I should not like to repeat," she said, fanning her face.

"You liked it."

She opened her mouth to deny it, but at that moment Danny heard his name. Turning, he spotted a few apprentices and a mechanic moving toward them.

"All right, Danny?" Lucas asked. His brown hair had been slicked back, and his eyes were bright. He sounded friendly enough, but made no attempt to hide a smug smile.

Danny recognized this group. They weren't exactly the kindest crowd in the Mechanics Union. A blonde apprentice clung to Lucas's arm, eyeing Cassie. The girl's upper lip curled.

"All right," Danny replied cautiously. "Didn't know you'd be here, Lucas."

"Sure. Smart thing to do, isn't it? Socialize, meet other successful young people like ourselves. Well, nearly all of us, anyway."

Danny narrowed his eyes. "Are you suggesting something?"

"Oh, not at all. You're a young mechanic, Danny, and plenty successful. Bar that one minor incident, of course." He tapped his chin, and Danny wished he could cover his own. "Some of the others, though . . ." Lucas followed his companion's gaze to Cassie, who tightened her hand on Danny's elbow. "What's this? I thought you weren't for the ladies, Danny."

"I'm his friend," Cassie said, her voice cold enough to ice over the punch bowls. "We've known each other since we were children."

"How sweet," Lucas said. "Now I see why you don't like ladies."

Danny shook off Cassie's hand and stepped forward. He was as tall as Lucas, but that's where their similarities ended. Lucas boasted a broad chest and thick arms. Danny wouldn't last long against him.

"Don't!" Cassie whispered. "It's not worth it."

"What did you mean by that, Lucas?" Danny growled.

Lucas held up his hands. "Only that with such a fine lady in your sights for so long, all other women must have been spoiled for you." The others grinned.

Damn Lucas. Damn him and his stupid, long eyelashes.

"How have the assignments been?" Lucas asked. "You were in Enfield, weren't you?"

The town's name made Danny's heart stutter.

"I was in Guildford, myself. Rather nice clock tower there, if

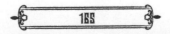

you haven't been. But that's beans compared to the new assignment they've put me on."

"And where might that be?"

"The new Maldon tower."

The room came to a standstill. Though others danced and talked and laughed all around them, Danny stood in a pocket of stillness, deprived of his senses except for the ring of one crucial question: *Why?*

"He's chosen you?" The words strangled his throat. *"You?"*

"Why, Danny, I thought you'd be happy for me." Lucas's smile turned cruel. "Maybe if you're extra good, I'll tell the Lead you ought to assist me there. Teach you a thing or two. After all, you need more friends."

"You must be his only one," an older apprentice said to Cassie. Danny remembered him from his classes. "He never visits anyone else except that old washed-out mechanic."

"And an unknown chap in Rotherfield," Lucas added with amusement.

"Stop it!"

"There was that one fellow," Lucas drawled. "Barnaby, was it? You two were rather close, weren't you? Until they relocated him, anyway. Such a sweet little couple, we always said."

Danny flushed, then turned pale. The sudden shift was so similar to the heat and chill of a fever that his body began to tremble. Lucas had been walking down the hall when Barnaby had given Danny his second-ever kiss. Lucas had looked into the empty classroom just in time to see it.

That had been before Danny had felt comfortable with others knowing his secret. They'd begged Lucas not to tell.

Danny should have known better.

"Bit brave of you, doing that in a classroom," Lucas went on. "We all thought you and Barnaby were such shy little things. Imagine my surprise when I saw him pawing at you like an animal!"

They laughed at Danny's stunned face.

"Darling, I think he's about to burst into tears," Lucas's companion loudly whispered into his ear.

Danny did nothing of the sort. Instead, he grabbed Lucas by the shirt and punched him in the eye.

The people around them screamed. Lucas staggered and nearly fell, but Danny caught him and clouted the side of his head. Lucas regained his senses and sank a fist into Danny's stomach, winding him. Cassie wrenched Danny back as a whistle sounded. Two chaperones elbowed the crowd out of the way.

"He *hit* me!" Lucas whined. He had dropped dramatically to the floor upon their arrival, one hand covering his eye, hair in disarray, companion fretting at his side.

"Explain yourself," a chaperone demanded.

"It's not his fault," Cassie pleaded when Danny remained silent. "This lot was provoking him!"

"That's no reason to come to blows. Come along, then."

"But he hit back!" Cassie pointed at Lucas, who had somehow managed to work up tears. He should have been a bloody actor.

"Did anyone else see this young man fight back?" Of course, Lucas's friends shook their heads, even though Danny was doubled up clutching his stomach. "There we have it."

The chaperones escorted Danny out of the building. It seemed he'd found an escape route after all. His head spun, and the dark, narrow streets of London blurred together. He shrugged their hands off his shoulders.

"Give us your pass, please."

He thrust the crumpled paper at them.

"Daniel Hart?"

He nodded.

"We'll be letting your parents know about this."

Danny turned toward his auto. *Go ahead,* he thought, *tell them. One of them doesn't give a damn, and the other is frozen in time.*

He kept clenching and unclenching his hand. The other—the one he'd slugged Lucas with—throbbed painfully, and his stomach ached where he'd been hit. Danny had never punched anyone in his life before tonight. Matthias had once taught him how, in case he found himself in a situation like this one, but he had never warned Danny how his knuckles would bruise and split.

He had to get away. Looking around, Danny realized an unsettling yellow fog had descended. It was the type of fog people could get lost in. In fact, several had ended up drowning in the Thames this way. His lungs hurt, and his head was woozy, but there was no way to tell if it was from the poisonous fog or his own desperation.

Finally, he recognized his auto and hurried to it, guided by a desire as sharp as hunger. He wanted to drive through London, through the fog and the night, all the way to Enfield. He wanted to see Colton.

The new idea took hold and he ran faster, wincing when his stomach protested.

Enfield. To hell with what the Lead said; Danny would go tonight. He'd stay with Colton in his tower, learn how to be a shut-in, a recluse. They could have all the next day to practice reading, and Danny would tell him stories of London, and listen to the local gossip.

Danny hopped into the driver's seat. The auto gave a promising little jump, then quieted. He tried again and again, but it wouldn't start. The fog had done something to it.

He yelled into the night air, then got out and kicked a tire in vexation. His toes twinged, but he couldn't stop.

"You damned—piece of—rubbish!" He punctuated each breath with a kick. "You're never—here—when I need you!"

What did any of them know about him? That he preferred blokes, that he had no friends, that his father had left him forever.

The saddest thing about it all was that his father wasn't even dead. No—his father was trapped in time, unmoving, a memory.

And now he couldn't do the one thing that might free him. He had been too caught up in himself, in Colton. Putting Enfield before his own father.

"Oy, what's going on here? This your auto?"

Two constables had seen what he was doing and approached

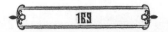

to investigate. Danny stood panting in the cold night air, glaring at them both, his breath bursting into white clouds.

"Yes, it's my bloody auto," he said. "'Course it's mine, it's a piece of shit, isn't it?"

"That's quite the mouth on you, young man."

"Shove off."

They were threatening to take him in when they heard the rapid clatter of a woman's shoes. Cassie emerged from the fog, out of breath.

"Please, he's had a rough night," she told the constables. "I promise I'll see him home." They grumbled for a moment, then let him go with a warning.

Danny straightened his jacket and turned to Cassie. Her face was blank, but he could tell she was disappointed in him.

"Auto won't start," he said, looking away.

She went to the boot for her tools. They had expected something like this to happen. As she propped the bonnet open and began to tinker, Danny leaned against the auto. Now that his anger had burned off, he could feel the cold and started shivering. Even the throbbing in his hand grew more intense, a sickening starburst of pain.

"I'm sorry," Cassie said. "I know how badly you wanted the Assignment."

"It's fine."

"Sure. Beating on a bloke tends to mean everything's fine."

"It's just . . ." He dragged his uninjured hand through his hair, clutching it until his scalp ached. "What the hell am I supposed to do now? I can't go to the Maldon tower. I can't even go to Enfield."

"Is it really so hard for you?" Cassie asked, glancing at him as she worked. "Not going to Enfield."

"You wouldn't understand, Cass."

"Wouldn't I?"

"No, you wouldn't. No one does." Except for Matthias, he remembered with a pinch of shame. Matthias would know how this felt.

He watched the brick wall across the street and listened to the clanks and scrapes of Cassie's work. There was a pause, then she swore. Danny turned and saw her staring at the internal components, her shoulders shaking. She went back in and checked every piece, every connection, every screw, every valve. Then again. And again.

"Cass." Danny gently pried her tools from her hands. Her white gloves were now stained with grease. He wrapped one arm around her, tucking her under his chin. It was the way he'd held her when she told him William was dead. She breathed hard, and he could feel the cold sweat on her temple.

"You've done enough," he told her. "It's fine. I'll be all right."

They stayed like that as the noxious fog rolled in, thick and oppressive. Eventually, Cassie swallowed and stepped back. She ran her sleeve under her nose, an unladylike gesture that would have given both their mothers conniptions.

"Thanks," she said thickly. He nodded. "Listen, Danny . . . if it's so important to you, then why don't you just find out who the new mechanic is and ask to switch?"

He leaned back on his heels. "What?"

"Find out who's going to replace you and convince them to let you go instead. Whatever assignments you get, they can have, and their Enfield assignments can be yours." She took a deep breath. "Right," she said to the auto, closing the bonnet and kissing the top. "That's a fix for you, then. And you?" She looked at Danny. "Is that a good enough fix for you?"

He thought about it, then nodded. "Cass, you're brilliant."

"Don't tell me what I already know."

He had been wrong about his mother not caring. When she got the call about Danny's behavior at the social, she ordered him to sit at the kitchen table. She lit a cigarette. The smoke wafted his way and he coughed.

They were silent for a long time. Finally, Leila said, "Why?"

"He was being an arse."

"Danny, please."

"What do you want me to say, Mum? He was being rude to Cass. How could I let him get away with that?"

"Hitting him was not the solution. You should have reported him to a chaperone."

Danny almost laughed at that, thinking back to Rotherfield

and how the constable had been willing to accept Lucas's word over his own.

"Oh, now it's all so clear! Let me just pull apart time and go back to that moment—"

"*Danny!*" Her voice cracked, and he winced.

"Sorry," he mumbled.

She took a long pull off her cigarette, then snuffed it out on a copper ashtray. "What did he say to you?"

He watched her expression as he told her, but it didn't change.

"Don't waste your thoughts on him, Danny. He isn't important."

"You agree with them, don't you? You think it's strange, me being this way. You think I do it just to make your life harder."

"I never said that."

"You think it."

She took out another cigarette.

You lost your temper, the gesture said.

She lit a match.

You told him to go, the flame whispered.

She took a long, slow drag.

He's gone because of you, the smoke sighed.

He stood up from the table. "I'm heading to bed."

"Danny . . ." They stared at each other, but Leila eventually looked away. The unspoken whispers followed him out the kitchen, up the stairs, orbiting above his bed like twin desolate planets.

Your fault.

AETAS AND THE SKY GOD

Aetas had never stood on a cloud before. The desire coursed through him with a sensation humans might have likened to hunger, so he emerged from the ocean and called for his brother.

Caelum descended from the sky. He soared on wings that branched from his arms in feathers of deep topaz streaked with veins of silver, like the halo of a storm cloud when the sun sits behind it. His skin was the deep blue of the night sky, freckled with white star-like diamonds. They winked and shone as he turned toward his golden brother.

"Will you take me up into the sky, Caelum?" Aetas asked. "I have never been, and I would like to explore your domain. I have seen Oceana's world, and Terra's, but now I would like to explore yours."

"It would be an honor, Brother."

So Caelum held Aetas and beat his powerful wings to launch them higher, away from the water and earth that Aetas loved and up into a colder world, thin of air and thick with moisture. They landed upon the ridge of a cloud, and the gods' feet settled on swirling iridescent fog.

They were sailing on an insubstantial ship, and the world below was their sea. Lights shuttered and blinked beneath them, and the cold darkness above swallowed sound. Aetas could see into the heart of that darkness, into the galaxies of paintbrush colors and the swirling trembling masses of stars dying and being born. Somewhere beyond rested Chronos. He'd grown weary and had long ago left his four creations to care for the world in his stead.

"What do you think of my domain, Brother?" Caelum asked. His eyes were clear and silver, refracting light like shards of glass. They reflected the fires and the lights below, the people small as weevils, their tiny homes and their structured lives.

"It is a good place," said Aetas, "if a bit solemn."

"I enjoy the quiet," Caelum said. "The restless energy of the world and the restless energy of the galaxies meet here in this sliver that is mine."

Aetas thought it was a noble place to stay. But even as he thought this, Caelum pointed down to earth.

"Something is wrong," he said. "Aetas, where is the morning?"

Aetas had been standing here for so long, he didn't know how much time had fled from his body. Panicked, he reached for the time threads that connected him to earth. They were stretched too far, too thin. Their light turned pale like wheat bleached from the sun.

"I must return," he said.

Caelum nodded and took him from the cloud, and together they flew back to earth. Aetas wound the threads around himself as they went, pulling in the night, bringing in the morning. Time shuddered and seized, stubborn at first, then giving in with a sigh.

Standing on the shore, Aetas watched the crescent of the sun begin to rise.

Caelum looked at him, worry creasing his brow.

"My brother, you seem tired."

In case Chronos was listening, Aetas said, "I am fine now that I have returned. Thank you for showing me the sky. I will never forget it." But deep within his core he felt the weariness building, the tremor of the time threads, the fear that he would run out of strength to maintain this beautiful earth beneath the stars.

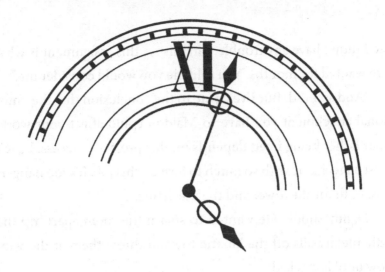

P lease, sir, tell me it isn't true."

The Lead stood at his window, smoothing his mustache with thick fingers. It was odd to think those fingers had once been in the field, delicately fixing clockwork. Most mechanics' hands were slender, like Danny's.

"Sir," Danny tried again, sitting on the very edge of his seat. "Please."

"Daniel," the Lead sighed, finally turning to him, "what do you expect me to do? You're the best in your class, it's true, but Lucas is more qualified to assist the other mechanics at the new Maldon tower. He has a good disposition for it. More than that, the Enfield assignments were difficult for you, and I don't want you under more strain."

"They weren't difficult. If you read my reports again, you'll see I didn't have any trouble. Sir, this . . . this assignment is what I've wanted for months. You told me you would consider me."

"And so I did. But I've come to the conclusion that the emotional attachment you have to Maldon could affect your work. Your father being freed depends on this project's success. I can't trust a mechanic with so much to lose on this job. It's too dangerous, both for the tower and the mechanic."

Danny shook. He wanted to smash the room apart, rip the little metal balls off the kinetic toy and throw them at the window until it cracked.

"More than that," the Lead went on, sitting, "you hit another mechanic. Lord knows your reasons, but I feel the stress may have gotten to you. You'll be put on suspension for a couple of weeks."

"Lucas provoked me!"

"That's not a good reason, Daniel."

A scream built in Danny's throat, but he held it there, trapped, and it burned his vocal cords. Nobody believed him—nobody cared. But if he didn't do something soon, Colton might hurt himself again.

Danny stood and grabbed his bag. The Lead called him back, but Danny pretended not to hear. He was already in trouble. What else could they do to him?

He slammed the door on his way out. The secretary jumped, but he ignored her, too. He ignored everything except the gripping impulse that told him what he had to do.

It was harder than he thought to find the mechanic who had replaced him. Danny wandered the office asking this secretary and that, but they all shook their heads or shrugged.

He stopped short when he spotted Matthias down the hall. He wasn't alone. Tom and George crowded him, speaking in low voices.

Danny didn't want to make himself known, not after what Tom had said to him last time, but the sight unnerved him. Matthias said something that made Tom clench his fist. George caught his friend's arm even as Matthias stepped back with hands raised in supplication. Tom spat a few words, turned, and clomped awkwardly down the stairs, George trailing after him.

Matthias heard Danny's careful approach and lifted his head. His face was flushed from the encounter, or maybe because Danny had witnessed it.

"What did they say to you?" Danny demanded.

Matthias rubbed the back of his thick neck. "Nothing of consequence." At Danny's frown, his lips twitched. "They knew I was snooping in their offices."

"Snooping?"

"Well." Matthias crossed his arms and leaned in, though there was no one else around. "To be honest, Danny, I don't trust them. Never have. And what with Tom being at Shere before you, it's too much of a coincidence. So I went into his office, thinking I could find some sort of hint. But there was nothing."

"I found something," Danny blurted. Matthias's eyebrows shot upward, and Danny figured he might as well admit to the

rest. "Or, at least, what I found was strange. Tom had a bag full of pipes in his office."

"Pipes?"

"Does that mean anything to you?"

Matthias shook his head. "No. Not a thing."

Danny swallowed his disappointment.

"You look pale, Danny Boy. What's the matter? Want to come down to the café with me?"

"I've already had tea, thanks."

"Is it about your mum?"

"My—? Oh, no." She was the furthest thing from his mind at the moment, though he couldn't help remembering her look at the kitchen table the other night.

"I saw the mouse you copped on Lucas. What're you up to? I thought you were better than that."

Danny pressed his lips together. "Says the man who does it for fun."

"Used to, Danny, used to. I'm different now." He seemed disappointed about it, too. Danny thought back to Tom's fist and how Matthias had forced himself to raise his open hands, to step back.

"*You* taught me how to fight."

"Yes, and now I'm regretting it." The corners of Matthias's eyes softened. "Come with me. Let's talk."

Danny would have. He wanted to leave this place and talk to Matthias, maybe even tell him about Colton. But just then Danny spotted a familiar gray vest down the hall.

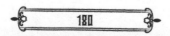

"Brandon!"

The apprentice looked over his shoulder. Danny waved frantically, signaling him to wait. The boy rolled his eyes.

"Sorry, Matthias," Danny said. "Some other time."

Danny ran down the length of the hall toward the gray-clad apprentice, who didn't seem particularly thrilled to see him.

"I'm glad I caught you. There's been a problem."

"Enfield again, is it?"

"Well, sort of. Here, let's step out of the way." He looked down the hall, but Matthias was gone.

As Danny explained what had happened, the apprentice's eyebrows furrowed. Danny probably sounded like a first-rate crank, especially if word had gotten out about him hitting Lucas.

"Why's it so important to keep this tower?" he asked when Danny wrapped up his fumbling plea.

"It's hard to say. I just feel rather attached to it." When Brandon didn't react, Danny realized he'd have to dig deeper. "They think I'm weak. That I can't handle it. Ever since my accident in Shere, the Lead's been treating me like I'm this fragile creature who'll break at the first sign of strain. I want to show him different. But I'll need help."

Brandon thought it over. His eyes trailed from right to left, looking between two answers. "I don't think there's much you can do once it's assigned. Sorry mate, but I've got an assessment coming up, and I don't want to get in trouble."

As he spoke, Brandon took out his tiger's eye and rolled it between his fingers like a priest handling rosary beads. Danny didn't even think before he snatched the marble from Brandon's hand.

"Oy—!"

"I'll give it back if you agree to help me."

"What are you, a child?" Brandon made a grab, but Danny hopped back a few paces.

"Brandon, *please*. I swear this won't come back to you. If I'm caught, I'll take all the blame. I'll say that I lied to you, that I made you think the Lead reassigned Enfield to me. You'll be clear for your assessment."

Brandon exhaled angrily through his nose. Danny knew that the boy could easily take him in a fight, but Brandon didn't seem the fisticuffs sort. Finally, after a minute of deliberation, Brandon nodded once. "All right. I'll ask around. If I find out the new mechanic's name, I'll send word."

Danny thanked Brandon profusely, gave him back the marble, and left before someone like the Lead saw him lurking around the office.

At home he walked from room to room in a daze. If someone found him out, he would be in serious trouble. He was already on a two-week suspension. Then again, if his relationship with Colton was exposed in any way, or if the mysterious bomber decided to turn to Enfield next—

He stopped dead, shivering all over. It only occurred to him

now how odd it was to say *bomber*, singular, when it could easily be *bombers*, plural. If people who were unhappy with the towers got ideas . . .

The telephone rang. He almost ran into the wall in his hurry to reach the receiver.

"Hello?"

"Danny, is it?"

It was Brandon's slow drawl. Danny deflated in relief.

"Have you heard anything?"

"They said there's an Enfield job next week, something about cleaning the clockwork."

I already did that.

"The new mechanic they're pairing me with is Daphne Richards."

Danny must have groaned, because Brandon made a sound of amusement.

"I asked her for a drink at the Winchester to get to know her beforehand. Tomorrow at six."

Danny could have reached through the receiver and kissed him. "I owe you a drink myself. No, five drinks."

Brandon huffed and hung up.

Danny stared out at the thick gray rain, thinking. How could he possibly convince someone like Daphne Richards to hand over a job based on some wish-wash? Especially if he was on suspension. Especially if she hated him.

But then he thought of Colton's smile, and his resolve hardened.

His mother didn't come home until late, and by then he was already in bed. He listened to her heels clacking against the hardwood floors as the rain continued on into the night. When she finally came upstairs, he expected her to go to her bedroom. He startled when she knocked on his door.

"What, Mum?"

She eased the door open and looked inside. "Are you all right, Danny?"

"What d'you mean?"

She took a hesitant step toward him, a dark form relieved only a little by the watery moonlight. "You've been acting odd lately. Something must be going on."

Danny slumped against the headboard, glad that she couldn't see his face. "I'm fine, Mum."

"Do you . . . want to talk about it?"

"There's nothing to talk about."

It wasn't a good feeling, lying to his mother, especially when she was trying. Why was she even trying? Why now? Why not three years ago, when he had needed her most?

Besides, he couldn't tell her the truth. Not yet. Maybe not ever.

She waited a moment, sighed, and the shadow of her head nodded.

"Let me know if you change your mind."

She left, and he wanted to call after her—say, maybe, that he wasn't upset with her, but that he was too busy with his own life to try understanding hers. Or to give into a childish yearning and ask her to sit beside him, to hold his hand until he fell asleep. To feel her cool fingers on his brow before she swept his hair back and kissed his forehead good night, as she used to do.

The door closed with a soft *snick*.

The rain had flooded the auto, and for a while it wouldn't start. When it rolled down the street it hiccupped a couple times, and Danny wondered if the world did not want him to succeed at anything.

He still managed to get to the Winchester with time to spare, so he sat in the auto and planned what to say. He had written his argument down, repeating the words until he had them memorized.

"Miss Richards, I respect our profession as clock mechanics and would never do anything to harm either of our careers. However, the clock in Enfield is my project and, therefore, my responsibility. I think you're a much better mechanic than most—better than me—but I understand how this clock works. So if you don't mind, I'll let the Lead Mechanic know we've spoken and head up there next week. You don't want Colton Tower, anyway; it's a dingy clock in a dingy town. I'm sure you'd much prefer grander assignments. Of course, I don't mean to cheat you of your earnings, so we could switch jobs or I can pay you something upfront. Oh, no, it wouldn't be a bribe! Merely a gift of thanks. I'm sure you understand."

His timepiece read five to six. He took a steadying breath and walked into the pub.

It was already crowded with patrons and noise, the smell of food and drink mingling with the scent of bodies after a long workday. Danny scanned the crowd until he saw her at a round table. He recognized Daphne by her long blonde hair and the diamond-shaped tattoo beside her right eye. The apprentices always made up stories as to why she had it; no one in the Union knew the real reason.

She was dressed in a dark jacket that buttoned diagonally, and she'd tied a blue kerchief around her neck. She attracted a few stares from men and women alike. Danny knew from his own mother's muttering that some women thought wearing men's clothes was beneath them.

Danny squeezed through the crowd, murmuring apologies and getting beer spilled on him until he reached her side. She ran frosty blue eyes over him like a cat evaluating a mongrel's size and potential for trouble. Danny tried to smile, and she scoffed.

"No thanks. I'm not *that* desperate."

"What? No, I'm here to talk about Enfield."

"Enfield?" She looked him over again. "Brandon Summers was supposed to meet me here. Not you."

"Well, it's me you're going to get." Danny sat beside her, but not too close. "Seeing as I'm the current Enfield mechanic."

This was a bold thing to say, since technically he wasn't the only mechanic who could be called to Enfield. It was rare for someone to be assigned to a clock tower full time.

Daphne raised an eyebrow. "You're the current mechanic." He couldn't tell if it was a question.

He thought about his speech, the one he'd planned so precisely in his head. He opened his mouth and took in a breath to begin, but all that came out was, "You can't go to Enfield."

Her high, smooth forehead wrinkled in a frown. "Of course I can."

"You shouldn't, though, is what I'm saying."

"What are you talking about?" Daphne hadn't finished her drink, but she looked ready to bolt.

"I've been working in Enfield lately, and I know that clock tower better than anyone. It was a mistake to assign you there."

"A mistake?" Her voice turned low and her long, pale fingers curled around the tabletop's edge.

"What I mean is—you're a wonderful mechanic. You might even be better than me. I mean, wait . . . you *are* better than me—"

"How would you know? You've never seen me work. And for that matter, yes, I'm a better and more qualified mechanic than you are. Why are you wasting my time?"

His plan was going to shambles. Danny imagined Colton's disappointed face, the Enfield tower exploding. He gathered himself for another attempt. "But that's it exactly! You're much too qualified to be stuck with a lousy, small clock like the one in Enfield. You deserve better projects, better towers, which is why I'm offering to take this assignment. Trust me, you don't want to work in a place like Enfield."

Her eyes never left his face. He schooled his expression into what he hoped was concern, the face of a young man who would never lie.

Finally, she said, "You never told me what you were doing in Tom's office."

Danny stomped down the urge to scowl. "I think we're about even, don't you?" When she looked confused, he clarified, "You told the Lead."

"I didn't tell the Lead anything."

Now it was his turn to be confused. If she hadn't told the Lead about being in Tom's office, then why had he taken Danny off the Enfield assignment?

She traced the outline of her glass as she stared at him. "If you take the Enfield assignments from me, how am I supposed to get paid? I have to feed myself."

"Why don't we switch assignments? Or I could pay you. Here, I'll even buy your drink." He tried not to cringe at the thought of more lost money.

"Are you cracked or something? I told you I'm not that desperate."

"Keep your skirt down, I prefer blokes."

With her bill settled, he walked her outside. She stopped at a chrome-plated motorbike, and Danny had to look twice. Even the sight of it made his stomach squirm. He preferred his father's jalopy compared to this vehicle of certain death.

"I know more about you than you think," she said suddenly. "And what people say about you. They feel sorry for you. Maybe I do, too, a bit."

Danny didn't say anything. Daphne unstrapped her helmet and sat astride the hulking machine.

"I understand, a little, what it's like." She paused, her breath hanging before her in the cold. "People knowing something about you that's invisible. The way they look at you, as if they can see it if they stare hard enough."

He felt his heartbeat in his stomach. He wanted to ask her if anyone ever did see it. If she *wanted* them to see it.

"I'm sorry, but I can't agree to do this. It's too risky, and I can't afford to lose my job. It's all I have."

Danny fumbled to pull a fiver from his pocket he'd been saving for his next auto repair installment. "Look, I can pay—"

"No." She shook her head. "I'm sorry, but no." Daphne hesitated, perhaps debating whether to say more, but she just sighed and strapped on her helmet. With a kick and a rev of the engine, she was speeding down the street, taking his last hope with him.

Well, not quite his last hope.

"Danny Hart, you are a fool," he mumbled as he hid in a stairwell of the Mechanics Affairs building the next morning. Biting

his lower lip, he peeked down the hallway. All along the back wall were folders, and in those folders mechanics received mail, quarterly reviews, turned in case reports . . .

. . . and received assignments.

A mechanic lingered in front of her folder, then walked away with her attention fixed on a sheaf of papers. Danny swallowed hard and snuck into the hall. His boots squeaked against the freshly polished floors.

A bead of sweat was already rolling down his temple when he reached his folder. There would be no assignment because of his suspension, though he checked anyway out of habit. But there, toward the end: Daphne's.

And inside, an Enfield assignment waited.

He wavered, visions of consequences teasing his mind as his fingers brushed the edges of the paper.

The sound of footsteps decided things for him. Danny grabbed the assignment and hurried away, crushing the paper to his chest.

So Danny, not Daphne, set out for Enfield the following week. Any shame he felt for what he'd done was shoved to one side, overshadowed by excitement. He was returning to Enfield. To Colton.

Despite the rain, the drive was uneventful, except for a swerve to avoid the usual bump in the road. The sight of Colton's tower melted away the dread that had settled on Danny like frost, a window bright with hearth fire, a welcome beacon urging him to hurry up—you're almost home.

Stepping inside, he relaxed as time wrapped him in its comforting embrace. *Want* purled through him as the fibers wound around his body, hugging him, greeting him.

At last, he could draw a full breath.

Brandon looked unsurprised to see him. Danny smiled and turned to the clockwork, which was already quite clean thanks to his earlier efforts, but a thin film of dust had once again settled. They brought out ladders and wiped down the highest gears. At one point Danny looked down, unsettled by the height, and saw Colton jokingly hand him the micrometer. Danny laughed, startled out of his fear, and Brandon gave him an odd glance.

"Not as dirty as all that," Brandon said when their task was complete, with a sense of pride that Danny thought highly undeserved. "Guess that leaves us a bit of time to relax."

"You can if you want to," Danny said. "I'll go check on everything else." Brandon shrugged and headed down the stairs.

There was a ripple through the time fibers. Danny felt the pull of him through the air, a gentle tug on his limbs like he was a moon being drawn into orbit.

He turned and saw Colton standing there. Golden and beautiful, ancient and new. The shining apex of the world. And when Colton smiled the light burst stronger, filling the cold cavities of Danny's chest where no sunlight had touched for so long. It ached. And it was sweet. And it was ancient and new.

They stared at each other for minutes that were wordless, but not silent. Their eyes were having a discussion of their own, a simple hello, a tangible relief. But Colton couldn't stay ignorant for long. As they walked through the tower, under the patter of the rain, Danny told him what had happened. Colton's lips dropped from his usual smile into a grim line.

"Won't you be in trouble?"

"Only if I'm caught. Besides, I doubt they'd want to get rid of me."

"They can do that?" Colton took a worried step back. "Maybe you shouldn't be here."

"It'll be fine." Danny took Colton's hand, and the space shifted around them. The air flowed over Danny's skin and time fibers wrapped around his body like rope, as if to keep him there forever. "I want to be here."

"Are you sure?"

"I wouldn't have done this if I wasn't sure."

Colton's smile returned slowly. Danny watched in subdued wonder as strands of golden time threaded across Colton's body, weaving under and around his arms, around his neck, hugging his torso, looping curlicues between his fingers. Danny had a sudden and irrational jealousy, then. He wanted to be that golden and that close. He wanted to wrap himself around Colton's body, to be everywhere, all at once, and feel the strength and power of him.

Danny looked into the spirit's eyes instead. He realized it was the closest he would ever get to that feeling.

Colton broke their gaze when he lightly touched the bruises on Danny's knuckles. "I can't believe you hit someone. I'm sure he deserved it."

"He did." Danny didn't repeat what Lucas had said. He was sure Colton wouldn't understand half of it, anyway. "They've suspended me for a couple of weeks, though. And I got a talking-to from the Lead Mechanic."

Remembering that conversation caused a hard lump to form Danny's stomach. Lucas working in the new Maldon tower, responsible for freeing his father—it was unbearable.

"Won't the other mechanics be angry that you hit someone?"

"Half of them would probably applaud me. Lucas is an idiot. It doesn't matter, anyway. None of them like me to begin with, except Matthias." When Colton frowned, Danny bit back a curse. He shouldn't have said anything.

"They don't like you? Why not? You're smart, and funny, and kind. And your eyes are so green. Why wouldn't they like you?"

"It's just how it is." Danny turned to the window. Though the jagged edges of a bad mood pressed into him, he couldn't quite get past Colton's comment about his eyes. "Since Dad left, I haven't wanted to be around them."

"Why not?"

"How should I know?" Colton's silence made Danny sigh. "My life's pretty pitiful at the moment. I don't want others to see that."

Colton joined him at the window. "You let me see."

Danny caught Colton's eye, then looked away. "You're different."

Colton leaned his shoulder into Danny's. They stared out at the rain, listening to each drop echo through the wooden hollow of the tower.

"It's sad and happy at the same time," the spirit said. "Rain." When Danny nodded, Colton asked, "Why do you talk that way about yourself? You don't deserve it."

"Maybe I do." He thought about stealing Daphne's assignment. "Maybe I'm a villain and don't deserve a happy ending." Danny chipped his thumbnail against a splinter in the window frame. "I'm no prince, that's for sure. I'm not handsome or special or any of that. I'm hopeless."

"That's not true," Colton said. "You're everything. You're . . . You're chaos and order and everything in between. Like sunshine kept back by clouds. Like the entire world's imploded inside you, but all I see are the stars are sewn into your skin. You're filled with soft, dark music." His smile was gentle. "I hear it all the time. Your music."

A timid heat rose inside him. Danny's thumb kept chipping at that splinter, eyes fixed on its point. "What does it sound like?"

Colton's eyes drifted back out the window. "It sounds like rain."

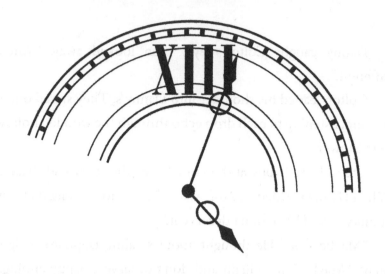

anny wrote up Daphne's Enfield report and turned it in the next day. The protesters outside threw rubbish at him as he was leaving, like they knew exactly what he'd been doing and decided to add their own commentary.

Every week the group seemed to grow more violent. It didn't help that a rival group was starting to form as well, protesters protesting the bloody protesters. The two sides got into shouting debates that could be heard on the third floor. The arguments always amounted to the same thing: *we need the towers to live; let's find an alternative time source.*

"Why are towers being attacked?"

"Don't you know this is going to cause another Maldon?"

"Why is no one stopping this?"

It grew tiresome.

Thankfully, now he could escape to Enfield. Danny couldn't properly describe what he felt when he visited Colton. He usually went alone, but Brandon accompanied him whenever Daphne was given a small assignment there, which Danny continued to slip from her folder. He tried to go in the early mornings to escape notice, worried the Enfield citizens might grow suspicious, but whenever they spotted him they only greeted him with nods or small waves.

Colton's beaming welcome always warmed away the autumn chill. Their talks grew longer and deeper as Colton came to learn more about the world outside of Enfield. In return, Danny asked him how a clock spirit lived.

"Do you ever get hungry?" Danny asked once.

"No."

"Thirsty?"

"Never."

Colton didn't need to breathe or swallow. He blinked simply because it had become a habit after watching humans do it for so long. When it came to the more complex questions, such as how Colton could disappear and rematerialize at a thought, Colton couldn't provide detailed explanations.

It took considerable courage for Danny to ask, "Have you ever kissed anyone before me?"

Colton thought, then shook his head. "I don't think so. I've thought about it, though. There used to be a girl down the street who was very pretty. But that was a long time ago."

Danny, who hadn't anticipated this answer, took a moment to reorganize his thoughts. "So you would have kissed me if I was a girl?"

"I would have kissed you if you were a girl. I would have kissed you if you were purple."

Danny wasn't quite sure what to do with this information.

He brought his father's copy of *Alice's Adventures in Wonderland*. When Colton stumbled over the poems, Danny laughed and said he had trouble with them as well. As he read them aloud, Colton closed his eyes and listened. Danny glanced over at him every so often, Colton's eyelids the color of dawn, his lips curved upward like a bow.

Danny had most certainly fallen down the rabbit hole. He didn't know if he ever wanted to return.

His mother began to notice his frequent trips. He told her he was seeing Cassie or another old friend he never spoke to anymore. Cassie sounded skeptical whenever he asked her to cover for him.

"If my mum calls your house, you have to tell her we're busy."

"Why? Can't you tell her the truth?"

"You know how she is."

Eventually, the date of his mother's interview in Chelmsford arrived. Danny waited at the house until she returned, pale and tired. He rushed to get her tea.

"What did they say?" he asked as she sipped from her cup. The wind had ruffled her hair, which hung around her face like plump, curly vines. She would have made a good Medusa.

"They said they won't make a decision for another fortnight at least."

Danny sighed quietly in relief. A little more time to sort things out. Though his mother leaving would hardly be the end of the world, it still hung like an unpleasant threat, but he hadn't the faintest idea how to convince her to change her mind.

As November rolled on, and the weather grew even colder, Danny's suspension came to an end. He heard Lucas had gone to the new Maldon tower, but tried not to listen to any news unless it happened to be "the tower is working."

Something pulled restlessly at him, fearful and urgent. He was losing his train of thought much more easily these days. His mind was in a summer's haze, focused on Enfield, drawing unbidden smiles to his lips. Those small, unconscious smiles came with a price, he realized. He was losing sight of what had driven him to this point. The thing he and his mother needed most.

While he was with Colton, Maldon was still trapped.

While he smiled, his father was still lost.

His desires couldn't seem to coexist. Desperation or relief— one or the other, they demanded. You can't have both.

I'll be lost without both.

To Danny's surprise, Matthias willingly brought up Maldon as they played checkers in the park one afternoon.

"I'm still miffed the Lead didn't consider you," Matthias said as he glowered at the red checkers. He made a slow move forward. "I mean, of all people, *Lucas*. You or Daphne would have been a far better choice."

Danny's lips thinned at the mention of Daphne. "Can't do anything about it now."

Matthias registered his flat tone. "You should talk to the Lead again. He could reconsider."

Danny fiddled with his black checker. "Maybe." He raised his eyebrows at the pinky finger Matthias held out to him.

"Promise you'll come to me if you need help," Matthias said.

With a small, breathy laugh, Danny wrapped his own pinky finger around Matthias's and shook. "All right." He looked back down at the checkerboard. "Hey, do you mind if I take this?"

He brought the checkerboard to Colton's tower and taught him how to play. He also taught him piquet and Beggar My Neighbor.

Running, his inner voice scolded. *You didn't get the Assignment, and now you're running away to sulk and play card games with a clock spirit. You shouldn't be here. You know the rules. This isn't going to end well for either of you.*

He ignored it.

Colton had his own games, such as walking quietly behind Danny as he climbed the stairs and then startling him at the top, or trying to get Danny to catch him and winking out of sight, only to reappear on a rafter high above.

"That's cheating!" Danny called up, his voice echoing. Colton

stuck out his tongue, something he had seen Danny do once and which was now his favorite expression.

The planes within Danny shifted and overlapped. Before, his world had just been *I*. Now it was expanding into *we*.

Danny knew the shape of Colton's lips, the arch of his eyebrows, the whisper of his hand as it slid into his own. The calm measured beats of his voice. He knew the strum and twist of time, the spark of recognition instead of fear. His panic slumbered, tucking its head down.

For the first time in three years, Danny did not have to force his laughter.

But every so often, he remembered they still had to be careful.

It happened once during a game of hide-and-seek. Colton gave Danny a hard chase, standing up above the pendulum before winking out of view to reappear on the stairs. Danny cursed and ran after him, and Colton bolted. The spirit laughed, the sound like an echoing hum throughout the tower. The clock tower itself was bright, golden, filled with an energy that made the air crackle.

Danny was out of breath when he reached the top. He looked for Colton in the clock room but saw no sign of him. A few steps in, he smiled.

The longer he spent in this tower, the easier it had become for him to sense Colton. Rather, to sense Colton moving through the time fibers. He felt the shift just behind him, preparing to catch him by surprise.

Before Colton could grab him, Danny spun and seized him first. Colton yelped and they toppled to the ground, laughing.

Then one of the tower bells rang. Danny jumped and looked at the clock face. It was only 1:23.

"Colton, stop!"

The spirit quickly sobered at Danny's tone. "What is it?"

"The bells. You made them go off."

Colton, lying on the floor, glanced at the clock face. Much to Danny's alarm, and not so much to Colton's, the minute hand had moved. The clock now read 1:27.

"It's preparing for the half-hour ring," Danny said. "You made it speed up."

Colton's eyebrows furrowed. "I can't help that."

"Well, fix it!"

The spirit sat up, his hair a mess, and closed his eyes. Danny watched as the minute hand slowly crawled back until it read 1:24.

"Better," Danny said.

Colton opened his eyes. "I really can't help it. It's just a reaction. Like humans crying when they're sad or happy."

Danny wanted to be upset, to validate himself with anger, but instead his panic raised its head to sniff the air again. "I know," he said even as his pulse beat a nervous rhythm. "It's not your fault. We just have to be careful."

Colton nodded with a faint frown, as if he didn't quite understand the word.

Martinmas came and went. Toward the end of November, Enfield started to prepare for St. Andrew's Day. Colton told Danny that the townspeople always made a festival of it, and he enjoyed watching the fun from his tower.

Danny could hear the celebration as soon as he drove into town that day. The village green was decorated with banners and wooden arches woven with purple and white flowers. Some of the townspeople played music, and a group of eight—all couples, including the recently married pair—were dancing in the middle of the green to the accompanying claps of the onlookers. Danny stopped and watched, and joined the applause when the dance finished. The couples were flushed and high-spirited, their eyes gleaming from the well-deserved attention.

"The men, now!" someone shouted. Other dancers came proudly forward, and the band prepared another song. A few saw Danny and beckoned him over, so he stepped onto the green.

"Join us in a dance, will you, love?"

"Oh, no, I'm horrid at dancing," he said truthfully. "I'd like to watch, though."

"Come on then, just one."

"But—"

"It won't hurt!"

"Really, I—"

Someone grabbed his arm. It was the handsome young man who had smiled at him before, all grins now. His brown eyes promised mischief.

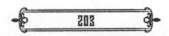

"Just one dance," the young man pleaded.

"I . . . oh, all right."

The crowd cheered as Danny was led to the center of the circle. His face grew hot, but the young man squeezed his arm in encouragement before his hand slipped away.

The first note struck the air and the men took their poses. Danny was slow to follow and some of the watchers laughed, but unlike the laughs of Lucas's cronies, it was an affectionate sound.

"Watch me," the young man said with a wink.

The music directed their feet. Danny turned and lifted his arms when he knew he should, and though he stumbled, a beat off from the others, he really wasn't all that bad. The young man grinned, and when they were paired, turned him around to begin the steps from the opposite side.

When's the last time I danced? Danny wondered. He couldn't remember.

He was flushed by the end, but more from exertion than embarrassment. He shook a few well-meaning hands and suffered some chatter, occasionally meeting the eye of the young man who had roped him in.

When he got Danny alone, he said his name was Harland. "You shouldn't be cooped up in the tower today." Another dance started, this time for the women. "Stay out here and have fun."

"I'll come back," Danny promised.

It took another five minutes of wheedling to escape the green and head for the tower. He took the long way around so that no one would follow him, walking between neatly trimmed hedges

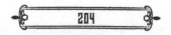

spotted with white honeysuckle, breathing in the scent of flora under the sharp chill.

Something caught his eye and he slowed to a stop. Between the hedges stood an old, weatherworn statue.

Another shrine.

Danny studied the figure as he approached: a man standing with his palms supine, his face as blank as an automaton's save for a bump that used to be his nose. A few fingers had crumbled from his hands, and a large chunk of stone was missing from his left leg. This close, Danny saw that the dais the man stood on was actually a clock face.

Aetas.

Carefully, Danny brushed his fingers over the smooth stone, feeling the indentation where the god's eyes had been carved. The statue was forgotten here, tucked away in one of Enfield's corners. He wondered if anyone came to visit it, if anyone still prayed to it. Then again, who would pray to a dead god?

Danny shook his head and moved on to the tower. His giddiness steadily returned as the music from the green grew louder. He took off his coat and draped it over his arm as he bounded up the stairs, humming the song the band had been playing.

"Colton!" Danny walked into the clock room and threw his coat on the box beside the door. "Colton?"

The spirit stood at the window that overlooked the green. Danny joined him there, smiling.

"They always have so much fun today," Colton said without a smile of his own. "They used to have two festivals, but the second

one was too rowdy. Couples ran off into the night. Some drank too much. It was taken away, eventually." He turned to Danny with a weak smile at last, but it dropped too soon. "You looked like you enjoyed yourself out there."

Danny's heart sank. Of course Colton had watched him dance. He wished he could bring him outside to join the festivities. Or just to watch, if he preferred. Danny wanted the townspeople to know their guardian, and why he was to be cherished, protected.

Danny looked into Colton's eyes, a much lighter shade than Harland's, and wished—not for the first time—that things did not have to be so complicated.

He thought back to another time they had been standing at this window, Colton's words slow and uncertain. "I want . . . well, it doesn't matter what I want."

But it did matter. It mattered to Danny.

Danny opened the window wide to allow the music to drift in with the breeze, then held his hand out. Palm up, expectant. Like Aetas standing in the hedge.

Colton gave it a strange look, asking him a silent question. Danny waited. After a slight hesitation, Colton lifted his own hand and slid it over Danny's. He curled his fingers around Colton's and led him to an open area of the clock room.

"What are you doing?" Colton asked.

"Dancing. I'm sure you've seen it enough times."

Colton's eyes widened slightly as he glanced at the window. There was something determined behind their glint now, something in the way they reflected the winter-bright sky outside.

The first note unraveled through the air. They shifted into the starting pose, Danny's hands above Colton's hips, Colton's fingertips against Danny's shoulders. Though they hadn't moved yet, Danny began to breathe a little harder.

The song took off and they slowly navigated the opening steps. It felt a little awkward, stiff with novelty, but at least they knew which foot went where.

Then Danny tripped and Colton laughed, a clear chime echoing through the tower. Encouraged by the sound, Danny put his arm around Colton's waist and turned them in time to the music.

It was how he had imagined it at the social: a swirling freedom, light gilding their edges as they turned. A deep and implicit merging of their souls to music, their bodies to movement. Each of them attuned to the other, eyes meeting, falling into sync.

They circled and lifted their forearms to touch palm to palm. Time shivered. Danny did too, from the top of his skull to his tailbone. Time brushed over his skin, making him long for more, for this one moment to never end. A visceral ache, like thirst.

The music stopped and so did their feet. They dropped their hands, but kept them clasped together.

"I've never danced before," Colton said softly.

Danny brushed his thumb over Colton's knuckles. "First time for everything."

He was cleaning Colton's clockwork when he nicked his thumb. Danny grunted in annoyance. This was what he got for leaving his gloves at home.

"What's that?" Colton knelt beside him and took his hand. "Blood?"

The spirit's curiosity had taken a morbid turn. Danny couldn't tell if Colton was excited or shocked at the sight of his blood, but either way, it fascinated him. Danny tried to pull his hand back. "Yes, it's blood."

"Does it hurt? Are you all right?"

"I'm fine."

Colton frowned thoughtfully at the red bead quivering on the pad of Danny's thumb. "What an odd thing."

Danny pressed a handkerchief to the wound to stop the bleeding. "I suppose clock spirits don't have fluids?" *Fluids? What had possessed him to say* fluids?

Colton shrugged. "I suppose not. My body's not like yours." He touched his chest, then touched Danny's. When he felt Danny's heartbeat, he pressed his palm against it, mesmerized. "You're a marvel."

Danny wanted that hand to stay there forever. Counting every beat. The air was warm and thin in the half foot that separated them. When Danny kissed him, Colton made a surprised yet happy sound, framing Danny's face with his hands. He felt willingly trapped, caught in Colton's grasp. Danny reached out a hand to steady them against the wall.

The air pulsed and Colton cried out. Danny removed his hand at once.

His bleeding thumb had pressed against the clockwork. He'd left a smudge of crimson there.

Colton reacted strangely, his eyes wide and his body shaking. Maybe it was only Danny's imagination, but he thought that time gave a little skip around them, like it had gotten snagged on a thorn. The air pulsed again. They were inside a struggling artery, being squeezed from all sides.

Danny hurried to wipe his blood off the gear. Colton relaxed a little.

"What was that about?" Danny asked, his voice hushed.

Colton shook his head, just as confused. They stared at the turning gear.

"Are you all right?"

"Yes." But Colton touched his chest again, as if expecting to find his own heartbeat there.

Danny decided that he needed to ask Matthias about the strange reaction at Colton's tower. Matthias was finishing a class when Danny arrived, so he waited by the door as the man summarized the apprentices' latest lesson.

"And remember, always keep a log. It's important for other mechanics to see what work you've done." Good thing Danny

had been submitting reports under Daphne's name, though shame gnawed at him each time he did. "For next week, I'd like you all to read the chapter on Newton's laws of time and space, as well as the one on Nicolas Fatio de Duillier and his use of jewels as wheel bearings. Both very important mechanics in their time."

The apprentices filed out, a mix of boys and girls around twelve or so, eyeing Danny curiously as they passed. There were some whispers—"I heard he hit another mechanic"; "I thought the Lead demoted him"; "Do you suppose he got that scar in a fight?"—but Danny forced himself to smile. That seemed to scare them more.

A couple apprentices stayed behind to ask Matthias questions about their latest assignment. When they left, Danny entered the classroom.

"Hello there, Danny Boy. I feel as if I hardly see you these days."

"I'm sorry, Matthias. I—"

"You don't have to explain to me," Matthias said, shuffling his papers. "You've got a lot on your plate. You have a certain look, though. Has someone caught your eye?"

Danny blushed to his roots. *It's that obvious?*

"You'll have to tell me all about her. Rather, him," Matthias amended with an apologetic smile. "Sorry. Sometimes I forget."

"It's fine." Danny picked at his shirtsleeve. "I just wanted to say hello, and to ask a quick question."

"You have more exciting things to do than to talk to an old

man, I know. At least you have more time to rest now that you don't have those awful Enfield assignments anymore."

"I don't need—" Then the words registered, and a strange ringing started in his ears. "How do you know I'm no longer assigned to Enfield?"

A small shift in Matthias's eyes revealed the truth.

"*You* told him," Danny said slowly. "You told the Lead to take me off that job."

Matthias took a deep breath, as if he'd expected him to figure it out sooner or later. "Danny, I was worried about you. You looked ill, and from what you told me, it was obvious you weren't fond of those assignments. What with the clock falling apart, I thought it was too much for you, considering everything else that's happened. You being hurt, your mother—"

"That's none of your concern!" Danny's voice burst out of him, too loud, too angry. He tried to rein it in. "I can make my own decisions."

"I'm sorry. I thought I was doing the right thing. I thought it would give you some time before Maldon to recuperate, but then you went and hit Lucas. That's not like you, Danny." Matthias paused as if waiting for him to respond. "What's so important about Enfield? It's just a little town. You said so yourself."

Danny forced himself to breathe evenly, wanting the ringing in his ears to go away. His anger blew out just as suddenly as it had come, and he was left feeling achingly empty.

"Sure," he mumbled. "Just a town."

"Danny—"

"Stay out of my affairs, all right? I don't need you and Mum looking over my shoulder every minute."

Before Matthias could apologize again, Danny turned away.

On the stairs, each step was a clap of thunder through his body, drowning out the question he had come to ask. All this stress, all this trouble, all this subterfuge, just because Matthias still saw him as a sickly boy who should stay in bed.

As if that were going to stop him now.

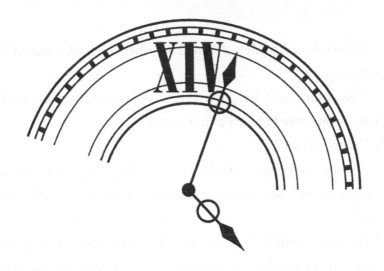

T he atrium was blinding, the sun absurdly bright despite the freezing temperature outside. In his rush to get away from Matthias, Danny hadn't even bothered to wrap his scarf around his neck before he burst out the doors.

It was a mistake. As soon as he emerged into the din of the protesters, two armies split by the entrance, someone grabbed his scarf and pulled. It slithered off his neck and the cold pierced the skin of his throat.

"Hey!" He reached for his scarf, but an obscenely tall young man held it far above his head. The young man's brown hair was shaggy, his grin toothy.

"We finally have someone's attention!" he crowed.

The others on the anti-tower side hooted as the young man spun the red scarf above his head like an American cowboy with a lasso. Danny clenched his hands into fists.

"Give it back," he demanded. The others tittered, amused by his rage.

The young man wrapped the scarf around his own neck. "Only if you agree to listen to our terms."

"What terms?"

A stocky ginger girl sidled up next to the young man. "We've submitted a petition to stop the building of the new Maldon tower."

Danny scoffed. "Good luck with that. The tower's practically finished." Each word was a splinter drawn painfully from his skin. *And I couldn't help at all.*

The tall man flipped the end of Danny's scarf at him. "Then maybe we'll find another way."

The way he said it sent a slimy feeling down to Danny's stomach. It didn't help that the ginger girl was smirking like she knew a secret he didn't. The glint in their eyes, the hunger of the small crowd at their backs, made him take a step back. He bumped into one of the anti-protesters, who grabbed his shoulders. "Leave the mechanics alone!" the woman yelled. "They aren't doing anything harmful."

"They protect the towers," a man at her side agreed, "which protects everyone."

"Protect?" The ginger girl snorted. "Dictating time is protecting?"

"We don't *dictate* anything," Danny snapped, shrugging away from the woman's clutches. He could feel everyone's tense breath around him, see the vapor leaving their mouths. "We don't control time. We fix it."

"If time ran free," the tall young man countered, "there would be no need to fix it in the first place."

The anti-protesters laughed.

"Time *can't* run free!"

"With Aetas dead, how do you expect to accomplish that?"

"Yeah, he went and got his head chopped off and fed to a shark."

"What? I thought he was turned mortal and drowned."

"That's nonsense. Aetas never existed."

"He did, but his throat was slit and his blood leaked into the sea—"

"And that's why it's so salty," Danny mumbled to himself, momentarily transported back to his father's story, to a simpler time. He shook his head. "Listen. You can bicker all you want, but leave the mechanics and the towers out of it. You harm them, you harm everyone else."

"*They're* the ones harming people!" The anti-protesters jabbed accusing fingers at the opposing crowd. "Who knows what they'll do? Maybe they're the ones responsible for Maldon in the first place!"

An icy hand squeezed Danny's heart. "I don't think—"

"Maldon wouldn't have even happened without the bleeding towers!" the protesters yelled back.

"Please—" Danny tried, but it was no use. The crowds came at each other, pushing and clutching with fists cocked back, nails ready to gouge. Danny was jostled between them, shoved this way and that until a fist connected with his rib cage. He grunted and doubled over, but that just made him an easier target for someone to bash a knee into his chest.

He would have fallen had he not caught himself on the arm of the tall young man. Danny yanked his scarf from his neck, nearly choking him. "You bastard," he yelled over the commotion. "Look what you started!"

Other mechanics streamed out of the entrance to break up the fight. Danny thought he heard a constable's whistle in the distance. But the young man seemed unfazed. He even gave Danny a cheery wink.

"Don't think this is finished," he said. "This is just the beginning."

"Beginning?" An elbow rammed into Danny's side. "The beginning of what?"

The elbow knocked into him again and sent him sprawling, scarf clenched in one fist. Someone stepped on his legs. He tried to get to his knees, but all around him was chaos. Screams. The wild heat of the fight.

Then another noise broke through the fray: the rev of an engine. Shouts turned to yelps as a chrome-plated motorbike pulled up in a screeching arc, causing protesters to scatter. Atop the motorbike sat Daphne.

"Get on!" she ordered. Danny scrambled to his feet and threw a leg over the back of the seat.

"I don't have a hel—" He gasped as Daphne throttled the

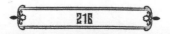

engine and they sped off. He wrapped his arms around her middle and held on tight, eyes pinched closed as the world flew by all around them. Autos honked and a horse shrieked in surprise as they zigzagged through traffic.

The ends of Daphne's blonde hair thrashed in the wind and stung his face. He opened his eyes for a moment and saw his own pale reflection in the back of her black helmet.

"Where are we going?" he yelled over the roar of the motorbike. He gasped again when they took a sharp turn and his grip on her tightened.

"I can't breathe," she growled.

"Sorry." He unwillingly loosened his arms.

Finally, they began to slow down. She took an easier turn into a quiet street and parked by the curb. Even when she killed the engine, Danny's body continued to vibrate.

"You can let go now," she said.

"What? Oh." He snatched his arms back. "Sorry."

She pulled the helmet off. Her hairline was slick with sweat. "First time on a motorbike?"

"How could you tell?" He tried to get off the seat, but his sore legs wouldn't cooperate and he ended up nearly falling on his backside. Daphne looked on, unimpressed.

"What the hell was that back there?" she asked. "I was passing by the square and saw them go at one another."

Danny explained what had happened, only then realizing he still held his scarf in a white-knuckled grip. He tied it around his neck. The ride had completely chilled him.

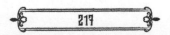

"They can't keep doing this," Daphne mumbled. Her blue eyes were sharp with concern. "It's only a matter of time until those idiots do something violent."

"My bruises say today was plenty violent."

"No, I mean something more. Something dangerous." Daphne looked down the street, and only then did Danny think to check their surroundings. Somewhere in Aldgate, maybe. Down the street was a large house that read St. Agnes's Home For Women. Why had she taken them here, of all places?

"You didn't park your auto outside the Affairs building, did you?" she asked.

"No, I took the bus. I'll take one home." He put a hand on his aching side where he'd been hit. Beneath the ache was familiar, writhing guilt. "Um . . . thank you. For getting me out of there."

She could have left him to be trampled, and would have likely thought good riddance. It's what he would have done.

No it isn't, a faint voice whispered. *You're better than that.* But the memory of stealing Daphne's assignments told him different.

"I'm sorry," he mumbled to the curb.

"Don't be sorry. Just be careful around those people." She put her helmet back on, but didn't fasten the strap. "See you."

He turned to walk to the nearest omnibus stop, but looked over his shoulder. Daphne only rode her motorbike to the end of the street, where she parked outside St. Agnes's. Danny paused, curious, but made himself turn back. He'd already invaded her life too much.

Don't think this is finished. Danny had no idea what it meant,

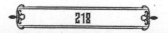

but Daphne might be right. If unchecked, there was no telling what these protesters would do. Or what they would set their sights on.

Lucas watched the two mechanics bicker about the clockwork before them and gently prodded the skin near his eye. The bruise was finally gone after Danny Hart had punched him, but he sometimes wondered if the damage lingered, if others could see his humiliation just as clearly as he still felt it.

Danny Hart. The poor, fatherless mechanic. The best way to get back at him for what he'd done was right before Lucas's eyes. Danny's father was trapped in Maldon; everyone knew that. And everyone also knew that Lucas, not Danny, had been chosen for this assignment.

Mull on that, you little Mandrake, he thought with vindictive glee. *Your father will be indebted to me, and so will you.*

It had been difficult to catch up to Danny Hart, the star pupil, the "prodigy." Lucas had been at the top of his own class, but Danny, a full class lower—both in age and society—had outstripped him with embarrassing ease. Only late nights and overtime training had pushed Lucas slightly ahead.

There were still some who said Danny had more natural talent, whatever that meant. Actions spoke louder, and now Lucas Wakefield, not Danny Hart, stood on the threshold of the most important job in recent history.

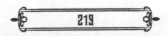

"It won't make a difference if you install the central cog last," said Tom.

"Fine." George gestured at the wall of cogs and gears. "Be my guest."

Lucas watched as Tom limped to the clockwork, his metal leg thumping loudly against the wooden floor, and began to fit the central cog to the frame. The clock room of the new tower was spacious and smelled of oil and iron. The fields around the isolated tower rippled with a strong wind that whistled shrilly through the tall, thin windows.

Lucas peered out. It was common for the London protesters to demonstrate near the tower, kept a safe distance away by guards, but today was oddly silent, not a body in sight. Beyond, he spotted the gray, impenetrable wall that closed in Maldon.

"I'm telling you, something's off," George said, shifting on his feet. "I don't feel anything."

Lucas didn't either, but hadn't wanted to be the first to say it. When he walked into a tower, time was all around him. Even just walking into a town set off the sensation. Here, near the closed-off territory of Maldon, time was stale. There was no life in it.

But today, finally, the central cog was being installed. Maybe that would change things.

Tom, bent over the cog, shook his head. "You're overthinking it." He adjusted a couple of things, then stepped back. "There. Let's get it started."

All three mechanics placed their hands on the clockwork and

closed their eyes. The metal was cool and unresponsive under their hands. Lucas concentrated on the time fibers around him, though they were thin and pale. Frowning, he pulled them forward and attached them to the clockwork, willing it to start. Pulled and attached. Pulled and attached.

The mechanism shuddered, jerked, and slowly began to move.

"Ha!" Tom exclaimed. "There it goes!"

But something *was* wrong. Lucas could feel it now, and the hairs on his arms stood on end. The clock ran, but it was dead. It wasn't creating an area of time, but rather feeding off the existing time around them, blocked by the indomitable Maldon barrier.

And then they all heard it: a ticking noise. But not the ticking of a clock.

"Wait," Tom said as the whistle of the wind grew louder. "I don't—"

Everything went white as the clockwork exploded.

Lucas must have screamed, but he couldn't hear himself over the roar. All senses were stripped from him, and there was terror in that unknowing, unfeeling suspension, lost in shuddering white chaos. Sight returned first, and he watched cogs and gears bounce and fly and break apart through the smoke. Gray and black replaced shocking white, his lungs filled with burning ash.

Then, as if using the eyes of another person, he looked down at the gear embedded in his chest.

He inhaled brokenly, gurgling over the coppery blood that rose in his throat. As it dribbled from his slack mouth, a rumble grew beneath him, and the tower trembled.

For a moment, time started. It flickered into existence like a guttering candle. But just as quickly as it had ignited, it blew out, the light extinguished for good.

The tower began to fall.

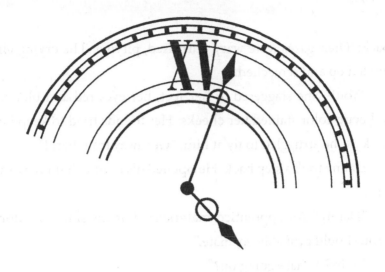

anny was relieved to see no protesters outside the Mechanics Affairs building the next morning. He hid a yawn behind his hand; it was early, but he had to check Daphne's folder.

He hoped he wouldn't run into Matthias. Danny was still upset with him for what he'd done, and for all the trouble it had caused him. But it wasn't Matthias he found in the hall. In a small alcove by a window, a girl sat sobbing into a linen handkerchief. A group of mechanics and apprentices surrounded her, murmuring among themselves.

Danny cautiously moved forward and realized the girl was the one who'd been attached to Lucas's arm at the social. The one who had sneered at Cassie.

So he's cut her loose, has he? But that didn't explain why everyone looked so grim.

Someone noticed him and gasped. The small crowd drew

back. Their gazes were wary, surprised, pitying. The crying girl looked up and screeched.

"You!" She staggered to her feet, her eyes red and blotchy as hectic color stained her cheeks. Her friends tried to keep her back as she struggled to fly at him. "Get away from here!"

Danny took a step back. He opened his mouth, but no words came.

"Danny." An apprentice materialized at his side. Brandon. "You should probably go, mate."

"Why? What's going on?"

"He's *dead*!" the girl screamed. "Lucas is dead because of that clock tower! Are you happy now? As if hitting him wasn't enough for you! I wish you'd gone instead of him, that you were the one to—that you were—" She collapsed back into sobs.

People were muttering, some trying to pull her away. Someone tugged on his arm and he obediently followed, too numb to resist.

"Bloody hell," Brandon muttered. "It can't get any worse."

He led Danny to an unused classroom and closed the door behind them. Danny sank into one of the desks and stared blankly at its surface.

"What was she talking about?" Danny rasped.

"Thought someone would've told you by now," Brandon said. "The new tower was destroyed. The older mechanics got out, but they're fair banged up. Lucas . . ." Only a shift of his shoulders told Danny he was steeling himself for the next blow. "A gear struck him in the chest and he was crushed by debris."

At first, Danny thought he'd heard incorrectly. That this was a test or a joke of some sort. But the boy's eyes didn't flinch, his face as grim as the ones in the hall.

Danny's stomach rose into his throat at an alarming speed. He shot out of the desk, fell to his knees beside the rubbish bin, and heaved.

Everything came rushing back in cruel, relentless detail. The sharp gear slicing his chin open. Blood on his skin, hot and slick. Bitter ash in his mouth, the hair-raising scream of grinding cogs. The smell of burning oil, smoke, sweat, terror. The shudder of time crawling to a standstill, the way the fibers had woven around him, squeezing, as if wanting to stop his heart. Danny whimpered, his body wracked with spasms.

I was in an accident. I got out. I'm safe now.

Was he really?

As the attack slowly passed, he shoved the rubbish bin away and coughed, eyes watering. He gasped for air, unable to stop shaking. Unable to stop expecting a death sentence to strike him down.

"The tower . . ." His voice came out raw. "It *fell?*"

Brandon nodded. Danny ran his hands through his hair and gripped tightly. He could barely feel the pain along his scalp.

"They found bombs hidden throughout the tower and behind the parts they'd already installed. Tom and George are going to be questioned. Lucas's funeral is in a few days."

Danny hid his face in his knees. He thought of Lucas's body

being stuffed into a coffin. He saw himself in that coffin, a gear buried in his chest.

"They don't blame you," Brandon assured him. "Not really. You wouldn't blast apart a tower that could've saved your dad. But you did hit Lucas, mate."

Danny stared at his apprentice until his words made sense. "You think I would kill Lucas?"

"No, frankly, I don't. The Lead's saying it's far more likely the protesters had something to do with it, and anyone that's been seen outside the office is to be found and interrogated. That's all I know."

Brandon opened the door. "All the mechanics and apprentices are invited to the funeral. You'd best come." He lingered in the doorway. "D'you need anything?"

Nothing you can give me.

"No," Danny whispered. "Thank you for telling me." And for not looking at him the way the others had.

Brandon nodded once and left.

Danny wanted to stay tucked away in this corner forever. If he didn't move, nothing would happen to him. His mother would go about her life, his father would stay trapped, Enfield's clock tower would go on ticking, and no one else would blame him for anything. A lifetime of regrets and fears ended. His thread uncut, his destiny unfulfilled.

The light in the room faded into the blue and gray bruise of dusk by the time he could stand. He thought he might retch again, but his stomach was hard and hollow.

Lucas was dead. The new Maldon tower—all of their hard work—destroyed. Bombs planted, but by whom?

He touched the scar on his chin. The shape and promise of a nightmare.

The funeral was held two days later in Highgate Cemetery, a sprawling place overcrowded with trees and ferns. It looked more like a forest than a graveyard.

He hadn't wanted to come, but he wanted to get away from his mother. The fragile hope she insisted on carrying had shattered when he told her about the tower. He had heard her sobbing long into the night, and in the morning, he couldn't convince her to leave her bed. He'd made her tea, but it had gone untouched.

"Mum, you have to eat something," he had told her in the dim light of her bedroom.

But she had just stared at him as if he were the ghost of a bad dream, as if this were somehow also his fault.

He had to escape that look, had to stop the sharp stone of guilt from reforming in his stomach.

So here he was, in his best suit and standing with his eyes lowered. He tried not to pay attention to the people around him, but someone came and stood on his right.

"I didn't think you'd come," Matthias said.

A flare of anger licked up Danny's ribs at the sight of Matthias,

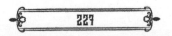

but it was weak and dissipated quickly. Danny watched mourners congregate around the recently dug grave. Lucas's parents stood at the front, their faces pale and expressionless as though carved from stone, like the weeping angels throughout the cemetery.

"Didn't think I'd come, either," Danny said, looking away. A mechanical raven was perched on a tombstone nearby. Come nighttime, it would be alert for grave robbers.

Danny swallowed painfully. "Matthias . . . who would do this? If it was the protesters, *how* did they do this? They—They *killed* someone."

Matthias's breath caught, and when Danny turned, the man's eyes were brimming with tears. Danny had never seen Matthias cry, and it made him avert his eyes again.

"I don't know." Matthias swallowed hard. "The Lead might try to build another tower."

"After this? Unlikely. Besides, you heard what they said. The tower didn't work."

"The towers are a lost art," Matthias agreed. "I wonder . . ."

He trailed off, and Danny glanced at him. But the man now had his eyes fixed on the coffin being carried by pallbearers to the grave, and they said nothing more.

The dark wooden coffin was lowered. Lucas's mother sobbed loudly as she watched what was left of her son disappear under the earth. Each sound tore a new hole in Danny's chest. He wondered if the clocks in their house were all stopped at Lucas's time of death, the time the tower had fallen, the exact moment a dream had ended.

Lucas was in an accident. He didn't get out. He's dead now.

"Be careful, Danny," Matthias whispered as the priest uttered words of blessing and tossed the first handful of dirt into the grave. "Until these people are caught, no clock tower is safe."

People.

"Matthias," he said slowly, softly, "what sorts of bombs were found at the tower?"

Danny wasn't sure where the question came from, but Matthias's knowing expression told him he'd been waiting for it.

"Pipe bombs."

Those two words possessed him.

Danny stood in the hospital entrance, blocking foot traffic. Those who passed shot him dirty looks and jostled him to get by.

Maybe this was a bad idea.

But he needed answers.

It had been months since he'd been to the hospital, and he remembered the smell immediately: chemicals and urine. It made his nose itch and his stomach hurt.

His stay here had almost been worse than the explosion itself. The way his mother and Matthias treated him like a china doll, the sympathy in everyone's eyes, the way the doctor approached his side as if he were unstable.

Then again, Danny's nightmares had tended to wake the entire ward. And he'd tried to escape. Twice.

"May I help you?" a nurse asked at the front desk. Thankfully, he didn't recognize her.

"Yes. I was looking for my, er, uncle. Tom Hawthorne?"

She checked the files and directed Danny to a room on the second story. He walked up the stairs, his heart pounding. The floors creaked under his boots, and he felt as if just by looking at him people would know what he was up to. But he went largely ignored, the staff far too busy with their own concerns.

When he reached the right room, he braced himself before entering. It was worse than he thought. Legs and arms were splinted, George's head bandaged and bloody, Tom's face bruised. At the sight of Danny, they tensed.

"What are you doing here?" Tom growled. Even his voice sounded bruised.

Danny tried to swallow past his dry tongue. "I know what's going on."

The two men exchanged a look.

"About the clock towers," Danny clarified.

"Then would you do us a favor and tell *us*?" George said.

"You two are in on it. Together."

Tom managed to croak out a laugh. "Lad, the hospital fumes must have gotten to you."

"He's always been like this," George muttered.

Danny came closer, trying to make himself taller. "You were at Shere before I was. You had access to the tower blueprints. There were pipes in your office, and pipe bombs destroyed the new Maldon tower. I bet Lucas saw something while he was in Rotherfield, and you two killed him at Maldon to keep him quiet. I don't know why you're doing this, if maybe you sympathize with the protesters, but it stops now."

"Danny," George said slowly, "you're not making sense."

"After Rotherfield, you said that something *needed to be done*."

"I was talking about finishing the Maldon tower. Tom was upset. His sister lives in Rotherfield, and when the bomb went off, he was terrified of the town being Stopped. And as for the pipes," George said, glancing at Tom, who was pale under his bruises, "Tom was re-plumbing his house."

Danny hesitated, his limbs buzzing with warning, with the need to do something. George could easily be lying.

"Those are convenient excuses," he said at last. "I don't know why you two are doing this, but I'm going to tell the Lead. I'll tell the police if I have to."

"You're out of your mind." Tom called for the nurse, who came to the doorway. "This young man is bothering us. Please escort him out."

"No!" Danny started forward. "I know you have something to do with it!"

The nurse yelled for help. George was yelling, too, but Danny couldn't hear the words above the roaring of his blood.

"Stop lying to me!" Danny screamed. "Just tell me that you did it!"

"Danny!" Tom shouted over him. "Let it go. The Maldon tower is gone." His face shuttered with grief, with regret. "I'm sorry."

Someone dragged him from the room, hauled him down the stairs, and shoved him into the street. A stocky man with a beard warned him not to come back.

Danny ran down the street and around the corner. He kept running until he smacked into a brick wall. Danny pressed his forehead to the gritty surface and pushed down a scream. He punched the wall over and over until his knuckles split and bled. Until he could convince himself the tears on his face were from pain.

Aetas and the Sea Goddess

T he sea churned and frothed the more Oceana paced before her brother. Her hair rose and floated like seaweed, waving slowly through the water and then touching the broad slope of her gray shoulders. Her dress of kelp and cockles rustled when she moved, and occasionally a small cardinal fish swam from one of the many folds.

"You must consult with Chronos first," Oceana told her brother. He had just admitted to how poor his grasp on time had become.

It had begun the day he journeyed to the sky with Caelum. Since then, time kept thinning, unraveling, until Aetas struggled daily to rein the threads in. Mornings flickered and nights wavered. Humans found themselves in the same spots they had inhabited twelve minutes before. Animals went missing. Crops grew too fast and withered prematurely.

"I have a plan to help control time," said Aetas. For he was learning more and more that it was a wild thing without cause or patience. Of all the elements he and his brother and sisters maintained, time, it seemed, was the most unruly.

"But it will anger Chronos. You know this. Speak with him instead. Perhaps he will end his long rest to assist you."

"No. I must do this myself."

Oceana's anger battered against the shore, waves rising and crashing above their heads. "Brother—"

But the shadow of a ship passed over them, and her sea foam gaze lifted. The ship was being knocked between waves like a plaything.

Oceana rose from the ocean floor and Aetas followed. She spread out her hands, attempting to smooth the waves she had created in her agitation. Aetas broke the surface and watched the men aboard their ship fumble for lines and call out helpless orders. The waves were too strong; Oceana would need time to calm them.

Aetas drew in the time threads around himself, the ones that dove into the water and wrapped around the ship like golden twine. A sailor fell into the angry waters below. Aetas plucked a thread, and the man shot back onto the ship's deck as if he had never left it.

Oceana joined her brother. "Aetas," she warned, but he ignored her and continued to weave the threads into a new pattern.

At first, the pattern appeared to work. The ship began to right itself. The waves grew smaller. But then Aetas slipped, just a fraction of a fraction, and time pulsed around him.

Suddenly, the ship was gone.

"Brother, what have you done?" Oceana regarded him as if watching the end of the world. "Where have they disappeared to?"

Aetas did not know. The sailors could be anywhere in time, or perhaps they no longer existed.

Sick and weak, Aetas dove back into the cool, dark waters. Oceana followed.

"The power is too strong," said Aetas. "I must do this."

And perhaps his sister knew a fraction of a fraction of Chronos's wrath, for she dipped her head and spread her hands. "Do what you think is best, Brother. I will assist in what ways I can."

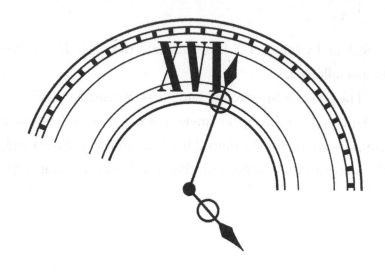

A week passed. Danny wanted to see Colton, to warn him about what had happened to the new Maldon tower, but he couldn't find the strength to leave the house. There were more guards around Big Ben than ever, and the Lead was tearing his hair out.

Miraculously, neither Tom nor George had made Danny's episode in their hospital room public, though they'd given his name to the nursing staff and, for whatever reason, asked that they go easy on him. Now Danny had a fine for disturbing the peace on top of everything else.

When his mother found out about the hospital incident, she didn't even care. The Maldon news had disturbed her on some deep level. He found her sitting in the dark kitchen one day, her face twisted in confusion, as if she'd forgotten why she was there. He made her breakfast, but she only nibbled at it.

Nightmares sank their claws into him, and most nights he woke with a scream trapped in his throat. Sometimes he dreamed he was Lucas, watching the tower explode from the inside. Other times he dreamed he was outside, watching some nameless, faceless villain throw explosives at the tower; or a shadowy crowd picking the tower apart piece by piece. His father stood in the distance, a prisoner behind glass. Danny clawed at the barrier, desperate to break through, wondering if he saw his father or only a reflection—wondering if he was the one trapped. Christopher pounded on the glass and yelled for Danny to run, but his voice was muffled, his hands leaving smears of blood that spread and covered all of Maldon with a sinister scarlet shadow.

He wandered London in a daze, staring at the homeless urchins, grimacing at the helpful automatons. The stench of coal smoke made him think the whole city had caught fire. It ensnared him like a vise. The only relief came when he closed his eyes and thought of Enfield, the chime of clean wind through tree branches and lazy sunshine on thatched roofs.

It was hard to admit life ended. It was harder still to admit it went on. His melancholy gradually turned into acceptance. The new Maldon tower was gone, and Lucas had died. There was nothing he could do about either. He had to focus on what he could do: protect Colton and keep an eye on his mother. Try to change his fate.

"Are you sure you're all right?" Cassie asked one evening in the Harts' sitting room. She had dropped by for dinner, a regular occurrence due to her parents' lack of culinary skills. Danny flipped through a book on his lap, though he didn't bother reading. His mother was already in bed.

"I'll be fine."

"Will they try to rebuild the Maldon tower, do you think?"

"I don't know." He stood and shoved the book back onto the shelf. "They'll do whatever the Lead says."

"Danny, I want to help you. What do you need?"

He needed Colton. He needed these attacks to stop. He needed his father.

"I don't know, Cass."

She played with the end of her braid. "Will you go to Enfield?"

"Why do you ask?"

"I was wondering if I could take a look at your auto again." She held up a hand when he opened his mouth to protest. "I have an idea I'd like to test out."

"Oh, Lord." Images of his auto exploding flashed through his mind.

"It's harmless," she insisted. "I won't do anything to the internal mechanics. It's . . ." Cassie's eyes clouded over. "A safety device. William's accident made me think of it."

Danny rubbed the back of his neck. He couldn't deny her that. "All right. But why did you ask about Enfield?"

"You're always going there to see your blond bloke. I wondered if visiting him might help."

"Maybe. Yes. I mean . . ." Danny passed a hand over his face. "I don't know."

He felt as if there was too much to do, but when he stopped

to think about it, the list vanished from his mind. His days were both endless and fleeting. One week crept into another.

There comes a moment when time seems to slip faster, running long then short, shadows shrinking as the sun climbs. It's the moment, he decided, when you're no longer a child. When the concept of time and the need for more of it come together and make you powerless. Make you yearn for the longer days, the lazy days, before you knew what time passing actually meant.

Eventually, Danny did go to Enfield. The townspeople knew what had happened in Maldon, but didn't know of Danny's connection. They asked if he'd heard any news. He mumbled no and hurried on.

Something shimmered on top of the tower. Colton had climbed onto the roof. Danny slowed to a stop, gazing up at the golden figure. Colton stood staring at the sun, as though in competition with it. A silent challenge. The remnant of a god.

As Danny watched, Colton lifted his arms. He stood that way for some time, arms up, palms out, holding up the world.

Danny's father had always told him the most incredible sights were right before his eyes.

Colton looked down and saw him. His smile was broad and messy with relief. Danny moved toward the door as the spirit climbed back through the window.

Colton knew something was wrong before Danny even

opened his mouth. "I overheard them talking," he said, nodding toward the window. They sat against the wall opposite the clock face. The light shining through the glass outlined Colton's face in gold. "They said a tower fell."

Danny said nothing.

Colton moved closer, eyebrows furrowed. "Is it true?"

When Danny remained silent, Colton wrapped his arms around him. Maybe it was the sight of him, impossibly and unfairly beautiful, or the desire to shed the weight that had been sitting on his chest all week, that allowed Danny to sag in his arms, making a pained noise as if someone had struck him.

In broken sentences, his head resting on Colton's chest, he told him about the fall of the new Maldon tower. Colton's arms tightened around him, and Danny wished he could hear something against his ear—the beat of a heart, the whistle of breath. It would have comforted him more than anything.

"I don't know why this is happening," he said. "The other two towers were small, out of the way. Why target that one?"

Colton shook his head. The spirit's fingers wove through Danny's hair. "I'm sorry. I wish the tower had worked."

Danny sat up. "Do you know anything about how the towers were made? How *your* tower was made?"

Colton straightened Danny's collar, his amber eyes downcast. "I don't."

"Are you sure?"

"Danny." Colton met his gaze, steady but remorseful. "The truth is, I can't remember that far back. I don't know how long

I've been here, or even how old the town is. All I know is that the towers were built when Aetas died. Like you told me."

"Right. Sorry." Suddenly restless, Danny stood and began to pace. Colton leaned against the wall, watching him.

"I've never seen spirits in other towers. I don't think the new Maldon tower even had a spirit before it fell. Do you think without spirits, the towers can't function?"

Colton lifted his shoulders in a slow shrug. "You're the mechanic. I'm just the clock."

A bubble of laughter escaped Danny. It was laced with panic.

"My tower will be fine," Colton said. "I'm sure of it."

"But you can't know that. The other towns couldn't predict that their towers would be attacked." Danny resumed his pacing, biting a thumbnail. "Damn it. If only I had a hint. Maybe if I find out more about Tom and George, try to blackmail them into telling me—"

"Danny, please stop." Colton joined him in the middle of the room and placed his hands on Danny's shoulders, forcing him to stand still. "I'm sorry," Colton said again. "I'm sorry I don't have the answers, and that I'm only making this harder."

"You're not ma—"

Colton pressed a finger to Danny's lips. "I am. And I wish I could help in some way, but I'm . . . well, I'm stuck here." He dropped his hands to Danny's chest. "I wish I could do more."

Danny's panic eased away, like water washing over his frantic footsteps. He put his hands on Colton's waist and pulled him closer. He wanted to tell him everything. Tell him about the burning in his heart, in his stomach. When Colton held him, it was as if the small, dark things that rattled inside him were gathered up and turned to gold. All melted down and forged into something brighter.

"Colton." It was all he could say, but it was enough.

The spirit rewarded him with a faint smile. "Danny."

They brushed noses before they kissed. It was slow and hesitant at first, but then it grew deeper, forming a conversation of its own.

I'm worried about you.

I'm fine.

I'm not going anywhere.

They fell into a rhythm of heat and pressure. When Danny needed air, Colton brushed kisses against his neck. Danny grabbed the back of Colton's head and crushed their mouths back together, desperate for contact.

But Colton jerked his head away, toward the stairs. Danny followed his gaze and choked on a gasp.

Cassie stood there, staring at the two of them with her mouth hanging open. "Da-Danny? What on earth?"

Colton disappeared in a blink. Danny felt oddly exposed without him.

"What are you doing here, Cass?" He tried to make the words loud and accusing, but they came out as a ragged whisper.

Her eyes were fixed on the spot where Colton had been a second earlier. Her voice sounded faraway. "You were acting strange, so I thought I'd . . ." She gripped the end of her frizzy braid. "I wanted to make sure you were all right. I followed you here. I thought it might be a nice surprise, you know, to see you and . . ."

She trailed off, her eyes taking in the clock room. She had seen Colton, Danny was sure of it. Which meant she had also seen him disappear.

"Where did he go?" She turned in a full circle, the end of her green scarf sweeping behind her.

"Where did who go?" *Oh God, am I really doing this?*

Her cheeks reddened. "Don't play the idiot with me. I just saw you and another boy kissing like it was the end of the world." She fought to swallow. "Please tell me what's going on?"

She stared at him, silently begging him to explain. He sighed and turned to the clock face.

"Colton? Please come back."

It took a moment for him to notice Colton standing beside him again. The spirit's expression was cautiously blank.

"Colton, this is Cassie. I told you about her, remember? My friend?"

Colton nodded.

"Cassie, this is Colton. The 'blond bloke.' And . . . a clock spirit."

He didn't think her jaw could drop so low.

"No," she said firmly.

"Yes?"

"He's a *clock spirit*?"

Danny winced. "Shout it a little louder, I don't think the people in London heard you."

"Danny, this is—"

"Stupid, I know. I'm an idiot for keeping this from you. But you understand why, don't you? Do you realize what'll happen to me if I'm found out?"

Cassie looked from Danny to Colton. Her shock gradually faded into curiosity. "Your name is Colton. Like the tower. You're a . . ." She fumbled over the words. "A clock spirit."

Colton glanced at Danny and nodded.

She studied him a moment, trying not to let her wonder show and failing miserably. "It's . . . er . . . nice to meet you at last. Danny's told me about you. Just not everything." She glared at Danny, and he shrank back.

Colton's wary expression broke into a tentative smile. "He talks about me?"

"All the time."

"What does he say?"

"Where do I even begin?"

Danny watched, struck dumb, as the two suddenly started talking at a fearsome speed. When he tried to get a word in, they barely acknowledged him.

"He was so flustered when he told me about that first kiss—"

"Said you live down the street from him—"

"Have all *sorts* of embarrassing stories to tell you—"

Danny sank onto a box and put his head in his hands. He had expected anger, fear, betrayal. This was far, far worse.

244

Although Cassie put on a bright face for Colton, which had done wonders to break the awkwardness between them, she turned stony when she and Danny left the tower later that afternoon.

He stepped toward his auto. "Guess I'll just—"

"Danny, get in my auto." Cassie was giving him a look, one she'd learned from her mother, that bored straight into him.

He did as he was told. She started the engine, which ran smoother than his own, and they drove down the narrow streets of Enfield to the outskirts in silence.

After a while she said, very softly, "Why would you keep this from me?"

"I already told you why."

She took a deep breath through her nose. He couldn't stand the expression on her face, the hurt he'd caused.

"I'm sorry," he said. "I wish I had told you sooner. I trust you, Cassie. I do."

"It's not that." She tightened her hands on the steering wheel. "You're behaving exactly like Matthias did."

Danny's heart gave a single painful thud. "You think that hasn't crossed my mind?"

"What are you thinking? Whatever Matthias did, if he actually loved a clock spirit like he told everyone, Maldon was Stopped because of it. He was exiled, Danny. You've told me over and over again how miserable he is, and how much it hurts you to see him that way." Her voice thickened with tears. "Didn't it

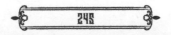

cross your mind that the same thing could happen to you? That I would have to see you that way?"

No, it hadn't. He had been so focused on his fear of losing Colton that he had never considered how he might end up hurting Cassie.

He looked out the window and frowned. "This isn't the way to London."

"I know. We're going to Maldon."

"What?" His fingers twitched. "No, we can't. I don't want to go there."

He had only gone once, right after the town had Stopped. All that stood there now was a gray domed barrier, an opaque bubble that enclosed the entirety of Maldon.

"Not the town," she clarified. "The tower. The new one."

"It's ruined, Cass. There's no point."

"I know you want to go. So we're going."

He opened his mouth to argue, but she was right. He did want to go, no matter how many ghosts stood in the way.

They drove in silence. Danny stared at his lap and wondered if there was a way everyone could win—a situation, however implausible, in which everyone he loved could have a happy ending just like in Colton's fairy tales.

"Here we are." Cassie parked the auto a short distance from a sectioned-off plot of land, blocked from prying eyes by tall canvas dividers. Beyond those dividers lay the rubble of the tower.

A few miles away, Danny could see the ominous gray dome of his father's prison.

"You're the best mechanic in your class," Cassie said. "Maybe something here will help you understand. Maybe it'll help save Colton from the same fate." Her hand slowly found Danny's and squeezed. "I don't want you to be wracked with guilt like Matthias is. Like I am."

It's too late for that, Cass.

Danny closed his eyes for a moment. He didn't want to see the wreckage, the ruined dream he'd shared with his mother. But he had no choice. The attacks wouldn't stop unless someone figured out what was causing them.

He opened his eyes and nodded. They slipped out of the auto.

Danny and Cassie lurked behind the bonnet, surveying the site where a few guards were patrolling.

"I think I can get us through with my mechanic's badge," Danny said. "Want to give it a go?"

When they approached an opening in the canvas, a guard with lips like a fish stopped them. "Hold on there. No one gets through without identification."

Danny showed his badge. "I'm a mechanic."

The guard scowled. "'Course you are, and I'm a ballerina." He pointed sternly at the auto. "Out."

"You don't believe me?" Danny shoved the badge in the guard's face again. "I'm a bloody mechanic. It says so right here."

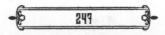

It was his age again. The guard had taken one look and dismissed them as children.

The man pursed his thick lips in irritation. Cassie plucked Danny's sleeve and they turned back toward her auto.

"What, you're just going to give up after driving all the way here?" Danny demanded.

"No, I have an idea."

He didn't like the look in her eyes. "Cassandra . . ."

"Daniel."

"What are you going to do?"

"You'll see, my chuckaboo. Wait here."

She hopped into the auto and started the engine. With a wink at him, she sped off. Toward the barricade.

"*Cass!*"

The auto hit the edge of a canvas divider and dragged it several feet, creating a wide opening. Guards shouted and ran after Cassie as she drove in circles. Danny caught a glimpse of her face and laughed. She was enjoying the hell out of this.

Before anyone could see him, he ducked through the gap.

When he laid eyes on what was left of the tower, his breath caught. He wasn't prepared for the reality of the tower's destruction that now spread before him.

Rubble was everywhere. The base of the tower was intact, but stood sadly empty, the rest of the structure lying in jagged pieces like a neglected puzzle. He walked through the debris, kicking up mortar dust that stung his eyes.

"God," he whispered as he sank to his knees. He touched a loose brick and shivered. *What if this had been Colton's tower?* Pressing the back of a hand against his mouth, Danny closed his eyes and fought the rising panic within him.

When he'd composed himself, he pawed through the rubble searching for something helpful. Wooden beams jutted up from the base, broken and skeletal. Shards of metal glinted in the sun. Danny found a small gear and picked it up.

A sensation rippled up his arm, there and gone too quickly to process. It was almost like how the air warped when he touched Colton, subtle but powerful. In this case, it was barely detectable. The air smelled sharp and metallic, the scent before a lightning storm. His scalp prickled.

Had the tower worked, then?

He remembered when he'd accidentally cut his thumb in Colton's tower. He thought about Lucas in this tower, a gear slicing into his chest, spilling his blood. His own blood seeping onto the floor of the Shere tower, time flickering around him.

Danny dropped the gear.

What does it mean?

"All right, you've had your fun." A guard grabbed his elbow and dragged him out of the enclosure. Fish Lips had a hand wrapped around Cassie's arm outside.

"Hand over your identification without fuss," Fish Lips growled. "We'll be informing your parents about this little adventure of yours." Cassie groaned.

"Be thankful we're not hauling you off to the jailhouse," Danny's guard said. "We see you here again, you'll have more than the Lead Mechanic to answer to."

Cassie met Danny's eyes and shrugged in apology.

But he had found something, even if that something only meant more questions.

Danny used the mechanics' library to hide from the world and think. The room was dim and crowded with shelves, perfect for secreting himself away. He found a table in a chilly corner and barricaded it with books. Books he'd already read, books he'd studied for classes, books he hadn't even touched yet.

He scoured them all, fingertip edging down the pages, but he found nothing useful. Nothing about what he had felt at the Maldon ruins or what had happened when he nicked his thumb in Enfield. There was a list of Stopped towns and cities around the world: Sorell, Yangzhou, Kaplice. None of it explained how to free them.

There was one book, written by clock enthusiast Phoebe Archer, that he pored over the most. She had written about Aetas, detailing the fall of the Gaian gods from modern religion, and how he had been killed by his own creator. How the clock towers had produced not only time, but an increasing demand for technology, feeding into a long and prosperous Industrial Revolution. She described the clock towers being tied to the composition of the human physique. Maybe she meant the spirits. Maybe she meant something else.

No closer to an answer, Danny closed the book with a loud *thud*.

There were no protesters when he left the office and boarded an omnibus. There had been no demonstrating at all, in fact, since the fall of the new Maldon tower. Now that they'd gotten what they wanted, maybe there was nothing left for them to do. Maybe they were scared to come back and face the wrath of the mechanics.

When Danny got off the bus a little ways from his house, something compelled him to look across the street just as his mother disembarked her own omnibus.

He ducked behind a letter box. He had no idea why; he would see her at home. Yet the thought of meeting her in the street was odd to him.

Part of him, a stupid, childlike part, still yearned for his mother. The old Leila—not this new, hollow one. A Leila who thought her son could do no wrong. Who had once made him feel safe. In another life, he could have gone to her about Colton. He could have confided in her how each senseless bombing set off an earthquake in his chest.

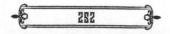

But that Leila had long ago disappeared.

Danny watched as she spoke with a friend at the curb. Her lips turned up in a smile, deepening the lines around her mouth. Danny had forced enough of his own smiles to recognize one when he saw it. The other woman put a hand on Leila's arm before turning away.

Leila stood there a moment longer, her hat crookedly perched on her head. The sight of it pained him. His hand twitched, longing to jog across the street and straighten it for her.

She heaved a sigh and slouched forward, pulling a hand-kerchief from her sleeve and dabbing her eyes as her shoulders jerked in a quiet sob.

Go to her, Danny told himself. But he couldn't move.

Sniffing, his mother turned to trudge the rest of the way home. She slowed when she noticed the confectionery shop, disappearing inside and emerging a few minutes later with a small wrapped parcel.

Danny waited a moment before following at a slower pace. At home, a lamp in the kitchen had been lit, but a creak upstairs told him she was already in her bedroom.

In the kitchen, a square of gingerbread wrapped in cloth sat waiting on the table.

"You can't eat all of it," his mother scolded from the past, even as he had grabbed for it with the small greedy hands of a child. "Save some for after supper."

But then she would turn from cooking and find his face

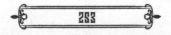

sticky with crumbs and the gingerbread completely gone, and she'd laugh helplessly.

The echo of laughter faded until the kitchen was silent and cold. He touched the edges of the cloth.

Nothing was ever simple.

Danny climbed the stairs with the gingerbread, unable to eat it yet. At his mother's door, he hesitated, then lifted a hand and quietly knocked.

Leila opened the door, looking as surprised as he felt. "Danny. What's wrong?"

"Nothing. Uh . . ." He cleared his throat. "How was your day, Mum?"

"Oh. The usual sort of nonsense." She paused. "Lottie is still dull as a pickle. Mr. Howard had a shouting match with the secretary." Leila shrugged. It was his own shrug, sharp and quick.

Danny knew she wouldn't say more. Wouldn't talk about the long periods of drowning silence, or the weight she had lost. He nodded absently. "Good. Um, thank you. For . . ." He lifted the gingerbread.

She smiled, a small thing, but this time it wasn't forced. It was softer. More like the old Leila.

"You're welcome." She lifted her hand, perhaps unthinkingly, and paused again. When she reached out and swept the hair off his forehead, it was almost as if a ghost was carrying out the action. "Get to bed. You look exhausted."

He would never have his mother back the way she used to be.

But the old Leila was still somewhere in this house, held in the cracks and the foundation.

The Lead had reprimanded Danny for visiting the ruined Maldon tower a few days before. He'd issued no punishment this time, on account of Danny's "personal interest" in the tower. His reprimand, however, was followed by uncomfortable questions about Danny's health, a punishment in and of itself. Danny had said whatever was necessary to get out of the Lead's office as quickly as possible.

Then there was Cassie, who used every meeting as an opportunity to demand more information about Colton. She said an explanation was the least Danny could offer, after the constable had stopped by and her mother had given her the tongue-lashing of a lifetime.

Desperate for a reprieve, Danny sighed in relief when he found another Enfield job in Daphne's folder. The gear chain needed to be checked and the clock face needed cleaning. Danny all but flew to the town.

When he arrived at the tower, Colton was standing at the window. Spotting Danny, he raised the sash and leaned out.

There was no one on the street or on the village green behind him. Overcome by sudden giddiness, Danny struck a gallant pose. "Rapunzel, Rapunzel, let down your fair hair!"

Colton grinned and shook his bright blond locks. "Too short for that, I'm afraid. You'll have to use the door."

"That's not very romantic."

Danny hurried inside and bounded up the stairs, eager to be with Colton before Brandon arrived. He had brought a book of Norse mythology and wanted to take his mind off of everything that had happened, if only for an hour.

Unfortunately, Brandon was waiting in the pendulum room. Danny stopped short.

"'Lo," said Brandon. "We'll wind it first, yeah?"

"Uh, sure."

They got right down to business, and Danny's heart weighed heavy again with disappointment. Brandon was abnormally chatty as they worked. He had been kinder to Danny since Lucas's death, or perhaps he had simply become used to Danny's oddness.

Cleaning the clock face was the longest and hardest process, something the maintenance crew hated doing. Danny couldn't blame them; the height never got any easier. Thankfully, he had something to distract him: every time he looked up, he caught sight of golden hair as Colton waved.

Tired but satisfied, Danny and Brandon pulled themselves back inside the tower. Brandon stretched his arms with a satisfied groan. "What're you doing after this?"

Danny looked up from rolling down his shirtsleeves. "I thought I'd—"

"Stay up here like a hermit? Come to the pub with me. You owe me five drinks, remember?"

Danny tried to think of a good excuse to stay behind, but Brandon had already shrugged on his coat. Danny looked around and saw Colton standing near the door, frowning.

"I'm not sure . . ."

"I won't bite your head off," Brandon said. "Come on." He turned to walk down the stairs.

Danny grabbed his coat, hesitated, and spotted Colton close by. His nearly-invisible eyebrows were set at a gloomy angle, his mouth turned down in disappointment. Danny gave him a helpless look, whispered, "Sorry," and descended after Brandon.

His feet thumped heavily on each stair. Brandon snorted at his expression. "Don't look too put out."

"Sorry. I was just thinking about something."

"And what would that be?"

Danny didn't want to bring up the Maldon tower or Lucas, so he settled for one of his lesser fears at the moment. "My mother interviewed for a job a couple of weeks ago . . ."

They walked to the pub, hands in their pockets and heads bent against the wind. It was growing dark already, the clouds on the horizon stained pink. When they opened the door, lively noise escaped and sucked them inside.

The townsfolk roared with approval at their presence, beckoning the pair to join them. They sat at a small table near the back and were plied with drunken praise and well-wishes until a tall woman pushed past the worshippers to take Danny's and Brandon's orders.

Danny sat passing his beer mug from hand to hand, legs fidgeting under the table. He wanted to see Colton before he left for home, but if he got in too late, his mother would worry.

"So you don't want your mum to run off," Brandon said.

"I'm just not sure I want to live alone."

"And you don't want to move with her?"

"God, no. I never want to leave London. It's my home. It's—well, it's *London*."

Brandon nodded. "I'd never leave London if I could help it. Got my brother and sisters, though, so I don't have to worry about that." He took a sip. "I'm sorry, mate. About your father and all that. Lost my own dad some time back." Brandon took out his tiger's eye marble and began to roll it between his fingers. "Not in Maldon, though. The white plague."

Many in the city had died of consumption, the illness stripping flesh from bones as their bodies wasted away. He could only imagine what Brandon must have gone through as his father lay coughing away his life.

"Don't have much of him now, save for a box of his old things. I found this in there a month after he died." He showed off the black and amber marble. "I used to play marbles with him all the time. I snatched it before the younger ones could take it."

Danny lowered his eyes, feeling a twinge of guilt for having nicked it earlier. "I'm sorry for your loss."

He knew what would come next. Brandon would say Danny

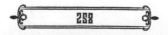

was lucky his father was still alive, just unreachable. Others had said the same, not knowing the words landed like knives.

But Brandon only sighed and shook his head. "Damn shame."

They sat in easy silence until Danny asked about Brandon's family. Brandon was more than glad to list them off, from his older brother who flew airships for the military to his youngest sister who was barely out of nappies. Whom he liked best, whom he liked least, and why he would fight to the death for them either way. Danny was both fascinated and jealous. If he had a brother or sister to share the house with, his mother leaving wouldn't have been so painful.

If only Colton could leave his tower.

The conversation shifted from high to low places, from amusing stories to sad ones. When Danny finally looked at his timepiece, he groaned.

"It's nearly eleven! I need to head home."

Brandon checked his own timepiece. "Ah, look at that."

"Er . . ."

"Yes?"

"I'm a little confused," Danny confessed. "About why you did this tonight."

"How long has it been since you've made a night of it?"

Danny didn't answer, but it was as good as an admission. Brandon shook his head.

"I was the same after my dad passed. Wouldn't let myself have fun, or talk to my friends. You can't let it take over your life. Your dad wouldn't want that, I'm sure."

Why were others always telling him what his father would or would not want?

Still, Danny knew Brandon had a point. He fiddled with his timepiece before pocketing it. "I suppose I do need to get out more."

"Sure do. Elsewise you'll end up making enemies left and right. Give others a chance, yeah?"

Danny wondered if this had been Brandon's idea of making Danny feel better. "I reckon I should. Thank you."

"Don't thank me; you bought the drinks." Brandon scraped his chair legs back to stand. "Until next time."

They parted at the door. The streets were dark and quiet. Danny shivered; the pub had been warm, but out here the icy finger of winter stroked down his spine.

As he headed for the clock tower, a hand touched his arm.

"Danny, is it?"

It was the young man who had danced with him on St. Andrew's Day. Harland. His teeth shone like pearls in the moonlight. Danny returned the smile, still a little woozy.

"What are you doing out so late?"

"I was having a pint."

"Want to take a walk and clear your head? Looks like you need it."

Danny wanted to go to the tower, but Brandon's words about giving people a chance were still busy in his head, so he agreed. They started down the road and around the corner, toward the shops. Danny didn't come this way often, and he let Harland direct their feet.

"The whole town admires you, you know," Harland said suddenly. Danny nearly tripped.

"I doubt that, what with all the problems the tower's had."

"They admire your dedication. You come here just to make sure the clock's running. No other mechanic would do that."

Danny was sure they wouldn't be nearly as impressed if they knew his real reasons, but before he could say anything Harland took his arm. He led Danny behind a shop, where an awning shadowed the ground from moonlight.

"What's the real reason you come here so often?" he asked.

Danny opened his mouth, shocked. Had he caught on? Did he know about Colton?

"I just want to fix the clock," Danny said feebly.

Harland leaned in closer. "I think there's another reason."

Danny's heart was pounding. He felt sick. Harland knew. He would tell someone, and then Danny would be exiled, and—

"It's to see me, isn't it?"

Neither said a word for a moment. Then Danny snorted, and tried to cover it up with a cough. "I think you have the wrong idea."

"Why else would you come?" Harland demanded. "I see the looks you give me." He stroked the side of Danny's face with slow, steady fingers.

Their faces were very close, now. "I . . ."

"Yes?"

But Danny couldn't speak, and in the silence his mouth was covered by Harland's. He inhaled through his nose, remember-

ing the way Barnaby had kissed him, soft and uncertain. Harland was a boy who knew what he was about.

He pressed Danny against the wall. Danny made a muffled noise, surprising himself. It felt nice, the chill replaced with welcome warmth. Danny closed his eyes, forgetting where he was.

The thunderous clang of tower bells struck the air.

Breaking open the night.

Danny's eyes flew open. He tried to squirm out of his hold, but Harland was determined. Danny grunted in annoyance as Harland parted his lips with an insistent tongue.

He did the only thing he could think of: he bit down.

Harland yelped and backed away, stumbling from the shadows into the moonlight. He touched his tongue to see if he was bleeding, then glared at Danny.

"What was that for?"

Danny fought for air. "You've got the wrong idea."

"You were just kissing me."

"That was a mistake."

"What, don't like blokes?"

"No, I—I have someone else."

"Then why did you lead me on just now?"

"I didn't. You assumed."

They stared at each other. Then Harland stood straighter, pulled on his shirt, and ran a hand through his hair. "So it is the clock," he muttered. "You're in love with that old thing."

"Don't talk about it that way," Danny snapped, then bit his lips.

Harland's eyes widened. "I was joking. *Are* you in love with the clock?"

"Don't be ridiculous."

"Well, I'm sure you've heard about Maldon." Danny flinched. "Can't blame me for wondering."

"I work a lot. I need to distract myself from other things, so I work a lot. That's all it is."

Danny held his breath in the new silence. Finally, Harland looked down.

"Fine. Forget this happened."

Danny watched him walk away. He didn't know what to feel: embarrassment, anger, or regret.

You've heard about Maldon.

Danny walked back to his auto. He stared at Colton Tower and thought he could see someone in one of the small windows. Danny wanted to go to him, and at the same time, he wanted to drive away as fast as he could.

His lips still warm from Harland's kiss, he got in his auto and drove back to London.

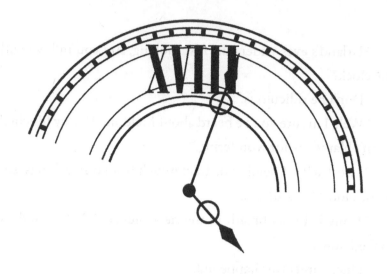

XVIII

Danny didn't know what to expect when he drove to Enfield two days later. He hadn't been able to think of anything besides Colton, Lucas, and the destroyed Maldon tower—unless that thing happened to be Harland.

He didn't want Harland. That wasn't the issue. But with that small interaction, Danny had once again been reminded of his stupidity. A relationship with a clock spirit was dangerous. What did he think would happen? That he could live his life with a spirit for a lover and never tell anyone? What sort of life would that be?

Matthias's life, he answered grimly. *And look how that turned out.*

Danny sighed and parked the auto. The town was quiet today. Hardly anyone was outside.

When Colton laughed, the tower was bright and hummed

with power. Now it felt cold and barren. Danny shivered as he climbed the stairs, dread deepening with each foot's landing. By the time he reached the clock room, he had prepared himself for the worst.

"Colton?"

He took off his coat and turned. Colton sat on a box, staring at him, bereft of his normal smile. For the first time that Danny could remember, Colton's face was perfectly blank. It scared him.

"What are you doing here?" Colton asked. His voice was flat.

Danny fiddled with the chain of his timepiece. "What do you mean? Of course I came."

Colton glanced at the clock face. "The tower doesn't need repairing."

The chill in the room intensified. Danny was sure he wasn't imagining it. "Don't you want me here?"

"Is that the only reason you came?"

Danny took a few steps forward. He didn't like the distance between their bodies. "No. I wanted to see you. Did you . . ." Heat crawled across his face, almost painful against the cold room. "Did you, um, see what happened with Harland?"

Colton's eyes hardened. The *tick* of the clock grew louder.

"That didn't mean anything. He had the wrong idea. I don't come to Enfield to be with Harland, I come here to be with you."

"But you said—" Colton clenched his jaw and his fists. "You still kissed him. I saw you. You liked it, too."

Guilt hooked Danny's navel and pulled. "All right, maybe I did, but I'd had a few drinks and—"

"You kissed him and said you don't care about the clock tower."

"What?" Danny almost wanted to laugh. "That wasn't what I—"

Colton winked out of view. He winked back so close that Danny could see the hurt in his eyes. Danny made an effort not to take a step back.

"Tell me the truth," Colton demanded. "Would you rather be with him? Another human?"

"No! It's not like that at all."

"Then why don't you kiss me like that?"

Danny gaped at him, silently adding this to the list of things he had never expected to happen: being confronted by a jealous clock spirit. "I wasn't sure how."

Colton's eyes shifted, but his face was unyielding. He appeared to think something over, then nodded to himself and came closer. "I've seen it enough times." Colton grabbed Danny's vest and pulled him in.

The kiss thrilled him, but in a terrifying way. Colton pressed Danny in closer and closer until he thought he would break. Part of him wanted the breaking, the snap and pain of it, the surrender. Danny couldn't get any words around Colton's lips. He pushed back, and they lost their balance and fell to the floor.

Colton pressed him down with his hips and something exploded through Danny's body, dangerous and burning. They had never kissed this way before—greedy, demanding, rough.

He liked it.

Colton's fingers slid over Danny's bare stomach even as his tongue slid into his mouth. Danny shuddered and gripped his arms hard enough to leave bruises, if Colton had a normal body. He knew this should stop, but another part of him was entranced, asking, *What next? What's he going to do?*

Danny wanted to find out.

It didn't feel like it had with Harland. That kiss had been disposable, there and gone like melting snow. This was a sunburn. Lingering. Scorching.

Colton's fingers slipped into his trousers.

He arched his head back and Colton kissed a path down the exposed slope of his throat, nipped the beating pathway of his pulse. He couldn't think. Nothing in the world existed except for Colton's mouth and his hand. God, his hand. A word left his mouth in a whisper—"please," maybe, or Colton's name. Colton answered by fusing their lips back together.

Danny's lungs screamed, but he didn't dare stop. He traced the hard lines of Colton's collarbones, the smooth plane of his neck. He buried his hand in the spirit's hair and sighed against his mouth. He would gladly give him all his air, if only that's what it took to breathe life into him.

Time compressed around them. It lay against his skin, then sent a jolt deep into his chest. Not its usual, gentle hold, but a jagged pain like teeth being pulled.

Danny winced and looked out of the corner of his eye. The hands of the clock were zooming around the face, the light outside dimming rapidly.

With Herculean effort he wrenched his mouth away. "STOP!"

Colton looked at the clock face in horror. He crawled off of Danny and sat on the dusty floorboard, holding his head in his hands, eyes closed tight. Danny sat up and watched him, breaths coming in short gasps.

Slowly, gradually, the clock hands stopped. They quivered in indecision, then began to move backward, the light outside brightening from night to late afternoon. The *tick tocks* resumed once the hands found their rightful place earlier in the day.

They sat unmoving on the floor, too afraid to speak. Danny slowly put himself back together, his lips swollen. He could feel his pulse in them. Could feel his pulse everywhere, even in the churn of the clockwork below.

The silence was loud and oppressive. He stood on weak legs and grabbed his coat.

"This can't go on," he said, his voice wavering.

Colton didn't look up, didn't move. Danny turned and made for the stairs.

A small crowd headed by the mayor had formed outside the tower, demanding to know what had gone wrong. Their day had suddenly turned into night, time slipping by with frightening speed. Danny apologized and told them something had happened to the pendulum while he was straightening up. But it was all right now, really. His mistake. They patted his back and nervously said that he would learn; no harm was done.

You're wrong, he wanted to tell them.

Too shocked to drive, he turned for the pub. The other patrons left Danny alone when they realized he was in a bad mood. He guzzled two pints, barely pausing for air. Then he laid his head on his arms.

It was mad to have these feelings for a clock spirit. Seeing this new side to Colton, this startling jealousy, confirmed there was no going back on his emotions now. Just as Matthias had been ensnared by the spirit in Maldon, so too was Danny caught by Colton. And if anything should happen to Danny—if he left— Colton might do something they would all regret.

But he promised. He loves the town too much.

If only Danny could talk to the spirit of Maldon, and ask how one prevented grief.

Danny finally mustered up his courage to return to the tower. By then dusk had naturally faded into early night, and the wind was freezing. He stood in the road and sighed, watching his breath become vapor, like he had turned into a steam-driven machine. He caught motion out of the corner of his eye and turned his head.

Colton stood behind the hedge, looking at him.

Surprise jolted Danny from his stupor. He didn't feel himself move when the spirit beckoned him over. Colton's skin and hair glowed faintly in the moonlight. He gave Danny a tiny, tired smile.

"What are you doing out here?" Danny demanded, shock quickly making way for fear. "I thought you couldn't leave your tower."

Colton shook his head. "I can leave, but not for too long. The farther away from my clockwork I am, the weaker I get."

Looking more closely, Danny realized that Colton seemed to be drooping ever so slightly, his voice a little slower and strained at the edges.

"How long have you been out here?"

"Not long." Danny should have known not to ask. Days felt like hours to the spirit.

"You shouldn't have done that," Danny scolded, but gently. "I don't want you doing anything that will harm you."

"I'm not harming myself." At Danny's look, Colton sheepishly averted his gaze. "Not now, anyway." He took Danny's hand and the air warped around them. "Come on."

They walked along the hedge, down the lane to the church garden. Danny saw the shadow of Aetas's shrine, the god's hands lifted in either offering or forgiveness. The honeysuckle's white petals seemed to reflect Colton's faint glow, a glow that was getting weaker by the minute.

"Colton . . ."

"Don't worry, I'm fine." He faced Danny, his expression grim. "I'm sorry. I don't know why I did that. When I saw that other boy kissing you, I felt this horrible . . ." He pressed a hand to his chest. "I don't know what humans call it."

"Jealousy."

"Yes, that's it. And I didn't want to feel it. But then I was so angry. Not at you, or at him. Just angry. For this." He gestured toward the clock tower. "Angry that I have to stay here, and that you have to go. That I ruin time whenever I'm happy or sad. That I can't control what I feel to begin with. Clocks aren't supposed to feel, Danny. They're just objects."

Danny thought of the newly destroyed Maldon tower. Was that the difference, then? Clocks needed spirits to live, or else they were just objects.

Colton reached into Danny's pocket and drew out his timepiece. He opened it and watched the second hand tick around the face. "Look at it. It's lifeless. So why am I like this?"

Danny wrapped his hand around Colton's. Together they closed the timepiece with a soft *click*. "Clocks aren't lifeless, Colton. They *are* life. Time makes things grow, and it makes them die. Time moves everything forward."

"But that's just it," Colton whispered. "Someday, you'll be gone. You should be with that other boy. You'll both age, while I . . ." He lowered his eyes. "Why do I have to be this way? I want . . ." He trailed off, and Danny thought of the last time he had said it. *It doesn't matter what I want.*

"I want to be normal," Colton said instead.

Danny stood at a loss, unsure what to say. He glanced at the shrine, at the form of the god Colton had descended from.

He pocketed his timepiece and swept back a lock of Colton's hair, touching the side of his face. Colton pressed his cheek into Danny's hand, hungry for contact.

"Can I tell you a secret?" Danny asked. Colton nodded. "I don't want you to be normal."

The spirit frowned. "Why?"

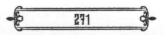

"Because that's why I liked you in the first place. You're not normal. There's only one of you in the whole world. There's a spirit of a boy, who is also the spirit of a clock, and his name is Colton." He swept his thumb over Colton's cheek. "And he's mine."

Slowly, the spirit smiled. There was too much left unsaid, so they didn't say anything.

Eventually, Colton took Danny's hand and laid something on his palm.

"I wanted to give this to you."

Danny held it up to his eyes. It was a tiny cog, about the size of a sixpence. The spokes were caked in grime, the metal rusting.

"I found this the other day in some crevice. Another mechanic removed it a long time before you came, so don't worry, I'm not missing any parts. He just forgot to pick it up when he replaced it with a new one." Colton smiled again when Danny looked up from the cog. "I thought you might like to have it."

Much like touching Colton, holding the cog gave him the feeling that time was aware of his existence. The sensation felt so familiar, so comforting, that he wondered why people feared its passing. He took Colton's hand in his free one, strengthening that feeling until he was convinced that so long as they stood there, between the hedge and the night-blooming flowers, time would be kind and allow them to stay this way for as long as they desired.

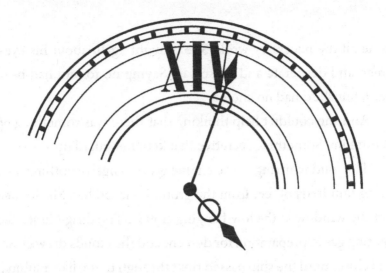

The dirigible wasn't as crowded as a public transport airship, but Daphne still felt claustrophobic. She kept twirling a long strand of hair around her finger—around and around and around—and then letting it unravel like a skein of yarn. She had seated herself in a pocket of the dirigible's gondola, the only passenger in the small cabin.

Daphne had always been fascinated by airships, but that wasn't why she rode one today. She had an assignment all the way in Dover. Things had been a little off at the clock tower. There were mechanics in the field who could pop over and have a look, but London was the clock mechanic hub of southeast England, and the Lead preferred to send his mechanics to investigate disturbances.

Strangely, though she'd been assigned to Enfield, she hadn't received any assignments there. Maybe Danny Hart had already done all the necessary work. She thought again about his eyes, green and desperate and so, so sad. Saying no to him had been hard, but she'd had no choice.

And she couldn't help thinking that there was something *off* about him. Something secretive that kept her guard up.

The loud whirring of the engine was strangely soothing, and being hundreds of feet from the ground relaxed her. She looked out the window at the low-hanging clouds. The dirigible started venting gas in preparation for descent and the clouds drew closer and closer until the ship passed right through them, like a submarine sinking into a cottony sea.

Once out of the clouds, she could see Dover below. It was a small town at the very edge of the country, right where land met sea. Beyond the sheer white cliffs of the shore lay the Strait of Dover, and beyond that, France.

The dirigible would land just outside the town and an auto would drive her to the tower. This was a one-day job; Daphne disliked overnight assignments. The London office usually made sure their mechanics didn't need to be away longer than absolutely necessary, just in case something happened in the field.

She thought about Lucas and shuddered.

The whir of the dirigible grew louder as it landed. Steam belched from the engine and the ground crew ran about in preparation below. When the ship came within a dozen feet of the ground, the engine sputtered and came to a stop as the gas did the rest. The ship slowly drifted down, where the crew grabbed hold of its mooring ropes to secure it to the mast. Daphne collected her bag and slung it over her shoulder.

"There you are, miss," the pilot said as he emerged from the front cabin, pulling up his aviator goggles. She noticed a tattoo on the inside of his wrist, a set of wings to symbolize Caelum, Gaian god of the sky.

Many pilots used it as a good luck talisman. Her father had had one in almost the same spot, an inch above his wrist. She remembered being small and tracing the black lines it made on her father's ochre skin.

"Was it a good flight?" the pilot asked.

"Very good, yes." She caught a glimpse of the copilot inside, an automaton fastened to the seat beside the pilot's. The automaton turned its head this way and that, as if surprised to be on the ground again. "You'll fly me back this afternoon?"

"Of course, miss."

Outside, the bright sunshine was deceptive; a cold wind came up from the sea, and she was thankful for her thick trousers and coat.

The man sent to greet her stood just off the gangplank. He looked her up and down with consternation, blinking repeatedly. "Ah . . . Daniel Hart?"

She frowned. "No, Daphne Richards."

His eyes lingered on her trousers, a corner of his upper lip curling. "Ah. Would you be the apprentice, then?" He looked back at the airship, as if expecting Danny to walk out after her.

Her voice came out frostbitten. "I'm the mechanic."

"Oh. I see." Now he was determined not to look at any part of her. "Well then, Miss Richards?" He gestured to the auto.

Daphne sat in the back as the man drove her into town. He glanced at her a few times in the rearview mirror, but she invited no conversation. She had experienced this before—men and women disapproving of her clothing and her profession. They would be shocked if they could see the other women of London: auto mechanics with grease in their hair, fisherwomen in from the coast with tattooed arms.

Matthias had told her what to expect when she had been his apprentice. That the men, especially the older ones, would look at her as if she were a joke. Or an insult.

"But I'm not doing anything to them," she'd argued. "I just want to be a good mechanic."

"And that's all that matters. Don't mind anyone else or what they think. You do what's best by you."

Daphne tried not to think of the driver's face when she'd said she was the mechanic, the way he had waited for a man to come and announce he was her escort.

Why did he think Danny Hart was coming with me, though?

The town didn't take long to drive through, and soon they were at the base of the clock tower that overlooked the sea. The two faces, one facing north and the other south, gleamed in the sunlight. Although she noticed the limestone had eroded away on one side, likely from sea salt, there were no crumbling bricks or obvious signs of neglect.

"Here we are, Miss Richards. Bernice Tower. Beautiful, no?"

"Very." She opened the auto door without waiting for him to do so for her. "I won't be needing assistance. I should be no more than two hours."

The driver stammered a little, but under her cool stare he simply said, "Aye, Miss Richards."

She walked to the tower entrance and breathed in deeply, enjoying the briny smell of sea air. It made the town feel fresh and clean. Daphne allowed herself a moment to think about how much her mother would enjoy the seaside.

She entered the tower through a well-oiled door. From what she'd seen so far, it appeared there was nothing wrong, but the report said various little hiccups kept occurring. The escapement for the pendulum had gone off, making the clock sputter. Life moving in jerks rather than the smooth flow of seconds. But another mechanic had cleaned that up.

She had come today to clean the clockwork and check for anything out of the ordinary. The maintenance crew reported that the cogs were grinding together and the gears were struggling to turn. She could feel it the closer she came to the clockwork, a tug that didn't feel normal. Like wind pulling instead of pushing.

Climbing the steep wooden stairs, she set her bag down on the landing and looked out one of the narrow windows. The sun sparkled on the ocean's surface.

Far below stood a tall statue of a woman. Her dress was etched with the scalloped pattern of seashells, her hair long and flowing like seaweed. She pointed a stone finger toward the sea.

Oceana. Dover had maintained the old shrine as well as they had maintained the tower.

Daphne turned and got to work. She laid out her tools and studied the clockwork. It was impressive, and she took a moment to appreciate the cogs and gears and chains that worked together to pull time forward.

But there was a tiny catch. Near the central cog, something clicked, and the surrounding gears had slowed as a result.

"Hmm." Daphne crouched before the central cog. "What's the matter with you, then?"

She closed her eyes and touched it, but couldn't feel anything wrong. "Must be something stuck inside," she said to the clockwork. "All right. Let's have a look."

Her mother had once said Daphne liked clocks more than she liked people. Daphne had never argued the point. That had been years ago, before her father died. When they still attracted curious gazes on the street, a family of odds and ends—a girl who wore trousers, a man with one foot in England and the other in India, and the woman who somehow found herself attached to them. It had gotten to her mother over time. The looks and whispers.

Then Daphne had been accepted as a clock mechanic apprentice, a profession her mother frowned upon. "First trousers, now this," she'd muttered. "Thank God you have my coloring, at least."

But when her father died, the accusations and the paranoia had grown worse, her mother's mind deteriorating until the slightest provocation had made her attack Daphne with a knife.

Now that she was in the asylum, Daphne used her love of clocks to pay for her mother's treatment. But funds were running low. She would have to ask the Lead for more assignments soon.

Daphne carefully removed each part to get to the heart of the problem. She cleaned the components as she went, time slowing as she did.

The clicking sound grew louder. Daphne frowned and unscrewed another gear.

"Be careful."

Daphne whirled around. A little girl stared at the clockwork, her amber eyes wide. Blonde hair fell to her waist, sleek and shining. She wore a white pinafore with a bow on the back.

"What are you doing up here?" Daphne demanded. "This tower is for mechanics and maintenance crew only."

The girl never took her eyes off the clockwork. Unnerved, Daphne glanced at the gears.

"Do you know what's causing this?" she asked.

The girl finally met her eyes. She had a strange glow to her skin that Daphne couldn't attribute to sunshine alone.

"Help," the girl whispered. She pointed at the central cog. "You have to find it before—"

A metallic scream drowned out the rest of her words. Something struck Daphne and sent her sprawling across the room.

The air pressed in hot and close. Daphne's mouth opened and closed until she could manage a ragged breath. She coughed, struggling to sit up, but a sharp pain in her shoulder made her cry out and fall to the floor.

Shouting. Churning. Daphne opened her eyes to slits and saw the little girl, bathed in ghostly gray light, still pointing at the clockwork. The girl was . . . *flickering*. Daphne's ears rang, and all she heard was *central cog*.

She looked up and gasped. Cogs and gears littered the room. The clockwork frame was smoking, the air reeking of ash and melted iron.

It was then she realized what caused the strange grayness around her. The town of Dover had Stopped.

Time no longer m o v e d, was something she could no longer control. A dream—a hallucination—a nightmare. Her vision doubledbəlduob.

The little girl shouted, but her voice was fading and weak as she flickered again. Daphne struggled to listen, but the girl might as well have been chanting another language. Gritting her teeth, Daphne crawled toward the clockwork. Her shoulder ached, and desperation bit her palms.

Do something, she thought. *Have to do something.*

Panting, she located the central cog, which hung crookedly off its frame. Daphne wasted no time and grabbed her tools to reattach it.

Her scratched-up hands were shaking. Time distorted, made her pick up her tools three times in a row three times in a row three times in a row, made her crawl across the floor again.

made her crawl across the floor again.

The little girl picked up the loose pieces and brought them to Daphne's side.

Once Daphne attached the central cog, she focused on the others, working layer by layer. She was mesmerized by the blood pounding in her ears, a drumbeat keeping her on course. Slowly, the clockwork moved forward—one second one second, and then another. Daphne's vision grew dark as she hurried to attach all of the pieces, to get them in the right order before she went under completely.

When every piece was in place, she put her hands on the central cog and closed her blurry eyes. The time fibers surrounding her writhed in turmoil, the ends frayed and stiff. She jerked them back together, and tied off the loose ends.

Something lit up inside her as her heart pumped, as her body struggled to remain upright, a tense power breathing down the back of her neck. Slowly, painstakingly, the fibers wove together in the pattern that should never have been broken.

She opened her eyes and swayed. The clockwork jerked, jerked again, and began to move.

The grayness lifted.

Time resumed.

Daphne took great shuddering breaths, her heart fluttering in her chest. She looked down at herself and saw patches of spilled blood. Her blood.

She toppled to the floor.

Footsteps thundered on the stairs, but she couldn't turn. The little girl stood before her, amber eyes still wide. No longer flickering.

Daphne blinked, and the girl was gone.

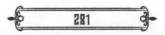

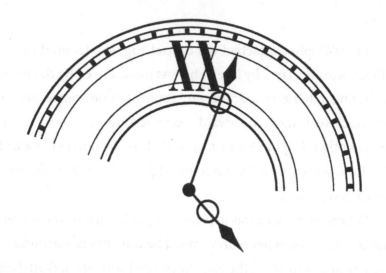

anny had taken a bite of toast when he received a call to come into the office.

"As soon as you possibly can," the Lead said. He sounded grim, and suddenly the idea of Danny finishing his toast was rather unappealing.

He didn't want to know what had happened to make the Lead sound like that. Ever since this whole affair with Colton began, Danny had been terrified he might receive a call like this.

Maybe Harland rang and said I looked suspicious, Danny thought as he drove toward the Parliament building, which cast a long golden reflection on the Thames. *Maybe he did see me with Colton.*

"Don't make assumptions," he muttered as he parked the auto.

As had been the case for the last several days, no protesters were outside the Mechanics Affairs building. Constables lined the front in case any decided to show up.

Yet the more Danny thought about it, the less sense it made for the protesters to have been involved. Maldon had been guarded night and day.

Unless they were only a distraction.

Danny climbed the stairs and greeted the Lead's secretary, who showed him into the office. She acted kind enough. Perhaps there was nothing to be concerned about after all.

And then the door opened.

The Lead looked up from his desk. Daphne Richards sat in one of the chairs before him. She turned and stared Danny down, her eyes like blades of ice; the kind that could pierce the hulls of ships.

He had a feeling he was about to be sunk.

Danny swallowed and walked inside. The secretary closed the door behind him.

The Lead gestured to the vacant chair. "Sit."

Danny hesitated, then pulled the chair a little farther from Daphne's before he took his seat. Her hands were covered in bandages, and she had scrapes on her cheek and neck.

"Daniel," the Lead said, lacing his fingers together on the desk's surface, "you've been lying to me." He glanced at Daphne. "Both of you have."

Danny began to sweat. His tongue flattened under the weight of apologies and excuses, but he said nothing. Likewise, Daphne remained silent.

"Are you aware of what happened in Dover, Daniel?"

He shook his head.

"You were assigned to go to Dover and clean the Bernice Tower clockwork. Instead, without my consent, you traded the job with Daphne."

"Sir, I—"

The Lead held up a hand. "While she was there, a peculiar thing happened. A bomb was hidden behind the central cog. The clockwork she was repairing exploded."

Danny inhaled sharply. His chin stung with the memory of Shere—of Maldon's tower falling, the gear gleaming in Lucas's chest. He looked at Daphne, who continued to stare straight ahead, her jaw clenched. She could have very well been lying in a coffin today.

Because of him.

Your fault.

Danny's fingers twitched as he fought the rising horror inside him. Over and over, he had sent others to their destructive fate. His next breath was a ragged sound torn from his chest, loud enough that Daphne looked at him.

I'm sorry, he mouthed. She turned away.

"Daphne was able to replace the central cog. Otherwise, she likely wouldn't be here." The Lead leaned forward. "Daniel, did you have knowledge of this?"

Danny's body buzzed. He shifted his gaze from Daphne to the Lead and shook his head.

"Don't lie," Daphne snarled. "You wanted to trade jobs with me for a reason. First Lucas, and now me."

"You think *I* killed Lucas?"

"It's simple, isn't it? Lucas and I were your competition, so you decided to do away with us for good."

"Of all the idiotic—"

The Lead slammed his hand on the desk and they jumped. He glared at them, mustache quivering.

"Listen to me, the both of you! This is a most serious matter, and I will not have you squabbling like children. Four clock towers have been attacked and there are bound to be more. Two mechanics are hospitalized, and another is dead. You two could have died as well.

"Daniel. Please, tell the truth. Why did you switch assignments with Daphne?"

Danny's mouth turned dry. He rubbed clammy hands against his trouser legs. "Sir . . . it's hard to explain."

"I don't care. *Explain.*"

He sat stupid and uninspired until he blurted out, "I have a lover in Enfield."

The room fell silent. Then Daphne scoffed.

"You wanted to trade jobs so you could get cozy with some Enfield boy?"

The Lead massaged his temples. "Is this why you requested to remain on the Enfield assignments?"

Danny nodded, blushing. The Lead sighed.

"You had no authority to trade assignments with Daphne without my consent."

She bared her teeth at Danny. "Aren't you going to question him? It's suspicious, isn't it? First he goes to a village that Stops, then he's seen snooping around where he shouldn't be, Lucas dies, and now this! And let's not forget his father's trapped in Maldon."

Danny stood so fast his chair toppled over. "Don't you dare bring my father into this! If you think I had a hand in that—"

"I don't know a thing about your father. For all we know, he beat you and you fixed it so he'd never return."

"Enough!" the Lead roared, standing. "Daphne, I agree that the circumstances are odd, but I believe Daniel had no part in what happened. Did you?" Danny shook his head, breathing hard through his nose. "Lord knows I should reassign you both to some godforsaken corner of England, but I'm afraid I have to take more drastic measures.

"Daniel, Daphne, you are both hereby dismissed from the Mechanics Union."

The maroon carpet tipped under Danny's feet. The whole damn world tipped.

"No," he whispered under Daphne's "What? But I didn't do anything!"

The Lead looked as though he'd aged ten years in ten seconds. "I can't be certain you aren't lying about switching assignments. With the state of things, I can't take any chances."

"But, sir, the committee." Daphne's eyes were wide. "The

foreign exchange program. I need—I mean, I thought I was—I wanted—" She couldn't finish.

The Lead drew a deep, weary breath. "Maybe when this whole mess is cleared up, I'll consider reinstating you. For now, your hospital bills will be paid for, but you are no longer members of the Union. I'm sorry."

Daphne was told to go home and rest. She turned to Danny with hate in her eyes, but whatever she wanted to say wouldn't come out. She stormed from the office with a muffled sob. Danny hung back, certain that the Lead wasn't through with him.

"I'm going to ask you one more time," the Lead said softly. "Did you have any knowledge of the attacks?"

"Sir, you can't really believe I had a hand in this."

"What Daphne pointed out is incriminating. You know that, don't you? Lucas said he thought your behavior was suspicious, and I must admit I wasn't too pleased to hear you'd been to the Maldon site. And let's not forget your little incident at the hospital."

"But Tom and George were *right there* at the tower. They had access to the blueprints. Tom was at Shere before I was. He had pipes to build bo—"

"Do you have proof, Daniel?"

Danny's silence was answer enough.

"You will leave those mechanics alone. Is that understood?" He waited for Danny to nod. "Now, answer my question. Did you know?"

Danny took a shaking breath. "No. I didn't know anything about the attacks."

The Lead didn't look convinced. "Daniel," the man said gently, "you're going through a difficult time. Your mind may not be completely sound."

"Sir, please, don't do this." Danny's voice broke. "I'm begging you."

The Lead passed a hand over his eyes. "I'm sorry, Daniel. I really am. But you can only have so many chances, and you've squandered your last one. I hope one day you'll understand."

AETAS AND THE END OF TIME

etas stood upon the solemn shore with outstretched hands, the time threads extended from his body as if he were a loom ready to be used. He didn't dare stroke a finger across them to feel them vibrate with possibility as he once had. Now there were too many possibilities, and he had only one choice.

He cast the threads out. They traveled from his body into the depths of the world. They snaked over Oceana's waters. They ran through Caelum's sky. They climbed over Terra's mountains.

They struck humans, twining around bodies strong enough to carry them. Those humans felt a great movement within them, apart from them, in the oceans and the sky and the mountains. In the depths of Aetas's heart.

When enough threads had been siphoned off, Aetas cut them from his body and they continued to thrive, to pulse, to glow. Time went on. He held the rest of them, the smaller number of threads he could maintain on his own.

"Hold these threads to you," Aetas told his followers. "Protect them. Feed them into the world. Ensure time continues to unfold. If you grow weak, come to me where I stay with my sister beneath the water. I will give you what strength I can."

His followers flocked to the shore. They cupped their hands in the water and whispered their hopes and fears to Aetas, who smiled at them from below.

Several years passed in this way. Time servants visited the

shores and prayed to Aetas, and fed their energy into time. Every second, every minute, every hour of every day was a blink and a breath to them, necessary and instinctive.

Then the sky began to darken, a rumble deep and building, and lightning sliced into Caelum's domain like a serpent's tongue.

Oceana knew it was Chronos. "He is waking up," she told Aetas. "He must know what you have done."

Aetas knew this, and knew he could not run from Chronos's wrath. He had done what was necessary to make certain the earth would be well kept. If he was to be punished for his care, so be it.

The sky growled and lightning bit. The waters boiled. The earth shook.

Aetas stood on the ocean floor as the water above him parted, revealing a storm dark and looming. He told his sister Oceana to run, to find shelter from their creator.

On this spot, he waited for Chronos to descend.

Danny played with the cog in his pocket as he walked through Hyde Park. After Colton had given it to him, he had polished the cog until it shone. He would often take it out to spin it with his fingers, or roll it around his palm, but never in public in case anyone happened to see.

But as he walked through the park, taking in the couples strolling together, he reached into his pocket for its comfort.

He was on his way to see Matthias. Danny had been furious when he learned that Matthias had suggested taking Danny off the Enfield assignments, but after some thought—and after losing his job—he realized his bruised feelings were the least of his problems. He needed someone to talk to. He needed his friend back.

It was time to tell Matthias about Colton.

Matthias would help him. He had been down this uncertain

road, had faced the possibility of losing everything. Hopefully they could prevent history from repeating itself.

But when Danny knocked on the door of the white and blue house, no one answered.

Danny fiddled with the cog as he stared at the park, wondering if he could go to Enfield. But the Lead might be tracking his movements now, making sure Danny never stepped foot in a clock tower again. The reality struck low and hard, winding him. No more clock towers. No more time fibers winding through his fingers.

No more Colton.

"Damn it," he whispered, putting his head in his hands.

He really was losing everything.

The door's lock scraped, and Danny started. But it wasn't Matthias behind the faded blue door. A woman peered out from the shadowed crack, narrowing her eyes against the brightness outside.

"Oh. Hullo." Danny checked that he had the right house. "Is Matthias in?"

She stood a little straighter and shook her head. Danny shifted on the step, wondering how to make a polite getaway. But the woman leaned forward suddenly, scrutinizing his face, and then waved a small white hand at him.

"You may come in and wait."

"Will he be long?"

"Not long."

Danny stepped inside and thanked the woman as she closed

the door behind him. She wasn't dressed like a maid, and she couldn't be Matthias's housemate. To avoid staring at her, he looked around the house with a sudden thrill. He had never been inside before.

The hallway was narrow and painted almost the same shade of blue as the door. The stairs on his left were dark-stained wood, and a blue carpet runner stretched from the front door to a sitting room at the back of the house. The woman showed him to this room before she disappeared into the kitchen.

Danny was slightly disappointed; it wasn't how he'd imagined the inside of Matthias's home. For one thing, the man had grossly exaggerated the state of the house's disrepair. Danny didn't notice a single thing out of place. He examined paintings of seaside landscapes that hung along the hallway, all quite similar to one another, before he passed a few framed sketches of a clock tower. Matthias's signature darkened the bottom right corners.

In the sitting room, Danny lowered himself onto a settee and waited for the woman to return. *Or does she mean to leave me here?* His leg bounced up and down as he eyed the trinkets on the bookshelves and read the spines of the many books collected there. Matthias and his father had loved collecting books. He saw a tome of classical mythology and touched the cog again. It could have been his imagination, but he swore that the small clock on the mantel ticked louder.

He turned and noticed the woman was standing in the doorway, staring at him. She held a tea tray in her hands, her head cocked slightly to one side. The pose tickled something in Danny's memory, but he couldn't think what.

"Tea," she announced with a small smile.

He stood politely when she walked into the room and set the tray down on the low, wooden table in front of the settee. He could see now that she was a tall, willowy woman, with golden hair and sallow skin. Her eyes were a very light brown.

She sank gracefully into the armchair behind her, and he sat as well. The woman was wearing a lavender dress that fell to her ankles, but with no stockings or shoes. Her bare feet were graceful, like a dancer's. Since she made no move to pour her own cup, Danny sat forward to pour it for her; it was what his mother would tell him to do. The woman leaned forward to accept the offered cup.

"Thank you for the tea," Danny said. "Are you, um—are you Matthias's housemate?" She nodded. "I know you've been living with Matthias for a while. I had no idea you were a . . . I mean, I thought Matthias lived with another man. Are you his . . . companion?"

She smiled, but he couldn't tell if it was out of amusement or politeness. "I'm a bit of both."

"Oh." Danny furtively glanced at her chest. Why would Matthias say "he"?

This was also the first Danny had heard of Matthias having a lover. It shocked him, to be honest. For years Danny had seen the quiet, longing sorrow that dogged Matthias like a second shadow. When had this woman come into his life?

Silence filled the room as they sipped their tea. The clock ticked on in the background. Looking more closely, Danny saw that the woman wasn't well. Her eyes were sunken, her skin pale like she hadn't seen the sun in some time. No one saw the sun for long stretches of time in London, but this seemed a different sort of pale, more gray than blue.

"Are you Danny?" she asked suddenly.

"Yes. How did you know?"

"Matthias talks about you. He's very fond of you."

Danny smiled. "I'm glad to hear it. I'm fond of him as well."

"I've always wanted to meet you. I'm glad I finally have the chance." The words struck Danny as odd, but he couldn't put his finger on why.

Her gaze trailed over his chest and paused on the timepiece chain hanging out of his left pocket. Her eyes flitted to the right pocket.

"You have something there," she murmured.

Startled, Danny put his hand over the slight lump where the cog rested. Unsettled by her gaze, he drew it out and held it on his palm.

"Are you a mechanic?" Danny asked. "How did you know I had this?"

"Did you steal it from a clock?" she demanded.

He leaned back at her sudden change in tone. "No. The clock . . . gave it to me."

It sounded ridiculous, but it was the truth. For some reason, he had no urge to lie to her.

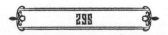

The woman stared at him, then at the cog, then back at his face.

"Why did the clock give it to you?"

Danny wrapped a protective hand around the cog and put it back in his pocket before she could snatch it away. "Because he wanted me to have it."

He must have sounded defensive, for she eased back in her chair. "I see. That's all right, then." She returned to her tea, sipping daintily, as if they had just spoken of crocheting rather than the gifts of clock spirits.

But then, as he watched her, an awareness slid into place. At first Danny dismissed it as impossible, but the thought came creeping back, begging to be looked at. The more the idea took root in his mind, the harder it was to breathe. His skin prickled, the hairs on his arms lifting as if he were about to be struck by lightning.

Danny lined up the pieces: the louder ticking of the clock in her presence, her golden features, the way her voice sounded like slow gears in need of oiling. The way she regarded things, tilting her head in innocent curiosity. He had seen all of that before. In Colton.

His mouth opened, and he was distantly surprised to hear words come out of it. "You're a clock spirit."

The woman peered at him over her teacup. She carefully put the cup and saucer down on the table. He could see now she hadn't drunk a drop. After all, her kind didn't need food and drink. She must have had a lot of practice at pretending.

"Yes," she said.

He gripped the edge of the settee as the clock's overly loud *ticks* stabbed him. "Your name?"

"Evaline."

The world darkened. When it came back as color and shapes, Danny was still sitting on the settee, still staring at the woman who stared back, unruffled.

"You can't be," he rasped. "Evaline is the name of the clock tower in Maldon."

"It was," she agreed sadly. "But no longer. Evaline is here, now."

Danny put his head between his knees, as his grammar school nurse had instructed him to do when dizzy. "That can't be," he whispered to the floor. "You can't be Evaline."

"Why not?"

He lifted his head. "Because the clockwork fell apart!"

She kept her hands in her lap, her fingers rubbing nervously over her knuckles. "That's not quite what happened."

Words were difficult to come by as the world unraveled around him, but he tried anyway. "Then tell me what did happen. Please."

"I shouldn't. I shouldn't have even brought you in here, but . . ."

Danny found another painful similarity to Colton in her eyes, a certain shade of loneliness. Not a prisoner in a tower, maybe, but stuck in this house while Matthias was gone for hours at a time, with no one to talk to.

"I can leave if you want me to," Danny said slowly, hating himself when he saw the distress on her face. "Unless you'd like to tell me what actually happened to Maldon."

Evaline bit her lower lip. She looked around the room, as if for inspiration. "Matthias was my mechanic," she began softly, dreamily, like Matthias used to do when Danny was younger. "He seemed sad, and I wanted to know why, so I showed myself to him. We talked about *everything*. I was so fascinated by his stories, especially those about London. He said he wished he could take me there, if I wasn't bound to the tower.

"He told me about his late wife and how she had died. The poor man had been lonely for so long. All I wanted to do was make him smile. I tried so hard, until one day I saw it. That smile lit up the whole world. I made him feel something he said he hadn't felt in years."

Her eyes were inwardly drawn to that golden, faraway moment. Though Danny didn't want to, he thought of Colton. Had his sadness been the reason Colton had shown himself? Had Colton, like Evaline, only wanted to make him smile? Danny dug his fingers harder into the settee's cushions.

Evaline's expression slowly hardened. "Matthias said that mechanics were not allowed to be with our kind. He and I, we didn't care. We were happy. But we were also reckless. Another mechanic saw us, and reported us.

"I didn't see Matthias for a while. Then that other mechanic came and told me what had happened to him. That he was exiled. I was . . . devastated." He watched as her memory turned from that golden moment to this gray one, and Danny could imagine the same terror of abandonment in Colton, the drastic urge to break and rip himself apart instead of facing that gaping loneliness again.

"I took apart my clockwork and walked to London to find him." A small smile, perhaps unbidden, curved her mouth upward. As if she was proud of herself. "Matthias had a bit of a shock, but he's been happy to have me here. I miss Maldon every day. But I would miss him far more." She looked Danny in the eye, daring him to say otherwise.

Danny sat there, stunned, the word TRAITOR bold and stark before him like a newspaper headline.

He jumped to his feet and knocked over his empty teacup, spilling the dregs. Evaline tensed as he kneeled before her and took her cold hands in his. Time didn't shiver the way it did with Colton, but it jumped, like the static shock of touching a fingertip to metal.

"Youcan'tstayhere," he said.

"What?"

"You. Can't. Stay. Here. You have to go back to Maldon."

She tried to pull her hands away, but he held on tighter. "What do you mean?"

The words wanted to tumble from his mouth. It took all his strength to get them out in the right order. "Do you know what a Stopped town is?"

She shook her head.

Fighting another wave of panic, Danny explained what her

disappearance had done to the town she'd left behind. "Because you left, the town is Stopped. Time is frozen and can't move forward. My father—and all those people—are trapped inside Maldon."

Evaline had gone as gray as the clouds outside. She gripped Danny's hands so tightly he worried his fingers would break.

"That can't be right," she whispered. "Matthias would have told me. Why didn't Matthias tell me?"

Yes, why *hadn't* Matthias told her? He had been questioned extensively, had said he knew nothing about Maldon Stopping. And yet for three years, he had hidden the spirit of Evaline Tower in his own home.

"How could you not know the town Stopped when you left?" Danny asked. "Didn't you feel it happening?"

"I thought they would install another central cog, and another spirit could live in the tower. That's what Matthias told me."

"We tried that, in a way," Danny said, thinking of the new Maldon tower. "It didn't work. There was no spirit in the tower." Who would ever think a tower would need a figure believed to only exist in fairy tales?

She opened her mouth, then closed it, thinking something over. "Being outside of my tower has weakened me," she said eventually. "So, for the last three years, Matthias has been trying to find a new one for me. He's been exiled from Maldon; there's no chance of going back there. But if he installs me in another tower, then we could be together without hiding. The search hasn't been going well, though."

Danny frowned, trying to make sense of the idea. It didn't seem possible. There were no abandoned clock towers, only broken ones, and those were locked within Stopped towns. If Matthias wanted to install her somewhere else . . .

A cold realization yawned open within him.

No.

And yet, Danny could see the effect of those three years before him. Evaline was vulnerable without her tower, and likely getting weaker every day. Her grayish skin, her slow voice, the weariness in her eyes—all rungs in the ladder that could lead to Matthias's desperation.

Don't look at it now. I can't.

This time he let her pull her hands away. Danny leaned against the armchair as Evaline covered her face with her hands. She could have been a statue for Lucas's grave. Danny was just wondering how long they would stay like this when Evaline stood and slowly left the room, as if sleepwalking. It all felt like a dream, like a twisting nightmare that wouldn't let them wake up.

Danny paced the room, his breath deafening in his ears. Matthias had held the key to freeing his father all this time. This entire time.

Three.

Whole.

Years.

How could he? *How could he?*

Danny snatched a teacup from the table and hurled it against the wall, where it shattered into a dozen pieces. The second one joined it, splashing tea against the sun-bleached wallpaper. Danny choked on his fury, throwing books off the shelves, barely looking at the things he broke before they joined the mess.

He slumped against the wall and covered his mouth with a shaking hand. When Evaline returned, she paused, taking in the damage. She was carrying a cog. Her central cog.

"He lied to you as well," she said. Danny nodded. Looking down, Evaline lifted the cog before her. "I took this when I left. It's the only thing keeping me stable. This, and the energy of the London clock tower. If I walk into Maldon holding this, the town will be restored?"

Danny dropped his hand. "I believe so. Humans can't pass through the barrier, but you did. The central cog needs to be reinstalled, and you can bring it back. The clock has to run for the town's time to restart. My father will be able to help." He moved toward her. "Please, you have to go. We all thought you were destroyed, but you're here, and—and something can be done. Please, I'm begging you."

Her eyes widened, as if amazed by the rawness in his voice, and perhaps at her own ignorance. She looked at the cog in her hands.

"I'll speak to Matthias when he returns," she said. "I don't know why he would let those people suffer, but there has to be a reason. I can't just leave without saying a word. We'll figure this out together."

Danny didn't want words, he wanted action—to push her out the door, steal the cog, throw her over his shoulder and run to Maldon. But he could do nothing except shake in the shadow of three long years of despair and guilt.

"When Matthias returns," she repeated, almost to herself. "Then we'll sort this out."

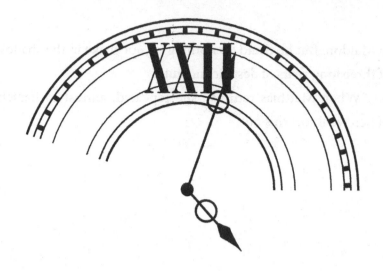

XXII

Danny went to the office. He had to. He felt outside himself, existing above his skin, mouth dry and heart made of paper. Nothing seemed real, even when he touched his fingertips to the wall. Every breath etched hairline cracks into his lungs.

The secretary told him the Lead wasn't in.

The air blew out of him and his paper heart crumpled.

What was he supposed to do now?

Danny searched the building top to bottom, hoping to find the Lead, Matthias . . . someone. But no one was there. No one he could trust.

Which was how he ended up at the Winchester, nursing a drink.

He rested his forehead on the sticky tabletop and moaned quietly to himself. Twitches had taken over his body, his legs jumping up and down. He needed to do something, but *what*?

He couldn't go to Enfield; Cassie had his auto at the shop overnight. She wanted to install her new safety device, some sort of seat holster.

He could try going back to the office and camping in front of the Lead's door until the man showed up. But maybe he shouldn't, not until Matthias spoke to his . . .

"His clock spirit." An unhinged laugh escaped him, verging on mania. "Oh, damn. What'll I tell Mum?"

"What are you telling her?"

Danny sat up and blinked at Brandon Summers. He stood beside the table, mug in hand.

"What are you doing here?" Danny asked.

"A crime to get a pint, is it?"

Danny rubbed the back of his neck and pushed out a chair, silently inviting Brandon to sit. The apprentice settled down.

"You look a right mess," Brandon observed, blunt as ever. "What happened, girl get tired of you? Er, boy?" Danny felt the return of his mania and ruthlessly pushed it down.

"Rough day." Danny held his nearly empty glass between his palms and thought about how Matthias would react to the chaos in his sitting room. His stomach squirmed.

Brandon quietly drank for a couple of minutes. "Do you fancy going to Enfield tomorrow?"

"What? Why?"

"I've got my first assessment coming up. I wondered if you'd give me some advice."

Danny's anxiety scooted over to make room for flattered sur-

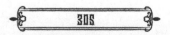

prise. An apprentice had to undergo three separate assessments before becoming a full-fledged mechanic. If this was his first, that meant Brandon was aiming to become a novice mechanic soon.

He probably didn't know that Danny had been sacked.

Danny thought he should stay in London, find the Lead or Matthias as soon as he could. But fear seeped into the cracks in his lungs. He wanted to speak with Colton. To clear his mind, to explain everything that had happened. *He* was someone Danny could trust.

Danny sighed. "Where can I pick you up?"

The day dawned cold and bleak, and soot hung in the morning sky from coal fires. Danny had tossed and turned the entire night, and the weather did little to improve his spirits. It was bad enough being tired and miserable and full of nervous energy; even worse would be having to drive this way.

As his mother waited for her interview results that morning, Danny couldn't bring himself to tell her about being sacked. Or about Evaline. The latter still felt too dreamlike to have been real, and Danny didn't want to raise his mother's hopes—and his own—until he understood the situation entirely.

He felt a similar frustration as he waited for a call from Matthias that never came. Both members of the Hart household stared intently at the telephone that vexed them with its silence.

On his way to Enfield, he occasionally glanced at Brandon,

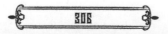

who had taken to complaining about the auto every two minutes. It sputtered crankily despite the new boiler. Cassie had
dropped it off that morning and showed him the new leather holster, demonstrating how it rested diagonally across his chest and
attached to a mechanical seal by his hip. He'd barely paid attention, but thanked her when she was done. It cut into his chest
now, and he felt a bit ridiculous.

"Careful, mate!"

Danny narrowly avoided the bump in the road he always
managed to forget.

Brandon cursed at his side. "Maybe this was a bad idea."

"I'm sorry," Danny said. "Look, the town's just there. I promise your life's in good hands." Brandon didn't seem convinced.

Since Brandon looked ready to leap from the auto rather
than stay in it another minute, Danny parked on the outskirts of
Enfield. Danny removed his goggles and followed his tall apprentice toward the green. The weather had driven nearly everyone
inside, and the abandoned look of the place didn't make Danny
feel any better.

"What can you show me that'll be on the assessment?"
Brandon asked once they'd climbed the tower steps. Danny
unbuttoned his coat and thought about what would take the
least amount of time.

"How about I show you a trick with the mainspring?"

Danny felt Colton's eyes as they worked. He sometimes
looked over his shoulder and saw the spirit leaning on the wall
directly behind him with arms crossed, or sitting far above them

on a beam. Danny explained the procedure as best he could, but he could barely hear his own words.

"Rather than directing time, you have to listen to it. It'll tell you where the rift is, or where it's torn. Time's like threads woven into a pattern. It's your job to understand the pattern and make sure you patch it up right. Some mechanics think you can control time, but that's not how I see it. Time is in control of *you*. You just have to know how to let it guide you. How to *feel* it."

Brandon had always seemed intelligent, but Danny knew from the look in his dark eyes that he understood exactly what he was saying. Brandon would pass his assessment easily.

Brandon insisted they go to the pub for lunch, but Danny saw Colton's impatient face over his apprentice's shoulder and felt his own matching tug of frustration.

"In a minute. I'm going to take a quick walk to clear my head."

Danny waited until Brandon was gone before walking down the stairs. He sensed more than saw Colton follow him, barely noticing when Colton held up his coat so he could push his arms through the sleeves.

He stepped outside and shivered, his face already raw from the wind. Colton, at his side, probably didn't feel a thing in his billowing shirt. The spirit met Danny's eyes with a small shrug, as if asking, "What now?"

Not wanting to stray too far from the tower, Danny took Colton's hand and steered him toward the hedge. No one would see them there.

Danny wasn't quite sure where to begin, so he asked, "How've

you been?" It felt stupid, but as automatic as putting a teaspoon of sugar in his afternoon tea.

"The same as I ever am."

They turned the corner, heading in the direction of the Aetas statue. "Something's troubling you," Colton said as they slowed to a stop. "Can you tell me?"

Danny nodded and took a deep breath. It came in starts and stops, many of his words half-formed. He told Colton everything he'd learned: that Matthias had been lying to him—to everyone—and that the Maldon clock spirit was not destroyed, but in London.

Colton's eyes were wide when Danny finished. "If she's alive, she can fix her clock. You can free your father!"

Danny remained silent, and Colton's elated smile began to fade.

"You can't?"

"I don't know." Danny turned away. "The thing is, I trusted Matthias. I went to him when I missed my father, when I needed someone to tell me what the right thing to do was. He was always there for me, even when I didn't want him to be. To find out he was . . . all this time, he was hiding *this* . . ."

Danny's voice began to shake, and he coughed to hide it. "If Evaline can't convince him to let her leave London, what can *I* do? How do I even speak to him?"

Colton put his hands on Danny's shoulders. The air shivered around him, soft and comforting, like a cat's vibrating purr against skin.

"From what you've told me, Matthias sounds like a good man. Even if he's done this, there has to be a reason."

"Yes," Danny said, voice low. "He loves that spirit. He loves her so much he would sacrifice an entire town for her." *More than one town?* his mind whispered, but he shoved the idea away. "That's not being good. That's being bloody *selfish*."

He turned and ripped off the nearest clump of honeysuckle. He thought, coldly, that love was simply that—a handful of bruised flower petals. Beautiful and terrible and fleeting. Too easily snatched away, too easily ruined.

"Danny, stop." Colton took the crushed flowers from his fingers. His eyes were pinched and his voice sounded a little slower. "You'll find a way to solve this, I know you will. And I'll help. What can I do?"

Danny ran his hands through his hair until it stuck up in the back. He was wasting the time he had with Colton to complain instead of focusing on his next steps.

"I know what you can do." He brushed his thumb across Colton's jaw. "You can keep telling me what an idiot I'm being."

"You're not an idiot," Colton said. "You're upset. What's your plan for when you go back?"

Danny lifted his arms, like the Lead did when stumped. "Try to speak to Matthias, I suppose. If he won't listen, I'll have to tell the authorities, and I really don't want—What's the matter?"

Colton had suddenly convulsed, and shock overtook his face. His eyes grew pale and distant. He reached for Danny, but as soon as his fingers touched his shirt he jolted again and fell to the ground with a scream.

"*Colton!*" Danny fell to his knees beside him. Colton writhed against the ground, clutching at his chest. His eyes rolled toward the back of his skull.

Danny froze when he felt it. Not the pleasant shiver he experienced at Colton's touch, but a terrible shudder that jarred him to his marrow. Not a skip in time, but a total plunge into nothingness.

He looked up as a gray mantle spread across the sky, forming an unnatural veil that hid Enfield from the rest of the world. A concealing web of time.

I was in an accident.

Brandon came hurtling down the lane.

I got out.

Townspeople ran from their houses, staring up at the sky or looking toward the clock tower.

I'm safe now.

The lie drowned under the thundering of his heart as Danny struggled to lift Colton from the ground. He fumbled with the tower door and fell through the entrance when time looped, and he fell over and over until he was finally able to stumble inside. Brandon ran in after him, his eyes so large they were more white than brown.

"What happened?" Brandon demanded. "Who the hell is that?"

Danny held Colton protectively to his chest. But the truth

couldn't be hidden now. With a creeping sense of dread, Danny explained the truth about the limp boy in his arms.

He didn't think Brandon's eyes could get any bigger. "You— this thing—he's been here the whole time?"

Colton feebly stirred, trying to say Danny's name. He pointed at the stairs, or at least attempted to. Danny bounded up, Brandon following close behind.

"How long've you been keeping this from me? How come I've never seen him?"

Danny stopped in front of the clockwork. He took a few leaden steps toward the mechanism and sank to his knees, laying Colton gently on the floor. The spirit opened his eyes long enough to see what Danny saw: the stopped gears and cogs, and the empty space where the central cog normally turned.

Colton groaned and closed his eyes.

Danny didn't bother to check his timepiece. There was no point.

The town had officially Stopped.

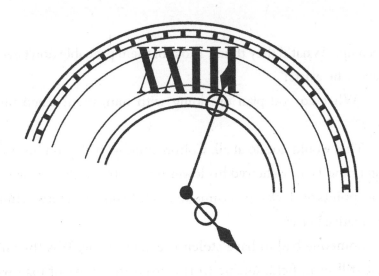

If time were still a moving thing, Danny would have said that with each second the crowd outside got bigger as Colton grew paler.

The clock had come to a complete standstill, and the town sat like a frozen gray bubble in the English countryside. Just like the moment when Shere had Stopped. Just like Maldon.

Danny could hear the frenzied townspeople beyond the door. He had brought Colton downstairs and lingered inside the tower with Brandon, trying to figure out what to do. With the buzz of the terrified people and Colton's strange shivering, it proved difficult.

"We can't just ignore them," Brandon hissed. "They have to know."

"They don't have to see him," Danny said, gesturing at Colton, who sat slumped on the stairs. He could barely keep his head up. "What'll they think? Most of them probably don't even believe he exists!"

"What do you plan on doing with him, then? Keep him here?"

That would not do at all. Colton couldn't be left on his own right now. Danny chewed his lower lip, frustrated that while the finer points of clock repair came so easily to him, he was woefully uncreative in a crisis.

Someone had to have stolen the central cog. Was the culprit still in Enfield, unable to run from the scene of his own crime? Or had he already left? Evaline had been able to escape a Stopped town, crossing the time barrier to the outside world. Was it because she was a spirit, or because she had been holding her cog? Yet the people in other Stopped towns, no doubt with access to their tower's central cog, had never been able to escape.

Danny clutched his head and groaned. He didn't *know*.

Time w^{ar}b^{le}d and they found themselves by the clockwork again, then everything ^{til}ted and they were back downstairs.

When he recovered, Brandon glanced at the door. "Maybe one of this lot stole it and now he's blending into the crowd. You know, to avoid suspicion? It's what I would do, if I'd done it."

"And did you do it?"

Brandon lifted his arms. "Search me all you like, but I don't have it."

Danny had seen Brandon run from the direction of the pub, not the tower. Danny looked at Colton, whose eyelids flinched in pain. He rubbed at his chest as if his heart was bothering him. In a sense, it was.

"All right," Danny said, "I think I know what to do. Brandon, do you trust me?"

The apprentice hesitated. "I suppose."

"You have to carry Colton to the outskirts of town. Right to the edge of the barrier. Wait there for me while I try to explain what's going on."

Brandon nodded. He bent to pick up Colton, but the spirit tried to push himself away.

"Colton, let him carry you. I promise I'll be right behind you."

Their eyes met, Colton's once-bright amber irises now dull. The spirit slumped, allowing Brandon to scoop him up, one arm under his legs, the other supporting his shoulders. Danny opened the side door and watched as Brandon slipped behind the hedge.

He gathered his courage and walked in the opposite direction, toward the raised voices. When the townspeople saw him, they immediately swarmed, as frantic as rats on a sinking ship.

"What's happening? Where's the time gone?"

"Can you fix it?"

"Are we trapped here are we trapped here are we trapped here are we—"

The questions kept repeating, and people winked in and out of view just as Colton did in his tower. One blink

here, another blink

there.

Danny held up his hands to ask for silence and miraculously

received it, except for the one man who couldn't pull out of his "are we trapped here" shouting loop. Clearing his throat, Danny touched his pocket where he could feel the indent of the small cog. It gave him resolve to speak.

"I know this is a frightening situation, and you want to know what's going on. The truth is, I can't tell you. I came here to check the clock, stepped out a moment, and came back to find the central cog missing." A few dismayed groans rose from the crowd. Mayor Aldridge started wringing his hands. "Whoever took the cog may still be in town. Everyone should be on the lookout for the thief and the central cog. When you find them, bring them here. My apprentice will know what to do."

The crowd split at once, like children on Easter morning to find eggs hidden around the yard. Danny slipped away.

He couldn't stay here. He needed answers, needed to confront Matthias. He also needed Colton in order to cross the barrier, yet the farther Colton was from his cog, the weaker he would become, and Danny didn't know—didn't want to find out—what happened to a clock when separated too long from its life force.

But in London, where time ran smooth and strong, Danny might have a better chance. The energy of Big Ben alone could power three clock towers, and Evaline had said it was a great help to her. If Evaline could survive with her cog and Big Ben nearby, surely Colton could feed off of the clock's power until his own was restored.

Danny's walk to the outskirts was warped. He sensed himself walking forward, then passing the same house three times, ...ed the village green then not recalling when he crossed the village green. The time fibers were frozen, gray, dead. He checked his timepiece. Time had Stopped at 11:14 in the morning. No matter how much time passed outside, in Enfield it would remain 11:14 until the cog was replaced.

Brandon waited just beyond the town line, where Enfield Chase became Greater London and the two time zones met. The border was divided by that strange gray wall. Colton lay on the ground, his skin now the shade of Danny's own.

Danny knelt beside him and swept his hair back, afraid for a moment that Colton wouldn't stir. But the spirit's eyes fluttered open, searching frantically for him. Danny tried to smile, and Colton's lips twitched in a heartbreaking attempt to return it.

"I know this'll make no sense," Danny said, loud enough so Brandon could hear as well, "but I have to take you out of Enfield."

Colton struggled to keep his eyes open. "Danny, no—"

"Are you mad?" Brandon snapped. "You know nothing can come in or out!"

"I have a theory I'd like to try. I think that so long as I'm holding onto a clock spirit—" he nodded to Colton— "I'll be able to pass through the barrier." After all, Evaline had done it.

"What'll that do to the town?"

"Nothing. I know it won't, because it's been done before." Not sparing much time for details, he filled Brandon in on what

he'd discovered in Matthias's house and how Evaline had escaped Maldon. The apprentice stared at him with parted lips.

"Come off it. There's no way that's true." Brandon glanced between Danny and Colton. "Is it?"

"That depends on how much you trust me."

Brandon was silent for a while, eyes flitting between the two of them, before he sighed. "You're too bleeding insane to be lying. Damn it. What'm I to do, then, while you're out there playing detective?"

"Danny, no," Colton whispered again. He plucked weakly at Danny's sleeve. "I can't."

"It's the only way I can get to London," Danny said. "Besides, you might be safer there. Brandon and the others will search for your cog."

Brandon grabbed Danny's arm. "You'll come back, won't you? You won't leave us here?"

"I'll be back. I promise."

Danny carefully lifted Colton. The spirit turned his head at the sound of the townspeople's voices. Danny saw the desire to stay in his pale eyes, to not abandon the people he had grown to love, generation after generation of Enfield families all watched over by a spirit who mourned their deaths and celebrated their births. Danny almost turned around, almost gave in to the same longing.

He forced himself to swallow. "We'll be back soon."

He hoped his theory was correct. Colton sagged in his arms as Danny pressed their bodies against the barrier. He braced him-

self to be rejected, electrocuted, something—but his shoulder sank into the grayness, and he gasped. Holding Colton tighter, he plunged through the barrier.

Colton's influence helped them both squeeze through the murky ocean of gray threads. It was a muted, colossal space, an impossible distance to cross. Veins of gold shot through the gray, slivers too thin for him to touch or feel, and in the distance he heard a muffled sound like waves crashing. There was a horrid weight in his chest, pressing all his organs together until he couldn't breathe.

And then they were on the other side.

Danny stumbled. When he turned, he faced a wall of gray, rising up into a dome with no hint of the town beyond. The familiar sensation of Big Ben's energy washed over him.

He let his forehead fall against Colton's. The spirit felt even lighter now, like his entire substance was dissolving. Danny drew in a shuddering breath and turned to where his father's auto sat waiting.

As he laid Colton in the backseat, the spirit opened his eyes. Danny stared at him for a helpless moment and touched the cog in his pocket. He drew it out and pressed it against Colton's palm. The pale hand closed around the little cog like a lifeline.

Halfway to London, it began to snow. Danny worried that Colton

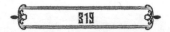

would catch his death of cold until he remembered that Colton did not function the way humans did.

Danny himself was frozen inside and out. He couldn't erase the image of that gray nothingness from his mind, the feeling of time stiff and strange as he passed through the barrier. Had the protesters snuck to Enfield? Why hadn't there been a bomb? Who'd want to steal a central cog?

He thought of his father, of Matthias, of the clock spirit who had started all of this. Evaline might not have a face that could launch a thousand ships, but Matthias had found reason enough to allow hundreds to suffer because of her. The fall of Troy, indeed.

Evaline had said Matthias was searching for a new clock tower for her. The suspicion that had latched onto him in Matthias's house reemerged.

One thing at a time. One bloody thing at a time.

A few hours had passed outside of Enfield before Danny crossed the barrier. Afternoon light was already fading to evening by the time he reached Kennington and rolled to a jerky stop in front of his house. He looked around in case anyone happened to be watching, but only spied a shadowed couple with a poodle on the corner and the tail of a neighbor's cat disappearing behind the next house over.

Danny clambered out and ripped his goggles off. He leaned over Colton, his breath bursting into clouds before his face, but the spirit didn't stir. The glow had finally left his body; he looked like a pale, sickly boy. The cog, however, seemed to have done some good.

Colton murmured Danny's name as he scooped him up in his arms.

"You're all right," Danny said, minding his head as he backed away from the auto. He checked the couple at the end of the street, but they were still lingering over their conversation as the poodle lifted its leg beside a letter box. "Come on. You'll have to meet my mother sooner or later."

Danny fumbled with Colton and his key, then pushed inside and shut the door with his back, calling for his mother. Judging by the clanging of pots in the kitchen, Leila was preparing dinner. She walked into the hall with a hard shove at the sticking kitchen door.

"There you are. I've been dying to tell you—" She stopped at the sight of her son carrying another boy in his arms.

"'Lo, Mum." Danny felt like he was ten again and had brought home a muddy frog. Except now the frog was a clock spirit. The situation was suddenly so ridiculous he couldn't stop a small laugh, which sounded dangerously like a sob. Leila hurried forward.

"What's all this, Danny?"

"He's sick. I'm going to carry him up to my room. Could you bring—?" He would have asked for a hot compress, tea, something of the sort, but those were for humans. What would an ailing clock spirit need?

His central cog, Danny thought bitterly.

Leila put the back of her hand against Colton's forehead. "He's like ice! Get him under the sheets quickly. I'll get the hot water going."

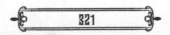

Danny did as his mother ordered, carrying Colton upstairs. He was glad he didn't have to answer questions right now, though knew he couldn't evade them forever.

His room was a mess, the floor littered with dirty socks, shirts, and crumpled bits of paper he'd used for meaningless sketches. He kicked away some of the debris as he made his way toward the narrow bed, which he hadn't bothered to make that morning. He wondered when he had last washed the sheets. Setting Colton down, he wished he had something better to offer.

Danny stared down at him, the once-golden boy now lying in the spot where Danny's nightmares found him, a manifestation of a new nightmare. Colton's eyes were always open, his mind always whirring. Now he was utterly still. Even though the spirit lay right before him, even though Danny could touch his cold cheek, he'd never felt so far away.

Danny had spoken of the riches of London, of the fantastical places beyond Enfield. What good were they if Colton was dying?

Dying. The word tore him open.

Still wearing his coat and cap, Danny drew the blankets up to Colton's chin and knelt beside him, taking his unresponsive hand. His mother appeared with a hot water bottle. She gave him a bemused look before placing the bottle under the sheets. Danny doubted it would have any effect, but didn't have the heart to say so. Colton was a son of time; he had no mother to care for him.

"Danny," Leila whispered, kneeling beside him. "Who is he?"

"Do you remember when I found out that Father Christmas

wasn't real, and you tried so hard to make me believe again?" She nodded, confused. "I imagine this is exactly how you felt then."

And he began to explain, right from the moment he accepted his first job at Enfield. Leila listened with pursed lips. She hadn't taken her hair out of its chignon yet, but a few curls framed her lean face. Her eyelashes quivered every so often, as though she wanted to react but prevented herself from doing so.

"I don't know why this is happening," he said, turning to Colton so he wouldn't have to take in her dark eyes. "This'll be news by morning. The Lead might call me in, and if Matthias is somehow involved . . . Mum, what do I do?"

He sat hard on the floor and pressed his forehead to his knees. His mother transformed from a statue to a woman again and tentatively touched his back.

"So they're real," she murmured. "Clock spirits. Your father mentioned them from time to time, and there was that whole affair with Matthias, but I didn't know . . ." She stared at Colton as her eyebrows furrowed, and he half worried she was about to tell him off for what he'd done.

"Are you sure, Danny? Do you really think Matthias has Maldon's clock spirit hidden here in London?" When Danny nodded, her breath caught.

"What do I do about Matthias? I can't just betray him." He turned cold again. "But he betrayed us, didn't he? He acted so sympathetic, and all this time—"

"Don't pass judgment yet, Danny." Yet Leila's face was firm, and he could see the lines in her skin like deepening cracks in fine china. "Let's try to settle this between us before we involve anyone else. I'll try giving him a ring."

"No, don't. I don't want him to know what we know. Not until I can track him down."

His mother gazed at Colton's prone body on the bed. Danny knew her focus wasn't on the clock spirit, but leagues away, on Maldon. Lost in the possibility of her husband's return. Danny kept one eye there, and one on Enfield—on the heart of the town itself, whose own heart was missing.

Danny wished he could offer his own as a replacement.

"Hello then, you've finally thought to ring me?" Cassie's voice, normally able to fill a room, came out strangely muted through the telephone wire.

He clutched the receiver in one clammy hand, holding the other end close to his mouth. "Cass? Listen, I've got to ask you a big favor. Will you come over?"

"What's the matter? You sound odd. Not the auto again, is it? Have you tried out the holster?"

"Can't explain through the telephone. Just come over." There was a pause, and he added, "Please."

"Hold on, I'll be over in a mo.'"

Danny hung up and peered out the window, catching a glimpse of ominous clouds. It would snow again today.

The house was freezing, so Danny wore his coat loosely over

his clothes. Climbing the steep stairs, taking care not to slip in his socks, he pushed his bedroom door open only to find Colton in the same position as he had left him.

Colton's skin was pale, as were his lips, and even his hair had lost its luster. A piece of metal in need of polishing. Danny pulled over his desk chair and sat. His body ached from lack of sleep.

The proximity of Big Ben seemed to be working. Sometimes Colton woke and had been able to exchange a few words with Danny over the course of the stressful night. Leila had been present for one such conversation, looking greatly disturbed when the spirit spoke. But Colton had politely said hello, and that it was nice to meet the mother of Danny, before he passed out again. Leila had tucked him in more thoroughly afterward.

Danny would never have been able to pass through Enfield's barrier without Colton, but he wondered if it had been a mistake to bring him here.

If all of this had been a mistake.

The guilt that weighed heavily on him was a hand against his chest, pushing him back, making him look at all that had happened since he first stepped foot in Colton's tower. This, too, he thought—*my fault.* He'd known that a mechanic and a clock spirit could never be together. But one kiss had tossed that knowledge like ashes to the wind.

He'd been lost in a chamber of his heart that bore no windows, blind to the outside world. His newfound happiness had burned so bright he hadn't seen the shadows it cast at the edges. Ignorant about what sacrifice truly meant until it was too late.

Because of his desires, Enfield had to pay the price.

But . . . that wasn't entirely fair. It wasn't only his desires. Colton had wanted it, too—had wanted to feel what the people of Enfield felt, the heat of laughter and the pleasure of dancing, the press of someone's hand against his own. To understand all of the emotions that had been denied him, to hold onto something as tight as he could as if that would make it his.

Surely that was worth something, even if it came at a cost.

Wasn't it?

Danny rubbed his dry, hot eyes and wondered if a fifth cup of tea would be appropriate. His stomach was too cramped to think of food.

Sighing, he checked to see that Colton was holding the small cog. That was also having a positive effect. Danny suspected that it acted as the central cog did for Evaline, although to a lesser degree.

Danny leaned over and touched Colton's cheek. Still cold, though he knew that didn't matter much to a spirit. It was disquieting to watch Colton and not see the rise and fall of breath.

"I could pretend," Colton had once offered, sticking out his chest and then drawing it back in. Danny had laughed until his belly hurt.

Why couldn't it be like the stories? In fairy tales there always seemed to be an obvious villain and an obvious hero. If Danny was the hero, who was the villain? Matthias? But he *knew* Matthias, and the man wasn't evil.

He hung his head, his thoughts a jumbled mess. Danny didn't

know what he would say to Matthias, or how to stop him if he tried to run away with Evaline.

Matthias had lied. His mother didn't understand. His father was trapped. Colton was dying.

Everyone leaves, in the end.

When he looked back at Colton, he thought of Sleeping Beauty and how one kiss had woken her from the enchantress's spell. Danny scooted to the edge of his chair and wiped sweaty palms on his trousers. He looked around. They were alone; his mother had reluctantly left for work. He swallowed and bent forward until his face hovered just above Colton's. Then, closing his eyes, he kissed him.

Even his lips were cold. When Danny broke away, there was no change, although Colton turned a little toward him. Danny shook his head, annoyed with himself for thinking a fairy tale cure could work.

The door opened below and Danny was beyond relieved to hear Cassie holler up. He jumped to his feet and met her at the bottom of the stairs.

"Will you tell me what's going on?" Cassie demanded. She wore her baggy work overalls, her hair done up in a thick braid.

Danny jerked his head toward the stairs for her to follow. Up in his bedroom, Cassie gasped at the sight of Colton.

"I didn't know what else to do," he said. He briefly told her what had happened in Enfield.

"Oh, Danny," she whispered.

At just that moment, Colton opened his eyes and searched

for Danny, frowning when he saw Cassie instead. Danny took his hand.

"I'm here."

"Are we going back now?"

"No, not yet. I have to find Evaline, the Maldon spirit. She'll be able to help. Cassie will take care of you while I'm gone." Colton looked at her again, and she waved weakly.

"I want to help," Colton croaked, attempting to rise to his elbows.

Danny gently held him down. "You can't do anything in the state you're in."

"But what if she's gone? If you take me with you, I'm sure I can find her."

Danny shook his head. "I don't think Matthias would let her leave the house."

Colton opened his mouth, but must have realized that Danny wasn't going to budge. He fell back against the pillow and closed his eyes with a grimace that twisted Danny's stomach even tighter.

"I promise I'll be back soon." Danny pressed his lips to Colton's forehead.

The spirit brushed his fingers over the back of Danny's neck. "Be safe."

Danny nodded and turned back to Cassie. "I know this isn't ideal, but I have to find Matthias and that clock spirit. It's the only way to understand what happened. Please, look after Colton until I'm back. He'll need protecting in case someone comes."

"Like who?" she demanded.

"I don't know, but I can't trust Matthias anymore, and I don't know if other mechanics can feel Colton's presence. If the Lead Mechanic suspects I did this, then the authorities might come, and . . . I know I'm asking a lot. You don't have to stay if you don't want to."

Cassie shivered, but not in fear. Not for herself, anyway.

"Will it be dangerous?" she asked.

Danny felt the burn of Colton's stare, waiting for his reply. "I don't know."

She breathed out through her nose. "Go on, then." She pulled a large wrench from her pocket and set it down with a satisfying *thud* on the desk. "We'll be all right here. Good luck."

Danny wanted to hug her, but there was only so much time. He nodded his thanks and hurried down the stairs. "And wear your holster!" she shouted after him.

Shoving on his boots, he pounded into the winter-clad streets of London.

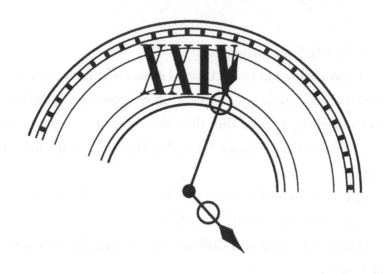

At this hour, Matthias was usually at the office filling out paperwork or training the apprentices. As Danny walked from his parked auto to the blue-trimmed house, he wondered which would be worse: not finding Matthias or confronting him on his doorstep.

Danny forcefully knocked. He stood there, tense, waiting to hear the scrape of the lock. It never came. Danny stepped away and tried to peer into the window, but the curtains were too thick.

The clock spirit was here, he was sure of it. Matthias would never allow her to roam London, especially not once the news that Enfield was Stopped began to spread, if it hadn't already.

Nothing for it, then. Danny breathed in deeply, steeled himself, and kicked the door.

"Mummy!" a little boy shouted. He was walking toward the

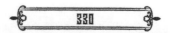

park, a woolen cap hiding the tips of his large ears. "That man is breaking in, look!"

The mother swung a suspicious glare on Danny.

"Ah—no," Danny said, perhaps a little too loudly. "I've only forgotten my keys, and my mother's out. I suppose I'll have to wait for her."

Danny settled down on the front step, feigning boredom. The woman stared at him a moment longer, then tugged the little boy along. Danny waited until they entered the park, then jumped to his feet and squeezed into the little alley at the side of the house.

Idiot, he told himself. *The police are going to come and haul you off at this rate.*

He found a rubbish bin in the alley and dragged it over to a small, square window. As he climbed onto the bin, it wobbled alarmingly under his weight. He pressed his hands against the wall with a moan of dread. Wishing he had an insect's ability to stick to walls, he reached up and banged on the windowsill with the heel of his hand. It took a while, accompanied by some pained curses, but eventually the window eased up enough for him to wiggle his fingers through.

Danny pushed the sash open. Hoisting himself up, he almost fell onto the bin, and scrambled to use whatever strength he had to maneuver his way through. He toppled forward into a tiled washroom, nearly smashing his head against a corner of the sink.

"Danny Hart, you are not made for burgling." He stood, wincing, and stepped into the blue-painted hallway.

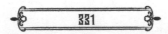

"Evaline?" he called, softly at first, then louder. He wandered into the still-messy sitting room and paused, taking in the destruction. The room was filled with the echoes of smashed glass and the sounds of his own rage.

Danny backed away and checked the kitchen, then eyed the stairs uneasily. The plots of detective novels passed through his mind, ones in which the detective thinks he's close to a clue and gets bludgeoned for his trouble. But though he took the stairs slowly, fist raised to strike a potential adversary, nothing happened. He lingered on the landing just to be sure, then peeked into the rooms. No one was here.

"Evaline?" he called again. He thought he heard a muted thumping from outside. Then he realized the sound was coming from right above him, through the ceiling.

He looked frantically for a way to get to the attic, racing back and forth along the landing until he noticed a cord. Tugging with all his might, the stairs descended with a drawn-out creak and a small cloud of dust.

He hurried up the stairs. The attic was a spacious upper room that Matthias used as storage space, judging from the boxes and bags flung haphazardly about. But there were new additions: a pallet on the floor, some books, a lamp, and a clock spirit.

"What are you doing up here?" Danny demanded as Evaline hurried toward him. "Where's Matthias?"

Her face fell. "Danny, I'm sorry. He's going to do something terrible. You have to stop him before it's too late."

Something beat low and dark in his chest. "It's already too

late. Where's your cog?" She grabbed it from underneath the pallet. "Good. Come on, I need to get you away from here."

"But Matthias—"

"There's a clock spirit who needs your help. Will you come with me or not?"

She looked lost, pale fingers curled between the spokes of her cog. Still, she nodded and followed him down the stairs. She disappeared into what he guessed was her bedroom and returned wearing a green dress. Her cog was in a satchel at her waist.

"He's done it, then," she said when she met Danny's gaze. He nodded, and she set her jaw. "Take me to this spirit."

The auto shuddered but accelerated quickly over the frosted pavement. Cassie's new holster dug into Danny's shoulder. At his side, Evaline's hands were folded protectively over the satchel in her lap.

"Why on earth did he lock you in the attic?" Danny asked. "I thought he loved you."

She gave him a tiny smile, as if to say that he had a lot left to learn. "I told him what you'd said, and how I wanted to return to Maldon. He . . . didn't take it well. When I asked why he kept the truth from me, he said he didn't want to upset me with the news.

"He knew it was wrong, he admitted it himself, but the thought of being abandoned—" Her voice cracked, and Danny squirmed uncomfortably in his seat. "He said he couldn't live

through that again. He couldn't survive being left alone a second time.

"I said I understood more than anyone, but that it wasn't an excuse, and I would return to Maldon. Matthias wouldn't have it." Her voice lowered. "He forced me into the attic. I begged him to stop, but he wouldn't listen. He told me not to worry, that his plan would work somehow."

"Plan?"

"He's told me about a faulty clock tower in Enfield. I thought the spirit had abandoned its tower, like I did mine. Maybe to transfer to the new tower being built. That's how he made it seem. But that isn't true, is it?"

"No," Danny said. "I told Matthias about the clock tower in Enfield. I was assigned there to help with repairs."

Danny felt dizzy, and it was all he could do to focus on the road before him. "I think Matthias planted the bombs." Even though he had no way to confirm it, voicing the thought felt finite, irreversible. "He wanted to get rid of another clock spirit to have a tower free for you. Maybe he thought if he broke a tower's central cog with a bomb, the spirit of that tower would disappear and he could install your cog instead. All this time I've been thinking the protesters had something to do with the attacks, or Tom and George, but Matthias could have easily used them as a cover."

Matthias had lined up the pieces for him like the mystery books he so loved, waiting for Danny to put the wrong ends together.

He swallowed hard. "And he couldn't use the new Maldon tower because he's exiled there."

"So there *was* a new tower?"

"Yes, but your darling Matthias destroyed it." But why, apart from not being able to use it? Another thing he didn't know. The blood pounded painfully in his head. "He killed Lucas. He nearly killed me, and Daphne."

Danny glanced at Evaline, the wind whipping their hair as the auto sped through the streets of London. Her eyes were round.

"What? He ..." She trailed off, wandering down that particular trail of thought until it came to its grim end. When she spoke again, she sounded leagues away. "He's been so strange these last few months. I'll catch him staring at nothing, or weeping, or locked in his bedroom working. And he doesn't even try to reassure me anymore. His eyes are emptier than when I first met him."

Danny's throat tightened. After a moment he said, "I understand how Matthias feels, you know. The spirit in that tower, he and I ..."

She nodded for him to go on.

"Matthias knew the bombs weren't working, so he stole the Enfield spirit's central cog. The spirit is with me now, in London."

"Without his cog?"

"My apprentice is searching for it. I wanted Colton—that's my spirit—to stay with me, to stay safe. You told me the tower here in London helps you. It's helping him, too."

They didn't speak for the rest of the drive. When the auto

shuddered to a stop, Danny turned to Evaline. She gazed solemnly back at him.

"I may be in the same position as Matthias," he said, "but I won't make his mistakes. He's going to try to put you in that clock tower, but if he does, Colton might disappear. I'm going to do everything I can to stop that from happening. Do you understand?"

She nodded. Without her tower, Evaline was as pale as Colton. Her tired eyes made her look older than the woman she would have been if she were human.

Danny called for Cassie as soon as he opened the front door. She came out of his bedroom holding her wrench and started when she got a look at Evaline.

"Blazes, that's her, isn't it?"

Danny didn't answer; he ran up the stairs to Colton's side. There was no change in him, though his eyelids flickered when he heard Danny's voice.

"He's the same," Cassie confirmed. "Hello there, are you Miss Evaline?"

The clock spirit had followed them, drawn to Colton's presence in the house. She gave him a brief, sympathetic glance before turning to Cassie.

"Yes, that's me. Do you know, too?"

"Cassie can be trusted," Danny said. "She's been taking care of Colton." He nodded toward the spirit in his bed. "If you wouldn't mind?"

Evaline drew near the edge of the bed. Colton struggled to

open his eyes, sensing her presence they way she sensed his. A tiny ripple went through the air as she walked, a slight tug from the cog. Even Danny felt drawn toward it.

Evaline leaned over Colton until he opened his eyes fully. When he saw her, he made a small noise of recognition.

"Evaline," he whispered hoarsely.

"Colton."

"Do they know each other?" Cassie murmured to Danny, who shook his head. They were products of time, more or less made of the same substance. Of course they knew each other. In a way, they were each other.

Evaline removed her cog from her satchel and set it carefully on Colton's chest. He tensed, fingers curling into the sheets, but his expression soon smoothed into relief. He opened his eyes and nodded.

"It helps him a little," she said, turning to Danny and Cassie, "but it's not a solution. Will you return to his town soon?"

"We have to. But I need to find Matthias first."

"I don't know where he is," she admitted with a frown. "He said he was going to the office to resign, but that was hours ago."

"He—? Damn it." Danny walked in a tight circle and pushed his hands through his hair. "If he *did* go to Enfield, we'll find him when we bring Colton back, but I can't risk leaving until I know for sure Matthias isn't in London. Otherwise I might never get Colton's cog back."

As Evaline tried to make Colton more comfortable, Danny led Cassie downstairs. They speculated on Matthias's whereabouts and wrote up a list of places Danny could check. Danny often looked out the window, half-expecting Matthias or the police to be coming up the walk. He crept upstairs to check on the clock spirits, but they never seemed to move. What was hours to Danny and Cassie was but a minute to the spirits.

Danny's mother came home in the early evening, her coat slipping off one shoulder and her hair a rumpled mess.

"The news is all over," she said, setting down her bag. "Oh, hello, Cassie. Everyone knows that Enfield is Stopped. You should hear them going on about it, not knowing a thing, and the protesters all up in arms again. I heard there was a riot in Hanover Square. It was all I could do to keep from looking like I knew something. Did you find Matthias? How's Colton?"

She was about to go upstairs to check when Danny blocked her way. "Matthias wasn't home. Colton is fine. I mean, he's not, but we're still sorting it out."

Leila clucked her tongue. "You best sort it out fast. I don't know how long we can keep this up." She headed into the kitchen.

He and Cassie shared a look. "I should be heading home," she whispered. "My mum'll worry. And speaking of mums, you need to speak to yours."

Danny wanted to cling to Cassie, to beg her not to go, but he knew she was right.

She wrapped her arms around Danny's neck and held on tight. "Ring if you need me." She promised to check on them tomorrow before she slipped quietly out the front door.

Danny squared his shoulders and walked into the kitchen.

His mother was nervously washing the dirty teapot, needing something to do with her hands. He tended to do the same thing.

"Mum, I need to tell you something."

Leila set the wet teapot on the counter. "What is it?"

Danny took a deep breath. "Evaline is here. The Maldon clock spirit."

It was a good thing his mother wasn't holding the teapot, or else she would have dropped it. She swayed and reached for the back of the nearest chair, leaning heavily on it.

"She's *here*? The Maldon spirit—here?"

"Yes. She's upstairs with Colton."

Leila stared at the tabletop. She pushed herself upright.

"She has to go back. You have to take her to Maldon, Danny."

"Mum, wait—"

"I swear, if you don't—"

He grabbed her arms. "Listen to me! She's our only chance to save Colton. If I take her back to Maldon, who knows what Matthias will do with Colton's cog? He might destroy it, and then Colton will . . ."

Leila grew quiet, and his hands slipped away.

"I know, Mum. I know it's hard. But we've got to let her sort things out with Matthias. If we take her to Maldon now, he'll do something rash."

Leila swallowed audibly. "Danny, how could you do this?"

The words reopened the wound inside him. It bled a fresh wave of fear through his veins, pulsing *your fault, your fault, your fault.*

It was a struggle to get the words out. "Do what?"

"You had to know what would happen, getting involved with . . ." She waved her hand at the ceiling, in the direction of Danny's room. "You've gone and tangled yourself up with a clock spirit, and now Enfield's suffering for it. Just like Maldon suffered when Matthias had his fun. How could you do it when you knew what would happen?"

They were the same words he'd told himself, but coming from his mother, they took on a whole new existence. They were living things with teeth, eating away at what precious defenses he had left. Danny held his elbows, staring at the floor. He saw what she could not: sunlight through a clock face, the pages of a fairy tale book, a dance across the tower floor.

"I'm so disappointed, Danny." Her mouth trembled. "Your father taught you better than this. If he could see you now . . ."

The frail cage Danny had built around himself crumbled with a breath. His nerve endings were suddenly exposed, electric.

"Do you think I decided this? That I woke up and thought, you know, that clock spirit's rather nice, maybe I'll fancy him? You know it takes more than that. It takes *time*. A shared look, a . . . a shared story. And before you know it, you're heading toward something you never saw coming, and when it's there, it's just . . . it . . . takes you away."

Danny had been shouting, but by the time he finished, his voice was little more than a whisper. He couldn't bear to look at her.

"I didn't choose this," he said.

The kitchen was silent for so long he thought they'd turned to stone. Then Leila said, haltingly, "I didn't say it was a choice."

"You may as well have," he growled. "I know you think it. And if you're going to hate me for it, I'd rather you forget I'm your son. Lord knows you've done a pretty good job of that already."

She took a step back, her eyes wide. "Danny, don't say such a thing!"

He glared at her, feeling not like Danny Hart, but someone else using his voice. "Matthias was selfish for keeping Evaline. You were selfish when you chose to go to Chelmsford. And I was selfish, too, wanting something I couldn't have. But I'm doing what I can to save Enfield *and* Maldon. In order to save Colton *and* Dad. Don't compare me to Matthias, Mum. Don't blame me for something I haven't done."

Leila looked away. Danny moved to the stove, angrily preparing another pot of tea. It came as naturally as breathing.

"It isn't his fault."

They both turned at the sound of Evaline's voice. The spirit stood in the kitchen doorway.

Leila opened her mouth, but Danny rushed to speak first; he couldn't trust his mother not to drive Evaline from their house. "How's Colton?"

"Worse, I'm afraid. If we find Matthias I can ask what he's done with the cog, but I don't think he would tell me. Not after—"

"Why did you leave?"

Evaline turned from Danny to his mother. Leila was breathing hard through her nose, her fists clenched.

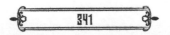

The clock spirit dropped her eyes. "It's difficult to explain."

"Difficult to explain? There's nothing *to* explain. The town's suffered—we've suffered—because of you. You have to go back. You have to free my husband!"

Danny stepped between them. "Mum, wait. She didn't know that the town would Stop, and Matthias told her it had been fixed. Blame him, not her."

"She's still responsible for her actions. Leaving . . . leaving Christopher there . . ." She almost gave in to tears, but collected herself at the last moment. "She's the most selfish of us all."

"If Matthias had just told her—"

"No," Evaline interrupted. "No, she's right. This is my mistake to fix." She closed her eyes, regaining control of herself, and then returned her gaze to Leila. "I'm sorry," she said, "for Stopping the town and for preventing your husband from coming home. If I had known, I would never have left. I only had eyes for Matthias, and I see now that I was foolish. Perhaps clock spirits are not quite so different from humans after all."

Danny touched his mother's arm. "It's not like we could help it. You said so yourself: wouldn't you do anything for the one you love?"

Leila looked at him. Her eyes were vague and somber, but gradually something shifted, a curtain pulled back. He caught her gaze flickering almost imperceptibly to the ceiling. Toward his room.

After a moment, she turned away, crossing her arms low over her chest.

"Just as long as you return to Maldon."

"I will," Evaline said softly.

Leila slumped down into a chair. Danny glanced at Evaline.

"Can you give us a moment?"

The spirit nodded. She returned to his bedroom, her step so light that Danny didn't even hear her on the stairs that normally creaked under his and his mother's weight.

"It all seems so impossible," Leila whispered. "I've spent three years trying to convince myself I'd never see him again. Now he's right within my reach, but I still can't touch him."

Danny knelt before his mother. "I haven't done a very good job filling in for Dad, but I promise we'll get him back."

She sniffed and dabbed at one eye with her sleeve. "What's this nonsense? Your father would be proud, seeing you take charge like this. You sounded like him just then."

Unable to meet her eyes, he stared at her shoulder instead. "It's my fault he went. My fault he's gone."

Leila grew very still. When he finally mustered the courage to look up, her tears had finally escaped.

"Why did I ever say that to you?" she asked, her voice thick. "I couldn't think. I couldn't do anything." She exhaled shakily. "Couldn't be the mother you needed."

She reached for him, hesitant, unsure if he'd let her touch him. But he didn't move, so she swept his hair back, just as she'd done when he was little. Tears continued to fall from her lower lashes. "I'm so sorry, Danny."

He kept blinking, his vision fuzzy. "You were right. It was my fault."

"No," she whispered. "It's not your fault, Danny. Your father was going to go to Maldon either way. Even if you'd told him not to go, it wouldn't have changed his mind."

He expected some relief—released pressure like a soap bubble popping—but all the conversation brought him was a weight heavier than before. The weight of three silent years. The weight of an empty house.

"Please forgive me," she murmured, her fingers trembling against his face. "Please."

The words were already waiting on his tongue. "I do, Mum. I forgive you."

The weight eased. Perhaps not entirely, but enough.

They both took a deep breath. Not an ending. Not fully a beginning. But something.

The kitchen door opened. Danny stood at the frightened look on Evaline's face.

"He's getting worse," she said. "He's . . . fading."

A jolt of terror struck Danny in the stomach. He ran past her, up the stairs, to Colton's side.

Evaline was right: he was fading. Danny could practically see through his blurred edges. Colton had a hand clutched at his chest, his face screwed up in pain. He flickered, his entire body stuttering like a lamp burning with too little oil.

Danny tried to touch him. It was like touching air. A burst of breath escaped him, a dry sob.

What do I do? How do I save him?

Distantly, across the river, the slow peal of bells began to sound. Big Ben was chiming.

Danny slowed his breaths. Fought to be calm. He turned and found his mother and Evaline watching from the door.

"We need to take Colton to Big Ben," he decided.

His mother blinked. "Big—? What, you mean St. Stephen's?"

"I think it'll give Colton the strength to return to Enfield. Besides, I've got to figure out what to do about Matthias, and Evaline can't stay here. If Matthias is in London, he'll check here, I'm sure of it. If not him, then the police."

Leila bit her lower lip, but Evaline nodded resolutely.

"You can stay with Cass," he told his mother. "Just in case."

"Matthias would never hurt us, Danny. He's done so much for us."

"Yes, like keeping Dad trapped." That silenced her.

Fighting down his alarm, he turned back to Colton and tried to smooth down his hair. Colton's eyes struggled open.

"We're going for a ride," Danny said.

"Are we . . . going to the London tower?" Colton asked in a slurred voice. "You told me about it. Big Ben."

"That's the one. Make sure you keep hold of that cog." He carefully scooped him up in his arms. The spirit weighed nothing at all.

At the front door, Leila hugged Danny as best she could with Colton in his arms. "Be safe. Come back as soon as you can."

"Mum? What news did you want to tell me yesterday?"

"Oh." She sighed. "They chose me for the job at Chelmsford."
It wasn't even painful anymore. "Will you take it?"

Her dark eyes rested on him, then on Colton, then on Evaline.
"I haven't made up my mind quite yet."

They filed out into the night. Danny looked around, wary.
Still no sign of Matthias. He settled Colton in the backseat and
prepared for the drive to Parliament Square, hoping for a smooth
ride and an easy entrance to the tower. More than that, he hoped
for Brandon to hurry and find Colton's cog before it was too late.

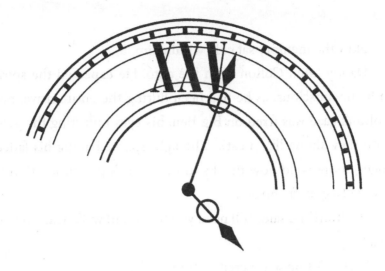

Τ he tower was lit a brilliant orange-gold, the clock faces shining like four separate eyes watching over a sleepy London.
Danny was not exactly sure what made the clock glow this way
at night, but he had a suspicion that the power of the spirit kept
it going.

Guards were posted at the entrances to the Parliament building. They would be more alert after the disaster near Maldon,
but Danny still had his mechanic's badge, which gave him access
to the tower at any time of day—or night. He hoped.

He had only ever visited Big Ben during daylight hours,
mostly for training. Once, before he had become an apprentice,
Danny had brought his father the packed lunch he'd forgotten
at home as an excuse to spend time inside the tower. Matthias
had been with Christopher then, the two men laughing as Danny
asked one excited question after another.

Now the memory sat cold within him.

Danny lifted Colton from the auto. He expected the spirit to be unconscious, as he had been during the entire drive, but Colton's gaze was fixed on Big Ben, his eyes reflecting the gold until they shone like a cat's. The light sparked along his faded edges, more solid now thanks to the tower's proximity. Danny released a grateful breath.

"Colton?" he said. "I'll need you to try and walk. Can you do that?"

"Yes," Colton whispered. "I think so."

Evaline stood to one side as Danny set Colton on his feet. The spirit wobbled, held onto Danny for a moment, then nodded as if to say he would be all right. Danny longed to keep the feeling of Colton's hand on his chest, but it slipped away far too soon.

The tower was huge. The base, like Colton's, was built of brick with limestone cladding; the rest was a spire of cast iron. The opal glass of the four faces, surrounded by large iron frames, beamed at the sprawling city below. Underneath each dial, a Latin inscription had been etched: DOMINE SALVAM FAC REGINAM NOSTRUM VICOTIAM PRIMAM.

Lord save Victoria the First. Queen Victoria had been the first to have her name carved into a tower, her name now etched into history and time itself.

He led the way to the tower's back entrance, the one reserved for mechanics. Two guards were stationed there. Danny broke out in a sweat as they approached. He could pass Colton off as

an apprentice, but Evaline was another matter. She looked older, like a mechanic, but had no badge.

Danny glanced over his shoulder. Colton was still a little unsteady, but his excitement gave Danny hope. He focused on what to say. *"Hello there, lovely night. No? Well, I suppose it is a bit nippy. Oh, them? Yes, they're with me, not to worry. I've been called over to give a quick demonstration, orders straight from the Lead. The boy wants to be an apprentice, but his mother's not so sure. Mind letting us in?"*

But when he stood before the guards, the words flew from his mind. They blinked owlishly at him.

"I need to get in," he said simply, showing his badge. They peered at it, gave a glance at the two figures behind him, and waved them through.

"That was easier than I expected," Danny murmured as they climbed the stairs to the belfry. The Lead must not have filed his dismissal paperwork yet. "Don't let your guard down. There may be mechanics up here."

As it turned out, there were none. The tower was empty.

The echoes of the tower's *ticks* and *tocks* were as soothing as the patter of rain on a quiet night. In the belfry, four quarter bells hung ready to chime the next hour. Danny spotted the Great Bell, or rather, the true Big Ben.

He was afraid Colton would have a difficult time climbing the stone steps, but the tower gave the spirit strength. His legs propelled him forward, the faintest hint of gold returning to his body. Colton gazed around in wide-eyed wonder. Danny felt a

twinge of sadness, and wasn't sure why until he saw the longing on Colton's face.

The clock room was more spacious than Colton's. There were no abandoned, empty boxes here, no dust building up in the corners. The clock faces surrounding them were a marvel. Danny remembered standing up here for the first time, simultaneously terrified by the height and awed by the spectacle. The faces glowed in the nighttime darkness, a reminder that that the city was safe.

The people of Enfield did not have that luxury.

Clenching his jaw, Danny directed Colton toward the middle of the room where he could best absorb the natural energy that flooded the space.

"Feel it?" Danny murmured, squeezing Colton's upper arms. The spirit nodded, his eyes brighter, more like their familiar amber shade.

"How can I not? It's everywhere. It's . . . life." Danny watched Colton walk from clock face to clock face, taking in the sight he had only dreamed of seeing. Evaline looked around, her face a little less grave.

"You've never been here, have you?" Danny asked her. "Even though Matthias has kept you in London for so long."

"I haven't been out much, no," she replied. "He's terrified of someone realizing. Too late for that, though." She gazed up where the ceiling arched. "It's a wonderful thing, isn't it? This tower. Mine seems so insignificant in comparison."

"So does mine," Colton agreed sadly.

Danny bristled. "Don't say that. You both have fine towers with fine mechanics looking after them."

Colton smiled. "Sorry, Danny. It's just so grand."

"It can be grand all it likes, but it doesn't make your towers any less impressive. You're important to so many people. Both of you are."

At the reminder, their smiles slipped and they each turned away, their relief short-lived. Danny could have kicked himself.

"We'll get this sorted out, don't worry."

"How?" asked Evaline.

"I . . ." There was a terrifying blankness within him, feeding on his thoughts and making them disappear like a magician's trick. As soon as he began to muster up an idea, it dispersed into smoke. "I don't know."

The words were small, but affected them all in some way. Colton lowered his head, Evaline closed her eyes, and Danny stood with buzzing fingertips and a creeping sense of failure.

"Would switching towers work?" Colton eventually asked.

Danny made an effort to catch and hold onto that thought, but it led down a dark road. "There's no record of it ever happening, and I'd rather not risk finding out. Even if it were possible, I'm not going to settle for that. Matthias is a criminal." He traced his scar. "He shouldn't live a carefree life in Enfield. And you wouldn't want to give up your town, would you?"

Colton shook his head.

Danny paced around the clock room, sometimes meeting

Colton's eyes. Every so often the spirit rubbed at his chest. That worried Danny even more.

I'm going to lose him.

It was a whisper at first, then thunder. Bringing Colton here was only a temporary solution, the same as running cool water over a burn and knowing that as soon as you took it away, the pain would come rushing back. Unavoidable.

The longer he stayed here, the less chance they had of making it through this.

Finally, Colton came to Danny's side and took his hand. "Stand still a moment. You'll get dizzy."

"I don't know what to do," Danny whispered, not bothering to hide the way his voice trembled. "Colton, I don't know what to do."

"How can I help?" Colton asked. "I feel so useless. It's *my* cog, and I should be fighting for it."

"I'm your mechanic. It's my responsibility to repair you."

"You've already done too much for me. Matthias was caught because he did too much for Evaline." He brushed a thumb over Danny's knuckles. "I refuse to get you in trouble. I can handle this on my own."

"Don't be ridiculous. You can't do anything in the state you're in. You can barely walk!"

He knew he'd said the wrong thing only when the words were out of his mouth. Colton's face shut like a door before he dropped Danny's hand and turned away.

Evaline looked between them. "Some advice: take whatever

time you have together before it's gone. In case the worst should happen."

Her words were stingingly blunt, but effective. Danny followed Colton to the southern clock face, where the spirit had retreated. His silhouette against the light made Danny's chest ache, as if he were already too far away, out of Danny's reach.

They stood side by side in silence and looked out over the city, the winking lanterns like fairy lights, the coils of smoke like the aftereffects of spells, the serpentine curve of the Thames glittering in the moonlight. The view from Enfield was so small and simple in comparison, but Danny couldn't help but long for it now, even with this vision spread out before him.

"I'm sorry," Danny mumbled at last. "I shouldn't have said that."

He wondered if Colton would have sighed, had he been able. "No, you're right. I'm next to useless. Even in my tower, all I'm good for is keeping time running. And I can't even do that properly."

"Don't say that. Look at all you do for Enfield. The people dancing on the green, the couples falling in love, the children growing up. That's you, Colton. You're giving them life."

Colton's eyes flinched with pain, feeling the pull of his town so far away, the need to bring that life back.

"We'll do this together," Danny said. It had been apparent from the start, he realized. Colton helping him during those first Enfield assignments, putting his trust in Danny. Only together could they mend what was broken.

"But what can I do?"

"When we find Matthias, you'll have to convince him to return the cog. Maybe if he sees what he's done to you, he'll change his mind."

Colton looked skeptical, but took Danny's hand again, threading their fingers together. There was something slow and somber in the touch, as if Colton thought what Danny refused to—that this could be the last time. Their last moment alone.

"I like London," Colton said, his eyes heavy and warm and golden, a late afternoon sun about to set. "I wish I could stay here."

If only he knew that the same wish was branded on Danny's heart. "I wish you could, too. I've told you so much about it, and yet all you've seen is my bedroom and this bloody old clock."

"Hey now, what's so terrible about this clock?"

Danny jumped. Behind them stood a tall, broad man with a blond beard. He wore a workman's outfit of brown trousers, white shirt, and tan vest. The man's light brown eyes traveled from Colton to Evaline before settling on Danny with a knowing gleam.

"S-sorry," Danny said, "I didn't think anyone would be here at this hour." Danny blinked once, twice. "Hold on, I know you. You're one of the tower mechanics." He remembered asking the man whether he preferred the name Big Ben or St. Stephen's.

"Not quite," the man said with barely concealed amusement.

"But I saw you when I was an apprentice here. I'm sure of it."

Colton tugged on his sleeve. "Danny," he whispered, "he's the spirit."

Danny stared. Looking closer, he saw that the man's shirtsleeves were rolled to his elbows, and a tattoo—or what looked like a tattoo—circled one thick arm: Domine Salvam Fac Reginam Nostrum Vicotiam Primam.

When the spirit who wanted to be called Big Ben winked, Danny rocked back on his heels, his face burning.

So much for being a detective.

"We're sorry to intrude," Evaline said, sounding humble in the man's presence, which was definitely big. His smile alone flooded the room like a blast of heat, and Danny swore the clock faces glowed brighter.

"No need to be sorry. I like the company. Couldn't help but overhear your dilemma, though. What are two spirits doing outside their towers in the first place?"

Colton and Evaline explained while Danny lingered shyly in the background. He wondered how many people Big Ben had revealed himself to over the years, and if any of them had been quicker to catch on.

"Well, now, that makes sense. I've felt you in the city for a while, but I wasn't sure why. I felt *you* just recently," Big Ben said, turning to Colton. "I know this mechanic fellow you talked about. I've seen him here working and training young mechanics. He didn't strike me as the type to turn rotten."

"That's just it," Evaline said. "He isn't rotten, not at all. He's only done something selfish. As have I."

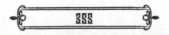

"As humans tend to," Big Ben mused, "but not so much spirits." Evaline ducked her head. "You love this human?"

"I do."

"But you also love your town."

She nodded, her long hair swaying. "Yes."

He turned to Colton again. "And you?"

Colton looked over his shoulder at Danny, longing in the shade of his eyes, misery in the shape of his mouth.

"Yes," he said quietly.

Big Ben rolled his eyes heavenward. "Hopeless creatures, the lot of you."

"We're aware of that," Danny grumbled, pulling Colton back and taking his place. "The question is what to do now."

Big Ben considered the matter. He began to slowly pace the room, and Danny worried the spirit might take hours before he came up with anything useful. But only a moment later he said, "There is no right answer."

"What do you mean?" Danny asked.

"I mean," Big Ben said, "that time itself is the answer. You can't force something to occur in the future because you'd like it to, just as you can't go back and force the past to change. There are many branches of time reaching from your bodies—I can see them attached to one another. Humans call it fate, but it's nothing so poetic as that. It's simply time. Time, and the decisions you make as it passes, which in turn make history. When one decision becomes impossible, the thread snaps, leaving you fewer and fewer choices.

"Anything can happen. You could return to Maldon, or your cog might be destroyed," he said to Evaline and Colton, respectively. "The men you love may die. Both, or just one." Colton gave Danny a horrified look. "You won't know until it happens, and that's when you'll know the right thing to do. Because it'll be the *only* thing you can do. And that becomes your fate."

"You're a real bloody comfort," Danny muttered, rubbing a hand over Colton's back. "What about an *actual* solution?"

"Thought I gave you one."

"No wonder they call you Big Ben. Big Headed, more like."

"Never heard that one before." The spirit smiled broadly. "Listen, mechanic. Time is the language of all things. It is everything you see, hear, touch. Treat it carefully."

Danny couldn't tell whether he meant time as a whole, or if he meant Colton. He supposed they were one and the same.

"And remember," Big Ben said, looking straight at Danny. "You have more control than you think."

The clock struck eleven and the four great bells began to carol the hour. Danny felt the floor vibrate with the chimes and stood rooted to the spot, surrounded on all sides by the booming, mesmerizing sound. In the chimes they heard something more than bells, something like what the spirit had been trying to tell them: time moves, and so does life, for good or ill. They could stay up here and wonder, or they could go and see what would come to pass.

When the last ringing echo faded into silence, they turned back to Big Ben, but he had disappeared.

Danny was reluctant to move and break the spell, but he roused himself with a shake of his head. "Right. We best be going."

"To Enfield?" Colton asked hopefully.

"To Enfield. But first I want to check if Matthias has been by the house."

"Yes," said a new voice behind them, "he has."

They whirled around. Matthias stood on the landing, blue eyes fixed on Danny. They briefly took in Colton and then settled on Evaline. His shoulders slumped.

"Why did you leave, Eva? You said you understood."

Evaline had frozen at the sight of him, but his pleading tone coaxed her to speak. "Matthias, this is wrong. You know it is. I thought I understood at first, but now that I know the truth, how can I?" She swung her head from side to side, a dreamer gradually waking up. "You've destroyed my town. All those people I loved and cared for are trapped because of you. And because of me."

Matthias opened his mouth to respond, but guilt stole his words. Danny saw it in his eyes, in the curve of his shoulders.

Evaline shifted her satchel behind her. "I have to fix things. If you truly love me, you'll let me do this."

Matthias took a deep breath. "If you go," he said, "I'll never see you again. You know that. Would you really leave if it meant never being together again?"

She turned her face away.

"Eva . . ."

"Don't do this to me, Matthias. Please."

"I can't be alone again. I can't lose you." He reached for her hand, then thought better of it. "When Alice . . . when she . . . I thought that was it for me. But now I have you. You're all I have left."

Evaline was silent. Matthias tensed, and Danny worried he would spring forward and drag her away from the tower by force.

"Matthias," Danny called. The man snapped his head around. "How could you do this to us? I thought I could trust you. You didn't just trap the people of Maldon, you trapped my father. Your *friend*. How could you look my mother in the eye with everything you knew?"

Matthias flinched. Not so strong after all.

"Danny, let me explain."

"I've heard it all from her. And I know what you've been doing to the clock towers. It's appalling."

Danny had hoped, in some small corner of his mind, that he was wrong. That Matthias wasn't the culprit, that it had all been in his head, like Tom and George. But the man's silence was as good as a confession. Something broke inside him, the crack echoing painfully through his body.

"Danny, look through my eyes for one second. You know what it's like to grieve." Matthias swallowed. "Losing Alice, I thought I'd never be happy again. And all that changed." His eyes flickered to Evaline. "But just like that, it was taken from me again."

Danny fought not to glance at Colton. He felt him at his shoulder, alert. "I don't need convincing. I've already made up my mind, and so has she. If you stand in our way, you're not proving your love. You're proving how selfish you really are."

Matthias's face hardened. "What do you know of love, Danny? You're just a boy."

Danny fumbled for Colton's hand and gripped it hard. "I know more than you think."

Matthias looked between them, his anger shifting to surprise. "You can't mean—*him*?"

"And why not? You talk about losing everything, but if you do this, we'll lose everything, too."

"Danny, it's not at all the same. Eva and I—"

"It's exactly the same, and don't you dare say otherwise!" Danny yelled, wondering how many of those threads Big Ben had described were attached to this moment. Colton gripped his hand tighter. "Tell me where you put his cog, Matthias. I'll make your life hell if you don't."

Matthias suddenly came forward. It took all of Danny's strength to stand his ground.

"*Hell?* You don't know what hell is. You know nothing of that place." Matthias reached for him.

Colton stepped between them and grabbed the man's wrist.

"Leave him alone, mechanic," Colton said coldly.

Matthias recoiled in surprise. He yanked his arm back and Colton stumbled, too weak to maintain his grip. Matthias turned as if to shove the spirit away, and in that instant one of Danny's possible threads snapped.

He lunged at Matthias.

There was a yelp of surprise, but he didn't know if it came from Evaline, Colton, or himself at his own daring. He had no delusion that he could do much damage; Matthias quickly regained the upper hand, pushing Danny to the floor and pinning his arm behind his back.

"No!" Evaline yelled. She held Colton back as he tried to come to Danny's aid. The more he struggled, the weaker he grew. "Stop this, Matthias! I'll go with you if you leave them alone."

Matthias paused.

"No," Danny croaked. "Don't—"

"Do you mean it, Eva?" Matthias demanded. "I'm only doing what's best for us. You understand that, don't you? This is the only way we can be together. I have to take you to Enfield."

Evaline steeled herself and nodded. She gripped her satchel with both hands. "All right, Matthias. If you can live with the guilt of separating these two boys forever, and for all that you've done, I'll go."

Matthias looked down at Danny and his eyes softened. He let go. Danny scrambled away, almost falling when he regained his footing.

"You're too young to understand," Matthias said.

Danny barely heard him over the horrible ringing in his ears.

"I'm sorry it had to be this way," the man added.

"I'm sorry we ever trusted you," Danny whispered back.

Matthias grimaced, then turned back to Evaline. Colton had sunk to his knees, swaying. Danny hurried forward to steady his shoulders.

"Evaline," Colton called out. She looked at them with regret, but there was something in her eyes like the substance of her tower, stone-like. It held them dangling over the pit of despair, not quite yet falling in.

"Go home to your mother, Danny," Matthias said, wrapping an arm around Evaline's waist. She clutched her satchel tightly. "She'll worry."

Danny watched them leave. In his mind, he ran after them. In his mind, he was racing off to Enfield to beat them there. He tightened his arm around Colton's shoulders. The spirit's head sagged onto Danny's chest.

"What do we do?" Colton asked softly.

Something winked in the corner of his vision and he turned to see Big Ben standing in front of one of his clock faces.

"You spoke about the threads attached to us," Danny said. "Can you see how many of those possibilities are still attached to me?" The spirit nodded. "How many have severed in the last five minutes?"

"Half."

Danny shuddered and pressed his lips to the crown of Colton's head. "We're going back to Enfield," he said.

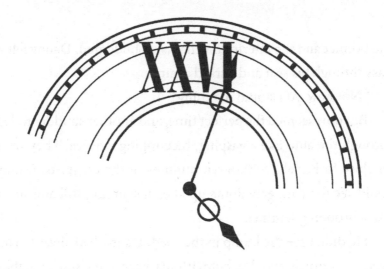

XXVI

The auto wouldn't start. Danny swore and opened the bonnet, poked around, slammed it back down, and tried again. It gave to eventually, and after he fumbled with Cassie's ridiculous holster, they sped off into the freezing night.

Colton lay in the backseat. He'd been awake as they were leaving Big Ben, but when Danny turned to check on him now, his eyes were closed. At least the small cog was still nestled in his palm, a tether to his tower.

It began to snow when they broke past London. Danny could hardly make out a thing in the dark, but he squinted into the pale moonlight, using familiar signs and landmarks to guide his way. Snowflakes met his face in icy kisses, gathering on his clothes and in his hair. They coated Colton's unmoving body.

"Hold on," Danny called to him. "Nearly there."

The auto sputtered and whined. Smoke belched from under

the bonnet and the interior mechanism shuddered. Danny felt it pass through his seat and cursed again.

"Not now, you stupid old thing!"

But now seemed the perfect time, and another shudder rolled through the auto like a gasping, hiccupping wheeze. They were so close to Enfield, within ten minutes of the outskirts. Danny could see the dark gray dome up ahead, standing still and silent like a brooding sentinel.

He didn't see the bump in the road. Danny had always managed to narrowly avoid it, but with his attention elsewhere, they hit it full-on and the auto's center of gravity shifted.

Danny cried out. The auto toppled sideways and he felt as if he were flying through space, the small white pinpricks of snow like cold, empty stars. Then he landed painfully on his side and blacked out.

He came to seconds later and groaned. A squeaking sound came from one of the tires rolling uselessly on its axle. The boiler under the bonnet began leaking, smoke rising as if from an infuriated dragon. Danny shifted himself and winced. He had hit his head, and when he touched the spot above his right eyebrow, his fingers came away bloody.

He tried to get up, but the holster around his chest kept him strapped to the seat. Danny fumbled with the metal clasp and breathed a quiet thanks to Cassie. If it hadn't been for this, he might have been thrown from the auto completely.

He kicked at the door above him until it gaped open into the night, then crawled out and fell to the ground below. Danny rubbed his arms and legs to restore circulation through his aching body before he forced himself to stand. He opened the back door and reached for Colton, dragging him away from the wreckage. The spirit hardly stirred, though he was still clinging to the cog.

Danny sank to his knees and shook him. "Colton? Colton!"

"Danny," he whispered. "All right?"

"Yes, I'm all right. We're fine. We're near Enfield. Can you feel it?"

Colton nodded.

"I'll have to carry you. Just hold on."

He gathered Colton in his arms. Pausing for a moment, Danny gazed sadly at the smoldering auto. No amount of repair work could fix it now. Maybe it was for the best. When his legs stopped shaking, he turned toward Enfield and ran without looking back.

Danny had never been a fast runner, and even in matters of life and death he was mediocre at best. He soon developed a stitch in his side and was gasping for breath. His head pounded and his vision swam. Matthias was probably just behind him, racing toward Enfield with Evaline in his faster, newer auto. They would overtake him at any moment. And since Matthias had a spirit with him, they would be able to walk through the barrier before Danny and Colton could.

Danny stumbled, then stopped. His breath hitched. They were alone out here, a tiny speck in an endless night.

"I'm sorry," he whispered, unsure whether Colton could hear him or not.

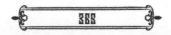

As if in reply, a hand grabbed his shirt. Colton met Danny's gaze, though he was struggling to keep his own eyes open.

"Don't give up." His voice fell upon the syllables like a slow-swinging pendulum. "You can't. You're Achilles and Perseus and Heracles." He struggled to smile. "You're the prince who saves the day, remember?"

Danny would have laughed had he been able to, but instead, his eyes began to sting. "Oh, hell," he muttered, and picked up the pace.

The gray dome loomed before them. Danny nearly toppled over with fatigue, but he pressed forward, drawing Colton's body close to his as they passed through the barrier. The sea of gray swallowed him, muted all his senses, until they sprawled painfully on the soil of Enfield and Danny earned a mouthful of grass.

"How can you be back already? You've only just left!"

Danny squinted up at Brandon's face. The sky overhead was bright, considerably brighter than the night Danny had just left. Of course—time was frozen. It would be the exact moment the thief had removed Colton's cog, 11:14 in the morning.

"How long was I gone?" he rasped, sitting up.

"I can't tell, can I?" Brandon said irritably.

"The cog?"

"We've only just started looking. Why are you wearing different clothes?"

Danny hid his face in his hands and laughed. He laughed until there was no more air in his lungs and he started to cough. When he regained his composure, Brandon was gaping at him.

"It's been more than a day."

"What? How?"

"The town's Stopped, Brandon."

Brandon helped put Colton in Danny's arms. The spirit's hair was tousled, and Danny smoothed it down.

"No time for grooming, mate," Brandon said. "What's the news?"

Danny explained what had happened as they walked toward the green. In his hurry, he forgot to hide Colton. By the time he realized his mistake, they were already in view of the searching townspeople.

They saw Danny immediately and rushed forward when they noticed the body in his arms, perhaps believing he'd found the thief. The back of Danny's neck prickled and his breath caught.

The people began to crowd around, chattering over one another, demanding answers. But then he saw the flash of understanding in their eyes, first in a woman near the front, then in a man with a worker's cap, on and on until the same thought ran across everyone's faces: this wasn't a normal boy Danny held.

The crowd hushed around him, a few figures winking out here and there as time looped.

Brandon shifted uneasily at his side, looking to Danny for a cue to do something. But Danny had to face them himself.

He took a deep breath. "Enfield," he said, "this is your clock."

There were gasps and murmurs as all attention shifted to the limp form of Colton. The spirit opened his eyes, saw what was going on, and squirmed in Danny's arms.

"Danny—no—"

"Let them see you," he whispered, then raised his voice for the others to hear. "This boy is responsible for your town. He's watched over you, mourned with you, laughed with you. He loves this town, and its people, and would protect it with his life. If you honor that, then help us find his missing cog and restore Enfield to what it was."

Danny wondered if he had done the right thing. Nobody moved or said a word. He almost preferred their questions.

Then one person broke from the crowd and approached him. Harland. Danny tensed, but Harland stopped just before him. He wore an expression of disbelief, but when he met Danny's eyes, there was also wonder.

Slowly, carefully, Harland touched Colton's arm. Colton allowed him to, staring up in his own wide-eyed amazement. Harland exhaled in surprise.

"He's real." Harland turned to the others. "He's real!"

The townspeople shouted and rushed forward, reaching for Colton in a shy, sacred way, like a religious ritual. Like they might have reached out to touch the shrine of Aetas hidden in the hedge. Colton could only stare at them, his lips parted.

"Hold on, lad, we'll find your missing piece."

"Hang in there!"

"Let's check the manor house."

The crowd broke apart and renewed the search with tripled effort. Danny was trembling, but he smiled. Colton still looked as if he'd been struck on the head.

"Who do you suppose could have done it?" Brandon asked.

"Someone in the town, maybe? Matthias could have bribed them. I don't think any of the other mechanics would do something like this, but none of the apprentices would be experienced enough. Besides, Matthias loves the apprentices. He wouldn't put one in danger."

Then again, he had killed Lucas. Maybe not on purpose, but it was something Danny couldn't look past.

As the people of Enfield searched the gardens, the houses, the hedge, Danny focused on Colton, trying to use him as a compass. It kept them near the village green, but he soon grew as frustrated as a dog sniffing the same spot only to find nothing new or remarkable about it. Time warped them out of

places   to

   they   them   places

      needed   returned   they'd

         to   and   already

          go   been.

Danny closed his eyes and focused harder. He tried to see the time threads stretching between him, Colton, and Brandon. What tied them together? What decision would set them on the right path?

Danny looked around. His eyes fell on the church.

"Has someone checked there?"

"I think so, but I haven't gone in yet."

"Let's see."

They walked across the green to the parish church. The nave and tower were formed from the random bits of rubble that workers had taken for good materials back in whatever long-ago century it had been built.

Danny walked inside with Brandon. The church was empty, the pastor out searching with the others. Colton stirred the farther in they went, restless.

"It's close, I think," Danny murmured. Colton's head tilted toward the steps leading to the church tower. "Come on."

They climbed the spiral staircase until they reached the tower room. Slats of gray light leaked through the window shutters and striped the floor.

Danny peered into the gloom and heard the scuff of a boot. He tensed, then set Colton on the floor with his back against the wall, out of harm's way. Danny exchanged a nod with Brandon and they advanced quietly.

A curse from a feminine voice broke the sanctified quiet of the church. Danny and Brandon lunged forward and each caught an arm, and the thief twisted and struggled. The sharp toe of a boot drove into his shin and Danny roared in pain.

The thief gouged Brandon's wrist and he quickly let go. "Damn!" She scurried backward, trapped.

When Danny's eyes adjusted to the dimness, he saw the thief's face. Specifically, the diamond-shaped tattoo by her right eye.

"Daphne?"

Her blonde hair was in disarray, her eyes wide and gleaming.

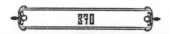

The blue kerchief she normally wore at her neck hung unevenly and the nails of her right hand were bloodied from clawing at Brandon. Some of her bandages had come loose.

"What are you doing here?" he demanded, too surprised to realize he'd used her Christian name.

She swallowed. "Stopping you."

"You—*what*?" He rubbed his forehead, wincing when he touched the cut there. "What are you talking about? Where's the cog?"

"I've hidden it," she said shortly.

"It's there, you dolt." Brandon pointed behind her.

And there it was, leaning innocently against the wall. She stepped back and spread her arms when Danny moved forward.

"You can't have it."

"Of course we can, it's the town's property! What are you playing at, Daphne?

"I know what you're doing to the towers, and I won't allow it."

"What are you talking about? Did Matthias put you up to this?"

She didn't move from her position. "You didn't give me a choice."

"What do you mean?"

She breathed loudly in the small space. "After the Lead fired us, I found Matthias. I told him about Dover and that you might be involved, and how I was afraid for Enfield because of your obsession with this place. He told me he was afraid for you—that you'd been distant and strange.

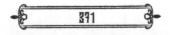

"He said you were going to take the central cog from Enfield to use it for the new Maldon tower they're planning to rebuild. I couldn't let that happen. He told me to remove the cog, to keep it safe while he asked the Lead for help."

"Did he think you'd get caught?" asked Brandon.

"He said I could just walk through the barrier with the cog, but I tried, and it didn't work. So I ran in here."

"I was right, then," Danny said, mostly to himself. "Only spirits have the ability to leave, and the mechanics who touch them." He refocused on the girl before him. "Didn't you stop to think, Daphne? The town's Stopped because of you. You've created another Maldon."

"Like you wouldn't have!"

Danny yelled in frustration. "Do you really think that *I'm* the one hurting the towers? That I killed Lucas and gave myself this scar? It's *Matthias*, Daphne! Matthias needs a new tower to use for the Maldon spirit he's bloody in love with!"

She blinked at him, not understanding. Danny told her everything he had unearthed about Matthias in the last forty-eight hours. Time warped a little, making him repeat certain bits over and over, but finally it was all out.

"That's . . . He wouldn't." Daphne's eyebrows furrowed. "Matthias would never do something like that. He . . . " Her voice lilted into a question. "He wouldn't?"

Brandon shook his head. "Let me guess: he also said he'd pay you for your trouble."

"You don't understand. My mother's in the asylum." Her voice caught, and Danny thought back to the day she'd saved him from the mob. St. Agnes's Home for Women. "I need money for her treatment, to get someone to take care of her. Yes, part of this was for the money, but I had to do something after you got me fired!"

More words with teeth, biting straight through him. He had caused all of this. Trying to alter destiny had led him to this moment anyway, drawing him closer the more he resisted.

"I'm sorry, Daphne," he whispered. "I . . . God, I'm just like him. I'm so sorry."

Brandon tugged on Danny's sleeve and jerked his chin to where Colton sat. The spirit had lifted his hand to reach for Danny.

"Come here, Daphne," Danny said.

She picked up the cog, holding it to her chest. "I won't go with you. Not until Matthias comes."

"Just come here, will you? I won't force you. I want to show you something."

Slowly, Daphne stepped forward. Brandon blocked the exit to the stairs as Danny knelt beside Colton. He took the spirit's hand and pressed it to his lips.

"Do you feel it, Colton?"

The spirit nodded, his eyes searching for Daphne.

When she saw him, she gasped. The glow returned slightly to Colton's body.

"This is the spirit of the Enfield clock tower," Danny explained. "And he'll disappear if you don't give that cog back to him."

Daphne stared at Colton. Colton stared back. There was a strange light in Daphne's eyes, a mesmerized sort of shock.

"You're the clock," she breathed. It wasn't a question. "The spirit, I mean. I've seen someone like you before. In Dover, there was a little girl . . ." She glanced at Danny. "When the clockwork exploded, she started flickering. She almost disappeared entirely."

They both knew without having to say it: Colton was fading, becoming more and more transparent. If he disappeared, Enfield would be trapped forever.

And Colton . . .

"I'm sorry about your mum," Danny said. "I'll help in any way I can, since I know this is my fault. But keeping the cog won't do any good. You can see that for yourself."

Daphne looked down at the cog. Danny crouched before her, ready to wrestle it from her hands if he needed to, but eventually she gave a shuddering sigh and nodded. Her hair swung forward to hide her face.

"I'm sorry," she said, holding the cog out to Colton. The spirit lifted pale, blurred hands to take it. "I'm so sorry. I—"

A commotion on the stairs made Danny turn. Brandon slid down the wall, groaning, as a hulking shape lunged toward Daphne.

"Matthias!" she screamed, jumping back. "Wait! You can't do this."

He came to a jarring halt. "Give me the cog."

"You can't put the Maldon spirit in the Enfield tower," Daphne said. "It won't work."

Danny and Matthias looked at her. Daphne's face was grave, her voice even. But Danny knew that she was bluffing. They didn't understand the complexities of the clock spirits, didn't have the right data to come to this sort of conclusion.

But she was Matthias's old apprentice, and the top of her class. She was appealing to his sense. Or what was left of it.

"Think about it," she went on breathlessly. "Nothing like this has ever been done in the history of the clock towers. There's no guarantee that installing the Maldon spirit's central cog will create the same area of time. It would all have been for nothing if it doesn't work. Both spirits will die."

Matthias paused to think, and Danny shifted slightly, ready to attack at the slightest motion. Colton held onto his elbow, keeping him back. He met Danny's eyes and shook his head.

"You don't know that," Matthias said.

"But do you really want to risk it?" Daphne asked.

There was a pregnant silence in the small tower room, time everywhere and nowhere at once, making the moment stretch. Danny's muscles coiled with tension.

When Matthias finally moved, Danny jumped to his feet and grabbed a handful of the man's shirt. Matthias grabbed the cog from Daphne's hands, knocking her to the ground. He turned and shoved Danny into Colton. Heavy feet thudded down the tower stairs.

Danny scrambled up and turned to the others. "Brandon! Take Colton and Daphne to the clock tower and stay there, no matter what."

"What, you're going after him?" Brandon demanded with a hand pressed dramatically to his injured head. "Are you mad?"

"I have to. Daphne, I swear, any funny business—"

"No," she insisted, crouching protectively over Colton. "Not from me."

"All right. Get him to the tower and—"

"Danny!"

He knelt beside Colton, who reached for him. Danny took the spirit's hand in his own and something scraped against his palm: the little cog. Danny leaned over and kissed him hard, refusing to believe it would be the last time.

"Go," Colton whispered against his lips.

Danny thundered down the stairs. When he burst from the church he saw a few townspeople on the green, still searching. But down the street he spotted someone running full speed toward the barrier.

Danny gave chase. A runner he might not be, but suddenly the buildings blurred and the shape of the man grew closer—time was warping him forward. Matthias turned to look for the source of pounding feet just as Danny barreled into him, sending them crashing to the ground.

The central cog flew out of Matthias's arms. Danny struggled to go after it, but the man pulled him back down.

"No you don't, Danny," Matthias panted above him. "I've waited too long for this chance."

"You're a murderer!" Danny yelled past his dust-clogged

throat. "You'll be killing Colton *and* my father. You've already killed Lucas!"

Matthias paused, his grip loosening. "Danny . . . I didn't . . ."

"Matthias, no!"

Evaline's voice. Of course, she had to be here for Matthias to have crossed the barrier. Danny twisted his head around to find her standing a short distance away, pale as a ghost.

Matthias let him go and grabbed the cog. Evaline kept her gaze on Matthias, who pretended not to notice her horror.

Danny lurched to his feet. A drop of sweat rolled down his forehead and dripped off his eyebrow. Time warped, and the drop rolled back up his face.

"I'm sorry, Danny," Evaline said. "I tried to stop him. He won't listen."

"You don't know what I've sacrificed for us," Matthias said. "I'm through living with so little hope. If I have to get my hands dirty, so be it." His chest was heaving as he faced Danny. "Even if it means going through you."

Danny reached up and touched the scar on his chin.

"You did this," he whispered. "All of it. And you let Daphne believe it was me. She trusted you."

Matthias couldn't look at him, his face rigid with emotion he desperately clawed back. "I . . ." He almost looked at Evaline, but couldn't bring himself to do that either. "I didn't know what else to do. Eva was fading. She needed a tower. I knew Tom was going to Shere, and I thought . . ."

A cold, brittle laugh escaped him. "I thought, if my plan worked, Tom would be the one getting in trouble. Not me. But the bomb didn't go off at the right time." Matthias glanced at Danny's scar. "God, you have no idea how much I—"

"Spare me," Danny growled.

The man nodded sadly. "I thought by giving you those clues about Tom and George, you'd find a way to help me convince the Lead they were the ones responsible. I saw the pipes in Tom's office and thought to use them as bombs. I didn't—" He swallowed. "I didn't mean to kill that boy. And I never meant to hurt you, Danny.

"But when Daphne came to me, convinced you were guilty, it was like a gift. I couldn't pass up the chance. You weren't supposed to be here when she took the cog."

"Matthias, why? What did I ever do to you?"

A muscle in Matthias's jaw ticked. "Not you, Danny. Your father."

"What does he have to do with this?"

"Everything." Matthias finally looked at Evaline. "Your father is the one who saw me with Eva. He reported me. He had me separated from her. From Maldon."

For a moment Danny could only focus on breathing in, breathing out. Was Matthias telling the truth, or talking him around to his side? Every word out of his mouth for the last three years had been a lie. Fabrications spun around a hidden truth.

"I couldn't let them build a new tower," Matthias went on. "If Maldon was freed, then your father would know Evaline had left on her own, and that she would be searching for me. They would arrest me and take her back to Maldon. The new tower had to be destroyed.

"All I need is another tower, another town. Once I install her cog, this will all be finished."

"What's the point, Matthias?" Evaline's voice shook. "Even if I'm in the tower, how do you know I'll be compatible?"

Matthias's gaze switched between Danny and Evaline, uncertain. Remembering Daphne's bluff. Danny saw the strain of desperation, a man used to fighting and hanging on by his fingernails. The threads he had to choose from were dwindling. Danny could almost see them detaching from his body.

"I'll do what has to be done," Matthias said at last.

Ice replaced the marrow in Danny's bones. The man he had known all his life was suddenly a stranger. It was like watching an egg fall, knowing what would happen when it hit the ground, yet being unable to move fast enough to stop its messy end.

Danny considered everything he wanted to say to Matthias, each angry, bitter word that gathered behind his tongue. He remembered how Matthias had comforted him with his fond smiles. How much he'd respected and admired him, and how badly it hurt to see him twisted by so much pain. How his father would not have wanted Matthias to grieve, but to do what he could to help his family. To do the right thing.

But all Danny could manage was, "I won't let you do this."

Matthias's face hardened. Still, Danny caught the flicker of regret in his eyes. "So be it."

Danny imagined himself as Perseus then, standing poised with racing heart and rapid breath, facing down an evil that needed slaying. Yet it was not a snake-wreathed Gorgon before him, but a man who had become like a second father, all too human and imperfect. And instead of god-given sword and shield, Danny had only a small cog hidden in his sweaty palm.

Matthias moved suddenly, and Evaline cried out in warning. Danny ducked instinctually as the man made a grab for him. He wrapped his arms around Matthias's legs to try and bring him down, but the man might as well have been a tree trunk. Matthias picked him up by the scruff of his collar and flung him to one side.

Danny had once seen a little terrier dog biting a man's ankles at a dinner party. The man would shake it off and smile awkwardly at the owner, who apologized over and over with increasing embarrassment. But no matter how that little, ratty dog persisted, it was always shaken off with muffled curses and looks of disdain.

Now Danny understood that little terrier and its frustration. He grabbed and clawed and jumped, but Matthias kept him down easily. Danny's arms began to tremble with fatigue, but still he tried to snatch the central cog. His left hand was too slippery, his right one wrapped around the tiny cog Colton had given him.

Finally, Matthias grew impatient and smacked him soundly on the head. Danny dropped and the world went spinning.

"Matthias!" Evaline cried. "No more!"

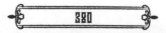

"He's come between us," Matthias panted. "He has to be stopped."

"No. I won't let you go any further."

Danny struggled to turn his head and open his eyes. His lungs were in shock, and pulling in air was difficult. But when he saw Evaline, he managed a choked gasp.

She knelt on the ground before her own cog. Unknown to Danny and Matthias, she had been carrying a chisel and a hammer in her satchel. Where she had found them, Danny had no idea; maybe in Matthias's toolbox. She gripped a tool in each hand, poised purposefully above the central cog that kept her and Maldon alive.

She glared defiantly at Matthias, who stood rooted to the spot.

"Don't," he said, his tone low and frantic. "Eva, you're being irrational."

"*I'm* being irrational? Look at you—you're destroying yourself! Look at all those you're making suffer because of your own desires. I fell in love with a man who was selfless and passionate, who told me about London and the life we could live there. But it's nothing like you said, Matthias. And you're not that man anymore. I don't know who you are, but you're not the person I met in Maldon."

They stared at each other, Evaline ready to end her own life if that's what it took to stop him. Danny struggled to his elbows.

"Evaline," he whispered. "Please, don't do this. You'll kill my father. You'll kill Maldon."

Her eyes met his, lost. Danny could see in them the urge to give up hope, but he shook his head, silently telling her that not all the threads had been cut yet. Matthias looked from Danny to Evaline and his body relaxed.

"No, you wouldn't sacrifice your town," Matthias agreed.

"I'll leave," she threatened. "Even if I'm somehow compatible with this tower, I'll just remove my central cog again and leave."

"And Stop Enfield like you Stopped Maldon?"

That made her pause. She again looked at Danny, but he had no solution to offer.

"I'm sorry, Danny." Matthias's eyes shone with fervor. "I know you won't forgive me. I don't deserve forgiveness. But please, don't get in my way."

Matthias left Danny in the dirt, moving toward Evaline. She shrank back, but Matthias only knelt and gently took her central cog from her. Evaline dropped her hammer and chisel to reach for the cog, but Matthias stepped out of the way.

"Trust me, Eva."

Danny tried to grab the man's ankle as it moved past him, but his body wouldn't cooperate, curled into a pained comma.

He saw Colton in his mind. Saw the curve of his smile and the glint of his amber eyes, a spark of life so bright that Danny had never seen its like in a human being. He felt him in the tower now, fading, dying, that spark about to be extinguished for good.

Danny pushed himself to his knees, shaking. He took a deep

breath and asked his head to kindly stop spinning. He had a town to save.

Something bit into his palm and he hissed. He unfurled his right hand to see that the tiny cog had punctured his palm. A bright bead of blood welled up and rolled into the sweaty creases. It touched the cog, spread between skin and metal.

Danny remembered the moment when a drop of his blood had touched Colton's clockwork. The shudder of power, the skip in time. The hint of it at the ruined Maldon tower. The blood he'd spilled in Shere.

Aetas's blood spilled into the ocean, and that's why it's so salty.

Danny closed his fist around the cog. Blood seeped onto the metal.

You have more control than you think.

He thought of time, of fibers and threads and the small cracks in between. He thought of *ticks* and *tocks* and the sound of air when a pendulum swings through it. He thought of movement, and of hands of black iron making a circle, now standing still. He held the cog tight and cut himself deeper, drawing the fibers closer.

His vision darkened. When it cleared, he inhaled sharply.

He could see the threads between him and Matthias, and between him and Evaline. He saw one, thin and faded, that stretched toward the clock tower. Toward Colton.

Danny stood. He looked all around him, noticing in a distant, offhanded way that he was the only thing moving in Enfield. Everything else had become motionless.

Time fibers crisscrossed one another, like the woven pattern of a tapestry. Danny could see them, the normally pulsing, bright fibers that now thrummed with each pump of his heart.

He was connected to time.

Matthias had stopped mid-step. Danny parted the fibers suspended in the air like they were made of gossamer to reach him. Matthias's face was determined, his mouth pinched and wrinkled at the corners. Both cogs—Enfield's and Maldon's—were nestled in his arms, similar in shape but slightly different in color.

Danny looked around again. The town at his back was frozen. Evaline was crouched, one hand extended to Matthias, her mouth open to call him back. Danny waved a hand before Matthias's face. Nothing happened.

"Oh God," he whispered.

This isn't possible. Maybe he had taken one too many blows to the head. To control time, to make it stop completely, was . . . was . . .

Possible.

As he focused on his connection to the time fibers, he could feel Colton fading faster. Danny was borrowing the spirit's power, or perhaps Colton was giving it to him. The longer they stayed connected, the more life he leeched from Colton.

Time to get to work.

He tried to pull the cogs from of Matthias's arms, but with no luck. He tugged and tugged, but there was no give. Danny opened his hand and gazed at the little blood-smeared cog, thinking. He got an idea and ran toward the village green.

Danny searched frantically, barely taking in the people stuck in strange positions. Eventually, he passed a house with a small picket fence. In the yard lay a cricket bat.

He hopped over the fence with a groan. His body ached. He plucked at the fibers and allowed time to move for just a second, enough to lift the bat from the ground. He froze time again with another quick pluck and headed back for Matthias.

Danny stood to one side of the man, considering his options. He patted the cricket bat against the sole of his boot, dislodging clods of dirt. When he felt ready, he turned his attention to the time fibers around him and let them drop.

Matthias had only just finished taking his step when Danny swung the bat with all his strength and landed a juicy *thunk* on the man's skull.

Matthias fell hard. The cogs spilled from his arms, dirt billowing where they skidded along the ground. Before Matthias could recover, Danny pulled in the fibers and everything stopped again.

Danny walked to the cogs. The dust hovered above them in immovable clouds. He tried to dig his fingers under Colton's cog to lift it, but it seemed permanently attached to the earth. Danny glanced over his shoulder at Matthias. He could start time and grab the cog, just as he had done with the cricket bat, but that would leave Matthias free to escape once the central cog was installed.

Colton was fading even faster.

Danny ran off again. He peeked inside houses, front doors

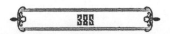

still open after their owners had run out at 11:14. He finally found what he was looking for: on a table beside a box of tools rested a coil of rope. Danny allowed just enough time to pass for him to grab it.

When he returned, he slowly circled Matthias's prone body. This decision required more courage than the last one. Taking a deep breath, Danny started time.

Matthias lay dazed on the ground, but was soon squirming in agony. Danny had only precious seconds, and he quickly grabbed the man's thick wrists, pulling his arms up until they stuck out behind him. Just as Matthias made to jerk them away, time froze.

Heart hammering, he wrapped the rope around Matthias's wrists, leaving just enough slack so that when he restarted time, he was able to cinch the knot tightly.

Danny pocketed the tiny cog and stepped back to examine his handiwork. Matthias writhed against the ground, rolling onto his side, testing the rope at his wrists.

"What did you do?" he demanded, more stunned than angry. "Danny?"

Danny ignored him and walked to the fallen cogs. He picked them up and brushed them off, then handed Evaline hers. She accepted it with both hands, her lips parted.

"Danny, no!" Matthias yelled. "What did you do? Danny!"

He made to walk to the tower, Colton's central cog under his arm, but Matthias's cries snagged on the last shred of pity he had left. He stopped, sighed, and knelt a safe distance away. Matthias's hair was coming undone from its queue. His gaze was wild.

"I'm not sorry," Danny told him. "You could have made this right three years ago. It was already too late for you."

Too late for Matthias to have a happy ending.

Matthias kept blinking, his eyes gleaming. "I didn't mean for it to come to this. My fate was to be an old, lonely man with regrets. So I changed that. I had to."

He had certainly achieved that goal. But in changing his fate, he had created for himself something even worse.

"You don't understand," Matthias whispered. "Wouldn't you do anything for the one you love?"

"Yes, I would. And so I am."

Matthias stared at him, defeated, but still proud. Danny thought of all those promises they had made to each other over the years, their pinky fingers twining in their own secret pacts. All the times Matthias had said he would be there for him no matter what.

He considered breaking the man's pinky fingers.

"I've never told you how like your father you are," Matthias said.

"I'd rather you didn't." Danny stood and limped blindly to the tower. He followed the sound of Colton's voice, the thread between them bright and taut, urging Danny to find him. To be healed.

Brandon and Daphne were by the clockwork. Colton lay unconscious between them, transparent enough for Danny to see the floor beneath him. They turned at the sound of feet on the stairs, and Brandon raised his fists threateningly. When they saw Danny's rumpled appearance they relaxed, then cried out when they saw what he carried.

"Tools," he croaked to Brandon. The apprentice ran to fetch them.

It took barely any time. Danny's body still hummed with hyper-awareness from the fibers, and the thread between him and Colton grew stronger, brighter. He slipped the central cog back into its proper place and nodded to Brandon, who ran to the pendulum room below. The clock was wound—he and Daphne heard the chattering turn of gears—and Danny placed his hand on the central cog.

Calling in the fibers, time compressed all around them. A gear turned, and then another, until the cogs and gears rolled back into one large, functioning unit.

Time was released like the first gasp of life.

Colton's eyes flew open. He shuddered and sat up, his edges filled in, the golden glow returning to his body. He looked down at himself in amazement. Then he looked straight at Danny with a smile so bright it flooded the tower.

"You did it!"

Danny fell to his knees beside him. He grabbed Colton and they both toppled over onto the dusty floor.

"*We* did it." He took the cog from his pocket and pressed it to Colton's chest.

THE BOY AND THE TOWER

There was once a golden boy who lived in a golden tower.

The tower was wrapped with threads of time, so meshed and measured that the boy had to care for them lest they become tangled. The boy stayed in his golden tower as time ticked around him, as he felt the days end and the nights stretch on forever, the earth tremble and fall silent, baked by sun and blanketed by snow.

One day, a lost boy came to the golden tower. He was alone, and had felt the gentle tug of time. He followed it to the golden boy, and saw the future as he never had before.

Through this golden boy he saw the sun and the moon and the galaxies that had given birth to everything, the beginning of creation and the end of time. He saw how the world was supposed to be, hanging on every breath, every flutter of a heartbeat, as stars were born and died and born again. He saw the shutter of the sun falling and the whisper of the moon rising. Over and over, until gold and silver blended into a veil through which the world was perfect. A world that was ancient and new.

A world that was theirs.

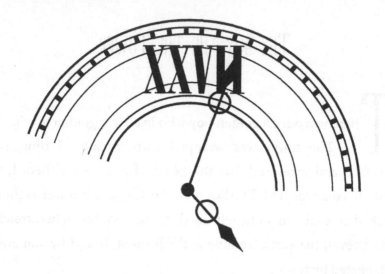

XXVI

anny watched the metal balls of the kinetic toy bounce back and forth, back and forth, click-clacking incessantly while he twisted a handkerchief in his hands. The window beyond the Lead's desk glinted with rare winter sunshine. Papers were scattered across the desk's surface. Danny tried to read them upside down, but it proved too much for his jumbled mind, and he returned to watching the toy.

The Lead had kept him waiting again. Danny couldn't help but think he did this to be dramatic. It was not appreciated.

Danny began chewing on the end of his handkerchief. He was dressed in his best suit, the silver chain of his timepiece creating a foil against the black waistcoat and trousers. His mother had even applied Macassar oil to his hair in order to make it lie flat, with little success. The battle with the comb had nearly made him late this morning. Not that it mattered now.

The door opened and he swung around. The Lead saw the handkerchief in his mouth and raised an eyebrow. Danny quickly stuffed it back into his pocket.

"Daniel," the Lead sighed, slapping a file onto his desk. "What are we to do with you?"

Danny swallowed. Although he had been fired from the London Union, there was still the possibility of applying to other cities. One word from the Lead, however, and no one would hire him again.

"Here you are, my boy. You'll need it."

A cup of tea was set down before him. He hadn't even noticed the Lead carrying it. He blinked at this offering and peered up uncertainly.

"Sir?"

"Drink, Daniel."

So he drank. The Lead looked through a few papers, signed a couple of memos. Finally, he reached out and stopped the kinetic toy.

"Tell me in your own words what happened."

Danny had already done this several times, even once to the London authorities. When they showed up at Enfield, they had driven him, along with Brandon and Daphne, back to the city. Another auto had taken Matthias and Evaline. At the station, they had given their witness statements while Evaline was put under close watch.

Daphne had been let off with a fine after Danny and Brandon vouched for her, and Matthias admitted to tricking her into stealing the cog. There was even a possibility of letting her back into the Union on a probationary period, so long as she kept her head down from now on. Danny had pulled her aside and said he would pay the fine for her, as he'd dragged her into this mess in the first place, even if it meant depleting the rest of his new auto savings.

She had demanded the full story from him, about how he'd defeated Matthias. "I felt something pass through the time fibers," she said, blue eyes glinting. "What did you do?"

He was tired of lying, so he said, "I controlled time."

Daphne sighed. "No more games, Danny."

"It's not a game. Believe me or not, it's the truth." He'd left with her staring after him, bewildered.

Matthias was to be tried, and likely had a long, hard imprisonment ahead of him. Danny ought to have felt sorry for him, but he didn't. Not really. He was only sorry to have lost the man he had admired for so long.

At least Matthias hadn't told anyone about Colton. Danny supposed he should be grateful for that.

When Danny wrapped up his account, taking care not to mention his more intimate involvement with Colton or how he'd connected to time—the latter he still didn't know how to explain—the Lead stared at his desk. Danny began fidgeting again, pulling at his too-tight collar.

"I'm sorry to have lost such a valuable mechanic," the Lead finally said, his words weighted. "He was a fine man, or so I thought. I never would have believed that all this time . . ." He shook his head. "Daniel, I'm truly sorry. I know the two of you were close."

Danny nodded, but said nothing.

"Maldon, of course, will be freed. You must be pleased."

"Sir," Danny said, "why don't you just tell me why I'm here?"

"Very well, then. After what's happened, I've done some thinking. Specifically, thinking about your future as a mechanic."

Danny gripped his knees. His fingernails pricked the skin underneath the fabric of his trousers. "Please tell me, sir."

And he was told. Danny sat for a moment and weakly asked for the words to be repeated. After a few questions, he left the office with his cap and his coat, neither of which he could remember how to wear. By the time he stood outside in the winter air, thoughts were flooding his mind all at once.

Danny looked across the square at Big Ben. And smiled.

"Oh, hell, get on with it!" his mother snapped at his side.

"Mum, stop it. You're drawing attention."

"I'll draw as much bloody attention as I please!" Leila took a final drag from her shortened cigarette and dropped it to the grass, stamping it out with a high-heeled boot. Twin plumes of smoke steamed from her nostrils. "They're taking forever."

They stood milling within the crowd that had come to witness the freeing of Maldon. It was rather a difficult thing to witness, as so many had come, and Maldon's time zone extended

quite a ways from the actual town. The authorities hadn't even brought Evaline to the site yet.

Danny looked at all the eager faces, some smiling like this was a treat, others as solemn and anxious as his mother. Many here also had family trapped in Maldon, had waited three years for this day to arrive. Danny's heart did an excited little turn of its own, but he would not breathe properly until Evaline walked through the barrier.

They weren't close to the ruins of the other tower. Danny still knew it was there, a landmark of their failure and of Matthias's betrayal.

He glanced again at his mother, wringing her hands like the mayor of Enfield had. He took one of them in his own and she looked up, startled.

"Don't worry, Mum. It'll be all right."

She smiled faintly and focused again on the barrier. Danny watched it with her, though there was nothing much to see. His eyes bored into the gray sheet that stretched across Maldon, hoping to sense his father beyond the dome.

"Oh!"

A train of autos headed for the crowd. The people cheered, and Evaline, in the front seat of the lead auto, looked around in surprise at the noise.

The guards helped the clock spirit out and escorted her toward the time barrier. Everyone backed away quickly. The ring of guards around Evaline glared at anyone who even looked her way. Evaline walked past the crowd, her head held high, but Danny could see it was not pride; she was facing her own humility.

Leila's hand nearly crushed his.

Evaline paused at the barrier, then scanned the crowd for Danny. When she spotted him she gave a small nod, grief still lingering in her eyes. It would fade, he hoped, in time. But what was time to one who breathed never-ending seconds, minutes, hours?

Evaline walked through the barrier. The grayness wavered and the people murmured, expecting it to fall, but it didn't. Danny knew they still had a long wait ahead.

"Come on, Christopher," Leila whispered. "You can do it."

Many sat, or spread out blankets as if to watch a fireworks show. Danny paced and bit his thumbnail for at least half an hour. Leila stood in the same spot as if transfixed.

Just as he was worrying that it might take hours or even days, suddenly the barrier wavered again. Then, in an instant, it fell. The field was finally exposed.

And beyond it, Maldon.

"He did it!" Leila screamed. "He did it, Danny!"

The crowd's cheers were deafening. Several people ran toward the town, even as the police tried to maintain order. Leila was one of them, Danny not far behind.

People slowly trickled out of Maldon, unsure of the sudden freedom they had been granted. Many ran back into town at the sight of the oncoming army of friends and relatives, but others hurried forward to be hugged and kissed and to exclaim over how much time had truly passed.

Danny guarded his mother from elbows and hands as she weaved through the crowd. She reached an empty clearing and looked around.

"I don't see him," she panted. "Do you?"

"No," Danny said, "but he's probably still in the clock tower. Let's just wait."

The crowd thinned. People were either entering the town or whisking away loved ones to continue their reunion in the field. Leila worried her lip so much that Danny feared it would start bleeding.

He was about to suggest going inside when an arm fell heavily across his shoulders.

"Hello, and who might this tall lad be?"

"Dad!"

"Christopher!"

They both turned and winded him with their embrace. Christopher Hart laughed and held them as tightly as he could manage.

"What're the tears for? It's only been a day."

"A *day*!" Leila repeated in a near-shriek. "You buffoon, it's been three bloody years!"

"Zounds. No wonder you look older."

When Danny stepped back, he had to wipe his eyes on his sleeve. Leila cried freely and tried to halfheartedly smack her husband. With her free hand she pulled him down for a rough kiss.

Danny quickly became fascinated with the grass at his feet.

Done for the moment with their reunion, Christopher pecked his wife on the forehead. She wrapped her arms around his waist.

Danny's father looked him over with a sharp, wide smile. His green eyes, like Danny's own, shone with joyful tears.

"The spirit told me what you did, Danny. Look at you!" He put a proud hand on his son's shoulder and shook it. "Saving towns left and right. Where did you learn to do that?"

"From you," Danny said.

With Christmas around the corner, and her husband safely home, Leila decided to give Danny his present a few days early. He woke one morning to find a new auto sitting at the curb.

"Mum!" he yelled as he ran around in his robe, hair sticking up in all directions. A girl riding by on a brass-plated bicycle giggled at him. "Mum, this is for *me*?"

"All yours," she said as his father inspected it. He had bemoaned the loss of his own auto, but now his face lit up like a boy's. "Had to put in a little extra time at work, but I thought it was time for a change."

Danny looked at her. All the late nights she was gone, Danny

had been convinced it was because she couldn't stand to be in the same house as him, when all the while . . .

"Mum," he began, but he couldn't find the words. She gave him a tremulous smile. There were still broken pieces at their feet, but in this moment he felt one slide back into place. It was only a matter of time before they replaced the rest.

After Danny and his father played around with the settings and took the auto on its maiden drive—it ran beautifully— Cassie came over to share in their delight. She immediately asked to take apart the engine, to which Danny gave a firm and non-negotiable *no*.

"It's one of the newer steam models," she said, stroking the bonnet. "Much more dependable."

"It's really a marvel. You were right, I should have gotten one sooner."

"See? And yet you never listen to me." She peered at the driver's seat. "Will you let me install a new holster?"

"Of course." He had seen Cassie since the freeing of Enfield, had tripped over his words in his haste to thank her, and to say that she had saved his life. He hadn't quite expected her to burst into tears and hug him so hard his ribs creaked. It wasn't the way she'd cried when William died; this time it was with relief.

Cassie leaned against the auto and folded her arms. "So what're your parents going to do now? Your mum still thinking of taking the new job?"

Danny leaned against the fence across from her. "I don't

think so. Not now that Dad's back. Honestly, I don't think she cares where she lives so long as he's there."

Cassie nodded, then ran her fingers over the auto's black finish, unable to help herself. "Well, she did a fine job, picking this beauty out."

"I think I'm in love," Danny said.

Cassie looked at him from under her eyelashes. "Speaking of which, what exactly is going to happen now?"

"What d'you mean?"

"You know. You and the 'blond bloke.'"

Danny looked up at the sky, which was churning with snow clouds that would unleash their burden sometime soon. He reached into his pocket to touch the small cog there, feeling along its edge with a fingertip.

"Did they suspect anything?" Cassie asked, worried by his silence. "Will you be able to see him again? Don't tell me they sacked you!" When Danny remained quiet, she shoved him. "Tell me, then!"

Danny breathed in deeply. He could smell the snow on the way. "Well . . ."

His father was told about Matthias, of course. There was no easy way to go about it. Christopher's disposition remained relatively somber for a few days. When that cloud passed, and they were all smiles again, Danny asked if he was all right.

"It's a shame that it had to happen to such a good man. He *was* good, Danny. Was. I don't know what happened to him."

"He fell in love. He grew selfish."

"True love isn't selfish, Danny."

They were in the kitchen, sitting at the table while Leila fried eggs. His parents exchanged a small, meaningful smile. "True love is self*less*. Sometimes it means you fight for it, and other times, it means you need to let go. You'll learn that for yourself, one day."

Danny bit the inside of his cheek. "Dad . . ." He cleared his throat when Christopher looked at him. "I'm sorry. About Maldon."

"Don't be sorry."

"But I told you to go. None of this would have happened if—"

"If Matthias had done the right thing," his father finished. "He should have known better."

Danny pushed the bacon around on his plate. He felt his mother's eyes on him, saying what Danny already knew: they couldn't tell Christopher about Colton. Not yet.

Not everything.

His father called him to the door when the post arrived. "Something for you."

"For me?" Danny never received letters except for payments, but he hadn't received any of those since being fired.

"Says your name right here." Christopher handed it to him with a sad smile. "God, every time I see you is a surprise. You've grown so much."

Danny flushed and took the envelope. On the front was

his name, but no return address. Someone must have shoved it through the mail slot.

"I've got an idea," Christopher said. "Let's take a walk to the confectioner's. Grab ourselves some gingerbread."

Danny returned his father's smile. "I'd like that." He slid his thumb under the flap and tore open the letter, which was only one page. While Christopher looked through the newspaper—"Looks like those tower protests have started up in India, can you believe it?"—Danny quickly read the short message.

Do not think this is finished.
You know something.
We'll be watching.

"Ticker?" His father looked up to see Danny standing rigid in the entryway, his face pale. "What's the matter?"

The hairs on the back of Danny's neck stood on end, and the scab on his palm itched. Somewhere, someone was interested in him. Interested in what he knew.

We'll be watching.

"Danny?"

He crumpled the letter in his hand. "Nothing. Just some rubbish."

It was amazing, the difference between the old auto and this one.

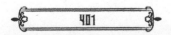

Danny wished he could have spent his first real drive in a better mood, but as it was, he muttered to himself most of the way.

"Can't believe—of all the bloody nerve—when I explicitly said—"

He steered easily away from the bump in the road. The old auto had been cleared away by now, and good riddance. Danny didn't need more reminders of that frantic drive.

When he reached Enfield and parked the auto, he grabbed his bag and slid out. The air smelled fresh and bright. Despite his mood, he stopped to inhale a lungful.

As Danny walked through the green, people saw him and cheered. He waved shyly. Somehow, he had become Enfield's hero. Although a little pleased with the title, he made sure not to let it go to his head.

Harland gave him a wink as he passed.

All right, not *too* much to his head.

His smile faded when he thought back to the anonymous letter. *We'll be watching.* As he often did now, Danny looked around, but all the faces he saw were familiar. No strangers watching him too closely.

Pulling his scarf tighter around his throat, he banished the thought. There were other things he had to take care of.

First, he stopped by the dilapidated statue. The faceless figure of Aetas stared back at him. Danny took out the small cog and held it to his lips, remembering the power that had ignited his blood. The thrill of time tangled within his veins.

"Thank you," he whispered.

Maybe one day he would understand. For now, this was between him and an absent god.

He turned away from the hedge. Within a minute he was standing before the clock tower. Looking up, he spotted the problem that had been reported just this morning after a lazy breakfast with his parents. A small chip of glass was missing from the clock face.

Danny's mutters began again as he climbed the stairs. He was supposed to have drinks with Brandon today, but upon accepting the job, his apprentice had most unexpectedly called in sick, even giving him a monotone cough through the telephone receiver. Danny had heard better acting from a puppet.

Reaching the clock room, he sighed and set down his bag and coat. When he turned, Colton was sitting on a nearby box. The sight of him made Danny ache.

"I hope you're happy with yourself," Danny said, rolling up his sleeves. He gestured at the missing sliver of the clock face. There was a mirroring scar on Colton's jaw. "The whole town's shaking their heads at you again. What have I told you about this? You said you'd never do it again."

"You were gone a long time. I was worried."

Danny bent down to take out his tools. "Even if I'm gone for a while, you still can't do this. It's not healthy for the town, or you."

Colton shifted. "I didn't know," he murmured, "if they would send another mechanic or not."

"They almost did. I wouldn't blame them, either." Danny

stood back up, screwdriver in hand. He pointed it at Colton. "But they seem to have had the same thought I did. Since you've been such a bother, the Lead's decided that a mechanic should stay here in town. Permanently."

The look of alarm on Colton's face almost made Danny smile, but he kept his face stern.

"Permanently?" Colton repeated. "Who?"

Danny flipped the screwdriver so that it now pointed at himself. "Me, of course."

There was a stunned silence. Colton's lips curled upward.

"So excuse me for taking so long, but it's a bit of a mess reuniting with one's father, learning to drive a new auto, and packing all in one go." He glared at the spirit, though his own lips were twitching. "Well? What do you have to say?"

Colton's grin burst like a firework across his face. Suddenly he was sweeping Danny up in his arms, and they spun dizzily across the floor. Their laughter lit the tower from the inside out, burning into a new star.

It wouldn't be easy. Being with Colton came with a price, but one that Danny was willing, even glad, to pay. They would be careful. They would be together. They would make it work.

Anything was possible.

A Note on *Timekeeper's* London

In *Timekeeper's* timeline, the construction of highly mechanized clock towers hundreds of years before the 1870s spurred the Industrial Revolution to happen a great deal sooner than it did in our own timeline. As a result, the England I portray benefits from technological advances that weren't invented or widespread by 1875. These advances are quite useful for the clock mechanics of London, as they need to relay information and travel quickly.

Below, I've listed what liberties I took in portraying this technologically advanced England:

Telephones

In 1861, Johann Philipp Reis developed an electromagnetic device that captured and transmitted sound, including musical notes and spoken phrases. Over the next several years, inventors experimented with audio telegraphs, some of which were achieved using the tones of tuning forks. Inspired by these attempts, Alexander Graham Bell began to tinker with harmonic telegraphs in 1873, which led to an 1875 experiment with his assistant, Thomas Watson, using the first functional telephonic device in recorded history.

Timekeeper takes place in 1875, so naturally, these inventors would have had made major breakthroughs several years earlier in the book's timeline. Telephones aren't common in the *Timekeeper* world, nor do they work particularly well, but mechanics are required to have one in their homes so they can be contacted in the event of emergencies (as we see with Danny and the Lead).

Cars

The first steam-powered vehicle was designed in 1672 by Ferdinand Verbiest, but it was Nicolas-Joseph Cugnot who built the first model in 1769: a steam-powered tricycle. He designed and built other steam-powered vehicles, but they had problems with water supply and steam pressure. Since then, various types of vehicles and engines were tested and tried, but the first motor car in central Europe wasn't constructed until 1897 by a Czech company called Nesselsdorfer Wagenbau.

Steam-powered vehicles did, in fact, exist during 1875, but they wouldn't have been the same models that are depicted in *Timekeeper*. The higher demand for technology launched factories sooner, and in larger numbers. With more resources than the Victorians in our world had, automobiles—or simply "autos"— quickly became a must-have commodity.

Women in Society

Technology and society are intrinsically linked. If one alters, so must the other. In this case, the Victorian society in *Timekeeper* differs from the typical Victorian culture we're so used to in many ways, the most obvious being how women are regarded in large cities. During the Victorian era, the issue of women's employment was fought by tireless feminists, including Millicent Fawcett and

Frances Buss. The Society for Promoting the Employment of Women was founded in 1859, led by the Queen herself.

The demand for more technology required more workers. In *Timekeeper*'s timeline, this prompted women, regardless of class or marital status, to leave the home and seek jobs in industries typically dominated by men.

We see this prevalently in the Mechanics Union. The ability to sense time is one both men and women are born with, which means that, as a matter of course, women should be allowed to become mechanics as well. Although faced with frequent criticism—even from other women in common society—and the stress of needing to prove their worth when their male counterparts do not, the female clock mechanics serve as a positive example for younger women who wish to break out in male-centric fields, such as auto repair. These young women are eager to deviate from their parents' conventions of dress, speech, and appearance.

Homosexuality

Before 1861, homosexuality was considered a crime punishable by death in England. Though the death penalty was eventually abolished in connection with this "crime," one could still be sentenced to prison if caught or suspected of homosexual behavior. The most notable example is Oscar Wilde's 1895 trial and subsequent two-year imprisonment for his relationship with Lord Alfred Douglas.

In *Timekeeper*, I wanted Danny to be part of a society that

was more indifferent than punishing. With the number of secrets he keeps close to his chest, I didn't want this important, fundamental part of him to be a secret as well. Therefore, just as women's roles have changed in a shifting society ruled by technology, so too have the laws regarding homosexuality.

There are quite a few differences between the real Victorian England and the one we see through Danny's eyes, all stemming from the creation of the clock towers and their impact on technology and society. I wanted to blend the traditional with the unconventional to create a strange era of contradictions: advanced technology combined with an old-fashioned aesthetic, evolving gender roles battling stubborn classism. Old and new coexisting in the constant stream of time.

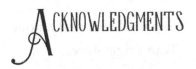CKNOWLEDGMENTS

I cannot believe that three years ago, this book was only a small, strange document on my computer. Now it is a physical thing you can pick up and read. How weird is that?

(Very. But also very cool).

Of course, I have to thank the many people who helped me in those three years:

First and foremost, to my amazing editor, Alison Weiss. Alison, you understood this book in a way I thought no one could. Maybe even better than I did. You pushed and challenged me (I might have also done the same to you—sorry), and your unwavering faith in me and this book is what kept me going. Thank you, thank you, a million times thank you. I'm still working on getting you a clock spirit.

To the Sky Pony team: Cheryl Lew, Bethany Buck, Jenn Chan, Georgia Morrisey for the lovely cover, Joshua Barnaby for the kickass interior design, and all the rest: thank you so much for your dedication. And William McAusland for that awesome map!

To my agent, Laura Crockett, who read this and somehow thought, Yup, this is something I want. I will forever be grateful for your support and enthusiasm. Thanks also to the rest of the Triada US crew: Uwe Stender, Brent Taylor, and Mallory Brown.

Liz Briggs, Pitch Wars mentor extraordinaire: I would never

have gotten this far without you. You picked this dusty stone from the ground and made it shine. #TeamBriggs 4ever.

Emily Skrutskie, the Cap to my Iron Man, the Burr to my Hamilton, the Hux to my Kylo Ren (yeah, I said it): thank you for putting up with this *gestures to self* and reading everything I shove under your nose, and overall just being a super cool person. Our crossovers will always be things of beauty. P.S. - Please don't blackmail me.

To Traci Chee, my favorite eighty-year-old woman, and Jessica Cluess, my favorite grumpy driver: you are my pillars. Your advice and wisdom and humor and friendship have meant so much to me. We'll always have the Circle of Ten. (Also: shout-out to Cole Benton, who got me that one ARC that one time and who sometimes carries my bags. You are one of the Good Ones).

To my fellow Sweet Sixteeners: I'm so proud to be in this group of amazingly talented authors. Thank you for sharing your stories and supporting mine. Special thanks to Heidi Heilig (you are a goddess), Alwyn Hamilton (road trip buddies!), Roshani Chokshi (the sun in my sky), Audrey Coulthurst (I'm dying to try the Timekeeper cocktail), Kelly Zekas (broody boys for the win!), and Kerri Maniscalco (honestly, how do you even exist?).

Victoria Schwab: thank you so much for the lovely blurb, and for being an incredible badass. You are an inspiration.

Thanks to the Class of 2k16 for all their work and dedication. I've loved being part of this group.

Tristina Wright: your excitement and support mean the world to me. You're such a wonderful human being. Also, you named your cat after one of my characters, and that is a bond that can never be broken. Mackenzi Lee: thank you for just being one of the coolest people I know. I'm so glad we bonded over mechanical arms.

To the Bay Area/NorCal authors: Stacey Lee, Stephanie Garber, Evelyn Skye, Sabaa Tahir, Sonya Mukherjee, Jessica Taylor, and Rahul Kanakia. You guys are so much fun. Thank you for welcoming me into this incredible circle.

To the Pitch Wars group (you know who you are): you are the best. What would I do without you?

To the booksellers, bloggers, librarians, and readers: I just want to shower you with love. Special thanks to Nicole at YA Interrobang, Allison at Old Firehouse Books, and Stefani Sloma at Caught Read Handed.

Becky Albertalli, Tabitha Martin, Michael Waters, Camryn Garrett, Katherine Locke, Shveta Thakrar, Tehlor Kinney, and Cindy Pon: you guys are super awesome. Just so you know.

To Olivia Berrier (who convinced me to keep writing when I thought I couldn't anymore), Jamie Lynn Saunders (who allowed me to find the inspiration for this story), and the rest of B3: you are stars. There are not enough words to explain how much you guys mean to me. To Alys Sink: the best London roommate a girl could ask for. Thanks for not killing me in my sleep. To the Hollins community: the closest I can come to expressing my adulation is screaming at the top of my lungs, so consider this my war cry of love.

To Ellen Gavazza (oh em gee bffs 4 lief), Carrie Gratiot (sushi and latte buddy), and Amber von Nagel (night cheese warrior): my life is so much brighter with you three in it. Never leave me.

Huge thanks to my family, who has always supported me no matter what. Special thanks to the Sekhons and the Gills.

To tea, without which I would likely be dead.

To Beka, my furry problem child.

And last but not least, to my parents, Harjit and Steve Sim. Thank you for everything you've done to get me this far, and for always believing I would get here.

Want to see what's next for Danny and
Colton? Find out in *Chainbreaker*.

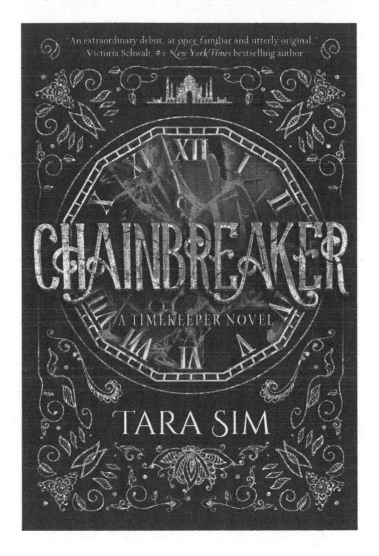

Turn the page for a sneak peek.

London, September 1876

The clock counted every painful second with ticks as thunderous and regular as a heartbeat. It was half past two, the hands slowly climbing their way up to three o'clock. Ten minutes hadn't yet passed, but already Daphne felt as if she had been sitting here all day.

It didn't help that the chair beneath her was uncomfortably hard. The plain, white-washed room contained better, padded seats than the wooden ones her mother had been slumped in when she arrived, but Daphne didn't want to drag over another and draw attention, lest it upset her mother.

St. Agnes's Home for Women was a quiet place, where residents woke at seven in the morning and went to bed at seven in the evening. After they performed chores and underwent treatment in the afternoon, they gathered in the parlor for tea and socialization. Over and over, the cycle reset every night to begin again at dawn, like the old Greek tale of a mechanical eagle pecking out the fire-stealer's liver.

The radio crackled and Daphne started; she'd forgotten it was on. The box beside them was a clunky, wooden-framed device that had grown popular in the last few months, a new marvel of telegraphy. The knobs were large and stained with greasy fingerprints. Her mother liked to turn it on after luncheon, according to the nurses.

"—it is, of course, quite an honor, and I'm sure I speak for everyone when I say that England is quite proud of Her Majesty. Only fitting she should officially be named Queen-Empress of India this year. She's done a marvel there already, even after the events of the Mutiny—"

The male voice coming through the radio's speakers was tinny and high-pitched. Daphne wished she could turn the dial down, but her mother raptly watched the radio, as though the words would form an image if she stared hard enough.

Daphne realized that her mother's fair hair was beginning to pale, her thin hands knobby and dry. A hawk-sharp face had grown even sharper in this place, her nose and chin more prominent, her eyes more sunken. Still, she had managed to hold onto a bit of beauty about her mouth and cheekbones, relics of a time when men's eyes would linger as she passed them on the street, even when she tugged her young daughter behind her.

Those other eyes had meant nothing; Daphne's father's had

been the only ones that had mattered. Until they'd closed forever, and her mother's had grown vacant.

"—so let's all congratulate Her Majesty on a job well done!"

Daphne leaned forward. "Mother," she said softly, "don't you want to speak with me?"

Her mother sighed, gaunt shoulders rising with the breath. "What is there to talk about?"

Me. My job. How the hospital staff is treating you. If they medicated you last night to make you sleep.

"We can discuss the news." Daphne gestured to the radio. "What do you make of it?"

"Make of what?"

"Her Majesty being named Queen Empress." The subject of India had always been a delicate one between them, yet Daphne still scrounged up a thimbleful of hope that this, at least, would spur her mother into conversation.

Her mother's shoulders lifted again, this time in a shrug.

Daphne leaned back, defeated. A year ago, she would have prattled on just to fill the empty space. Now she didn't bother. She could no more conjure hope than she could conjure birds from thin air. She'd learned too soon how painful it was to have disappointment constantly sinking its barbs into her. How they liked to twist and rip her open, filling her with holes.

A girl full of holes had no room for hope.

Daphne tried to visit St. Agnes's at least once a week, but she wondered if her mother would even notice if she stopped coming. Guilt choked her at the thought, and she looked down at the weak sunshine that touched the edges of her boots. The distant roar of a busy London rumbled through an open window under the radio's chatter. Daphne found it strangely soothing. She was unquestionably a child of London, bred from metal and steam and ash. All better caretakers than the woman before her.

Her whole life, her family had suffered echoes of the scandal caused when her English mother had married a man born to an English officer and an Indian woman. The struggle certainly had not improved after her father had passed. Listless days and frantic days and *kill me* days and *I hate you* days. Days when Daphne had been glad to be an apprentice clock mechanic, busy earning her own money, and days when she'd been reluctant to leave her mother alone to play with knives and hollow herself with hunger.

Doctors had advised committing her mother to the asylum many times, but it wasn't until she had nicked Daphne with one of her treasured knives that she'd finally condemned them both: her mother to this place, herself to loneliness.

Daphne looked around the room. A nurse shuffled to each woman, handing out little pills. A weary-looking woman with frizzing hair stuck her hand out for the proffered tablet, then knocked it back like it was a tumbler of whiskey.

"Dreams," her mother muttered. Daphne wondered if she had misheard. Then, again: "Dreams."

"Dreams? Of what?"

Her mother lifted a hand and let it fall back heavily into her lap. "I have them."

The nurse stopped beside them and offered a pill. Obediently, without even looking down, her mother accepted it and swallowed.

Daphne waited for the nurse to leave before she repeated, "Dreams of what?"

"My parents. My old stuffed rabbit. A silk fan my uncle brought back from China. James."

Daphne winced at her father's name. "Do you . . . miss these things?" Her mother nodded. "I'm sorry. I wish I could give them to you."

"So do I," she whispered.

They slipped into silence again, but it was a different kind; not the silence of deep water, but the silence of a lazy Sunday. Daphne almost felt pleased. It had been weeks since her mother had spoken so many words.

The radio warbled, and her mother instinctively leaned forward to adjust the knobs. When the channel returned clearly, the high-voiced announcer was still at it:

"—tell them to try Bill's Brake Solution, the only solution to all your automotive troubles. Now we—oh." The radio was unnaturally quiet for twenty loud ticks of the clock. "It seems we have incoming news from the jewel colony itself."

Daphne grew very still.

The announcer cleared his throat. "Early this morning, a protest broke out in the heart of the city of Rath, where their clock tower stands. In the midst of the commotion, there was a loud report, and a mechanism within the tower was blown to pieces."

Daphne couldn't tear her eyes away from the radio. Neither could anyone else in the room.

"Although the rioters were subdued, the cause of the explosion remains unknown. After consulting the local clock mechanics, it's been confirmed that the tower . . . has fallen."

Hushed whispers and gasps from the other women. Daphne's vision tunneled. Suddenly, she was back at that moment of perfect horror in Dover, frozen as the world went white and time shuddered to a stop.

Her body rang with an echo of that terror. As nausea clenched her belly, she swore she could smell blood.

"Soldiers helped the injured out of the rubble, but a search through the debris yielded no bodies. The central frame of the clockwork has not yet been located."

Muttering issued from the radio, the announcer conferring with someone just beyond the microphone. "At this time, there is no clear connection between the riot and the tower falling. The strangest part the soldiers have reported"—the announcer's voice faded—"is that Rath has not Stopped. There is no barrier.

"So far, time continues to move forward."

Daphne released a sharp breath, then inhaled another. The announcer must be mistaken. The news was coming all the way from India. Along the way, some piece of the report must have been misinterpreted.

It wasn't possible for a city to run without its tower.

"Unfortunately, we know nothing further regarding this incident, but we hope to have more information soon." There was a lengthy pause. "And now, the season's cricket rankings."

The room gradually stirred back to life. Voices rose in speculation, some entranced by the report, some startled, some skeptical. Her mother continued to watch the radio.

Daphne thought of the clicking sounds she'd heard just before the Dover clockwork had exploded. Of the little girl who had flickered before her eyes. Daphne rubbed her neck where a small scar lingered. There was a larger, more jagged scar on her shoulder where a gear had cut her, and it ached.

Music drifted from the radio. Or at least, Daphne thought it was coming from the radio until she realized her mother was singing.

"Hickory dickory dock, the mouse ran up the clock." Her voice was raspy and thin; she had not sung in years. "The clock stuck one, the mouse ran down . . ."

Daphne gaped at her mother, gripping the wooden armrests of her chair.

"The clock struck one, the clock fell down . . ."

Daphne stood, uttering a quick good-bye before she hurried from the room. Her mother didn't even look up.

The once-comforting roar of London became overwhelming as soon as Daphne stepped outside, swallowed by sticky heat and smoke and the odor of bodies. She was jostled this way and that, following the current like a clueless fish.

When she found her motorbike, she threw a leg over its metal bulk but didn't start it up. Instead, she sat waiting for her blood to settle and her pulse to grow quiet, staring at the macadam road beneath her as her shoulder throbbed.

The clock struck one, the clock fell down . . .

It was happening again.

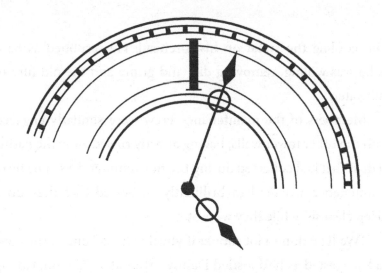

The view of Enfield from the top of Colton Tower was always lovely. Seeing it from this angle, however, was another matter entirely.

Danny Hart held on for dear life to the ladder propped against the tower wall. The ladder wasn't flimsy; it was an industrial metal contraption firmly suctioned to the ground below. Or so the maintenance crew had assured him, multiple times and with mounting impatience.

Yet the fact that he was perched nearly fifty meters above the ground, with nothing more than a thin rope attaching his belt to the aforementioned ladder, could not be overlooked. It was like being on the scaffolding, but worse. Much worse.

"Sod this," he muttered to himself. He tightened his grip on the brush as he slowly reached for the tower wall and carefully— very carefully—started scrubbing. A breeze ruffled Danny's dark hair, cooling the sweat on his forehead. He scrubbed as hard as he was willing, removing dirt and grime and the old film of rainwater.

Members of the maintenance crew were similarly engaged with the other tower walls, having already rinsed away the patina of dust that had collected during the hot summer days. The head maintenance worker had brilliantly suggested that they do a "deep cleanse" while they were at it.

"We'll be done a lot sooner if you'd help us," one of the crew had suggested as he'd jostled Danny's shoulder. "C'mon, lad, up for a little adventure?"

"In no way, shape, or form is this an adventure," Danny mumbled as he continued scrubbing, his arm already growing tired. "Don't treat me like a child."

Under different circumstances, the maintenance crew wouldn't have been nearly as familiar with a clock mechanic, but Danny had been living in Enfield for about eight months now. Not to mention he'd saved the town from being permanently Stopped the previous year. Did they make him mayor and award him a medal of valor? No. Did they insist he never pay for his own drinks at the pub? Yes, and God willing that wouldn't end anytime soon.

The breeze returned, carrying a wave of pollen with it. Danny suppressed a sneeze, but of course that only made the urge stronger. Unable to hold it in, the sneeze exploded out of him, and one of his feet slipped on the rung. Yelping, he scrabbled to grab hold of the ladder as his stomach lurched.

A hand caught his wrist. Looking up, Danny's breath hitched at the sight of Colton grinning down at him, hanging off the roof in a manner that would have sent any normal person tumbling to the ground.

"Having fun?" Colton asked, amber eyes crinkling.

Danny exhaled a small laugh. The quickening of his pulse wasn't only due to his near-fall. "Not in the least."

Colton reached for the brush. "Let me do it."

Danny held the brush out of reach. "Oh, no. This is my job, not yours."

Colton's blond hair stirred in the wind. He lifted one pale eyebrow at Danny. "It'll take you ages this way."

"Hope you don't mind if I grow a beard, then."

"Or: I find a better way and spare us both that image." Colton crawled forward, dangling off the lip of the roof with one hand, and grabbed the rag that hung from Danny's back pocket.

"You're going to make my heart stop one of these days," Danny said as Colton returned to the roof.

"I hope not." Colton leaned forward again, but not to perform circus tricks. This time, he planted a gentle kiss on Danny's mouth. Danny enjoyed it for two seconds, then broke away to quickly scan the ground.

"You can't do that out here. Someone might see."

Colton ignored him and began to scrub at his tower. "Less talking and more working, Mr. Hart."

"When did you become so bossy?" Danny attacked the wall again, a tiny smile wavering on his lips. He longed to be as carefree as Colton, but his concern was well-founded. Colton, after all, was not a normal boy.

He was a clock spirit.

Danny glanced up at him as they worked: a boy seemingly his own age, gilt-touched and bronze-skinned. A boy wrapped in the golden threads of time, the heart of an elaborate and terrifying tapestry. Without Colton's influence over Enfield's time, without the very tower they cleaned, the town would Stop altogether, just as it had months before.

Danny had been able to fix it then, but at a cost. When his father's old friend Matthias had stolen the central cog from Colton's tower, Enfield had risked the same fate as the town of Maldon, where time had been frozen for three whole years. But Danny had managed to get the cog back, and Maldon's clock spirit had returned to her tower, freeing both towns from time's punishing grasp.

If there was anything Danny had learned from the experience, it was that there was a barrier between *want* and *need*. Matthias had put his love of Maldon's clock spirit before all else, and now he faced a life of imprisonment. His longing had turned him down a darker path, one on which Danny never wanted to find himself.

But Danny was just as guilty, mistaking that diamond-hard barrier between *want* and *need* for glass, something he could easily shatter to make the two indistinguishable. The difference between him and Matthias—the thing that made him a hypocrite—was that no one knew. No one who would report him, anyway.

Now that Danny lived in Enfield, he was free to spend time in the tower with Colton, but he still had to be cautious. As it often tended to do, his mind drifted back to the letter he'd received eight months before, and the subtle weight of the threat it carried.

We'll be watching.

"That's cheating, Hart!"

One of the maintenance crew stood at the foot of the ladder, hands on his hips.

"What is?" Danny asked.

"Getting help!"

"He needed it," Colton called down, making Danny flush with indignation.

The man laughed. "I can believe that. Carry on."

"I am a very prestigious clock mechanic in London," Danny reminded them both.

"I know, Danny." But Colton couldn't hide his puckish smile.

A slow, grueling hour of work followed, and Danny was sore and sunburned by the end of it. Colton followed his progress down, leaving his perch on the roof to hang from the ladder rungs instead. The wind rippled his loose white shirt, and Danny could see hints of his back whenever he looked up.

"Back to join the humble ground-dwellers?" the lead maintenance worker joked as Danny's foot met sweet, solid earth.

"Hopefully for good," Danny replied. "Are the others finished?"

"Half an hour ago." Danny groaned, and the man laughed again. "You're handy with the clock, and that's what matters." The man nodded to Colton, who was now standing beside Danny. "Good work, son."

Colton waited for the man to walk away before he asked Danny, "Why does he call me son when I'm not his son?"

"It's just an expression. It means he likes you. They all do."

The Enfield folk had taken a great interest in their clock spirit once they'd learned he was more than a myth. There had been such a steady stream of visitors that first month that Danny had irritably asked Mayor Aldridge to make a rule: no one could enter the tower without Danny's say-so.

Besides, what if someone accidently walked into the tower while he and Colton were . . . not cleaning?

"Your face is getting red," Colton observed.

"Well, your hair is a mess."

"So's yours."

Just as Danny reached up to fix Colton's fringe, he noticed a young woman jogging their way. Danny quickly dropped his hand. The young woman's skirt swished in agitation as she stopped before them.

"Sorry . . . Danny . . . but . . . telephone."

"Hold on, catch your breath."

She nodded and fanned her face with one hand. Jane, the mayor's assistant, tended to handle her duties with an intensity that often made Danny worry after her health.

"Hello, Jane." Colton smiled.

She returned it with a faint blush. "Hello, Colton. Your tower looks lovely."

"Thank you. I helped clean it."

"What about the telephone?" Danny cut in before they got lost in pleasantries.

"The hub telephone rang for you. It's not the London office, though—I checked. The caller is waiting now."

Telephones were expensive and worked poorly in smaller towns like Enfield, which was why they had just the communal one located at the mayor's office. Anyone was free to use it, provided the calls didn't take too long. His parents didn't make it a habit to call him, as he frequently visited them in London. Cassie would only call in an emergency, and Brandon knew to ring him at his parents' house.

"I'd best see what it is," he said to Colton. "Go enjoy your clean tower."

Colton wanted to say something; Danny could see it in his eyes. But he only nodded and watched as Danny followed after Jane.

In the mayor's office, Danny closed the door to the telephone room. Picking up the receiver, he leaned toward the mouthpiece.

"Hullo?"

"Danny? It's Daphne."

He swallowed a curse. He hadn't spoken to Daphne Richards in months, and for good reason.

"Oh. Hello, Miss Ri—Daphne."

"Your father gave me the number. I hope you don't mind."

"I don't mind." He shifted on the bench, nervously tapping his fingers on the tabletop. "I don't mean to be rude, but *why* are you calling?"

They weren't exactly chums, but neither were they ene-mies—not anymore. After the mayhem of last year, when Matthias had tricked Daphne into stealing Colton's central cog, things had been awkward at best.

The line went silent. Danny started counting in his head, and when he reached seven, she spoke: "I need to talk to you. In person. Have you heard the news?"

"What news?"

"You haven't, then. Come to London. Meet me at the Winchester."

"Daphne, I have things to do."

"It's important." Then, softer: "Please."

Danny pinched the bridge of his nose. "Fine. Give me two hours." He hung up.

"You're leaving?" Colton demanded when Danny stopped by the tower afterward. The spirit sat on the steps beside the clock face. "I thought you weren't going to London for a few more days."

"I'll be back tomorrow morning. Why, is something the matter?"

Colton shook his head. The mirth of that morning was gone, as if his levity was a thing meant for open air and couldn't survive once his feet touched ground. "No. I just don't like seeing you go."

Danny wanted to tell Colton he'd rather stay, too. Instead, he held out his hand. Colton didn't hesitate to take it. That famil-iar spark flared between their skin, the acknowledgment of time.

It grew stronger with every resonant tick of the clock, traveling deep into Danny's chest and stilling the doubt he felt there.

"I'll be back soon," Danny said. "Wait for me."

"I always do."

Tara Sim can typically be found wandering the wilds of the Bay Area in California. When she's not chasing cats or lurking in bookstores, she writes books about magic, clocks, and explosives. *Timekeeper* is her first novel.

Follow her on Twitter at @EachStarAWorld, or online at **www. tarasim.com** where you can find fun *Timekeeper* extras.